Sea of Evil & Desire

J. STŘELOU

Copyright © 2025 by Julia Střelou

Cover art, interior art and design by Vivien Reis

Interior world map art by Gustavo Luzzatto Schmitt

Rune key by Julia Střelou and Karen Alarcon

All rights reserved. No part of this publication may be reproduced, stored in a retrieval system, or transmitted in any form or by any means, without prior written permission of the publisher, nor be otherwise circulated in any form of binding or cover other than that which it is published and without a similar condition including this condition being imposed on subsequent purchaser.

J Střelou/New Zealand

www.juliastrelou.com

This is a work of fiction. Names, characters, places, and incidents are a product of the author's imagination. Locales and public names are sometimes used for atmospheric purposes. Any resemblance to actual people, living or dead, or to businesses, companies, events, institutions, or locales is completely coincidental.

Sea of Evil and Desire/Julia Střelou.

Paperback ISBN: 978-0-473-73618-7

Hardback ISBN: 978-0-473-73619-4

Ebook ISBN: 978-0-473-73620-0

For all those who want to believe magic exists. This could happen to you.

Dedicated to my mom and sister. My sister and I started writing this as teenagers. We were inspired by the stories our mother wrote.

Author's note:

This book is a romantasy set in our world. That being said, I have taken full creative liberties when creating the fictional town of Ruadán's Port and the fantastical Kingdom of the Deep. So, if you're a scientist or marine biologist, or you happen to work for NASA—it's time to suspend your disbelief . . .

After all, none of us truly know what lies in the deepest, darkest corners of the ocean.

Sea of Evil and Desire is a dark romance fantasy. It contains mild sexual and physical violence, as well as references to domestic violence (not between main characters).

If you would like a detailed trigger warning, you can find it on juliastrelou.com/content-warnings

The Kingdom of the Deep

neptunus

uss phantom

wild west of the ocean

port royal

pacificus mer kingdom

blackwater ghost

kaimana sīrēnēs

the lost horizon

niveus mer kingdom

unus castle

Ruadán's port

lugh sirenes

dom

renes

Thálassa mer kingdom

the Icarus

Sundara Sirenes

Okeános mer kingdom

mer kingdom

ss midnight gale

N
W E
S

Krumós mer kingdom

Map

- Cemetery
- Bayside Shopping Center
- Ferris Wheel
- Samscary St.
- Mékir
- Finn's House
- Merrow Rock

Ruadán's Port

Morgana's house

bookstore

The Port House

Cró St.

Oblivere place

...na's jetty

...ghthouse

Runes of the Ocean

Glossary

Aigéan (Ah-gee-ahn) Origin: Irish
Agápē (Ah-GHAH-peh) Origin: Ancient Greek
Aranare (Ar-ah-nar-ay) Origin: Minoan
Archōn Agorá (Ar-kon A-go-rah) Origin: Ancient Greek
Ătlanticus (At-lanti-cus) Origin: Latin
Iona (eye-OH-na) Origin: Gaelic
Krumós (Kru-mos) Origin: Ancient Greek
Kyano (Ki-a-nos) Origin: Ancient Greek
Lugh (Loo-gh) Origin: Irish
Manannán (Man-nuh-náhn) Origin: Irish
Naútēs Diábolos (Now-tace Dia-bol-os) Origin: Ancient Greek
Neptūnus (Nep-tune-us) Origin: Latin
Niveus (Niv-EE-us) Origin: Latin
Okeanós (Oh-KEE-a-nohs) Origin: Ancient Greek
Pācificus (Pa-chif-i-cus) Origin: Latin
Pisceon (Pis-ce-on) Origin: Latin
Ruadán (Roo-ah-dan) Origin: Irish
Selich (Sel-itch) Origin: Scottish
Thálassa (Tha-AH-la-sah) Origin: Ancient Greek
Therme Skótos (ThER-me SKŌ-tos) Origin: Ancient Greek
Sundara (Sun-de-ra) Origin: Sanskrit

Prologue

King Neptūnus had a feral glint in his eyes when he handed me over to the prince. I could see it even though I was barely conscious, scarcely drawing breath in my watery surroundings.

I never thought I would die like this . . . not in my wildest human dreams. But I wasn't human anymore, and here we were in the Kingdom of the Deep.

Edward let out a noise of terror. It was my fault that he was here; now, he too would have to suffer at the hands of the prince.

The last time we'd seen Prince Aigéan, I had thought him beautiful, with his dark hair floating in the swell, his crimson-tipped tail, and the packed muscles in his glistening, inked torso. Now? Now, all I could think about was the claws he'd exhibit when he tortured me. What would they feel like raking through my flesh? A chill skittered down my spine as I continued to take ragged inhales.

I would die immediately, but Edward was Drowned. His wounds might heal, and the prince could hurt him again and again—just as he had José.

None of this would have happened if I hadn't moved to Ruadán's Port. Would I take it all back if I had the chance? No. I had started to feel like there was a place for me here, however short-lived.

I did have some regrets, though. I wished I could have learned more about my family and this world I never knew existed. Been the one these people needed   I wished I could have known the intimate touch of a man, as I was about to die a virgin.

The prince's cold, clear voice echoed from the back of the great hall. A guard grabbed me by the hair, and my trembling body was drawn from the floor to face him.

PART ONE

Ruadán's Port

1.

MORGANA

The ringing seemed shrill and urgent. I was overwhelmed with a sense of dread. For twenty years, I'd been plagued by the feelings of others. I hoped they were wrong this time, but in my experience, they were always right.

"I'll get it, Morgana." Mom gestured for me to stay seated for dinner and moved toward the phone.

I knew the caller would either be my grandparents or a telemarketer—they were the only ones who ever rang the landline.

My apprehension deepened as Mom listened to the person speaking. She turned pale and stifled a howl.

I dropped my fork.

"Dead? No, that can't be right! She was old, but she wasn't sick. She always seemed younger than other women her age." Mom pressed her forehead against the stained kitchen wall. "Tell me everything."

I crept into her bedroom to pick up the other receiver. I was used to hearing my grandmother's warm Scottish accent on the other end of the line, asking me about school, recommending books to read, or telling me about her travels to faraway countries.

"Robbie found her and called us," a man with a brogue accent said as I lifted the phone to my ear. He sounded like a deputy—professional, polite. I found myself thinking of what my grandfather's face must have looked like when he discovered her. I didn't know him well, but now, I pictured him crumpling. My heart was hammering, and the corners of my eyes stung, but I couldn't put the phone down.

"Where is my father? Can I speak with him?" I could tell Mom was trying to be strong, but her voice was breaking.

"Sorry, Mrs. Scott. He's not able to come to the phone. In shock, I don't doubt. That is why I am making the call."

How many calls had the deputy made like this? If he was struggling, he didn't show it.

"So, she had a cardiac arrest. Is that what you're saying?" Mom—the most analytical, unemotional woman I knew—was choking back tears.

"Aye, the paramedic said her heart stopped."

Mom didn't reply. She was drawing shuddering sobs. I picked at some loose threads on the red woolen blanket at the end of her bed.

"There was water on the kitchen floor when we arrived, but your mother's body was bone dry," the deputy continued, his tone flat, as if listing routine facts. "We searched for signs of electrical shock but found nothing. There was a deep cut on her right palm. We thought maybe she'd slashed herself and taken a fall, but there was no bloodstained knife to be found anywhere in the kitchen."

"Wait a minute." Mom's voice was sharper now. "Are you saying there is a possibility this was suspicious?"

I stiffened. My eyes were still burning, but I hadn't shed a tear. I could only listen and pick at the ugly red throw.

"Robbie said the doors were locked when he arrived home. There was no sign of forced entry, so we are ruling out foul play. Though I'll admit, the cut was a bit strange, given the absence of a knife. And there was a smell—"

"Okay, I don't need to hear this." Mom sounded angry now.

"You've got me wrong. I meant there was a smell in the house, like seaweed or fish," the deputy stammered.

"I . . . Ah, well, that must be from Robbie. He spends most days at sea."

"Aye, that would make sense. Look, Mrs. Scott, Robbie's no' doing well. He's barely saying a word. Could you get someone to come stay with him?"

Mom was silent.

I sucked in a breath.

My mother grew up in Ruadán's Port, a small coastal town in Scotland situated on the Western tip of the Isle of Islay, but she left before I turned one. I'd always suspected her move to the Midwest had something to do with my father, but she refused to talk about him. She gave me her last name and never mentioned his. Even now, she couldn't bear to return. Although my grandmother would visit us during her travels, I hardly knew my grandfather, who hated flying.

Mom still hadn't answered the deputy, but I could hear her inhaling sharply. Perhaps she was hyperventilating.

After another awkward pause, he said, "I'd best be getting back. Please contact me at the Bowmore police station if you need anything."

Mom remained silent. The loose threads on the throw had become a hole, and I was curling my finger through it.

"And Mrs. Scott . . ."

"Yes?"

"I'm sorry for your loss."

Mom offered a strangled murmur before the phone clicked off. I was left sitting on the bed, unable to move, the dial tone blaring in my ear.

My mother begrudgingly drove me to the airport the next day. She couldn't argue with my decision to go, because Granddad had no one else, and she couldn't bring herself to return to her hometown.

I watched the houses of Kansas City suburbia fly by outside the car window, and I couldn't help but think about how different Ruadán's Port would be. My grandmother had told me stories about the place and its history. It had gotten its name in the 1700s, when it still operated a thriving seaport—one of the smallest in Scotland—but the port's decline began when the primary trade route to Ireland was redirected to nearby Port Ellen. The place was a ghost town now. Once or twice, I had asked my grandmother if I could visit her, but she was always adamant I would hate the place.

"Are you sure you want to do this?" Mom asked as we loaded my suitcase onto the conveyor belt.

I threw her an exasperated stare.

"What about college?" she persisted.

Deferring college was an easy choice as high school's sensory overload had driven me to avoid people entirely. As I walked down the corridor, I would feel it: the love emanating from a girl clutching her books against her chest, the arousal of a jock as he looked at his teammates, the suicidal thoughts of the boy trailing against the wall . . . It was all-consuming.

"Mom, I'm doing it for *her*," I said, collecting my passport back from the agent at the gate.

I'd always felt a strange connection to my grandmother. There was something about her presence I found soothing. I remember watching her move around our kitchen in Kansas City, her hips swaying and her long, gray-streaked hair falling gently down her back. When I was younger, she'd read me poems about the ocean and taught me how to draw mermaids.

Mom nodded and toyed with the ugly antique ring she wore on a chain around her neck. Her face remained hard, but I sensed her emotions: sadness, fear, and most of all, relief. Relief that it was me going and not her.

My mother and I were polar opposites, not just in our personalities but in how we looked. The only pieces I had of my father were my green eyes and red hair. The rest of the Scott family were dark. Sometimes, I wondered if my appearance was what made her so drawn around me.

Mom gave me a short, strained hug, more affection than she usually offered, and then stepped back. "I've enrolled you in Ruadán's Port Medical for your . . . condition . . ." she called after me as I slipped into the flow of people streaming through the gate.

I waved her off with a cheery, plastered-on smile. My "condition" was one of the reasons I wanted to leave this city, to leave her. I didn't want to see another doctor. My grandmother had never felt anything was wrong with me; she always said I was simply intuitive, which was one reason I loved her. I wished I hadn't taken no for an answer when she was alive and just gone ahead and visited her, but at least I could do this now.

It was an almost fifteen-hour flight—with a layover—from Kansas City to Glasgow, where my grandfather was going to pick me up with his friend, Barry. From there, we would drive the five and a half hours to Ruadán's Port.

A tangle of hair, sweat, and luggage, I finally boarded. Navigating the cramped aisle, I hauled my carry-on behind me, my satchel weighing down one shoulder.

"How are you?" The man in the seat next to mine grinned as I stowed my bag in the overhead bin. He had slightly crooked front teeth and the beginnings of a beard. His gaze moved slowly from my head to my waist as he took me in, and his desire washed over me. Fifteen hours ... of this.

"I'm fine," I muttered as I slid in beside him.

"Flying alone?" I sensed his glee at being seated next to a girl he found attractive.

"Yep." I shot him an awkward grin and started fiddling with the television screen, pretending I knew how to use it, but I'd never been on an international flight before.

The man continued to survey me, and I sensed his unfaltering attraction. I pulled my headphones out of my satchel, pressing play on my music. I should have been used to the emotions of others by now, but it never got easier, especially in such proximity.

On second thought ... I reached back into my satchel and grabbed my Xanax.

Mom had dragged me to multiple therapists, who'd diagnosed me with different disorders and prescribed me different pills. Some made me jittery, some sleepy, and others made me feel nothing. I didn't normally take them, but in situations like this, the Xanax helped.

I awoke drenched in sweat. It was the same nightmare—the black, swirling darkness, the same cries for help. There was a rushing sound, and red eyes peered out at me.

This was nothing new. The nightmares had plagued me for as long as I could remember, but a new character had appeared this time. A handsome man had stepped out of the darkness and smiled at me. His eyes weren't red; they were obsidian. I was drawn to this man in the dream, but at the same time, something about him flooded my body with warning.

I lost myself in the in-flight entertainment for the rest of the journey. When I finally landed in Glasgow, rain streaked the plane windows. The man I'd been seated beside tried to start another conversation as we waited for our bags, and relief coursed through me when mine was one of the first suitcases out.

I recognized my granddad as I pushed through the people streaming out the arrivals gate. He was standing next to a younger yet equally weather-beaten man with dark, graying hair and pale skin.

"You must be Morgana! I'm Barry." The dark-haired man pulled me into a big embrace. His emotions washed over me—a rush of sympathy. "How's Anna doing?" he asked as he let go.

"Mom's okay..." I thought of her steely exterior, which had reappeared as soon as she'd hung up the phone on the deputy.

I turned to my grandfather. I hadn't seen him in person for years, but he looked much the same, with tanned, battered skin and dark eyes. His once-ebony hair was almost all gray now. He nodded hello and gave me an uncomfortable hug, which he withdrew from quickly.

Barry drove a white truck, and he slung my two suitcases into the back, where they joined a collection of fishing tackle and buckets. Granddad hadn't yet spoken to me. Was he always like this, or was it grief? I was relieved Barry was there to diffuse the awkwardness.

I stared out the window, watching the scenery flicker by, and wondered if I had made the right decision coming here. Everything felt foreign: the rolling green hills and the weather, which had transitioned from torrential, stormy rain to a brilliant sunny day and then back to rain, all in the space of half an hour. I couldn't deny the place's magic as we whizzed past an old castle and more stone fences nestled amid the green, and passed a giant body of water—a loch. My grandmother had told me stories about them and the famous Loch Ness Monster.

"You ready to trade city lights for the sound of waves crashing against the rocks, lass?" Barry surveyed me in the rearview mirror as we pulled into Kennacraig, where we would be getting the ferry to the Isle of Islay.

"Honestly, I'm not sure yet," I confessed, peering over his shoulder at the dark waters ahead. We had been traveling for at least three hours now, and I was ready to stretch my legs.

"The sea has a way of growing on you. It's in your blood, whether you know it or not." My granddad's croaky voice caused me to jump. It was the first time he'd spoken.

Barry's truck rattled onto the ferry's metal ramp, tires splashing through puddles as the wind carried the scent of salt and diesel into the vehicle deck.

Leaving the truck behind, we climbed metal stairs to the open area, and a sudden rush of salty air stole my breath as the sea appeared. The wind tangled through my hair, lifting it in wild strands as if the waves were reaching for me. I'd never seen the ocean in real life before, and as it unfolded before me, a mass of deep blues and grays, I was transfixed. The scent of brine filled my senses, and for a moment, I stood motionless, drinking it in and letting the spray from the ferry pepper my face.

Two hours later, we were back in Barry's old truck, rumbling across the isle.

"You want a job, Morgana?" Barry's dark eyes found mine again in the rearview mirror as we passed a white, weather-worn road sign: "You are now entering Ruadán's Port."

"I— Ah—" Mom had been nagging me to hand my resume in at one of the Kansas City malls, but there were too many people there. But here, there were fewer people—fewer things to sense.

"I've got a wee souvenir shop at Bayside shopping center. My son Jamie's been running the place, but he can't stand it."

"Okay."

I found myself grinning. *Freedom*. That's what a job would offer me, along with some means to support my grandfather. We weren't dirt poor, but Granddad was retired on the State Pension, and Mom didn't have much money to spare as a single parent on a low-level accountant's salary.

We drove up the small hill where my grandparents' house stood. From the top, the town spread out beneath us. A cluster of whitewashed stone houses led to the sea.

"Shall we go have a look?" Barry asked.

I nodded, and he continued past the driveway he'd been about to pull into. The bay opened before us at the end of the street as Barry parked the truck in a spot facing the ocean.

"Ruadán's Port, eh? Not quite what you're used to in the big city, lass. No coffee chains, but we've a view that could make a poet out of anyone."

The town was nestled along a rugged coastline. The harbor was an inlet bordered by rocky outcrops, creating a natural shelter for small boats. The breakwater curved gently, hugging the sea and adding to the enclosed feel of the harbor, while the open water beyond stretched out to meet the horizon. Straight ahead was a gray wooden jetty, and beyond it, the Atlantic Ocean shimmered, a rolling, steely-colored expanse reflecting the shades of the overcast sky.

"Bayside is the town's only shopping center." Barry wound down his window, and I was hit with a gust of salty sea air as he gestured to the cliff face on our right.

Perched on its top, a carriage-less Ferris wheel loomed, its silhouette ominous against the tumbled gray sky.

"The Ferris wheel and those new houses were constructed three years ago to attract tourists, but they never did get the wheel working. Stupid spot to put it, if you ask me," he muttered.

A slew of modern large-windowed houses were nestled into the cliff on the slice of land making up the bay's right side. On the left arm, a mass of black rocks jutted into the ocean, and above them, an old stone lighthouse stood.

As I looked out over the view, thunder rumbled, and dark clouds moved in on the horizon. The wind blasted through Barry's open window, and the Ferris wheel on the cliff began to spin.

"Another gale, and they still haven't found those wee kids who were swept away," Barry said sadly as he restarted the truck's engine.

"There's no hope for them now," my granddad rasped. "The water's far too cold, even at this time o' year."

The hairs on my arms prickled. It was October—the end of fall. What would this place be like in winter?

"The sea gives us so much, but sometimes it needs to take something back." Barry sighed. "You'll want to steer clear of Merrow Rocks at night. This place is full o' strange tales. Not that you should believe half of what folks here say."

As we pulled away, I gazed at the cluster of black rocks stretching into the water. The waves tossed in the wind, leaving them glistening with spray.

Back in front of my grandparents' whitewashed stone home, Barry hauled my suitcases from the truck and turned to Granddad. "Shall we head out to sea when this bad weather clears?" he asked, leaning on his open door, squinting at the darkening horizon.

My granddad nodded, and I was shocked. He seemed too old to go out on the wild ocean. Then I thought about his strong, weather-beaten hands. The man had been at sea his whole life; why would he stop now?

Like the others on the street, my grandparents' house was old and whitewashed. It was stone, with small square windows hemmed by dark shutters. The roof was pointed for the most part, but one section protruded into a tower.

"Your room will be up there, adjacent to the attic," Granddad said gruffly, nodding at the tower. "You must be tired after your trip."

Evening had set in, and I *was* tired. Once I'd heaved my suitcases up the narrow, winding stairs, I found that my room and the attic were filled with boxes of my grandmother's treasures. The passing thought tightened my heart. She'd often brought me presents from her travels: a worry doll from Guatemala, Baoding balls from China, and a pashmina shawl from India. Now, I would be sleeping among the remains of her adventures, the things she had boxed up and brought home. I didn't mind; I thought it was the best room in the house, although it was permeated by a musky odor.

I stowed some clothes in the oak dresser adorned with three dusty mirrors and took in the rest of the room: white walls, a single bed with a patchwork quilt, an old wooden wardrobe, and a square window with lacy white curtains. My grandfather's room, kitchen, living room, study, and a shared bathroom were downstairs.

Thunder cracked, and rain beat against the window. The sound was soothing, and I sprawled on the small bed, falling asleep in all my clothes.

🐚

Cool morning light filtered through my bedroom window. I was drenched in sweat from my nightmares. How long had I slept?

Outside, the storm had passed, and the ocean was sighing behind the whitewashed houses leading down the hill. In the half-light, the waves looked mauve. It must have been early, perhaps 8 a.m.

I inched down the narrow staircase from the tower to the hall and crept along the dark passage toward the sound of faint chatter from the television in the living room. I paused as I passed some black-and-white pictures hanging on the wall. Even in the dimness, my grandmother's smile caught my eye. In the photo, she was wearing one of her linen suits and a white Panama hat with a black band that made her look like an archaeologist. She was holding my mother, who was wrapped in swaddling clothes.

I met my grandmother's dark gaze and whispered, "I'll take good care of him." But I wasn't sure I could deliver on that promise, as I often struggled with the simplest tasks, like finding two matching socks.

I reached the doorway to the living room and peered in. Grandpa was sitting in his armchair in the darkness.

He was rocking slowly, and I sensed his sadness. It filled the room and seeped out the door. It was suffocating. He had one of my grandmother's long furs splayed out over his legs.

As he ran his shaky hands over the coat, I wanted to grab it from him. I caught myself, gripping the doorframe. What was I thinking?

Hunger gnawed at me, and I crept behind him toward the kitchen. I should probably make something for us both to eat.

"Morgana, is that you?"

I froze. Granddad's armchair creaked, and the morning newscaster prattled softly as I moved to his side. He grasped me gently by the wrist, his hand calloused from years at sea, the television light illuminating his sorrowful face from one side.

"She'd have wanted you to have this." He gestured toward the coat, tears pooling at the rims of his dark eyes.

I clutched it to my chest. "It's beautiful," I whispered, fingering the soft gray fur. I was overwhelmed by a deep longing; it was as if he had just handed me something I had been searching for all my life. I held it close and breathed in its scent.

"Aye, she'd be happy I did this. Maybe she will forgive me now," he murmured, almost to himself.

I lifted my face from the soft fur, the memory of my grandmother, the smell of her. "There's nothing to forgive," I said. "She loved you!" I wished I had words to ease his pain.

"Aye . . ." He sighed, and his sadness now seemed heavier, mixed with something else: guilt. It was as if I had stepped into a vortex of emotions, and the combination nauseated me. I gripped the arm of his chair to steady myself, and I was surprised to feel his fingers atop mine.

"Now leave me," he said, and patted my hand.

A morning glow had begun to tease the edges of the horizon as I padded into the kitchen with the coat still in my arms. A fluorescent glare filled the room as I flicked the light switch. The simple wooden chairs cast outlines across the white lace tablecloth, which, now washed and worn, told the story of my grandparents' life here.

This was the room where they'd found her sprawled out on the floor next to the sink.

I threw the coat over a chair, pulled a box of cornflakes from one of the white wooden cupboards, and paused as I reached for the milk. The fur's mottled pattern caught my eye. Leaving the fridge ajar and the milk on the counter, I threw the coat over my shoulders. It held just enough weight to feel comforting, but not enough to bear me down. I slipped my arms down the sleeves. The lining was cool.

A beep from the open fridge reminded me of my half-made breakfast. I finished pouring my cereal, but I kept the coat on as I ate it and washed my bowl.

Granddad had turned up the television in the living room, so I returned to his side to give him a hot cup of tea.

"The search for the brother and sister believed to have been swept from Merrow Rocks has been called off . . ." the newscaster said somberly.

"We will scatter her ashes in the bay this morning if you want to come." Granddad's croaky voice penetrated the darkness as he took the tea in his shaky hands.

I nodded.

His eyes were on the coat. "It suits you."

"Thanks," I mumbled, and I found myself pulling its soft folds around me protectively, as if he might leap from his armchair and take it back.

I returned to the tower to dress for the funeral as the newscaster talked chirpily about sporting news. The lost kids were forgotten.

༄

I'd never been to a funeral before, but I'd seen my fair share of them on Netflix. I knew people usually wore black, so I hung my grandmother's fur coat in the wooden wardrobe and threw on a black dress. Glancing out the window, I pulled stockings and a jacket out of my bag.

Granddad and I walked down the hill in silence. Something about him seemed lighter, as if a weight had been removed from his chest when he gave me the jacket. I kept myself neutral as these emotions engulfed me, just as I'd done with his sadness. I had a fresh start here. I didn't want Granddad to start dragging me to doctors the way Mom had, although knowing her, she'd already warned him of my "condition."

The path wound down to the bay, where the briny tang of the Atlantic greeted the air. When we reached the jagged rocks that led to the gray sandy beach, I tried to help Granddad, but he brushed me away.

My grandmother's funeral was nothing like the ones I had seen on Netflix, which always included a somber procession of many well-wishers. There was no coffin. Instead, my grandfather drew a small silver box holding her ashes from beneath his arm. Only five people awaited us on the shore. I recognized Barry and his son Jamie, who had the same dark hair and sallow skin as his father. The other three people I didn't know.

Barry nodded at them as Granddad and I approached. "They're the Williamson family. They own half o' this town. Louisa was friends with your grandmother."

Louisa was standing between two brown-skinned men. Unlike them, she was fair, and she must have been old—perhaps in her seventies, as her shoulder-length hair was entirely silver. She wore a beige cardigan and loose slacks with a brown belt, like my grandmother used to wear.

One of the men had his arm around Louisa's waist. He looked younger than her, maybe fifty, with dark shoulder-length wavy hair. The second man was younger still—not much older than me. Perhaps he was their son. His amber eyes met mine, and he offered me a grin. He had a pleasant face, straight white teeth, and brown hair tousled by the wind.

Everyone was looking at my grandfather, who was still holding the box. He looked as if he might be about to say something, but when he opened his mouth, all that came out was a choked sob.

"F-forgive me, Iona," was all he could manage.

He tried to open the box, but his hands were shaking so badly that Barry had to help. As soon as the lid came away, the ashes were swept up by the sea breeze. The sun came out as the wind took the little gray flecks in its arms, and the sky became a brilliant blue. The grass on the clifftops was a lush green.

The sea rippled as glistening heads emerged. I gasped. *Seals!* Their dark eyes gleamed like polished stones in the morning light. They watched us with quiet curiosity, whiskers twitching as if catching secrets carried on the wind. Their eyes were so . . . human.

As the last of my grandmother was swallowed by elements, the seals slipped back beneath the waves. Granddad shook with tears, dropping the empty silver container onto the sand.

Barry put his hand on Granddad's back, and I retrieved the box. There was a carving on its lid. I ran my fingers across it. It was badly worn, but it looked like some sort of insignia. I could make out a circle with a wave in the middle, and around it, there were five pictures ... a skull and a mermaid, but the others were too faded to recognize.

"What is this box?" I asked, handing it back to my grandfather.

"It—it was hers. I think she got it on her travels," he rasped, clutching it to his chest.

His aching sadness washed over me, and in that moment of laxness, the emotions emanating from the rest of the group wrapped around me, suffocating and inescapable. As sentiments of sorrow and sympathy flooded my being, I faltered.

Barry was staring at me, concern knotting his dark brows. Tears burst onto my cheeks, and I waved him off.

The lady called Louisa was watching me, too, and her eyes widened with something—fear. It mingled with the sadness. Barry made as if to leave Granddad's side and comfort me, but I waved him off again. I did my best to make my face neutral, but the emotions were overwhelming. Nodding apologies, I left the group and wandered along the sandy beach. I made my way toward the end of the jetty that stretched across the ocean.

To my right, the Ferris wheel towered above on the sloping green clifftop, overlooking the concrete-framed inlet. Before me, the sea opened between the bay's two arms, rugged and empty.

I shoved my headphones in, escaping in my music, and loitered on the jetty until the other funeral goers and their emotions had dispersed.

I was returning to my grandparents' house when I noticed him—the man from my dream. He stood on the concrete boardwalk, watching me as I made my way along the sand. His arms were folded across his chest, and the wind pushed his dark hair about. He was wearing black jeans and a dark coat, just like in my dream. *Stop being stupid*, I told myself. *You don't just dream of people and then see them!*

A shiver raced down my spine as I stopped and dragged my gaze to his. He didn't look away, and I was overcome with the same urge to go to him I'd had in the dream, but also the same prickle at the back of my neck warning me to stay away.

I scrambled back up the black rocks that led to the boardwalk. When I reached the top, I looked for the man again, but he was nowhere to be seen.

2.

MORGANA

I liked the desolation of the Bayside shopping center. It was an outdoor complex, and the sea air seemed to soften the feelings of the shopkeepers. They disintegrated into clouds and cold. Behind the center lay a few industrial sheds, and cement bled into a grassy cliff face before the land fell away to the bite of the sea.

It was my first day at a real job, and I'd put some effort in, donning a dusting of mascara and throwing my grandmother's coat over my jeans and T-shirt. It felt luxurious, yet stirred a tinge of guilt, because I could tell it was real fur.

The center was gray like the rest of the town. Gray concrete met gray façades, which collided with a gray sky.

I grabbed the keys Barry had dropped off that morning and opened the door to Celtic Keepsakes. The store was lined with locked glass cases filled with Celtic jewelry, brooches, and figurines, and in the middle was a glass counter. The little lights that shone from beneath the panes gave the place an unwholesome fluorescent glow. The irony of being a tourist in this town and selling souvenirs wasn't lost on me.

"You must be new here. I got you a pastry!" A woman appeared in the doorway, clutching two white paper bags in her long, pink-nailed hands. Her raven hair was perfectly curled. She wore a leopard-print sweater and had a zebra-striped bag on her shoulder. I'd never seen anyone pull off double animal print, but somehow, she was doing it.

"Erm, thanks," I muttered awkwardly, taking the hot paper bag she held out to me even though my instincts to recoil had already kicked in.

"I'm Skye Davies. I work at Tartan Treasures next door." She extended her free hand and peered at me curiously.

"Morgana." I shook it, then quickly pulled my sweaty palm back and made myself busy moving things under the glass counter, hoping she would get the message.

She didn't.

"Shall we go and get coffee?" Skye moved from the doorway to lean on the counter, her many gold bracelets jangling.

"I have to work." I waved her off with a curt smile, glad I had a genuine excuse.

"Work?" She huffed a laugh. "We're lucky if we see five browsers a day. Some days, no one comes in." She crumpled her empty pastry bag and tossed it to me as if we'd been friends for years. Pulling a bubblegum-pink gloss from her purse, she slicked it over her lips and pouted at her reflection in the glass counter. "Come on." She grinned at me.

Then, she swished out the door. She was smiling, but I was overcome by the sadness emanating from her—a haunting sadness I didn't think she was even aware of. I hesitated, but my jet lag had kicked in, so I followed her to the coffee stand.

"My boyfriend, Parker, he's a lawyer. He's just been made partner in a firm in Campbeltown, so he spends most of his time there." Skye quickly began delving into all the details of her life. I listened silently.

The morning sun cast a cool glow over the center, and the shops on either side of us were springing to life when I noticed him: the man from yesterday. He was smoking a cigarette outside a shop called Ruadán's Port Pawn. A dark tendril of hair had fallen across his face, obscuring his features, but I knew it was him. He was wearing black jeans tucked into lace-up army boots and a hand-cut singlet that exposed his shoulders. One arm was covered in tattoos.

Suddenly, he looked up. His glance surprised me, and it was too late to look away. My eyes met his, which were black, crowned by black brows.

"The dream!" I gasped.

"No, it wasn't a dream. This happened," Skye exclaimed at my side.

"Huh?" I had forgotten she was there.

"My boyfriend's been acting shady since he got his promotion . . . Do you think he's having an affair?"

Skye followed my gaze, noticing the dark-haired stranger.

He was lingering out the front of the pawnshop. Maybe he worked there. The man looked up again. This time, I held his gaze as he flicked away the remains of his cigarette and squashed it under his boot. His eyes were cold. I flushed and turned to Skye.

"He must be new! I've never been into the pawnshop. The old man who owns it scares me," Skye whispered.

"Shhh, he'll hear you!" I smoothed my hair and chanced another glance. He was still watching us.

"He's kind of attractive in a dark I-want-you-to-do-bad-things-to-me way." Skye laughed.

"Let's go," I hissed, pulling her away and trying to focus on the quaint coffee cart before us, nestled between a souvenir kilt shop and a whisky store. I inhaled the rich aroma of freshly brewed beans.

Skye glanced back at the man as we joined the small line of other shopkeepers waiting by the cart. "Is he making you flush?"

My cheeks must have been as red as they felt. I found myself hoping that the growing rouge was bringing out the green of my eyes. My wild auburn hair, freed from the fishtail braid I had worn on the plane, prickled around my shoulders. I wished I had chosen to run a brush through it.

"No—I just feel like I know him from somewhere, that's all," I muttered, combing a hand through my curls and pretending to be fascinated by the menu on the side of the cart.

"Really?" Skye raised her perfectly threaded eyebrows at me. "He looks like a creep. You know what? I reckon he came out of his store to watch you go past." She smiled gleefully and said to the cart cashier, "We'll have two cappuccinos."

"Me? Don't be absurd." I looked back at the pawnshop; the dark-haired man had gone inside.

"He wouldn't be looking at me. Those hipster types don't go for me. Oh, wouldn't it be wonderful if you moved here and fell in love?" she crooned, clutching the hot coffee to her chest like a precious heirloom.

"Don't be ridiculous." I rolled my eyes as I took my coffee, but I felt jittery inside.

"Let's see if he comes out again when we walk back past the store," Skye whispered.

I sipped my hot drink and trailed behind her as she turned toward Ruadán's Port Pawn. Her sadness had turned to excitement at getting involved in my love life. Was this what having a girlfriend was like? It was kind of . . . nice.

The center was just as quiet as Skye had said. It was biting cold, yet the man had been wearing a singlet. Perhaps this was considered warm for the locals.

"He has to get a good look at us loitering outside." Skye grabbed my arm to slow my pace. I feigned interest in the windows of the clothing store across the way while watching the door of the pawnshop in their reflection as we passed. Unlike the other Bayside stores, with their gleaming modern windows and artful stone finishings, it must have been here before the development. It was whitewashed stone, and its windows were framed with blue wood. We continued to linger across the way, but the dark-haired man didn't emerge.

"Let's go. This is stupid." I blushed at my foolishness and pulled Skye away.

She pouted. "But I was hoping to play matchmaker."

"You don't even know me . . ." I trailed off as I noticed the dark-haired man slip out of his shop. I was sure his mouth showed half a grin. Heat blossomed in my cheeks. Had he somehow overheard our conversation?

I stole a closer glance at him. He was young—maybe a bit older than me. His skin had a pasty sheen, as if it rarely saw sunlight. His thick, dark locks looked slightly greasy, like they needed a good wash. And there were those eyes again. You couldn't miss them, even with the hair dancing around in front of them.

He was still staring. I don't know where I found the burst of courage, but I smiled widely at him. His face fell cold, and he went back inside.

"Well, that was awkward," Skye chortled. Once again, I'd forgotten she was there.

My face burned. *Of course he wasn't interested!* In this new town, I'd let coincidence and my love of films carry my imagination away.

"This is your fault," I grumbled at Skye.

"Oh honey, at least you tried." She slapped me on the back, still giggling.

My shoulders sagged as I returned to Celtic Keepsakes.

This was why I'd never had any friends—or boyfriends, for that matter.

I *was* different from other women in their twenties. Most of them had already had sex, for one thing.

It's not that I never had suitors. There was James, the boy who'd lived next door, who had shown seven-year-old me his male parts in return for a glance at mine. Then there had been Asher and Gareth. Growing up without a father, I found men foreign and inaccessible. Worse than this were the things I sensed in them.

As the afternoon progressed, I imagined my life as an arthouse movie—a slow-paced picture about a sad girl who worked in a souvenir store. Every creak would be emphasized, every rustle magnified. There would be shots of me doing something banal, like making coffee, but the whistle of the pot would sound sinister. The scene wouldn't cut until the water had actually boiled.

I let out a long, slow breath. Sea salt consumed my nostrils as I inhaled.

My pale wrist was resting on the glass counter, and I did a double take, holding it up to my eyeline to examine it—a shadowy patch on my skin. Was it a bruise? I didn't remember banging it on anything. I rubbed my fingers across the darkness, but it didn't fade. It was *textured*.

Shoving my hand underneath one of the fluorescent bulbs, I could see the hair—a small grouping not much bigger than a fifty-cent piece. I plucked at it, and the follicles jumped to attention. *Yuck!*

They say that hair starts growing out of strange places as you age. Was this happening to me now? Perhaps my lack of love interests had prompted early menopause.

Thunder rumbled battle cries as its army of clouds assembled on the horizon. They began to leave their war front, closing in on the bay as I settled at the jetty's end, wrapped in the folds of my new fur coat.

I plucked a bread roll and soda from the bag of groceries I'd bought for Granddad as the final glow of sunset tried to penetrate the inky clouds. The waves beneath me swirled like a black silk scarf around the jetty legs.

The storm was rolling in fast.

The jetty groaned under the ocean's pull, salty spray misting my face, but it made me feel alive.

Beyond the reach of the dock lights, movement stirred. Dark shapes glided below the surface, breaking through the water only to vanish again. My breath hitched but relaxed as a seal emerged, its head glistening in the evening light. It watched me with large, liquid eyes—human eyes. More followed. One by one, they appeared, a quiet audience of shadowed forms drifting in the swell.

A hand gripped my left shoulder, and I started sloshing soda down my coat.

"Sorry if I scared you."

It was *him*. Standing there. Grinning. His voice was deep and confident—one of those voices you can feel in the pit of your stomach, just above the loins. It was somehow smooth as silk and domineering at the same time. It reminded me of the sea billowing beneath us.

"You didn't," I lied. My voice came out high-pitched and shaky. I brushed the soda drops from my jacket.

A splash brought my attention back to the seals. The largest of the group tilted its head, almost questioning, before slipping beneath the waves. The others followed, their heads vanishing into the darkening water.

"I saw you working in the center," the man said. "I'm not very good at talking to people, but when I noticed you sitting here, I felt the need to come and introduce myself. I'm Finn."

"Morgana," I choked out as a breadcrumb lodged in my throat. I managed to shake his outstretched hand before spluttering into a coughing fit.

"Do you mind if I join you?" His voice was warm now, possibly amused, but it was difficult to tell from his inscrutable expression.

"Um, no, not at all." I shifted, pressing my back against the jetty's pole and letting one leg dangle from its edge.

Not good at talking to people? Yeah, right.

"So, do you come here often?" I heard a smile in his words as he moved to stand next to me. He looked down, and his eyes met mine.

My stomach squirmed. I found him attractive. Very attractive. The feeling melted over me like treacle, and my entire body grew warm. His coat was black, matching his eyes. They were the same color as the dark ocean, and the smile dancing around them reminded me of the playful licks of the waves against the dock. I tried to sense his emotions, but I couldn't feel anything.

I couldn't feel anything. Strange.

"I've just moved here, but I plan on coming here often." I wiped my cheeks with the back of my hand, sure they would be covered in flour.

"Is that so? This could get awkward, because I couldn't handle working in this place without coming down here to unwind." Finn leaned on the jetty post and looked out at the approaching storm.

"I could learn to share." I angled my head up at him. "So, you're new here, too?"

"I moved here last week." I couldn't place his accent.

"Where did you move from?" I narrowed my eyes, studying him.

"My family lives on an estate a few hours inland." He waved a hand, his casual tone contrasting with the building storm on the horizon.

"Why would you move here?" I wondered aloud. Surely, an estate was better than this sleepy town.

"I . . . *my father* wants me to get some work experience in Ruadán's Port Pawn. It's one of many . . . family businesses." I found myself liking the way his gaze traveled from my eyes and across my body.

"I've heard the old man who runs that place is scary." I laughed.

"Ah, don't worry about Mr. Inegar. He's an old family friend." Finn crouched down so that we were eye to eye. "But I must admit he scares me a little bit, too." He grinned, and his eyes crinkled in the corners.

Is he joking? I wondered if I should laugh. I couldn't sense mirth in him. I tried again to feel his emotions, but still, I sensed nothing.

"That's an interesting jacket." He surveyed my new fur, a flicker of desire in his eyes, but it was gone so quickly I thought maybe I'd imagined it.

"It was my grandmother's. She left it to me when she died." I instinctively pulled it tighter around me.

"Well, it suits you," he said, resting his forearms lazily on his knees as he crouched beside me.

Was he flirting with me? This wasn't too hard! Everything was so much easier when I couldn't sense other people's overwhelming emotions.

My sleeve slid up, revealing the dark patch of hair I'd noticed earlier. I hastily pulled it back down, glancing up at him from under my lashes. A smile was flirting with his lips as he continued to watch me.

I flushed, focusing on the swirling black water while pulling my coat sleeve further over my hair patch. The waves sighed at each other as the gathering wind rushed over them, and I was overcome with a deep longing to dive beneath them. A ringing pierced my ears, and I grasped the jetty's edge.

"Whoa, are you okay?" I heard Finn ask as a black mist blurred my vision.

The swollen waves seemed to be coming closer. *Closer.*

Splinters of wood lodged under my nails as my grasping hands briefly found the jetty. Then, they were clawing at nothing.

Finn's face faded, replaced by the churning swell beneath me. Salty spray misted my cheeks, and a bubble filled my head. Could I hear music?

Come, ye drunken sailors, to the bottom of the sea.

Come, ye sunken traitors, to swim eternally.

The tune seemed familiar, like an old song I had always known, yet I could not remember the first time I had heard it. Everything was beginning to spin. Was I falling toward the ocean, or had the sea risen to meet me?

3.

Morgana

What happened last night?

The fragments of the dream I had awoken from hadn't left me: a whirlpool of darkness, shadowy figures crying out, a rushing sound, blood flowing into the water. *My blood.* All the while, unblinking red eyes watched me. A chill ran down my spine as I recalled the sensation of something reaching out to me from the shadows.

Another cold, steely morning peeked through the curtains. I pulled myself from the bed and moved shakily toward the window. There was a song about drunken sailors stuck in my head, and I found myself humming it. I couldn't remember where I had heard it before. Perhaps I'd made it up in my dream.

Finn—that was the dark-haired man's name from yesterday. I'd been with him last night. Strange, I didn't remember leaving him. Had I come home and poured myself one too many red wines?

Shit, it was a workday.

I scrambled down the stairs. Granddad was not in his bedroom, and the rest of the house was dark. Barry must have come by to pick him up in his old truck while I slept. They would be out on the water by now.

The thought of seeing Finn ignited a flicker of excitement in my belly. *What is wrong with me?*

I didn't have much experience with men, but I was pretty sure that if you met a strange man and then woke up unable to recall the night's events, you should *not* be fantasizing about them.

I studied myself in the bathroom mirror; I looked pale. I rubbed my hands over my face. *Ugh!* The patch of hair on the back of my wrist!

I scrabbled in the bathroom cabinet for tweezers, wincing as I plucked it away hair by hair.

❦

Skye was chewing a pink piece of gum that matched her pink lips. Her dark hair was piled high on her head in an elegant bun. I had to admire the effort she put into her appearance each day. My hair prickled around my shoulders as I scoured my satchel for the key to Celtic Keepsakes.

"I thought you might have dressed to impress the dark and mysterious boy." Skye giggled as she stood patiently, poised, waiting for me to open the door so she could follow me inside and continue interrogating me.

"Geez, thanks. And his name's Finn," I muttered, fumbling with the lock until it opened.

"How do you know that? Don't tell me you *talked* to him." She rushed in after me.

"Yeah, briefly. Down at the jetty." I feigned business at the cash register.

"Well, what was he like?" Skye leaned on the glass counter and peered at me with wide nut-brown eyes.

"We didn't talk much—just exchanged names. He's just moved here, and then . . . I don't know. I think I fainted." Saying it out loud made me feel even more ridiculous.

"Oh my gosh! What did he think?" Skye squeaked. She was high on the drama.

"I don't know. I woke up in bed." I felt my face flush and wished Skye would return to her store.

"He could have drugged you, for all you know! He looks like the sort to do that kind of thing. He dresses strangely and hangs around all on his own . . ." Her reprimand trailed off into silence as the bell over the door jingled.

Finn smiled as he entered the store and strode up to the counter. "Hope I'm not interrupting anything."

"No, not at all," Skye muttered. "I was just leaving." She threw me a look of warning before turning and strutting out the door. The sound of her patent-leather boots only died away once she reached the carpet of her adjacent shop.

Finn's loose black sweater was rolled up at the sleeves, and the tattoos on his forearm were on display. I moved out from behind the counter, grasping his hand to get a better look, and he smiled down at me—an inviting smile. His skin was cool beneath my burning palm, and the rest of the shopping center fell away, replaced by our closeness. My blood seemed to be coursing faster than usual.

The tattoo was like nothing I had ever seen; it was a work of art. Around his right wrist was a cuff-like structure comprising three lines. On top of them were symbols. They looked like runes, but I couldn't place them. The rest of it wrapped elegantly around his upper arm, forming an intricate band of interwoven Celtic knots. Between the weaving, there were dark spots. Some were filled with strange markings, but in others, there was imagery. One encompassed a small cluster of fossilized shells; another looked like the moon above a dark horizon. The same strange runes that formed the bands around his wrists also ran up and down some of the arcs. The design was intricate, yet it had a raw, unrefined edge.

He stepped closer to me, and I liked the way he smelled. Something about it was familiar—like sea salt blowing off the waves. I pushed the sleeve of his sweater up further to see the rest of the ink, heat rising in my cheeks. The air grew tighter, *closer*, between our bodies.

"This is amazing," I breathed, unable to downplay my curiosity. The soft hum of the heating system was the only sound that accompanied the blood pumping in my ears.

Then I noticed the scars. They were barely visible under the ink, but I could see them in the bright light of day, winding around his wrist and up his forearm. It was as if the tattoo had been cleverly designed to cover them.

A shadow flickered across Finn's face as he caught my gaze tracing the patterns. He tensed as if about to pull his arm away but hesitated, then said, "Do you make a habit of latching on to handsome strangers?" His voice was an icy drawl. He rolled his sleeve back down, and his eyes met mine—cold, distant, as if my touch had repulsed him.

I was drawn from my trance as the leather goods shop across the way swam back into view through the glass windows. I was still holding his wrist.

Shit, shit, shit.

I let it drop, wiping my palms on the side of my jeans. Why had I grasped his hand in the first place?

Pretend you're incredibly interested in tattoos.

"Did a tattooist do that? I—I was thinking about getting one." A lie. I dug my hands into the pockets of my pants and glanced out the window.

"No, it was a friend of mine." He shrugged. Even in the daylight, his eyes were the ocean's black, but his irises had flecks of gray.

"How are you feeling? That was strange last night." He grinned as if shaking off the shadows.

That's right—*last night*. The touch of his skin had made me forget that I had woken up in my bed unable to remember how I'd gotten there.

"What happened?" I tried to act nonchalant, but the question cascaded from my lips in a gush.

Finn moved to lean against the glass counter, and his iciness was replaced with the same air of confidence he'd had at the jetty. "I suppose you could say you fainted toward the sea. I grabbed the back of your coat to stop you from falling in and then carried you away from the edge. The water here could give you hypothermia, and a storm was coming."

I searched his eyes and thought I could see something welling in them—it looked like curiosity.

"Oh." I blushed at the thought of being carried in his arms.

"I took you home. I didn't know what else to do. Your granddad let me in, and I sat by your bed for about an hour until the storm passed. When it looked like you were sleeping peacefully, I left." He stepped forward, and I thought he might reach for my hand. Instead, he seemed to think better of it and moved back, regarding my face.

"You sat by my bed?" My cheeks burned as I thought about the underpants that might have been strewn on the floor. "But wait! How did you find my house?" I tilted my head, studying his expression.

I thought I saw his cool exterior falter, but then he smiled. "You regained consciousness and told me. Then you fell asleep again in my arms. I think you were having a bad dream."

I remembered the familiar nightmare I had awoken to and hoped I hadn't been thrashing about.

"Is this the first time something like this has happened to you?" Finn's eyes seemed to bore into mine.

Each moment of silence echoed between us like a heartbeat. It was as if he thought my secrets would be revealed if he looked hard enough. I liked that he seemingly found me interesting. My body was responding to the stare in a way that I had never experienced, so I tried to sense his feelings despite myself. *Nothing.*

"I don't habitually faint into the water, if that's what you're asking." My emotions wavered between grateful and embarrassed. "Thank you," I added, as a shudder worked its way down my spine. What would have happened if he hadn't been there? The water was freezing, and I would have fallen into it while unconscious.

"I couldn't have my only friend here drowning now, could I?" He pushed off the counter, closing the space between us again.

At that moment, a couple of shoppers entered.

"I better go," Finn said. "I'll see you in a few days. I'm really glad you're okay."

He lingered for a moment, and I wondered if he would say something else. Instead, he gave me one last smile as he turned and stepped out of the store.

I was left speechless. My cheeks were hot, and my fingers were trembling. To my horror, I was sweating. *Gross!*

Why would he not see me for a few days? My body had become a shaky mess, but . . . I would miss this feeling.

"So, do you think you'll sleep with the mysterious lad?" Skye said, playing with the marshmallow in her hot chocolate.

She had insisted we meet for dinner at the café beneath the Ferris wheel. It was at the end of the lane, tucked behind the coffee cart. Glass panels extended from the weathered stone, sheltered by a tin roof shading retro blue patio furniture. We were seated in the outdoor area, a heater humming overhead.

"Just this morning, you were telling me he was dangerous!" I put down my burger and wiped my fingers on the blue-and-white napkin, which matched the table and chairs. "Like he would want to sleep with me anyway," I added. But my skin prickled at the thought of being in Finn's arms. I knew they had already held me, yet try as I might, I couldn't recall it.

"I think he does." Skye popped a fry between her pink lips without smudging her gloss. "Why would he have found you last night and then again this morning? Guys only want one thing." She giggled.

"Intelligent conversation?" I raised my eyebrows as I watched the sun dip behind the distant cliffs.

Skye must have noticed the grimace I was trying to hide, because she pressed, "Don't tell me you haven't done it before?"

My stomach turned, and I let my face answer the question.

"A guy like Finn would have slept with heaps of girls!" Skye chewed on her cheek before adding, "I bet he's the kind of guy who expects women to go all the way because he asks them to."

The nausea in my gut expanded.

"There's no way I'd go all the way just because he asked me to!" I folded my arms across my chest.

"But you're twenty years old . . ." Skye's nostrils flared delicately.

I laughed off her inquisitive stare, but my throat tightened.

There was no denying it: I *did* want to do all kinds of stuff with Finn, but there was a reason I was still a virgin. I thought back to my first sexual encounters. In these moments, the emotions had run so strong they blinded me. My fear and self-disgust were at the forefront, mingling with what I sensed. I knew this wasn't normal, because if it were, other people wouldn't enjoy foreplay or the act it leads to.

Skye must have seen a look pass over my face, because she said, "I didn't mean to upset you."

"You're right. Finn, or any guy I encounter at this age, is likely to be a hell of a lot more experienced than I am." I grinned as if to shrug the statement away, but it had been playing on my mind.

What if I sensed the same intense lust in him that I had found in the others? I hadn't been able to pick up on Finn's feelings at the jetty or in the store, but people's emotions always became more unguarded when they were aroused.

"But you have something wonderful to offer." Skye clasped her hands together in glee. "A virgin is a rare find these days, so don't freak out. I'll tell you anything you need to know." She gave me a little wink.

"You can't say stuff like that. It's not the Middle Ages. I am not a sacrificial token to be led to Finn in a white dress."

"Um, *hello*. I am comfortable in my sexuality. Don't slut shame me for speaking my truth!" Skye snapped her fingers at me in a way that said *I am woman, hear me roar* while completely missing the point.

A chilly ocean breeze ruffled our hair. I inhaled—salt mixed with seaweed and fish. Another gust of wind hit us, and I was overcome with an urge to kick over the table and run down to the shore.

"Are you okay?" Skye's concerned voice brought me back from my reverie.

My knuckles were white against the table's edge, and I had raised myself out of my seat. Was I going insane?

I whipped my head around the café. If the Ferris wheel had been active, it would have been the hottest eatery in town, but thankfully, tonight, it only held three other diners.

"I . . . I was just enjoying the wind," I muttered, immediately wishing I had formulated a less weird excuse.

"I think the dark and mysterious lad is starting to rub off on you."

Skye giggled, and my shoulders, which had become tense, relaxed. She scrunched up the wrapper from her burger and aimed for the waste bin. It ricocheted off the edge of a nearby table and tumbled to the ground. "Damn it!" She stared at me in a pouty way.

"There was no way you were going to make that shot!" I scoffed, gesturing toward the trash can on the other side of the venue in the wheel's shadow.

As I got up to retrieve the wrapper, the wind brushed against me, sending a chill up my spine. The hairs on my neck rose, as an eerie sense of foreboding settled in.

Behind me, Skye was bent over, texting on her pink iPhone in the open café's warm glow. I exhaled, tossing the rubbish into the bin, then froze. A flicker of movement stirred in the shadows beyond.

Was someone watching me? There, from the gloom around the pedestal of the wheel. I squinted into the dusk. I knew someone was there. *I sensed them.*

"What are you looking at?" Skye's voice made me jump. She had emerged behind me.

"Nothing. I thought I saw . . ."

Something moved again, followed by a flash of silver. I stormed into the darkness.

"Wait! Where are you going?" Skye was at my heels.

We reached the bottom of the wheel, and its white frame opened above us.

Skye let out a frightened gasp behind me as she, too, noticed the man.

Cloaked in black, he moved swiftly, the fabric gliding over the grass as he hurried away, but just before vanishing into the night, he glanced back, his gaze lingering.

Skye gripped the back of my arm as the meager glow from the café hit the inside of his hood. Her fear washed over me, mingling with my own. The man's face shone silver in the half-light, and I could see his cheekbones were sunken. The sockets of his eyes were colorless chasms. Then in a swish of his cloak he disappeared into the darkness.

I couldn't move, but Skye was dragging me toward the café. I stumbled after her, still I didn't take my eyes off the spot where the man had been.

"What on earth was that creep doing?" Skye was shaking when we reached our table.

"I don't even know why I chased him." I was astonished at my boldness.

"What is that awful smell?" Skye wrinkled her nose.

I sniffed. "It smells kind of like the sea."

"Aye, it smells like something died!" She dry retched. "I've officially got the creeps! I'm driving you home tonight. This town is full of weirdos." She gathered her stuff from the table, still scrunching her nose.

"Thanks," I muttered, slinging my satchel over my shoulder.

I didn't feel like walking alone on the cold, dark docks tonight. The hairs on my arms were still standing on end. There had been something unnatural about that man. I couldn't shake the image of his silver-tinged skin and how his cheekbones jutted, skeletal and hollow.

4.

Morgana

Drumming reverberated through the kitchen as I made dinner for my grandfather. It was October 31. In America, this was Halloween. Here, it was Samhain—the end of the harvest season and a time for welcoming winter, the darker half of the year.

"Make sure you set a place for her." Granddad nodded at the table as I began pulling cutlery from one of the wooden kitchen drawers.

"For who?" I opened the microwave, grabbing the frozen vegetables I had been heating up.

"For Iona," he said matter-of-factly, rapping his weathered knuckles on the table across from him where my grandmother must have once sat.

I paused mid-stir over the mashed potatoes, glancing at his face to see if he'd gone mad.

"Tonight and the three days that follow, the veil around this world and the other comes down. The souls o' those who have left us can visit, so we like to leave a place for them." Granddad surveyed the seat across from him with sad, dark eyes, as if he could see her sitting there.

I scrambled to get some cutlery and a plate for my grandmother. I chose one of the special ones with embossed lemons she'd undoubtedly picked up on her travels. This made Granddad smile, and my heart clenched.

The rhythmic drumming echoed through the kitchen while we ate our dinner in silence. I found myself glancing at the window and the empty place I had set, wondering if my grandmother would indeed appear to have dinner with us.

"You should go check it out." Granddad nodded at the window. "It's an old Celtic festival. Not many places in Scotland celebrate it any longer, but this town likes to keep with traditions."

Bonfires were lit on both arms of the bay. The drumming was coming from the grassy cliff behind the Ferris wheel, by the old graveyard, and I made my way up there.

Tears bit at the corners of my eyes as I thought about my grandfather eating alone, waiting for the love of his life to return.

Evening had begun to cloak the world in shades of indigo as I arrived at the Bayside shopping center. The café under the Ferris wheel was open, and for the first time, it was bustling. The young man from my grandmother's funeral was waiting tables. He had a stack of plates in one arm and a notepad in the other, but he smiled at me and nodded hello.

The usually deserted grassy cliff face behind the Ferris wheel was alive and alight with makeshift market stalls tonight. Bonfires blazed all along it. The nearest, set on the grassy strip to the wheel's left, was the largest. Drummers sat around it, their rhythms pulsing through the air. Further up the cliff, smaller fires dotted the landscape, trailing past the old graveyard like beacons of light against the darkening night.

As the last rays of sun penetrated the horizon, a gush of ocean wind hit me. I faltered as the smells washed over me. Perhaps a clifftop festival was not a good idea when my mind was so . . . fragile.

"Morgana!" A squeal rang out. Skye was coming out of the crowd, holding hot fries in a cone. "Why didn't you tell me you were coming? I would have gone with you instead." She jerked her head toward a man glowering at us beside one of the stores.

Parker. He was exactly as I expected: handsome, but too handsome. The kind of looks that create an air of cockiness. He had sandy hair, a cleft chin, and an aura of impatience. Arms folded, he watched us with irritation flickering in his baby-blue eyes.

"I—I better go." Skye looked crestfallen.

"I'm going to go check out the fires anyway."

The bonfire crackled, shooting flames into the darkening sky. Drummers were using wooden sticks to beat against round, hide-covered drums. Some of the leathers had patterns, a Celtic design, and a bird. There was a throng of people all moving back and forth to the steady beat. They were dressed up, I realized. A man with giant antlers wreathed with vine leaves on his head, someone wearing a cow skull, men and women bearing flags, and women in full-skirted dresses were all moving around the fire to the music. In my jeans and jacket, I suddenly felt underdressed.

"Morgana." I heard my name again—a man's voice. A horse skull was at my shoulder, colorful ribbons streaming from its sides. Someone was holding it beneath a sheet, giving the impression of a ghostly stallion.

"It's Láir Bhán—the white mare." Finn grinned as he threw the sheet off himself and casually placed the skull under his arm. "Supernatural beings and the gods of old are said to be abroad tonight, but these costumes can ward them off." He passed me the skull. Its eyes had baubles stuffed into them, and spirals were painted onto the bleached bone.

It had been three days since I'd last seen Finn. Now, firelight was illuminating his angular jaw and dark brows. My breath caught in my chest—not so long ago, this beautiful man had carried me in his arms away from the water's edge and saved my life.

"How was your time away?" I asked, passing him back the horse skull and wiping my sweaty palms on the legs of my jeans.

"It's always . . . difficult to go home." Finn smiled dryly, and I thought I could see a shadow flicker across his face—maybe the same darkness that had arisen when I'd noticed the scars.

What did he mean difficult? I hated that I was wondering what he was thinking about and trying to sense his feelings. *Still nothing.*

"What made you decide to go back to the estate?" I asked. The crowd ebbed and flowed around us between the market stalls and bonfires, drinking and dancing.

"Oh yeah, the estate . . ." He dragged his fingers over his lower lip. "My father wanted a report on how my new job was going." I liked how he talked: all proper. It was refreshing. I noticed again the lack of a local accent, or any accent I could pin down.

"Oh." I hooked my thumbs through the belt loops on my jeans and removed them, realizing how ridiculous I must have looked. Folding my arms, I surveyed the people gathered around the fire.

"Coming here and dressing up is a ritual for my cousin and me. He's here somewhere." Finn scanned the rest of the clifftop merrymakers; when he didn't see who he was looking for, he half yelled, "Do you want to get a drink?" over the drumming.

I nodded, and he shrugged off the sheet, letting it fall beside the skull on the grassy hilltop. Now, he was back in his usual attire: black jeans and a black sweater. We returned from the cliff's edge toward the bustling makeshift market stalls.

While we waited in line, I watched kids light wooden torches in the bonfire.

"People take flames back to their homes as protection." Finn's dark eyes reflected the fire as he watched the children.

<hr />

"I wonder where my cousin is. Off doing something debauched, no doubt." Finn chuckled.

Is that what Finn would be doing if I wasn't here? The thought caused my throat to tighten, and I sipped the soda he had bought me as we walked back toward the large bonfire and the merrymakers around it.

As we neared the cliff's edge, the sighs of the waves rose above the rhythm of the drums. Night had masked the sky, but the flickering flames bathed us in a soft light.

"Being here reminds me of my grandmother . . . of the stories she used to tell me as a child." My teeth sunk into my lower lip as I surveyed the scene.

"You loved her," Finn stated. He was staring at me in that all-consuming way. The way part of me liked, and the other part found unnerving.

"I used to cry for days when she returned home after visiting me in America." I sighed. "They say you don't forget the sound of someone's voice, but I'm starting to think I have."

My grandmother's stories of her travels and magical tales always captivated me. When she left me with my mother again after those trips, I felt more alone than ever.

"I lost my mother when I was young." Finn's tone grew rigid, and he paused. "Sometimes I imagine what her voice sounded like—soothing and sad, maybe like the ocean at night . . ." A shadow danced over his face.

We were silent as the waves crashed against the rocks below.

"Do you ever wonder if people we've lost can still see us?" I said. "Maybe they're watching from somewhere, even wishing they could say something?" I thought about my grandfather sitting next to the empty place setting.

Finn's black brows were drawn as he turned from me and looked out over the ocean. "Tonight, they *can* see us," he said.

"It's strange. I could tell my grandmother loved this town, but for some reason, she never let me visit."

Finn turned back to me again, his dark eyes flickering with something.

The bonfire behind us cracked, and I jumped.

"The fires mimic the sun," he explained, following my gaze. "They are a bid to hold back the darkness of winter."

Tears peaked in the corners of my eyes. Something about celebrating life and death, light and dark, embracing the supernatural and warding them off simultaneously was so . . .

"Beautiful," I said the word out loud as I surveyed the fires. I had always felt like an outsider, but in this small town—my grandmother's town—filled with superstition and tales of magic, I was beginning to feel less out of place.

Finn put his hand on the small of my back, taking in my expression. "Beautiful, yes"—his voice was quiet—"but also said to be a night of grave dangers."

But I was no longer watching the fires. I had turned to watch a man. He was wandering along the cliff's edge. So close to the cliff's edge. He stopped by the next fire over from ours and observed me. He was handsome, or so it looked in the half-light from this distance. He had a chiseled jaw and dark features, but his hair was light. His gaze flicked to mine, and I could have sworn his eyes flashed red, but then it was gone. Perhaps it was the firelight playing tricks on me.

Finn stiffened at my side as he, too, noticed the man.

I gripped Finn's arm. Suddenly, the man was . . . *gone*.

"Did he . . . did he just jump?" I started moving toward the cliff's edge, where the man had been only moments—seconds—ago, dragging Finn with me.

"I saw him slip into the shadows," Finn muttered. "It must have been a trick of the light."

I was at the cliff's edge now, and the man was nowhere to be seen.

"Morgana!" Finn pulled his arm from my grasp and rolled up his sleeve. Little crescent indents from my nails marked his skin, shining red in the flickering firelight.

"I'm sorry," I breathed. "It just looked like he disappeared, that's all." I peered into the crashing waves below, but there was only darkness. I shook my head, exhaling deeply. Perhaps I was losing my mind, but I wondered why, if that was the case, everything felt clearer than ever.

"I've got to find my cousin." Finn's tone was grave.

Before I could respond, he slipped away into the crowd, still swaying to the rhythm of the drums. I craned my neck to track him, but he had vanished into the shadows, just like the strange pale-haired man.

A prickle of foreboding licked at the back of my neck as I opened the door to my grandparents' house. They were familiar to me, these sensations. They usually meant something was amiss.

Granddad was in the living room next to a crackling fire. He nodded and gave me a small smile as I crept behind him to the kitchen, where the table setting I'd laid out for my grandmother remained.

I made myself a hot chocolate, relishing its creamy sweetness after the cold night, but unease gnawed at me. Finn and Granddad were sure our loved ones could visit us tonight, but what about the man I'd seen—the one who had seemingly jumped from the cliff?

Making a second mug of hot chocolate, I set it next to my grandmother's empty plate.

The prickle at the back of my neck intensified when I reentered the dark hallway. I found myself wanting to check every room in the house.

I pushed open Granddad's door first and flicked on the light. Relief flooded me as his simple queen bed appeared.

I checked the bathroom. Flick—nothing.

I went to the study. Flick—nothing. I breathed a sigh of relief. Perhaps the feeling had something to do with Samhain and the veils between worlds disintegrating. What was I thinking?

The feeling intensified as I climbed the winding stairs to the attic, and the fine hairs on my arms stood on end. My hands trembled as I flicked the light switch—I'd seen enough horror movies to know it's *always* in the attic! But I felt foolish when nothing but dusty boxes and my grandmother's old dresser were illuminated.

My room was also empty. I even opened the old wardrobe to check that nothing was hiding inside. I shook my head. I was acting crazy. But there had been so many strange occurrences since I'd been here: the fainting, the sunken-faced man, and now the beautiful disappearing man.

I threw myself on my bed and stared at the beams running across the dark wood ceiling. Then, out of the corner of my eye, I saw it. All of my dresser drawers were open, and I remembered closing them.

Ignoring the bed's groan, I leaped up and rifled through them. Nothing was missing, but someone had been here. I was sure of it.

Why had someone wanted to go through my things? Could it have been my grandfather? No, he had trouble with the narrow stairs, and the prickle at the back of my neck suggested it had been someone else.

Terror clutched at my throat as I flung open the wardrobe again. My grandmother's old fur coat was still hanging there. Relief coursed through me. I'd grown fiercely protective of the heirloom.

5.

Morgana

Finn was leaning against the glass doors of Celtic Keepsakes the next day, nonchalantly smoking, dressed in a khaki jacket, jeans, and boots. My palms grew sweaty, and warmth flooded my cheeks. It had been easier to be around him in the flickering light of the Samhain bonfires, but my heart started hammering now that I observed him in the light of day. I took in his dark hair, gently tousled, and his sensuous lips.

"You always smoked?" I asked, nodding and raising my eyebrows in a way that made me feel cool.

"Since I was a suckling babe." His cheeks caved as he took a draw. It made him look like someone from an old black-and-white Hollywood film.

"You know smoking isn't cool anymore?" I scoffed. I had my satchel slung across my chest like a side bag, so I wasn't really in a position to say what was and wasn't cool.

"I like to try new things while away from home." His mouth curved into a half smile. I liked how he stood, always straight-backed and confident, even with his shoulders resting on the glass—the complete opposite of me.

He ground the butt of his cigarette into the ashen cement with the heel of his boot, running a hand through his tangle of dark curls.

I wanted to say something intelligent—or anything at all—but I just stood frozen as we stared at each other. Finn seemed to flit between charming and arrogant to cold and distant. Both personas must be masks, but what was behind those masks? I *had* to know. Was this what it was like to speak to someone when you couldn't sense their emotions, or was it just him?

He seemed to want to be around me, though; this was the fourth time he'd sought me out, and the thought made my stomach flutter.

"Yes, well, I better open up now. If you would be so kind." I jerked my head to motion him away from the doorway.

He exhaled a breath but didn't move. We stood like that for a moment, and I stared at him. I knew I was feeding his ego, but he needed to move and let me into my store. I attempted to reach around his body to put the key into the lock, and his scent washed over me—sea salt blowing off the waves.

He grabbed my hand, and his eyes met mine. "Have lunch with me?"

My mouth fell open. I clamped it shut and collected myself. "Um, okay, sure." I wrenched my sweaty palm from his grasp as his lips tugged into a grin.

I inserted the key into the lock as he finally began moving away from the glass. My fingers were trembling, and it jammed. *Shit.* I wiggled it furiously. As his footsteps retreated, I relaxed enough to unlock the door.

"Oh, and Morgana!" Finn stopped and looked down at his feet as though suspended between wanting to say something else and needing to leave.

"What?" I was smiling now.

"Think of somewhere we can go that's not *here*." He gestured to the empty center.

☙

Peering into the dusty window of Ruadán's Port Pawn, I didn't see anybody behind the counter, so I entered.

The arrangement of odds and ends cluttering the walls made me feel claustrophobic. A bowl of coins on display caught my attention, and I plucked a piece from the pot. It was silver, just like the fifty-cent pieces I was used to, but different. Instead of the presidential seal or a monarch's torso, this depicted a fish, or something that looked like a fish. Its engraved tail was long and curved up one side of the coin. There was lettering around the outside. It looked like runes, but they had been worn smooth, and I couldn't be sure. I snatched another piece from the bowl. They were all the same, and they had all been badly worn.

Finn's voice emerged from the back room, and I froze to catch the conversation.

"Look, all I want to know is *what* my father is going to do with this information," his cold, clear voice said.

"I've already told you everything I know about this second job," a voice, which I assumed belonged to the old shop owner, Mr. Inegar, growled.

"You wouldn't lie to me for him, would you?" Finn sounded stern now. I thought this was strange, given that Mr. Inegar was his boss.

"I have tutored you since you were a lad. We're like family! If I knew more, I would tell you," Mr. Inegar replied.

"He's been acting . . . stranger than usual." Finn sighed.

"And you're dragging it out. *Why?* Surely, it can't be difficult," Mr. Inegar said gruffly.

"Of course not." Finn scoffed, "It's just a bit diffcrent, that's all . . ."

I had been absent-mindedly running my fingers through the bowl of coins, which now tipped and spilled across the counter with a clatter. The voices stopped. Finn and Mr. Inegar appeared as I scrambled to collect them.

There was something etched into the bottom of the empty bowl. My breath hitched. It was the same insignia from the box holding my grandmother's ashes—a wave with a crescent moon rising above it, surrounded by a mermaid, a skull, *a seal* . . .

Mr. Inegar rushed over, grabbing the bowl from me before I could make out the other images. He scooped the coins back in with a scowl.

Finn greeted me with a welcoming smile. "So, have you decided where we're going?"

"Yep." I grinned, wiping my dusty fingers on my jeans.

Mr. Inegar frowned at us over his shoulder. His brows were snow-white, and his skin was leathery.

"Wait, I think I would like to buy one of those coins—" I swung back to the mess I had left on the dusty counter.

"Not for sale." Mr. Inegar glowered.

"But why were they on display?"

He placed the silver bowl under the counter, continuing to glare at me.

"What country are they from anyway?" I shot him a smile in the hope of some reciprocity. He didn't return it.

"Don't worry about him," Finn said, gently tugging me toward the doorway. His touch made me forget all about the coins.

🐚

As we passed beneath the towering broken Ferris wheel, I glanced at its rusted beams silhouetted against the overcast sky. Streaked with mold, dirt, and seagull droppings, it was like a relic of a carnival long forgotten.

Ducking under one of the lower beams, I caught it sparkling in the sunlight. I reached up, running my fingers over its rough surface. There were messy silver markings streaked across it as if someone had painted them. *Silver.* Just like the face of the man I'd seen here.

"The wheel is impressive, but I don't know if I'd ever get the urge to stroke it." I sensed Finn's smirk behind me.

"There are markings on it." I turned to face him.

"Let me see that!" Finn's eyes narrowed, and he rushed forward. He ran his hands where mine had just been. His eyes moved to and fro like he was reading.

"Do you know what the drawings are?" I asked, shielding my eyes from the bright midday sun to squint at the white beam.

He ignored me, staring up at the top of the wheel. I followed his gaze but saw nothing unusual, only its carriage-less circle silhouetted against the clouds.

"You know, you're right." Finn turned back to me and grinned. "It's impossible to walk past this wheel without giving it a stroke." He brushed the silver designs on the beam in an exaggerated caress.

"Shut up," I grumbled, pushing ahead of him. I wondered if I should tell Finn about the man. But what would I say? That I'd seen a man with a silver face and sunken eyes? I was certain reaper-looking creeps weren't the best topic for a first date—but was this even a date? I wasn't sure.

We crossed the grassy area where the festival of Samhain had been held, but this time, we didn't turn toward the cliff's edge. Instead, I led us to a dilapidated fence marking the center's boundary from the industrial area. Behind it was a small concrete wasteland of deserted shipping containers

I had noticed the night before. They must have been hauled up here and left behind from the port days of trade.

"Are you enjoying working at the pawnshop?" I asked as I trailed down the fence line, looking for the perfect spot to cross. I was still thinking about the strange conversation I had overheard between him and Mr. Inegar.

"You never know what curious items someone might bring in. How are you liking this wee town?" Finn moved closer, his salty scent washing over me.

"Believe it or not, I like this forgotten outdoor center." I stopped at a spot where the rusted fence was sagging.

He grasped my hand as I stepped over first, and I flushed as a flash of excitement coursed through me. I turned to face him as he sprang after me, still holding my hand. The gray flecks in his eyes were sparkling. Could he tell how his touch made me feel? I couldn't sense his emotions, but sometimes it seemed as if he could read mine.

The emptiness of the industrial area, which bled into the rugged green cliffs beyond, now loomed before us, and Finn's shoulder brushed against mine as we surveyed the scene together.

"I like this place too," he said. "It offers me . . . well, freedom." There was a heaviness behind his reflective eyes. It was a feeling I thought I understood.

"Before coming here to look after my grandfather, I'd never left the Midwest. My mother has always been overbearing." I hooked my hair behind my ear and turned to him, thinking about how nice it was not to have her fussing over my "condition." Living here, it felt like a weight had been lifted from my shoulders. I didn't tell him I sensed college was not my destiny, but that maybe this town was. That would be way too weird.

"Are you and your mother close?" he asked, his eyes flicking to mine.

"No, not really. We are very—well . . . different." I thought about her again. "She's an accountant and practical to a fault. Everything's about what makes sense—numbers, rules, logic . . ."

My mother had no room for "feelings," whereas they consumed me.

Finn and I made our way between the scattered shipping containers, their rusted maroon and mustard pillars towering above us.

"At least she's consistent. One moment, my father's shouting orders; the next, he's cold and distant, like I don't even exist to him." Finn laughed sarcastically. "Your mother— does she care about what you want? Or is it always her way?"

"She'd say she cares. She wants me to get a good job, live a 'normal' life, whatever that means."

"I get it." He let out a low chuckle. "My family has money, and with that money comes duty. With duty comes sacrifice." He adopted a deep, would-be-fatherly tone.

The ground beneath our feet was a patchwork of cracked concrete and wild grasses that had claimed the land back from its man-made purpose, the air thick with the scent of metal and sea.

"What would you do with your life if you could do anything?" I angled my head to survey the side of his sharp jaw.

"Honestly, just this. I find beauty in the simplest things, like having lunch with a pretty girl and feeling the first autumn winds on my face." Finn turned on the spot, taking in our surroundings.

We reached the base of a large navy shipping container, and I imagined the cloaked silver-faced man crouching in its shadowy depths. In the light of day, I would have been able to see what was inside his hollow eye sockets.

But the container was empty; the daylight reached its dark back and showed that only sand and bird droppings had made it their home. I had chosen this container because it was the largest, and the smaller ones had fallen by its side, leading like a mismatched staircase to its roof. I scrambled up first, and the sea breeze caught me as I emerged on its top. I crouched down for fear of being buffeted straight off or, worse still, acting crazy and sniffing all its scents. The last thing I needed was for Finn to see me inhaling the wind like some frenzied animal.

From the top of the shipping container, the Ferris wheel, the Bayside shopping center behind it, and the two arms of the bay beyond stretched before us. I looked sideways at Finn, who had seated himself spread-legged beside me. His elbows rested lazily on his cocked knees. His jacket hid his tattoos today, but I tried to conjure the feeling of being in his arms—carried down the jetty, away from the water's edge.

"I like how you find beauty in the mundane." Finn looked out over the harbor, and the wind was in his hair.

Was it a compliment or an insult? I couldn't tell.

His eyes found mine with a turn of his head, and he looked sincere. "Now you have to let me return the favor. Would you like to come to my house tomorrow night to watch Netflix? I find myself quite fond of this platform you have here."

"Don't you have Netflix on your estate?" My eyes widened.

"No, it's quite archaic, really."

I had practically lived on the streaming service in Kansas City, but Grandpa didn't have a smart TV, and Mom hadn't let me take the laptop. I couldn't deny I missed watching movies. Movies and books had always been an escape for me. I couldn't sense the emotions of the characters, allowing me to interact with them in a way that was almost . . . *normal*.

"So, do you want to come?" Finn surveyed me, his black eyes narrowed. I thought about my dream and its warning but found myself nodding. I swallowed. It felt like a *real* date.

"See those houses?" He gestured to the luxurious buildings with big glass windows clustered around the bay's curve. "The largest one in the middle is where I live. I won't be at work tomorrow, but you should come over afterward."

My entire body heated up as I thought about being in his home.

"This place is so wild and empty," I muttered, looking away so he wouldn't notice the flush in my cheeks.

"I think you will like it here. Morgana means 'dweller of the sea' in Gaelic. We also have the Morgen—water spirits said to drown men." He chuckled.

"I had never seen the ocean before moving to this town, but I seem drawn to it." I smiled, thinking my grandmother must have had something to do with my name.

"You are unique, Morgana." Finn sighed as he surveyed me, and his cold hand brushed mine. "What's most captivating about you is that you don't even realize how rare you are."

I wasn't sure I'd ever felt like this. My blood was racing. I was used to being overwhelmed by emotions and wanting out of there as soon as possible, but I didn't want this to end. I wanted to *live* in this feeling. I wrenched myself from his gaze and squinted in the direction he had pointed.

"The pawnshop must be doing well if you can afford to live there."

"It's only one business of many..." I could hear the shrug in his words as I stared at the houses. Tomorrow night, I would be inside those walls with him.

6.

MORGANA

A nagging feeling settled in the pit of my stomach as I walked to work, a nervous excitement that I couldn't swallow or keep at bay.

I had taken some care in selecting my outfit. Skye said the trick of first dates was to "put a lot of effort into looking effortless." I wasn't planning on following her entire dating rulebook—I wasn't even sure if it *was* a date. Yet, my usually wild curls were straight and sleek this morning. They stuck to my glossed lips and tickled my cheeks in the wind. I had chosen black jeans and a tight white T-shirt to look acceptable at work. Then, I'd thrown my grandmother's fur coat over the entire outfit. I nestled my pink fingers deep within the pockets to avoid the cold.

The opulent houses crowding the bay's right fist were burrowed artfully into the small strip of land between the open ocean and the harbor. I imagined the views from them held nothing but the waves.

Finn had mentioned he wouldn't be in today. Was he up there somewhere, watching me from high above?

Warmth spread across my cheeks, and I pretended to admire the whole bay, focusing on the boats bobbing in the mooring area before me. The name of the only yacht caught my attention, "Parker's Wet Lass" traced down the side in red script.

I snorted. I did not doubt this was Skye's boyfriend's yacht.

"Nervous?" Skye asked gleefully when I arrived at Celtic Keepsakes. She was leaning against the glass as Finn had done the day before.

"A little," I confessed, rattling the store door open.

"Because you *know* what 'Netflix and chill' means. In boy language, that is code for 'I want to rip your clothes off,' and you're meant to understand that." She followed me inside. I wondered if she ever operated the tartan store.

I was kind of over Skye's constant desire to impart the wisdom she had gained from being five years my senior, but I knew she meant well.

When Finn invited me, he had seemed sincere and serious. Now, I pictured him giving me a knowing nod and a little half wink as he said, "Watch Netflix."

"I'm sure there isn't a code." I twisted my fingers together, which I only did when I was anxious.

"I learned it the hard way. Google it!" Skye giggled, her dark curls bobbing in unison.

Despite myself, I plucked my iPhone from my pocket and opened the browser.

"*Netflix and chill* is a slang term used as a euphemism for sexual activity . . ." I read aloud.

Oh, fuck. My stomach dropped as I slid my phone back into my jeans pocket.

"See!" Skye's brown eyes were wide with glee.

"He doesn't even have Netflix back on his estate! So I'm sure he is unfamiliar with using it as a euphemism." I tried to think back to Finn's invitation again.

"It's all the same thing." Skye stared at me momentarily, clearly trying to come up with another question or something else to say. Finally, she added, "If he wants to 'watch a movie' with you, he wants to sleep with you. Period." She did a little twirl, like a lawyer who had just delivered a victorious closing statement.

"I'm not sure I'm ready . . ."

My chest tightened, and I was back in the bushes at the prom after-party as Asher pushed me down. His arousal washed over me. It was suffocating. I had wanted this, hadn't I? I had kissed him and consented to being led into the bushes, but now that we were there, his emotions were too strong. Before I knew what I was doing, I had thrown him from me and raced away. I could still hear him muttering "You crazy bitch" as I fled the scene.

"But you like him!" Skye pouted. Perhaps, even though she went for guys like Parker, she held a secret candle for dark and mysterious men like Finn. The thought made me smile. Skye took it the wrong way. "I knew it! I knew you wanted to."

"I guess I do a bit," I admitted, thinking of how Finn made me feel. "But I will lose my virginity when I am ready, not when *you* tell me to, and *especially* not when a boy tells me to."

That was it: my nervous excitement had officially transformed into nausea.

Skye lifted her chin in thought. "I'll help you. I'm an expert." She was only hearing what she wanted to hear.

"Just because I haven't had sex doesn't mean I know nothing. And shouldn't you go open your store?"

She clomped back past my front window to the tartan store. Her practiced calves never faltered in her brown knee-length suede skirt and boots.

I counted the contents of the register and wiped down the glass around the counter. Outside, a seagull cawed aimlessly. It was as though this center was a place of waste: I wasted my life while the gull wasted its breath. Perhaps Skye was right. I should *just do it*.

I rapped on her window, and she emerged, clutching a pink handbag in her long-nailed hands.

"So, what's the plan then?" I asked, pulling my fur coat around me. It seemed colder than usual this morning, but perhaps it was my nerves.

Skye paused, rifling through her bag until she found a silver flask. "It's simple. Go in there, remove your clothes, and rock his world."

My gut twisted. It wasn't the act itself that made me uneasy. It was the thought of doing it with him; his presence made me nervous enough.

"Take this." She shoved the flask toward me.

"I've already done the drunken dalliances thing," I said, thinking again of Asher. I unscrewed the lid and sniffed. "Ugh. Scotch? Are you trying to turn me into a crazy woman?"

"It was all I could find in Parker's cabinet." She spun around excitedly. She was a whirlwind of movement—I wished I had half her energy.

"I think the real question is why you have *this*?" I rattled the flask at her.

"I—ah, well." She flushed and looked at her feet. "Sometimes, when Parker goes out and doesn't reply to my messages, I can't sleep, so I take a swig." She was finally still, as if awaiting my judgment.

"Skye . . ." I let out a long breath.

"Please, let's just drop it." Her expression changed, and sadness seeped out, but she quickly changed the subject. "I know you're all into the red wine, but drink this before you go, and I promise you won't be nervous." Her excitement had returned, and she looked at me like a merchant promising this snake oil could heal my incurable disease.

Asher swam into my mind again, how aggressive he'd been as he pawed my body. The alcohol hadn't worked to diffuse his emotions, or mine. Afterward, he had told the rest of the class that I'd attacked him. "That's what you get for trying to get it on with Mad Morgana," the other boys had guffawed.

Skye was still staring at me expectantly, waiting for me to agree to "the plan." She was really terrible at giving dating advice, but I didn't want her to be crestfallen.

"Thanks, I guess." I tilted my head and made a show of tucking the flask inside my fur coat pocket.

"Just tell me everything tomorrow!" She clasped her hands together before twirling on her heels.

"What's with Parker's Wet Lass?" I called after her.

She turned in the doorway, clutching her little pink bag in her long-fingered hands.

We both burst into hysterics.

"That stupid boat." Skye wiped tears of laughter from her eyes.

"Did he name it after you?"

"Aye, he says that he did, but I have a sneaking suspicion he says that to all the girls."

7.

MORGANA

Why was I so nervous? This was a completely normal activity that ordinary people did all the time.

I pulled Skye's flask out of my fur jacket and toyed with it. Opening the lid, I sniffed its contents. *Ugh.* I took a small sip and spat it back out. Now I remembered why I avoided brown spirits.

I tightened my coat around me and continued through the parking lot, keenly aware of its isolation. The emptiness amplified every sound, making my heart beat just a little faster.

Music wound its way through the darkening night so softly that at first, I thought I must be imagining it. But it became louder. It was the same song.

Come, ye drunken sailors, to the bottom of the sea...

A chill crept over me, and I spun around, searching the shadows for its source, but the lot was empty. Another gust of stormy sea breeze caught me. I inhaled metal gnawed at by the waves; the soft insides of barnacles; and the entrails of a fish a shark had consumed.

Was I going mad?

I walked faster, but the music swelled about me, filling me with yearning, a longing as deep and plaintive as the singer's to be among the waves. To be *with* these sunken traitors and drowned sailors. To be among the many tantalizing smells from the ocean's depth on the wind.

Okay, I am going crazy. These can't be normal thoughts. Can they?

I clamped my hands over my ears as my steps turned into a jog. Maybe my mother and the doctors were right. There was something wrong with me.

I was shaking when I reached the cement at the side of the small harbor where the moored boats bobbed. I couldn't turn up at Finn's house in this state.

I pulled the flask from my pocket again and took a second swig. It burned, but this time, I forced it down.

The sun had dipped below the horizon, and the shades of evening had turned to night. I sniffed at the wind and could no longer smell the scent of the sea. The Scotch had comforted my nerves, and I started to understand why Skye used it to sleep.

I was still shaking. *Confidence!*

I took a third sip of the fiery liquid and peered at the tops of the large stone houses above me. The lights were on in the gray one—Finn's house. I swallowed.

My cheeks warmed as I took another sip. Whisky was always glorified in adventure tales. Whenever the protagonists were cold and depressed, a bottle was passed around, offering momentary merriment. I pretended I was in one of those stories for my fifth sip. After that, one sip melded into another, and it didn't taste so bad. I was warm, and my moment of merriment began. I was no longer nervous; I wanted to see Finn as soon as possible.

I picked my way up the stone stairs from the harbor to the houses perched on the slice of land closing the bay. Grass sprouted from either side of the steps, and boulders had been tactfully arranged to give each fortress privacy.

There were three of them on the cliff face, but Finn's was the largest by far. The letter box that heralded the concrete path sloping toward the back of the gray stone structure was marked with the number two. What I'd thought was the hillside from afar was actually part of its architectural design—it had been embedded in the plateau. Grass covered the roof, and stone walls inserted the house into the clifftop. The front door was barely discernible in the dim light, a dark metal frame nestled between glass and stone.

"Come in." Finn's voice was distorted through the speaker beside the door, and a clicking indicated he had automatically unlocked it.

I better have one last swig.

Fumbling with the lid, I took a large gulp of the burning liquid.

When I stepped inside, I was met by a polished concrete floor. There was a mirror on the wall at the entrance, and I surveyed myself. My cheeks were rosy, but my hair remained sleek. I rubbed spit furiously onto a small stain on my white shirt.

"Thanks for coming." Finn met me at the entrance, a grin splitting his face.

When he took my coat and hung it by the door, our bodies brushed, sending an involuntary shiver through me.

As we walked through the open-plan living area, my breath caught in my throat. The kitchen, to my left, had a metal island that complemented the polished floor. To my right was a modern hearth crafted from an assortment of feature bricks in varying shades of gray, and a set of black leather couches framed a large flat-screen TV.

He was a minimalist. There was no mess no shelves, books, or clutter—just this sleek creation of grayscale design. Oh, wait, I was wrong. There was a telescope in the corner beside the window. Aside from that, the house looked virtually uninhabited.

Floor-to-ceiling windows looked out at the Atlantic, compensating for the lack of life in the decor. The sun had set, but flashes of lightning from the approaching storm penetrated the clouds.

"This place is so cool!" I pressed my nose against the window. Finn's family must be filthy rich.

"I'm glad you like it." His voice emerged from the kitchen and draped over me like silk. It was deep and comforting, familiar, and after my experience in the parking lot, I needed comfort.

"I would do anything for an endless sea view like this one." I dragged my gaze from the ocean to lean my back against the glass. Now I was facing him.

"Anything?" The hint of a smile flirted with his lips.

"Well, not— You know what I mean." I blushed and turned back to the ocean as thunder rumbled in the distance.

"Would you like a drink? Something tells me you're a Scotch drinker."

I turned to see him grabbing a beautiful glass decanter from a kitchen cupboard. I thought guiltily of the empty flask in my coat. Had he smelled it on me?

"So, what movie do you want to watch? Let me see . . ." His eyes glittered as he surveyed me. "I think you're a romance girl, but you like to pretend that you're not." He pulled the lid from the decanter with a pop.

"You choose." I swallowed. *The code!*

I stole a glance at him from under my lashes. He didn't seem to be giving me sleazy vibes. Tonight, he was wearing a hand-cut singlet and jeans, which he'd rolled up at the ankles. His feet were bare, and I could see his tattoo in full. His hair fell in arrows across his brow as he poured our drinks.

"I seem to have the same song stuck in my head, and sometimes I hear it in the wind. *Come, ye drunken sailors...*" I found myself mumbling the words at him. Oh dear, I was drunk.

He stiffened. *Shit. I've officially made myself look like a crazy person.*

He stopped what he was doing and observed me. My god, he was good-looking. My cheeks burned, and I averted my eyes, unsure how to return from this. Perhaps bringing up the song about drunken sailors was not the best way to enhance my reputation—especially when I was drunk myself. I almost giggled at the irony as I turned back to the window.

Lightning illuminated the sky, and the dark ocean was tossing under the pull of the wind.

Finn merely chuckled. "It is said the veils between this world and the other remain open for three days before and after Samhain." He moved to my side, handing me a glass, and we surveyed the approaching storm together.

After a few moments, Finn broke the silence. "You've never mentioned your father. Where is he?" he asked, which surprised me. It was a simple question, but it set my heart racing. It was something you'd ask someone when you wanted to get to know them better. Or to show that you cared.

"My father—well, I never knew him." I continued to look out to sea.

"You don't know who he is or just never knew him?" His eyes searched mine.

"I don't know anything about him. Mom says it's best to leave the past where it belongs, but I think he's why she refuses to return here." I hooked a strand of hair behind my ear and held his gaze.

He nodded. "I know what it's like to have only one parent. How about your grandmother? Does she have any sisters?"

I was silent for a moment, pondering the question.

"No. As far as I know, she has no other family."

Finn traced the backs of his fingers down my arm and back again, setting my skin on fire. When he reached my shoulder, he put both hands on me and drew me to face him. My stomach fluttered, and my lips parted. This was it. I wanted him to kiss me more than anything.

"So, tell me more about your family." He cupped my chin and tilted my head back so my eyes found his.

"There's not much more to tell." I shrugged but continued looking into his dark eyes, which were rimmed with black lashes.

Why does he keep pressing me about my family? Talking about my nonexistent father and dead grandmother did not set the mood.

He kept his hand on my jaw, holding my gaze captive. I swallowed as a throbbing sensation engulfed the space between my thighs. I clasped them together as desire flared in me in a way I'd never felt before.

His eyes moved to and fro, searching mine.

Why doesn't he kiss me? Should I kiss him?

I was about to go in for the kill when he pulled his hand from my face and turned away. "Strange," he murmured, almost to himself, as he stepped back from me. He furrowed his brow and rubbed his chin as if thinking.

"What's strange?" I asked, although I didn't care to talk. I wished he would touch me again.

His eyes found mine, and he stared so hard I felt it in my stomach. "I was just wondering, why are you so different?" He moved back to my side, and his hand brushed against mine. "I can't figure you out."

His words caught me off guard, and I spluttered over my drink.

"No, it's a good thing. I find myself unexpectedly drawn to you."

What did he mean by "unexpectedly"? Had he been expecting to meet me and not be drawn to me?

Confidence, I told myself as I wiped my lip and smiled apologetically.

"I feel the same way about you." The words tumbled from my mouth before I could stop them.

Is this a date now? I drained my drink, and the corners of Finn's mouth twitched with amusement as he took the empty glass from me.

Dizziness warped my vision as I gazed at the raging dark ocean—there was ringing in my ears, and for a moment, I thought I heard the song.

"Did you want to sit down?" It was as if he had read my mind.

I nodded, and he slipped his arm around my waist, guiding me to the couch.

I searched for the sickly feeling that usually accompanied these situations, but it wasn't there. Was it the whisky? Perhaps I had drunk just enough to replace the overwhelming sensations with the dizziness of alcohol.

The room swayed as we sank onto the largest leather sofa, but all I felt was the warmth of Finn's touch. He reached around and tucked a strand of hair behind my ear, and I took in his angular jaw, black brows, and the flecks of gray in his black irises. They were dancing like the ocean outside. *No, they can't be. It must just be the drink.*

"How old are you, anyway?" I burbled.

"How old do you think I am?" There was a faint gleam in his eyes.

I examined his face again, but the whisky was warping my vision. "Perhaps twenty-eight . . . ?"

Amusement danced in his eyes. "Good guess. I'm going to get my laptop from my room. I can't work out how to use this television." Furrowing his brows in frustration, he gestured at the large flat-screen.

He slipped through a hall behind the kitchen, which must have led to his bedroom.

This is it.

Skye's words echoed in my mind. *Confidence!* During the daylight, her advice had seemed terrible, but now, under the influence of the whisky, it seemed only logical.

I couldn't let Finn know this was my first time. A flashback to the taunts of my youth reached through the haze of liquor. I still felt like Mad Morgana, as the kids had unkindly dubbed me. The familiar self-loathing clawed at my ankles, but I brushed it off. Slowly and confidently, I made my move. Standing up, I unzipped my jeans, kicked them onto the floor, and pulled my shirt over my head.

Finn reemerged in the living room, and I smiled at him. I could do this. I reached around to unhook the back of my bra.

"Wait!" he cried, rushing over and pulling my hands into his. "What are you doing?"

"Aren't we going to have sex?" I asked, my throat dry.

His jaw tightened, the muscles in his arms standing out beneath his tattooed skin as he let his hands travel to my hips. My fear was gone, and I wanted him.

"Why did you have to be so damned beautiful?" His voice was thick and low.

The connection lasted only a moment before he disappeared into the hallway. He returned with a blanket and gently draped it over my shoulders.

This was odd. This was not how they initiated making love in movies!

"Sit down." He kept his arms around me and guided me back toward the sofa. Sitting beside me, he placed a silver MacBook on the coffee table.

The truth of the situation cascaded over me in a wave of embarrassment. "You actually wanted to watch a movie? I should go." I started pulling my discarded clothes toward my feet.

"Don't," he protested gently.

I ignored him and continued gathering my things.

"Morgana, you're drunk, and a storm is blowing up outside! I insist you stay here." His hand closed firmly around my wrist, and I let my belongings fall.

"I can't even imagine what you must think of me—getting drunk and naked my first time at your house." I put my face in my hands.

"Hey, look at me." He tilted my head toward his. "I *do* find you attractive, and quite frankly, I think the fact that you tried to get naked at my house is amazing." A wicked smile played on his lips. "But—" His face fell, and he paused. "But I am not a good person. You deserve better than me."

"What do you mean?" I breathed.

"I . . ." He sighed. "I am engaged to someone else." He expelled the last bit quickly, as if he wanted to gloss over those details.

Engaged! Just when I thought I couldn't be any more humiliated. A sliver of jealousy poked at my insides, churning the whisky in my empty belly. *Oh no! If I hurl, it will be much worse.*

"So, that's where you go those days you haven't been around?" I steadied my breathing as the liquor eddied to a nauseating pool in my stomach.

"I guess you could say that," he replied solemnly.

"I'm sorry. I thought this was a date, and I got nervous because I—I'm a virgin." Word vomit was spilling from me instead. I didn't know which was worse.

"Don't get me wrong. I'd like to fuck you, Morgana." His voice was low, edged with something dark, as his eyes swept over me. "Maybe if I'd been able to . . . Never mind. Something about you makes me remember my responsibilities," he said through pursed lips. "Sometimes, I forget myself in . . . this place." He waved a hand at the room as if his chic clifftop house caused him to act out.

"I don't understand why you invited me here if you have a fiancée." The whisky was curdling my embarrassment into anger.

Finn's jaw was hard as he stared back at me. Several beats of silence passed between us. Finally, he said, "I was hoping for a friend."

"But why would you call me beautiful if you only wanted to be friends?" Heat stained my cheeks.

"Like I said, it was unexpected."

"Why do you keep saying 'unexpected'? What *did* you expect?" There was a lump forming in my throat.

He moved closer to me on the couch, his thigh brushing against mine. I pulled away.

"I didn't expect us to have so much in common, both with only one parent and the other one . . . distant."

"What's your father like?" A subject change might help me fight the brewing waterworks.

Finn's eyes darkened, and then they narrowed a little. "I don't want to talk about my father."

I pulled the blanket tighter around me. He noticed, and his features softened.

"You're drunk, Morgana. Can we talk about this in the morning?" His eyes were pleading.

By the sound of it, this night had unraveled horribly for both of us. I rolled my eyes and tugged the cover up to my chin.

He snapped open the laptop and brought up his movie choice—*Ten Things I Hate About You*. Fitting.

I woke with my head nestled in Finn's lap.

Ugh. How did I find my way to him?

Removing his limp arm from across my body, I sat up. He was still asleep, and I had a splitting headache. I raised a hand to my temple as the horror of last night flooded back. My pile of clothes was on the floor at my feet, and I threw them on.

I cast a lingering look at Finn, whose head was resting on his fist, strands of dark hair splayed across the arm of the couch. His tattooed arm lay on the sofa beside him, the inked patterns and strange symbols drawing me in. An ache curled inside me—the urge to kiss him awake, to feel those arms tighten around my waist as I straddled his hips.

What am I thinking? He. Is. Engaged.

I shook away my dirty thoughts and tiptoed toward the door, grabbing my fur coat before shutting it carefully behind me. Was this what they called the walk of shame? If only I hadn't drunk from that stupid flask. What on earth possessed me to take my clothes off?

It was still dark, but the sun had begun to cast golden hues on the distant skyline. Everything was quiet after last night's storm. It was as if the sea and sky had thrown a temper tantrum that they now regretted.

As I padded toward home, the wind picked up. It whipped my hair in all directions and tugged at my clothing as if it had hands. I pulled my grandmother's coat tighter around me. The wind's caress brought Finn and his touch to mind, producing a flutter in my stomach, but the memory of last night's horror swiftly quashed it.

Dawn was on the horizon as I reached my jetty, and the gale was becoming unbearable, but I pushed on. I let the scents consume me: sulfur from an underwater volcano, fresh seaweed, and salt—so much salt. This time, I felt less afraid.

Maybe I was just different. There was no fighting it. *I am Mad Morgana.*

As I approached the jetty's tip, the gusts became so strong that I dropped to my knees and crawled. I clung to the edge of the planks as sea spray stung my face. My vision blurred, and the ocean and sky became one. The rough wood disappeared from beneath me. My hands grasped at nothing as I sank into darkness.

Come, ye drunken sailors, to the bottom of the sea.
Come, ye sunken traitors, to swim eternally.
Come, ye drowned with chests of gold.
Come, ye drowned, leave your mortal soul to the sea,
to the sea . . .

8.

Finn

I'm getting sloppy.
I brushed my hair back from my face and stretched out on the couch, scanning the room, but the girl had gone.

How late had I slept? The sun had long risen, the ocean glistening like quicksilver under its caress as I reached the kitchen counter and pressed my palms into it.

The storm had passed, but the gentle waves simpering at the horizon sent a sharp pang of guilt through me. I was no closer to understanding why the storms had been growing more frequent—or whether they were connected to him.

I padded back to the couch, opening my laptop on the coffee table. It was still paused on the movie's closing credits, and my mind wandered back to the girl. *Morgana.* I should be questioning why my gifts hadn't worked on her, wondering what I would tell my father. But all I could think about was how she'd looked up at me from under her lashes as she reached around to unhook the back of her bra.

Rolling my shoulders, I shook away the thoughts. I had failed, and my father would never let me forget it. I'd never failed a task for him before, but now, it seemed I was failing two.

I was a professional. The jobs never got to me, never unsettled me, no matter how much they screamed, begged, or pleaded. I was impervious. My father had made sure of it.

What was it about this girl?

Interrogation was usually easy with my particular skill set, yet it hadn't worked on her. This intrigued me. She was pretty, too, but it was more than that. I'd been with beautiful women before—lots of them. A smirk curled my lips at the memories. But no, there was something beguiling about this girl that drew me in the same way the moon pulled upon the tides.

A fucking human of all things, and she'd been immune. A nagging feeling in my gut warned me not to tell my father. Not yet, anyway. Still, I had to give him something. I pulled the laptop onto my knees, opening my browser.

What is that site called they all use? I can never remember. Ah yes . . . Instagram.

I didn't have a personal account, of course—social media is an absurd human plaything. But I did have a fake profile for situations like this.

I typed her name into the search bar. My heart quickened as a page appeared, and I gritted my teeth against the feeling.

Thankfully, her account wasn't private, but she hadn't updated it in years. She didn't have many pictures of herself, mostly posting moments of mundane beauty. I scrolled through the feed. A streetlight glowing against the evening sky, a rose holding a drop of dew, and a few shots of beautiful bookstores appeared. I paused at these. The girl liked to read. I thought about my family library, rows of books stacked as high as the eye could see above a polished stone floor. She would probably have to catch her breath at the sight of it.

One photo showed her in a black bodice dress, her long red hair draped over one shoulder. The caption said, "Prom night."

My cock pressed against the denim of my jeans as blood surged to it when I took in her plush lips, painted bright red. Who had escorted her to that prom? Did another man get to hold her close, slow dance with his face pressed to her cheek, feel her heaving chest as he gazed into her ocean eyes?

A muscle ticked in my jaw, and I slapped the laptop shut. Why should I care?

A normal girl, likes books, nothing unusual, but we should continue with the observations. That should satisfy the old man.

Inegar had accused me of dragging out the observation. I didn't want to admit it to myself, but he'd been right.

This should have been simple—I despised humans. They'd created the sickness that plagued my people.

But my gifts had failed on her. When they didn't take hold in the store or among the shipping containers, I brushed it off as a fluke. I never intended to watch a movie—though I do enjoy this human form of storytelling. The plan had been to get her alone, away from any distractions. But no.

I rubbed a hand down my face.

From the moment I'd met her to when she offered herself to me, her eyes had been completely clear. There was none of that hazy expression, a side effect of the allure they usually exhibited. Could that mean . . . she genuinely wanted to be around me?

When she had discarded her clothes, every bone in my body wanted her in ways I'd never experienced before. What would it be like, just this once, to be with someone who desired me for who I truly was? But it would have been wrong to take her when I couldn't make her forget—and the moment my gifts started working again, I would extract all the information I needed and be done with her.

I'd never had much of a conscience—my father ensured that. Why her, and why now?

The door flew open, and my thoughts disintegrated as my cousin, Pisceon, entered the room.

"Your father wants you to return home and provide another report." He grinned, casting his eyes across the space, looking for evidence of depravity.

"I gave my last report only days ago. Why is he so impatient?"

Pisceon shrugged, retrieving the whisky decanter from the cupboard, and poured two tumblers. He handed me one, and I swirled the amber liquid before sipping. It made me think of her.

"Why do you get all the fun jobs?" Pisceon's eyes fell upon last night's empty glasses. He linked his fingers together and stretched his arms, muscles bulging.

I polished off my drink, setting the empty glass back on the sleek benchtop. If only my cousin knew—nothing about my life has ever been fun.

PART TWO:

The Kingdom of the Deep

9.

MORGANA

What the hell? Was I lying motionless, or was I floating?

The same song had played again, and the tune lingered. Images of the jetty, the wind, and the sinking flooded my mind. It was so still now.

Had Finn found me and taken me home to my bed again? I opened my eyes a fraction, and a watery green light filtered in.

At first, I thought I must be in my grandparents' attic, because I was lying on a faded patchwork quilt, but when I sat up, I realized this one was tattered and coated in a greenish film. *Gross!*

The room was cramped, reminiscent of ship cabins I'd seen in films. The floorboards and walls were thick with grime. A round window cast shafts of emerald light, illuminating the dirt-streaked floor and a dresser, its mirror veiled in mold.

My eyes darted around the strange yet somehow familiar room, trying to piece together my surroundings. The oddest part was the sensation enveloping me; there was no wind, yet I still felt cool. *I am underwater!* I gasped. But the thought struck me as ridiculous.

Finn said the water here was cold enough to cause hypothermia, but I was comfortably cool, and I seemed to have some strange kind of oxygen reserve. I scrambled at my chest, exhaling a sigh of relief as I felt the slow thudding of my heart.

This is impossible! Perhaps I fainted, and this is all a dream.

That was it. I let out a long breath, sending a stream of bubbles swirling around me.

I gulped down my panic and leaped from the bed. My fingers slid through the water, and my long, red hair flowed behind me. I moved easily, not swimming, but walking.

My breath caught in my throat as I glimpsed my reflection in the grimy mirror. I rushed over, cleaning its surface. Scooping back my hair, I saw the fur. It covered my arms and stretched across my chest like a corset. I gasped as I took in the rest of my body—I was practically naked, aside from a covering of downy hair that accentuated my every curve. I stared, horrified, at where my breasts should have been. Now, there was just a fur-covered outline, my nipples still visible underneath the bodice of fur. It stretched over my torso and covered my legs, but it dispersed at my ankles, and my feet were bare. It was as if I were wearing a bodysuit like Catwoman's, but instead of leather, mine was fur.

My feet . . . I did a double take. My toes now sported leathery webs. *Ugh!*

I choked, lifting my hands to my face and then drawing them away in horror. My fingers had the same tough-skinned webs between them.

What the fuck? I was no stranger to weird dreams, but this one . . . this one took the cake.

Racing to the door, I flung it open. I was on the upper floor of a grand steamship lined with cabins. The hallway of doors stretched into inky darkness to my left and right. Little lights hung at intervals along its sides, illuminating streaks of a rust-like substance running down the walls.

Every muscle in my body went taut, freezing me in place as I locked eyes with a ferocious-looking fish hooked to the wall. Long, pale fangs protruded crudely from its gaping mouth, and a bulb hanging from its forehead was glowing. I'd heard of these creatures—anglerfish, found only in the deepest parts of the ocean. They had bioluminescent bulbs on their foreheads. *Someone, or something, is using them as lights!*

Wait a minute. My shoulders slumped in relief; knowing this was a dream meant I could control it.

I relaxed my body. Eyes shut, I willed myself to wake. But when I opened them, I was still in the dark hallway, the anglerfish's unblinking eyes fixed on me.

To my left, a staircase spiraled down into the murky darkness of the lower deck. The roof above was decaying in places, and shafts of greenish light fell right through to the compartments below.

I guess I have to brave the stairs.

I took a deep breath, edging my foot onto the first step.

It was almost too dark to see the sea life, but I felt their presence. A school of fluorescent fish darted to and fro around my ankles, and a crab scuttled sideways as my foot felt clumsily for the next step, but I continued down into the gloom. I willed my subconscious not to conjure anything scary down there.

I froze, ears pricked. *Music.* Deep and mournful, it wound its way up from the shadows. It was the same tune I'd heard upon waking, but there were no words this time.

The song swelled at the bottom of the staircase, and I found myself in another room. Tall wooden doors loomed before me, a deep-set engraving across them spelling "Davy Jones's Tavern."

Underneath the words was what looked like a roughly carved stamp. I ran my fingers across the grooves, which had blackened with slime. It was a circle, with some kind of runes running around the outside. In the middle was a carving of a crashing wave with a crescent moon above it. A paralyzing tension washed over me—it was the same insignia from my grandmother's box and the bowl at the pawnshop. Around the wave and moon, there were five carvings. They were roughly hewn and obscured by grime, but I could make out the skull, mermaid, seal, some kind of sea monster—a squid perhaps—and another mermaid-like creature.

I ran my hands over each carving, my breathing ragged. This was way too much.

The music continued to wind through the doors, and I pushed against them, fingers sliding in the goo. Inside, high stools lined a slimy counter, and wooden tables and benches littered the floor—a bar.

More anglerfish lit the room. They were shoved into glass jars on the tables and caught in fishnets, strung between tangles of sludgy seaweed vines on the ceiling.

A man was hunched over a piano in the room's far corner. Barnacles clung to the instrument, and seaweed swayed sadly to the man's tune, yet the keys remained clean, shining like polished marble as he caressed them. The man had black hair, most of it turned gray, caramel skin, and a soft white beard. He would have been handsome before age took its toll. A navy-and-white sailor's hat was perched crookedly on his head. He wore a matching uniform—captain's attire. Noticing me, he looked up and smiled.

I couldn't move. Only hours ago, I had felt Finn's touch, his warmth beside me on the couch. Now, I was here in this eerie place, and I wasn't waking up by the looks of things.

My throat constricted as a small sea snake popped its head out from the man's right eye socket, knocking a wooden eye to the floor, and then darted back in when it saw me.

"What is this place?" Fear clouded my subconscious, and although only bubbles exited my mouth, I heard my words come out as a high-pitched squeak.

"You are in the Kingdom of the Drowned, and you can call me the Captain." It came out as bubbles and strange gurgles, but my mind comprehended him in English. He had stopped playing, but his fingers still rested on the keys.

"Then I'm . . ." *Dead*. I couldn't bring myself to finish the sentence.

The Captain surveyed me with his one good eye. "You are curious to me, because you are neither dead nor dying, but you do have the mark of the sea on you." Once again, bubbles came out of his mouth, and my mind translated it—his accent was deep and husky.

"This is a dream!" I rounded on him, drawing myself up to my full height as if this would enable me to change my narrative.

I closed my eyes, desperately willing myself to be somewhere else, *anywhere* else, begging for control over the situation. Slowly, I reopened them, but was immediately disappointed as the green light filtered in. I was still in this . . . this . . . Davy Jones's Tavern.

"Wh-why do I look like this?" I stammered. My stomach felt like it was made of lead.

The Captain smiled again.

Why does he keep smiling at me? I glared at him.

He rose from behind the piano, the movement jolting me. His wooden leg scraped against the floor as he swung it in a wide arc, limping toward the bar.

Of course he has a wooden leg. I rolled my eyes despite it all.

"Well?" I followed him and slid onto one of the high stools, running my finger over the counter, which was coated in green slime. *Ugh!*

The Captain reached up toward the shelves behind him, which glittered with glass bottles, all different shapes, sizes, and colors. He grunted as he stretched, grabbing two of them and placing one underneath the tap of a large wooden barrel.

"Drink." He handed the bottle to me. It was green glass.

I lifted it to my lips but stopped, narrowing my eyes as the Captain retrieved his own bottle from the tap.

"You think I mean to poison you, child?" He raised his bushy brows. His good eye gleamed bright as topaz, but it was kind.

Still, I'd seen enough movies to know you didn't accept drinks from strangers . . . especially not *dead* ones.

"What is it?" I raised the bottle to the light, and a dark liquid shifted inside.

"It's only rum." The Captain grinned, taking a long swig from his. The little snake slithered around to the left side of his head, surveying me with crimson eyes.

Great, more brown spirits! It was the last thing I needed, but I took a little sip.

The warm, spiced liquid was unlike anything I'd tasted—smooth yet potent, with the familiar burn of rum but no need for a mixer. Strangely, it didn't feel like eating or drinking in a dream. As the liquid entered my body, I relaxed, if only slightly. I wondered if it had some magical properties, like the Drowned's version of Xanax. I couldn't help but smile at the absurdity of the thought.

The Captain was surveying me over the top of his bottle.

"How did I get here? How do I get out?" I leaned further onto the slick wooden bar and met his eye.

"I cannot tell you why you are here, Morgana. That is for you to discover."

"You know my name?"

"I know everyone who will pass through these doors before they do. You are not dead, but our world has marked you for some reason. Take a look." He gestured at my left shoulder. Pulling it forward, an inky likeness that hadn't been there before shone on my skin. It was a wave that curled around and came to a sharp point. A crescent moon rose above it.

"It's the same as the carving on the door." I swallowed. "What is that?"

"The insignia of the Kingdom of the Deep and all its houses."

My mouth fell open, and I clamped it shut. I didn't reply. I couldn't.

"The sooner you realize this isn't a dream, the quicker you'll realize your destiny," the Captain said matter-of-factly, and started polishing glass tumblers hanging on hooks behind the bar.

My destiny? How cliché.

"But this is not scientifically possible in any way." I gestured to the anglerfish squashed into the jar before me on the bar.

"Is it that unrealistic for the drowned to live on in the depths of the ocean?" The Captain raised his bushy brows at me again. "I am not here to give people the answers. I protect this place and the souls that come here. You are in the Kingdom of the Drowned now, and down here, many things you may not believe in are possible."

My throat bobbed as my eyes darted around the space. The rum had helped, but panic and disbelief were still roiling inside me.

"Ah, it is the drinking hour," the Captain said after a moment, rubbing his weathered hands together.

The windows darkened, but the room brightened until I could no longer see the fierce teeth or bulging eyes of the anglerfish tangled in fishnets on the ceiling. They were glowing, and the mottled roof resembled a sky full of stars.

People of all ages began entering the venue. Some came through the swinging doors at the front, and others used the big wooden doors I had entered from. They moved like they would on land—not floating, but walking, as if some magical force kept them anchored to the ocean floor. A man with dreadlocks wearing a pirate hat glared at me as he barreled past. I let the bottle of rum I was holding fall to the floor, and it smashed beneath my stool.

These people must be the Drowned.

They were not translucent like the ghosts in tales. They were opaque. None of them were furry like me, though. They all wore the tattered clothes they must have drowned in—some years ago or centuries ago, by the looks of things.

The Drowned began to make themselves at home. Chess sets were drawn from rusted chests in the corners and games started on the slime-covered boards. Gnarly sailors pushed at each other to get to the bar. Two schoolgirls wearing pinafores over white torn T-shirts, probably from the 1950s or thereabouts, giggled at a table, and a woman in a ripped beaded 1920s dress conversed happily with a modern-day girl beside them.

The Captain began to fill more glass bottles and hand them to the sailors jostling beside me.

I was frozen on my bar stool. *No way. This is way too weird.*

But it was happening. More and more drowned people emerged in the bar. Sailors pulled laughing women onto their laps, and everybody snatched up spicy rum bottles that the Captain sent sliding down the long wooden bar. A man in a stained white-and-blue naval officer's hat leered at me, his teeth green with algae. I careened backward, my stool clattering to the sandy floor.

The Drowned at the bar stopped to stare at me. I became acutely aware of the way my new furry bodysuit clung to every curve, wrapping my arms across my breasts as heat worked its way into my cheeks.

Some Drowned were good-looking and well-preserved. They had died handsome and young and were immortalized that way. Others were older, and some—who may have resided in this watery world longer—had missing teeth and dark rings under their eyes, as if the ocean had started to have its way with them. As the many stares of the Drowned devoured my fur-covered body, I realized *I couldn't sense their feelings.*

I let the upheaval of the bar wash over me. *Nothing.* Apparently my senses didn't work on the dead.

"How does the rest of the world not know about this?" I righted my stool but didn't sit down. The Captain passed out more rum bottles as the merriment became raucous.

"The living cannot see us! Only the dead and those of the ocean like yourself can. To the inferior eye, the inside of this ship looks as decayed as the exterior," the Captain yelled as he lined rum-filled tumblers along the bar. Despite his wooden leg and age, he was moving with a speed and agility that would outdo even the best young bartender in Kansas City's most fashionable nightclub.

The crowd around me was becoming increasingly unruly. I shrank into the far corner, between the piano and the swing doors. What would I find outside?

Peering over, I saw only murky darkness. I ran my hand along the slimy doors. They couldn't possibly have been here when the ship sank. They looked like something from a Western saloon. I wondered if they had been built by one of the Drowned or magically introduced.

What am I thinking?

A cry rang out as a pirate threw the man in a naval officer's hat against the bar using the ribbon around the neck of his uniform. My mouth fell open as he yanked on it, pulling it tighter and tighter until the officer began to choke.

"I thought I told you to stay away from my girl," the pirate snarled. He was wearing a white tunic and had long dark hair plaited down his back.

A woman was hovering nervously at the pair's side. "Cedric, don't," she whimpered. She was wearing a power suit and had a short blonde bob. She must have drowned in the last fifty years.

The man in the naval uniform, whom Cedric had pinned to the bar, spat at his attacker. Without hesitation, the pirate pulled out a huge, hooked knife from his belt and thrust it into the officer's gut. I gasped as the man cried out in pain, then slumped over the blade.

The woman let out a frightened squeak.

"Help him!" I cried, turning to the Captain, who continued serving customers nearby, unfazed by the scene unfolding beside him.

He chuckled.

Why is he laughing? This isn't funny! A man is dead. But wait—he was already dead.

As if on cue, the officer coughed and returned to life as Cedric the pirate pulled out his blade. He, Cedric, and the woman with the bob all looked at one another and roared with laughter. Cedric pulled the officer from the bar and slapped him on the back.

"That will teach you to sleep with my girl," he said, holding up his tumbler of rum. To my surprise, the naval officer held his glass up, too.

"I hear you, brother." He nodded, and the three of them roared with laughter again.

What the actual fuck? Did they just cheers each other for murder?

I pressed myself further into the wall beside the swinging doors.

Another fight broke out in one of the far corners, and a man in fisherman's overalls broke a chair over the head of a man in a kilt.

I peered into the darkness beyond the doors. Perhaps stepping outside would awaken me. My nightmare couldn't get any worse than this. Could it?

10.

Morgana

Remains from the shipwreck were scattered far and wide. Bits of rusted metal were poking out here and there, half-submerged in sand. Glowing columns of bioluminescent coral protruded on either side of me, marking the swinging doors as an entrance.

Casting my eyes toward where I was used to seeing the sky, I saw nothing but darkness. A heavy and unyielding silence gripped me.

How deep under the ocean am I?

Stepping back, I surveyed the ship. It was a mottled monster of dark bubbles and slices of corrosion. Mold and seaweed danced in shafts of light from the portholes above.

The bar must have been nestled in the hull, perhaps the second deck from the top in the middle of the ship, but the keel was almost entirely immersed in sand. The portholes began peeping out about a meter above the sand, and more decorated the upper decks.

The Captain had assured me this wasn't a dream, but to my reality-trained brain, it seemed absolutely mental. Yet I couldn't shake the feeling that the strange occurrences at Ruadán's Port—the ocean's pull, the music, the doctors and psychiatrists who had long names for whatever was "wrong" with me—all had something to do with this.

No. I shook the thoughts away. It was more likely I had succumbed to madness.

I sensed movement behind me and spun around. A forest of gnarled pillars loomed in the darkness, rising from the ocean floor like stalagmites. Plumes of hot water spewed from their peaks, giving the atmosphere around them a dreamlike quality.

The mottled pillars stretched into shadows, and I was surprised by how well I could see. A fish scooted past me to join others nibbling at the heat vents. Perhaps I had aquatic vision like them. Another absurd thought.

Curious, I followed the fish and reached into the glistening plumes. *Argh!* I snatched my hand back, and it instantly cooled in the crisp water surrounding the rest of my body.

What the hell? This was all too much. I would rather stay close to the Drowned and the Captain than take my chances in the dark forest of heat vents.

I plopped onto the sandy ground in the light of the portholes, pulling an object out from beneath me—an old boot. I chucked it furiously into the murky darkness, and tears pooled in my eyes. They burst out of me in a shaky sob.

How did I end up here?

The tears didn't feel nearly as satisfying as they did on land, dissolving instantly into the ocean. Sniffing them back, I glared into the gloom. Perhaps it would have been easier if I *had* drowned.

More tears appeared. This time, they felt angry—hot and furious like the hydrothermal vents dancing in front of me.

"I wept upon my arrival here also." The voice startled me.

A man around my age was standing over me, clad in a maroon porter's uniform with a white collar and matching cap. His bent name badge still read "Edward," and his bright orange hair contrasted against the green backdrop.

"Why would you cry? You're dead. You can't feel anything." I knew the words were heartless as soon as they tumbled from my mouth, but it was too late.

The man called Edward winced but didn't turn away. "The Drowned can still feel pain. We are souls, after all. Think of us like . . . vampires, but under the ocean. It's quite peculiar, really." He sat beside me, his red trousers hitching above his ankles. Barnacles clung to his leather boots, and the skin above his socks had begun to decay.

I thought of the naval officer I'd just seen stabbed in the bar, his face twisted in unmistakable agony.

"Was it hard to come to terms with your death?" I asked, making patterns in the sand with my webbed hands. *Ugh*, my webbed hands! A part of me still couldn't believe I was having this conversation. If I didn't look at the Drowned man beside me, he might disappear, and the real world would materialize.

"Indeed it was. Yet, it's a mercy to have one's soul intact. The fate of those Drowned whose souls have known too much evil is not as pleasant." Edward sighed.

"What do you mean, like Hell?" I stopped trailing my fingers and gave him my full attention.

"Not exactly. They become gems in the Garden of Mortimer. They are tortured inside but shine so clearly on the outside that their beauty can be seen through the waves. They have been the cause of many sailors' untimely deaths. They leap from boats to reach them, but instead find themselves a place in the garden." There was pain and fear in Edward's voice.

"What's the point of dying if you can still feel? If Mortimer is like Hell, what's this supposed to be—Heaven?" I scoffed, kicking the remains of the old boot further away.

"I do not think we are completely dead; as I said, we are souls. We can still feel pain and love, yet our hearts do not beat. I do not understand the intricacies of death. Does anyone? But I suspect we are here to pay our debts to the spirit of Manannán, God of the Drowned—Davy Jones, as some know him. He is a God of many names." Edward let out a weary breath. "Eventually, the wicked souls of murderers and rapists end up in Mortimer. Still, if the average Drowned sinner dies down here and has fulfilled their debt, we can pass on." He stared at the shimmering stalagmite forest.

"That doesn't make sense," I muttered as a tiny glowing squid propelled through the water before us.

"I've seen pirates tear each other apart with knives and then laugh about it afterward." Edward rubbed the side of his face, and I thought of the scene I had just witnessed. "But occasionally, a skirmish unfolds, and something most peculiar occurs when a fellow gets stabbed. Their body seizes, sighs in relief, and disintegrates into the surroundings." He looked at me earnestly, then shuddered. "A few times, I have seen them shrivel and shriek, disappearing to what I can only imagine is the Mortimer Garden."

"So, you're saying if I were to grab this piece of rusted metal," I said, gesturing to a twisted beam lying half-covered in the sand at our feet, "and shove it through your heart, one of three things could happen. You might dissolve into peace, or you might wither in pain and end up in this 'garden,' or the most likely scenario is that nothing would happen, and we would laugh about it afterward?"

"That's about the size of it." He chuckled. His full lips and freckles made his face look pleasant.

"Man, that's confusing. This God of the Drowned sure wants to keep you all on your toes." I shook my head in wonder. Everything seemed unbelievable, and this tale of the souls sounded exactly like something from the pages of myths and legends. I stared into the gloomy darkness and wondered what my mother, the accountant, would think about all this.

"You'll get used to it." Edward patted me on the back uncomfortably. "Plus, every time there are a lot of new souls, we Mourn together, which makes it easier."

"Mourn?" I sniffed.

"Last night's storm saw a cruise ship turn sideways onto some rocks. Some fifteen souls have now joined us. Even though you're not dead, the Captain asked me to take you along for the Mourning. It might aid acceptance."

Did I really want to "Mourn," or whatever it was, with the dead residents of Davy Jones's Tavern? The thought seemed so absurd I nearly laughed out loud. But perhaps it would help me discover why I was here. Or better still, wake me up.

"Is this where all Drowned people go?"

"Good heavens, no! We wouldn't fit. There are ships like this all over the world."

"And where exactly are we?" I swallowed.

"Deep in the North Atlantic, far off the coast of Scotland and Ireland, past the Outer Hebrides, where the ocean swallows all land."

Holy shit. I swallowed the anxiety that had clutched at my chest.

"You're from England?" I asked, finding solace in Edward's recognizable accent.

He nodded, gesturing to his uniform. "I was sailing from Liverpool to New York City via Belfast, working aboard a passenger liner when it went down."

The Drowned began emerging from the bar, and I instinctively pressed closer to Edward.

"The Mourning will make accepting this place easier," Edward said again, quietly. "I was never particularly close to my parents. It is my lover I miss most dearly. Have you a lover?"

I thought about Finn. Even though he was practically a stranger to me, there was something about him—a familiarity like I'd known him in a past life. I knew I would miss him for the rest of my days if I never saw him again.

Edward must have seen something in my expression, because he said, "Come, it is time. Maybe you will see them when you Mourn." He stood up and reached for my hand.

There was a gash in the material across his stomach. I wondered if it was from the cut that killed him or if it had been the water. Probably both.

My mouth fell open as light radiated through Edward's body. I tried to pull my hand free, but he held on tight. Around us, the other Drowned were glowing in the same way, but it wasn't their bodies. The light came from luminous orbs they held against their chests.

"Come, child," said the Captain, clutching his ball of light. "It's time for you to remember and Mourn. As we rise to the surface, we will serenade those lost on the ship and give them a chance to say goodbye."

My breath hitched as a glowing sphere appeared in my own hands. Had the Captain said we were rising to the surface? This could be my chance to escape!

"Don't let go of my hand. You're only a visitor to the world of the Drowned, and I don't know what would happen if you tried to Mourn on your own," Edward warned as though he'd read my thoughts. "Raise it skyward." He lifted his ball of light.

The Drowned were no longer jostling or squabbling—they were

focused on the little shining orbs dancing in their hands. Their eyes filled with something that looked like love.

I lifted my shimmering ball, awe washing over me as the bodies around me rose from the sandy seabed. Edward and I ascended together, carried by an unseen force.

We rose higher and higher. I gasped as the Drowned turned translucent, their forms fading into the water. Glancing at my hands, I saw nothing but the murky green of the ocean and the faint glow of the light guiding us. A chill ran through me. Had I become transparent, too?

A soft, plaintive wailing commenced, growing louder and louder. We were moving fast, and the sound was suffocating. Was I going to faint? Or would my head explode first?

The night sky unfolded above me as I broke the water's surface, and my headache eased as the howling was swallowed by the crashing waves and roaring wind. Twinkling stars stretched across the heavens. Had I been here for a full day already?

I saw nothing of my body when I looked down, only the crashing black seas below. The light that had appeared in my palms still floated beside me, guiding the way.

The sensation of Edward's cold hand clutching mine remained, but he and the other Drowned were invisible, their tiny lights twinkling like phosphorescence. Their lamenting engulfed me, and the glow dancing in front of me plucked at my heartstrings, willing me to remember. I saw my grandmother smiling at me, her thick black hair veined with gray. She faded into my mother sitting at her desk, poring over work documents. I felt compelled to call out to them.

"Mother," I tried to scream, "goodbye!"

The words formed in my mind, but they emerged as an eerie wail when they left my lips. I succumbed to the ocean's demands, crying out alongside the Drowned as I remembered my loved ones. My grandfather in his armchair, alone in the living room . . . Then, Finn appeared, his dark hair falling in arrows across his eyes. Would I ever see him again?

My little light danced in my free hand as I floated above the waves. I wept for all I was leaving and all I had lost. Around me, the Drowned did the same. Together, we filled the night sky with a beautiful, eerie sound as our many lights glittered on the surface.

It was over all too soon. The glow began to fade, and I was sinking back down. The hypnotic trance broke as the cool water touched the space where my waist should have been. I was still transparent. Would my body return if I stayed above the waves like this?

My thoughts turned back to my grandfather as my face slipped beneath the swell. Without me, he'd be left alone with only his broken heart for company. Our words may have been few, but he needed me. I had to try.

Taking a deep breath, I loosened my grip on Edward's hand. He wouldn't let go. I struggled against him, kicking at the water beside me where his body should have been. He flinched, but he didn't release his grip.

"Let go of me!" I hissed, a gargle of bubbles filling the space before me.

I kicked out again, but he held me tight. My feet met soft sand, and I knew we had sunk back down to the ship. The bodies of the other Drowned materialized around me, their lights fading into nothingness. Grunts and shoves erupted as they resumed their frantic scuffling, heading for the coral pillars marking the bar's entrance.

"I told you not to let go of my hand! Who knows what could have happened? You had no physical body. You could have just disappeared." Edward rounded on me, his blue eyes narrowing.

"I was trying to get home! You should have let me try." Tears burned my throat.

"I don't believe it would have worked. I brought you up to Mourn with the Drowned, yet you are among the living! Mourning is the only time we are permitted to rise above the waves, and the Captain told me never to let go of you, no matter the cost." His eyes filled with sympathy. I could tell he knew what it was like to yearn for a place up there.

"I can't go back home looking like this anyway." I sighed, remembering that I was now covered in fur and had webbed feet. "But perhaps you can help me find a way to transform back."

Edward nodded, but his eyes were sad.

"Do you Mourn after every shipwreck?" I raised my brows.

Through the glowing porthole, I saw the Captain behind the bar, handing out rum. A teenage girl caught my eye as she led a younger boy inside, his small hand clasped in hers. Their familiar faces struck a chord. Then it hit me—I'd seen them on the news. They were the kids who'd been swept from Merrow Rocks. A small smile tugged at my lips. Somehow, it was comforting to think they'd found this afterlife together.

"We Mourn after accumulating a collective of new members. It allows them to say goodbye and accept this new existence. Did it work for you?"

Edward and I were now the only ones still outside. The forest of mottled pillars continued to spout heated streams behind us. I did feel lighter. I drew in a deep breath of water and let it flow out. If my grandfather could handle himself at sea, he would be alright without me for now. As for Finn, well, he was *engaged*.

"I guess it did." I shrugged as a school of silvery fish scooted past. They moved like a disoriented cloud that couldn't decide which direction to float in. My stomach lurched. How long had it been since I'd eaten? I swallowed as the fish darted back and forth, their scales glimmering tantalizingly in the light from the ship's portholes. My stomach growled—I desired them.

What has become of me?

A large pale fish left the group to nibble at a sludge patch on the sand,

and I pounced. Before I knew what I was doing, I was holding the wriggling creature in my newly webbed fingers. Flesh melted in my mouth, and bones crunched between my teeth, but it tasted surprisingly good.

Did I really just demolish a raw fish?

I looked around guiltily for another as I let its skeleton fall, but the rest of them had vanished.

"I have been here a long time, and that was the most absolutely revolting thing I have ever seen!" Edward sniggered.

11.

MORGANA

"So, what's with the rum?" I held my brown glass bottle to the anglerfish lights strung in nets above us and examined it. There was no label, but it was polished perfectly.

Edward and I had tucked ourselves away at one of the rough wooden tables in the corner of the bar.

"I mean, you guys don't *need* to eat or drink. Do you?" I peered at him apologetically. Many of my questions involved reminding him that he was dead.

"Some say that the first sailor ever to drown was granted one wish, and he asked the gods for rum in the afterlife." He chuckled, raising his tumbler in cheers.

I laughed, clinking my bottle against his glass. "Do you sleep?" I asked, setting the drink down on the grimy table.

"No, no, we don't sleep," he said, shaking his head. "However, we are all given rooms, which some of us like to use to imitate repose. Others fill theirs with treasures or items they've been lucky enough to retain."

The little room I woke up in had resembled the one I left behind in my grandparents' house. I guessed it was now mine, wondering who my new next-door neighbors would be as I scanned the bar.

There were few modern folks around. More people would have died of drowning when boats were still an essential means of transportation and life-saving methods were primitive.

A man with a cool stare met my gaze, and I quickly looked back at Edward. Once the man had returned to his drink, I studied him. He was sitting in the corner beside the piano, exuding an air of careless authority. His clothing caught my eye first—a long black overcoat and tall black boots, their heels encrusted with barnacles. His feet rested lazily on the table, and a high black collar framed the white material bunched at his throat.

He must have drowned sometime in the early eighteenth century, because he looked like the men I had seen in *Pride and Prejudice* film adaptations. His features were dark, and the glance he'd shot me was one of pure disgust, as if I were an unpleasant odor wafting across the room. He was sitting with another man, this one dressed in modern attire—a faded suit. He had dirty-blonde hair tied back in a ponytail, and his pale skin and light eyes suggested daylight might incinerate him, yet he seemed perfectly at ease in this cool climate.

Edward peered over his shoulder at the men. "That's Donahue and Jackie," he whispered. "Jackie joined us about sixty years ago. He was a petty criminal killed by the Irish Mob, but Donahue drowned long before even I did. He must have migrated here after the ship became a portal."

I snuck another look at the two of them. Jackie was examining a small blade in the light of the glass jar on the table, but Donahue was now looking at the back of Edward's head, the traces of a smirk playing on his lips.

"Who did you hang out with before I got here?" I asked, scanning the rest of the bar.

"On my own mostly." Edward shrugged. "Although sometimes I play chess with Daniel." He gestured at a young man in military uniform playing the piano. He had a sweeping brown fringe and a full mouth.

An elegant woman at the bar, her loose gown covered in jewels, caught my attention. Her tight curls reminded me of Skye's. She was toying with her necklace and batting her eyes at some young men in brown wool caps.

"That woman you're staring at is Evelyn. She was a passenger on *this* ship," Edward interjected, following my gaze.

"And you said there are ships like this all over the ocean?" I asked, eyes wide.

"Yes—"

A blood-curdling wail pierced the merriment as a pirate burst through the swinging doors. Daniel's hands froze over the piano keys, and the bar fell into a heavy silence. All eyes flew to the man.

"I told him I didn't mean to do it. I didn't know I was on Mer territory—I swear I didn't." The man trembled as his eyes darted around the room. He pressed himself into the stained wall beside the doors and slowly sank down, grasping his face.

The woman called Evelyn rushed to him. Her jeweled dress pooled on the floor as she knelt beside him.

"I needed loot to pay my debts, I did. Didn't know it was Mer territory, honest . . ." he cried.

"Don't tell me mermaids exist here as well?" I hissed, thinking of the insignia I had seen engraved on the bar's door.

Edward had turned in his seat to watch the man. When he glanced back at me, his face was so pale all his freckles stood out. "They live in a castle not far from here. The Drowned and the Mer have never been friendly."

"What happened, José?" I heard Evelyn ask.

"The Mer Prince . . . every part of my body . . . he sliced into it and let it grow back before cutting into it again with his claws . . . *His claws!*" The man's wail filled the tavern.

The Captain and Evelyn hoisted the man up, dragging him toward a door behind the bar. He thrashed against their grip, his wails echoing through the room. A ripple of hisses passed through the crowd as Evelyn shut the door behind them.

"Fuck the Mer and their prince," a pirate with a black mustache snarled.

I swallowed as I glanced from one murderous-looking Drowned to the next.

"You'll get used to it. The Drowned hate the Mer, and the Mer hate the Drowned." Edward sighed. "It's been like that for thousands of years. José is not the first of us to have a run-in with Mer Prince Aigéan, but he will be okay after some rum."

The man's wails seeped through the closed door, tightening something deep inside me. I took a long gulp of rum.

"Would you like to see the rest of the boat?" Edward gestured toward the grand doors, trying to distract me from José's screams.

I followed him back to the gloomy room under the stairs, where he unhooked an anglerfish lantern from the array hung on hooks beside the door. I hadn't noticed them when I arrived because I'd been so fascinated by the insignia.

"This ship was similar to *Titanic* and also found itself at the bottom of the Atlantic," I could hear Edward say as he navigated the darkness. We descended a different staircase, which led not to the cabins but into the shadowy depths of the lower decks. "She was just as magnificent, but not nearly as famous, so we get no human investigation. Thousands of ships strewn around these waters will never be found." Anguish trickled into his voice.

"This was *your* ship," I whispered.

"*SS Jones's Lady*, she was called. I say it was the name that doomed her. She went down in February of 1914."

"How did it sink?" I asked as we veered left at the bottom of the stairs into more darkness.

Edward was sure to know his way around, but that didn't stop my heart from quickening as I followed his lantern into the gloom. Slimy shells crunched underfoot as I carefully felt my way. Now and then, he would help me skip a spot he knew had decayed completely.

"It was a cold night . . ." Edward's voice softened as he traveled back in time. "The sky was starry and clear, but a ghastly wind blew up. It howled through the great rooms. The guests grew apprehensive, so we had the pianist play a jig to distract from the wind, and we kept the whisky flowing. Everyone was having a smashing time when we felt the jolt and heard metal scraping against metal." He stopped, and I almost walked straight into him. "We rushed to the deck and saw that we had collided with a large bulk carrier ship." He shook his head. "I watched in horror as it sank in minutes before my eyes. Dread filled me. Drowning is awful, but it's that very moment when you realize it's about to happen that's the worst. Nothing can compare to it."

"What happened next?" I whispered.

"That was it for her." Edward shrugged. "The carrier had grated a big tear in the right-hand side of her hull. We slowly filled with water and were at the bottom of the Atlantic within hours. I stayed with the ship until she was swallowed by the icy depths, debris swirled around me. Something tore through my belly, and then, darkness. When I woke, I was here."

A shudder brushed my arms. Perspective—that's what Edward's story gave me. I was lucky to be alive.

He steered me through a broken doorway. A patch of the ship's side had been torn off here, illuminating the space with shafts of gloomy emerald light.

"I present the swimming pool." Edward swung his lantern around the room.

"Looks more like a garden now." I laughed, taking in the sluggish plants and crustaceans that had made the giant basin in the floor their home.

"This place is my favorite. Come on." Edward led the way to a doorway across from the pool.

I didn't need his light anymore. I could see even after he had steered his lantern elsewhere. I kicked off from the boat's surface and found that my webbed feet equipped me with an aqua ability I never had in any Kansas City pool. *Interesting. It's a shame they're so hideous.*

We passed a brass-doored elevator. Its twisted gates were locked, and I shuddered as I imagined the people who might have been trapped there.

"Are there bones?" I asked as something crunched under my feet.

"No. Bones dissolve after years of being in the deep." Edward's voice drifted eerily out of the shadows.

I followed his light through a murky hallway until a staircase emerged from the gloom, its once-grand design now deteriorated. It led to a room that must have been reserved for first-class passengers. A massive chandelier lay crashed in the center, its glass beads green with grime.

Viridescent light filtered through the cracked panes of once beautiful windows, illuminating the algae draped over everything below. The were other remains in the space, but the sea had rusted them into the unidentifiable. I stepped over a spoon and sent what I thought was an ashtray skidding. Gloomy jade light made its way through missing portions of the wall, and sausage-like sea plants hung in bundles from the dark corners.

"I spend time here occasionally, to remember."

I couldn't make out Edward's features, only his silhouette. Without the lantern and my new aqua vision, this room would have been pitch-black.

"It's beautiful in a haunting way," I breathed, casting my eyes over the shattered glass ceiling.

Something shone on the far wall. It looked like graffiti—the kind you would find under bridges on land. "KILL THE MER."

Edward let out a horrified gasp as he noticed it too. I propelled myself toward the wall. Darkness festered at its base, and someone had scrawled the words across its uneven surface.

"Was this always there?" I turned to Edward, who had frozen a few meters behind me in his pool of lantern light.

"No." His voice was sharp with fear as his eyes darted across the scrawl.

I inched forward, drawing closer to it. Written in light crimson, it glinted with silver under the emerald glow.

"How would paint even work down here?" I wondered aloud. The letters had been done clumsily, and droplets ran down from each one.

"Th-that's not paint," Edward stammered. "It's *blood*."

"But it's silvery?" I reached for the shiny substance.

"Don't touch it!" He cried. "It's Mer blood. Oh, this is bad. *Really* bad!"

"Are hateful acts like this committed often by the Drowned?"

He shook his head. "Mer blood holds immense power," Edward whispered. "Some Drowned trade for it at the Sunken Bazaar, but that power always comes at a cost."

I looked back at the blood, now shimmering with the hues of a pearl. "It's so . . . beautiful."

What kind of magnificent being could produce such a substance in their veins? A chill crept over me, pebbling the fur-covered skin on my arms. I pictured Walt Disney's Ariel when I tried to imagine these creatures, but somehow, I didn't think the Mer would look like that. José had mentioned claws.

"There used to be an alliance between the Drowned and Mer, but this was over three thousand years ago, in the Days of Gods." Edward shifted uncomfortably from foot to foot. "This was before the curse that started it all, of course . . ."

"The curse?" I furrowed my brows.

"After the Battle of the Caeruleus Templum, it is said the gods cursed the houses of Mer and Drowned. Since then, they have been feuding, but there hasn't been a battle in over three hundred years."

I looked back at the words, sensing their otherness. They changed from translucent aqua to silver to light pink in the murky light, the dark surface revealing all of the brush's sprays and flicks.

"Who do you think did this?" I thought of all the rugged candidates I had seen in the bar.

"Every Drowned whispers foul words about the Mer." Edward's eyebrows drew together. "But most Drowned are cowards. They mutter foul words and trade in bootleg blood from the naturally deceased but cower when faced with the Mer. No one dares provoke their wrath. You saw what happened to José."

"Let's get out of here," I said, rubbing chills from my arms as I returned to Edward's side.

He released a long exhale, a clear sign of his relief.

I stumbled over a rusted object, perhaps a twisted piece of metal. He grabbed my elbow to steady me.

"How is this room so decayed in comparison to the bar?" I grumbled, rubbing my knee.

"We use preservation potion—that and the Captain's magic as a Protector—but it can only go so far." He held his anglerfish lantern higher, and the pool of light illuminated the doorway ahead.

"Preservation potion?" I scoffed.

"It's made by the Mer House of Niveus in the Arctic Ocean. They allow the Drowned to purchase it in large quantities. Well—they allow the Captain to. Even this part of the boat would be more decayed without it." The words rolled as casually from his lips as if he'd been discussing the weather.

"You mean there is more than one kingdom of Mer?" My mouth fell open, and I banged my shoulder against the side of the door, some wood floating off into the darkness.

Edward turned to me in exasperation. "Do take care, won't you!" He took me by the hand and guided me back down the dark hallway. "There are currently seven great Mer Kingdoms—Krumós, Thálassa, Niveus, Neptūnus, Pācificus, Mors, and Okeanós." He rattled the names off like a kid in a classroom listing America's fifty states. "Each house wields unique powers drawn from the ocean within which it stands. The House of Niveus can command the power of the icy Arctic Ocean. Hence the preservation powder that allows us to freeze the erosion of time."

"And what about the Mer who live in *this* ocean? You said their castle was not too far from here. What power do they command?" I found myself swallowing as I asked the question, thinking of the fear I had seen in José's eyes.

"They are the House of Neptūnus, the largest of the houses, and they draw their magic from the Atlantic Ocean."

The skin on my arms prickled again. "What does that allow them to do?"

We had reached the outskirts of the room with the empty pool. Edward strode ahead of me, his maroon uniform billowing around him.

"Well, I'm not entirely sure of the particulars, but they can harness power from storms, ocean fogs, and, naturally, the tides." He shrugged.

Freezing, I pressed my hand against Edward's chest to silence him. A gasping echoed from the room we were about to enter. I peered in through the dark doorway as the cries grew louder—a woman's cries. Had these creatures, powerful enough to command the Atlantic, descended upon the ship to take retribution?

Edward listened momentarily before rolling his eyes and continuing on. I followed his lantern light, marveling at his daring. Were we about to walk in on the graffiti culprit or, worse still, the "Neptunes" or whatever Edward had called them?

The gasping transformed into shrieks, and a thudding noise made me think someone was being beaten. Edward disappeared through the doorway, so I stepped in after him. As I entered the space, he turned to me, barely suppressing a smile, and I saw the source of the sounds that had chilled my blood.

A woman in a ruffled eighteenth-century dress was down on all fours and almost smothered by her layers of clothes. Her tightly wound curls bobbed about her face as a gnarled sailor made love to her from behind.

"Oh my gosh!" I giggled into the darkness as Edward and I felt our way back up the stairs.

"You'll get used to it." His voice was cool.

"What?"

"The sex. All the Drowned do is drink, gamble, and nookie." He took my hand to guide me over an eroded step.

"So you can feel pleasure, then?" I scrambled up behind him, and our bodies were pressed against each other.

"Yes, we were granted that. Perhaps it has something to do with one's soul still being intact. Or perhaps one of the first Drowned suggested it when they made their deal with the oceanic gods. Drowning makes for a vulgar afterlife." He let go of my hand and propelled himself away from me up more slimy stairs.

"Do you ever do it?" I used my webbed feet to catch up to him.

"No," he said shortly, retaking my hand as we reached another missing step. His touch didn't evoke the all-over awareness that Finn's had.

While Edward found it distasteful, I thought sex in the next world was a good thing—it likely kept the Drowned from being even more aggressive and miserable. The woman we'd interrupted came from an era when promiscuity had been frowned upon. If she hadn't been married when she drowned, she'd probably been a virgin—just as I would be if I were dead now. If Finn and I shared this afterlife, I'd let him bend me over like that.

My cheeks warmed. I was becoming one of the vulgar Drowned.

That didn't take long.

Rows of identical doors stretched before me, distinguished only by their numbers. Which one was mine?

I needed some solitude to process . . . *everything*, but the thought of accidentally disturbing one of the grisly pirates from the bar sent a chill through me.

I only remembered the inside of my room—a patchwork quilt and a dressing table with drawers. As these images danced in my mind, I was drawn to 207, just to the left of the spiraling stairs.

I turned the handle, and the door creaked open. Relief washed over me as I stepped into the room I remembered.

How strange. It was as if I'd instinctively known which one it was. On land, I had read emotions, but I could sense other things here.

I closed the door behind me, leaned against it, and surveyed the space. The quilt was the same as the one I had on land. I ran my hands over it, climbing onto the squeaky mattress and wrapping the blanket around me. I stared at the grimy ceiling and blew out a long breath. *How did I end up here?*

If the Captain—who I assumed knew more than anyone—kept his secrets, how was I supposed to uncover what I was or why I was here?

I am not here to give people the answers . . . His words echoed in my mind. *Typical.*

I tossed off the fraying quilt and went to the dirty mirror. Flecks of green algae flowed into the water as I cleaned the glass. Scooping my hair back, I inspected the gray fur covering my chest and arms. Then I peered at my left shoulder, where the inky crescent moon rising above the rolling wave remained unchanged. The Symbol of the Ocean, the Captain had said—whatever the hell that meant.

I moved my hands across the fur on my right breast; the traces of a nipple peaked beneath it. My fingers traveled over my abdomen. The pelage stretched almost all the way across it, sleek and smooth under my fingers. I took a deep breath as I slipped my hands over my pelvis and between my legs. I exhaled in relief when I felt my human woman parts' warmth and familiar shape. Thankfully, from the outside, the thick fur suit obscured any defining contours.

I returned to the bed and curled up beneath the faded quilt. My eyes drooped with fatigue—at least I still slept. Some strange magic had brought me here. What else could it be? I'd gone from never setting foot in the ocean to finding myself deep beneath it. I wanted to believe this was all a dream, but I knew in my heart that it wasn't.

Though some of the Drowned bore signs of decay, they still seemed more human than I was now. I could already hear the whispers of "monster" and "freak" that would haunt me if I ever returned to the land.

I can never go back like this.

12.

MORGANA

"I need to get out of this ship. I have literal cabin fever!" I banged my fist on the table, rattling the chess pieces of our game. Restlessness spread over me. There was also something else: a tightness in my chest. Anxiety, perhaps.

We were in the games room directly above the tavern. Like the tavern, it had been magically preserved. There were polished dark wood tables standing at regular intervals across the space, with chairs grouped around them. Some had high velvet backs and looked like they matched the décor, but others must have been gathered from different wrecks. Wooden beams supported the ceiling, and the light came from a chandelier of anglerfish in its middle. Edward had explained that apart from when they Mourned, the Drowned did not possess the power of light. The Captain bought bottled light magic from the Neptūnus Mer—who could channel lightning hitting the Atlantic—and used it to enhance the fish.

A roulette wheel was the room's centerpiece, and the Drowned surrounded it, squabbling. Wooden chests lined the walls, brimming with games collected over centuries from countless ships. There were chessboards, dice, playing cards, marbles—I even spotted a Monopoly board. A thin layer of algae coated these things, but for the most part, they were well-preserved.

"For the hundredth time, we can leave the ship when the storm has passed." Edward's brow furrowed as he gestured to the storm globe. Its giant half-sphere was embedded in the roof directly above the room's entrance. Dark, swirling waters crashed around its insides, and lightning illuminated its glass circumference.

"How long do you think I've been down here?" I grumbled.

"We don't keep track of time. That's just depressing. But if I were to guess . . . around two days." He started to rearrange the chess pieces.

Two days. My heart clenched as I thought about my grandfather.

"I ain't giving you a cent!"

My shoulders hunched instinctively as a snarl echoed from the table behind us. I turned to find a pirate with matted hair brandishing a knife at his fellow poker players.

"Pay up, Rackham, you filthy cheapskate!" A pirate with a thick black mustache growled at the shaggy-haired pirate and flipped the table, sending cards flying and coins clattering to the floor around us.

I plucked one from the soggy carpet and examined it. It was silver, with the Ocean Symbol etched on one side. On the other side, an outline of a mermaid was engraved, and peculiar runes surrounded each picture. I flipped it back and forth with my fingers.

"The pawnshop!" I gasped.

"The what?" Edward pulled his attention from the chessboard.

"I saw some of these coins in a shop on land, but they were so faded I thought the mermaid was a fish!" I thrust the coin in his face.

"It's the ocean's currency," Edward said, looking at the coin.

How did they get to Mr. Inegar's shop?

"What does the lettering say?" I held it up to the light of the anglerfish chandelier.

"It is in the ancient Runes of the Ocean. We need a key to read it."

I grabbed more coins from the carpet at my feet. "This all spilled onto the ground when that pirate upturned the table." I gestured over my shoulder at the hulky man with the mustache. He had now righted the table and was intent on a new game.

"That's Teachie, and next to him with the shaggy hair and beaded braids is Rackham. They're from Port Royal, the sunken city, but they migrated to this boat about six months ago."

"What's the sunken city?" I asked, watching Teachie's face twitch as he glanced down at his hand of cards.

"Port Royal was once a pirate town in the Palisadoes. In 1692, though, it mysteriously disappeared beneath the waves." Edward's gaze flicked toward the pirates.

Teachie's scowl morphed into a grin as Rackham set down his cards. Stacks of the ocean's currency and shipwrecked treasures lay before each player.

"What would you even buy down here?" My focus returned to the coin, running my fingers over the intricate carvings adorning the silver. It looked like something archaeologists would dig up on National Geographic.

"Sometimes, we might buy things from the Taberna," Edward said, creeping one of his pawns forward.

"What's the Taberna?" My eyes widened, and Edward's brow creased.

"It's a shop run by an old merman who doesn't mind associating with all creatures of the sea. It's your move." He rapped his copper-haired knuckles on the table between us.

"Perhaps they have something that will help me get my human body back!"

"We can go when the storm has passed." Edward's eyes moved to the ceiling. The globe still showed chaos above, but it seemed to be subsiding.

Another eruption came from the poker table. Vindication spread across Rackham's face as he won some treasure from Teachie.

"Why must you stay in the boat when a storm rages above?" I asked. "Surely its turbulence wouldn't reach here." Even though the globe showed violent seas, the portholes only reflected blackness, but the water around us felt warmer, as if it had been stirred.

"We stay on the ship to avoid wandering into shallower water and being swept to another part of the ocean in its currents." Edward's eyebrows drew apart, and then his mouth tightened.

The nagging feeling was back—the anxiety. I pushed my velvet-backed chair aside and picked my way through the tables to peer out the nearest porthole, massaging my chest. Outside, the pillar forest admitted shuddering heat into the current.

The tightness jabbed at my ribcage, and I tripped over an open trunk, skidding onto my back on the slimy floor. My chest constricted again, and I rasped a shallow breath, but it felt incomplete, like the air wouldn't come.

I reached for the grubby porthole to pull myself up. *Damn it!* My hands slid on the slick algae, sending me skidding straight toward two men playing cards. I recognized them as Jackie and Donahue.

The side of my body collided with the wooden base of their table, and I watched in horror as cards spilled over the edge. A tattered pair of Oxfords and tall black boots hemmed me in on either side.

"You best watch yourself," said a voice above me—Jackie.

I began peeling myself from the slimy floor, but felt a blade pointed at my throat. Fear constricted my being. I had never come face-to-face with this kind of danger, and my body betrayed me with paralysis.

"You've lost me a fair bit o' money." Jackie had an Irish accent.

Legs splayed, he reached for me, his filthy suit rumpled, trousers hitched to expose moth-eaten socks. He jabbed the knife toward me, forcing me into the table leg. There was nowhere to go—the blade's tip found my throat, and I winced in pain.

"I . . . I'm sorry," I gasped as he leaned down to leer at me. His lips curved into a malicious smile, showing a mouth full of yellow teeth.

"Jackie, do refrain from vexing the seal slut," said the man with the tall black boots—Donahue.

Jackie's awful smile faded as he withdrew the knife, slamming it sulkily on the table. I brought my hands to my neck. Warmth. It had drawn blood.

Using the algae-slick table for leverage, I pushed myself out from under it, squeezing past them. Jackie shifted, spreading his legs wider, and my body grazed his pants.

Both men watched me now as I stood before them, wiping slime from my trembling knees. Donahue ran a hand through his dark hair, surveying me with equally dark eyes. I was acutely aware of the outlines of my fur-covered breasts.

"It's grand that you want to grind on me, love, but you're not my type." Jackie looked me up and down. The hunger in his pale eyes contradicted his words.

"Who is your type then? *Him?* Cute." I nodded toward Donahue and smiled coyly, but at the same time, I reached for my chest as the anxiety flared.

Jackie's grin contorted into a glare. "Your time's coming, bitch! Just remember, you can still bleed." His eyes flared.

Shit—he was right.

I returned to Edward, who had grown pastier than usual as he watched the event unfold.

"Are you okay?" He leaned forward, the words escaping his lips in a whisper.

"What's the deal with those assholes?" I glanced over his shoulder at the men. Donahue was reshuffling the cards, and Jackie's attention was now on him. His knife was still unsheathed on the table.

"Donahue was once an English nobleman," Edward mumbled, color staining his cheeks. "And Jackie is nothing more than Drowned scum." His mouth thinned.

I clawed at the skin above my left breast. It felt like someone was squeezing my heart, or was it my lungs? I couldn't tell, but it was getting worse. Bending over the table, I coughed as the discomfort became more pronounced.

"I . . . I can't breathe," I gasped.

Edward's eyes went wide with concern. "Hey, *HEY* . . . Something's wrong!" he called to the Captain, who was playing chess with Daniel at a table to our right.

The supply of oxygen I had been drawing upon seemed to have diminished and I was being slowly suffocated. I clasped my throat, knocking my bottle of rum to the floor. I inhaled deeply, but my lungs remained unsatisfied. If I hadn't been drawing oxygen from the water, then where had it been coming from? Edward's hand was on my shoulder as the Captain's wooden leg reached our table.

"What's happening to me?" I peered up at the Captain.

"It looks like you need to surface to replenish your air." His face was grave.

"Wait, what? *I can do that*?" I coughed as another wave of suffocation washed over me.

"B-but she can't go. There's a storm," Edward cried.

"She needs to go *now*," the Captain commanded. "I suspect Selkie's blood might run in her veins. If this is true, she needs to try to surface, or she will die."

"She's a Selkie? I thought they were extinct," Edward hissed, eyes widening with fear.

What the fuck was a Selkie?

"Go, child!" the Captain urged me.

Drawing a shuddering breath, I clung to the oxygen reserves I had left. My senses had been warning me for hours, and I had passed it off as restlessness. Another part of me was in a daze. *I can leave this place. I can surface.*

The storm globe showed that the turbulence above was easing as I bolted from the games room. I sped down to the bar, pushing past the rowdy Drowned, whose menacing grunts fell on deaf ears as I burst through the swinging doors.

I knew my senses worked differently down here. Perhaps they would lead if I could visualize where I needed to go. The only docks I knew were at the shores of Ruadán's Port, the sea gray like the sky and the waves lapping against my jetty. Beyond the bay's two fists was the Atlantic—which I was somewhere underneath right now—an ocean that stretched wild and vast.

Emptying my mind, I waited for my oceanic sense of direction to kick in. *Nothing. Come on, come on, come on!*

I let images of Ruadán's Port wash over me as I propelled myself forward across the forest of stalagmite towers, drawn by the invisible thread of instinct. My lungs seared with every stroke, a piercing ring fraying the edges of my consciousness.

As I swam diagonally upward, the darkness gradually gave way to deep blue waters, and I left the bubbling forest of hot vents beneath me. The feeling of suffocation was growing.

My stomach knotted as my chest tightened. I wouldn't make it to

Ruadán's Port in time, so I switched directions. Instead of traveling diagonally, I kicked upward. Schools of fish parted in my wake as the grip on my lungs squeezed tighter.

Up and up I went, and my surroundings became aqua.

Up and up. The ringing in my ears intensified, and dizziness consumed me. Seaweed moved in clumps left and right, strands brushing against my ankles. I shook them off to rise higher and higher . . .

I spluttered as I broke the water's surface, letting out a rasping cough and bringing my hands to my burning throat. Sea water slapped the sides of my chin and made its way into my gaping mouth. When I spat it out, I drew in deep, life-giving breaths from the atmosphere around me.

Wind caressed my face. Oh, how I'd missed its gentle embrace. It was dark, and stars twinkled above me, strewn between shrouds of clouds. Real stars! Not the eerie cosmos of anglerfish.

The cool breeze brushed against the wet fur on my shoulders. My heart beat excitedly as a barrage of thoughts raced through my mind.

I can surface! I have not been sentenced to an eternity with the Drowned.

I floated, basking in the moonlight, feeling my chest's rhythmic rise and fall as I inhaled the crisp air. I dived under the waves and breathed easily now as if my oxygen source had been replenished. Not only was I able to surface for air, but my life depended on it.

SS *Jones's Lady* must be nestled in one of the deepest, blackest parts of the ocean. I had surfaced in—what was it—half an hour or an hour? That meant I could move fast when I wanted to. How fast? Faster than a car or even a submarine, that's for sure. I found myself thinking of my mother. She would be able to do the math.

I didn't want to return to the deep, not yet. I didn't know if I *ever* wanted to go back there, but I couldn't go home either. I no longer looked like a human. But what if I returned to Ruadán's Port for a visit? The idea of seeing those familiar shores comforted me.

Perhaps I would see Finn as he walked down from his clifftop fortress to work in the morning. The thought coated my body in warmth, but the water lapping against my fur-covered breasts reminded me I would have to stay hidden. He couldn't see me like this, and what if someone else spotted me? They would capture me and cut me apart like a science experiment. I had seen enough Hollywood films to know what happened to creatures of the deep when someone from above caught them.

I propelled myself in the direction my senses were taking me, parting the swell with my webbed hands. One stroke and then another.

After traveling for an hour, the blue became monotonous. Aside from the odd fish I devoured, I lost interest in the multitude of sea life. I let my mind wander as I swam . . . and it found Finn. I pictured him strolling along the water's edge toward the jetty, his pants rolled up, his white shirt billowing in the breeze. The wind tousled his dark hair, and his gaze searched the sea as if looking for me.

Wait—was that Finn or Prince Eric from *The Little Mermaid*? I chuckled to myself. Either way, it was working for me. I imagined myself emerging from the ocean, water streaming down my fur bodysuit, as Finn's dark eyes filled with lust.

I swallowed hard as the sea floor became visible below me. My daydream had carried me into shallower water. Cans were scattered here and there, and I slipped between the two rocky arms that enclosed the bay. Twice, I passed the hulls of small boats heading out to the open ocean. I propelled myself deeper, almost crawling along the seabed.

My limbs were aching when the barnacle-ridden legs of my jetty materialized out of the gloom. I was home.

The waves lightened around me as the dawn broke. I popped the top of my head out of the water, revealing one facial feature at a time. The sun's rays were turning the waves around me crimson—that gorgeous ball of glowing light! Allowing my entire torso to break the water, I inhaled fresh air. I floated on my back as the sun made its way into the sky, and all the pink colors disappeared.

Something had changed. The sea continued to caress my legs, but they beat against it like they'd never had webs. I fumbled at my chest—my sleek fur was gone. Instead, my grandmother's coat was flapping uncomfortably around my shoulders. Beneath it, I was naked.

I dove beneath the swell, eyes burning with salt, and a swirling green mist of bubbles met me. A relentless urge to surface and breathe took hold, and my body remained free of fur.

I wrapped my arms around one of the jetty's slimy poles, ignoring the barnacles that dug into my thighs, and rested my head against the rough wood above the water. My chest heaved with relief. I was human again.

Was it all a dream, or am I losing my mind?

Someone was walking along the shore. I stiffened. They were wearing black jeans and combat boots. I knew those jeans. Those leather boots. *Finn.* A surge of emotion washed over me—comfort so deep it nearly stole my breath. What was he doing out at this hour?

He was dragging something black along the sand. The wind plucked at it—a garbage bag. I yelled out, but a strangled gurgle left my lips. The language of the sea was still on my tongue.

No, I can't think like this.

If I had descended into madness, I needed the rest of the world to believe I was sane. I tried again. This time, the gurgle seemed more intelligible.

Wait a minute. I swallowed my cry for help, my relief quickly soured by humiliation curdling into anger. The last time I'd seen Finn, I'd been drunk and naked in his house. I was nude again now. Heat flared in my cheeks as I pressed deeper against the barnacle-crusted pole.

I waited until his black-jeaned legs had disappeared before I grasped the end of the jetty and hoisted myself up. My arms felt like they had no muscles. *Work*, I willed them in frustration as I hung on to the edge. I had dreamed of feeling the wind on my skin, but it was causing me to shiver in the wet coat. *Work*, I thought again, glaring at my arms. This time, they responded, and I pulled my bedraggled body up onto the scratchy wood.

I slowly pulled myself upright. The harbor was coming to life, and some fishermen eyed me curiously from their boats as they chugged past.

"Morgana?"

I knew that voice and how it coated my body in heat, making my heart beat faster.

13.

Finn

She winced when I called her name, turning slowly. There was a flush in her cheeks.

I dropped the garbage bag and crumpled soft drink can I was carrying, folding my gloved hands across the chest of my black coat as I surveyed her.

The girl was sopping wet, wearing nothing but a fucking fur coat—the fur coat her grandmother gave her. *Interesting.*

Her cheeks grew rosier under my gaze. Perhaps she was remembering how she'd undressed at my house. I hadn't gotten the memory out of my head either. I had tried—trust me, I'd tried—but it seemed burned into my subconscious.

She pulled the folds of her wet fur tighter. Was she naked again now? My jaw hardened as I gritted my teeth.

"I—uh—" she started. Her teeth were chattering. "I was swimming. You know, the benefits of ice baths and all that."

Bullshit. I almost snorted aloud, but she started walking toward me.

Oh no, you don't.

"Your friend Skye's been looking for you." I took a sideways step so my body was blocking the space where the jetty met the sand. "She said you've not been at work in two days."

"I've been sick." She tried to push past me, but I remained in her path.

"Here." I pulled off my jacket, wrapping it around her shoulders, and she tugged her wet fur tighter underneath it. It was a gentle gesture on my part, but I needed her to trust me if I was going to try again.

She gazed up at me with wide green eyes, her lips tinged purple, her wet auburn hair tucked into my jacket. It was as if she were bracing for the inevitable question: Why had she been swimming in the freezing harbor while sick?

I said nothing. I now had suspicions, but I could find out everything I needed to know without asking if my gifts worked.

Her gaze lingered on me, tracing the muscles in my forearms before she quickly looked away, a flush rising to her cheeks once more.

Could it be my allure? No, she didn't have the same docile, foggy-eyed expression they usually got. This was different . . . *She desires me.* The thought caused a tremor in my groin, and I shifted from foot to foot, shaking myself.

"What are you doing?" she asked, eyes moving to the garbage bag, now deflated at my feet.

"Cleaning up the rubbish that careless morons leave scattered on these shores." A muscle ticked in my cheek.

"Oh. How often do you do that?" She nibbled on her trembling bottom lip.

"Pretty much every morning when I'm here." I shrugged, brushing my hair from my forehead with a gloved hand.

She stepped from the jetty, her bare feet sinking into the damp sand. Reaching down, she picked up the soft drink can I had dropped. "Here," she said, placing it into the bag as I opened it. Our hands brushed, and she didn't pull away.

There was that damned niggle at my cock again.

"Thank you." I swallowed as the side of my gloved finger met hers.

Images of that night at my house flooded my mind—her eyes locked on mine, hands tangled in her hair, her offering herself to me.

Oh, gods be damned.

"I should go." She made as if to remove my jacket from her shoulders.

I put my hand atop hers. "Keep it. I am sure I will see you soon."

It looked like she didn't know what to say or do—she knew this situation was completely absurd. She mumbled a thanks and pushed past me, her face burning.

This was perfect. I thought she had returned to America, but no. My father was right—there was more to this little human than met the eye.

I will get her alone again without distractions. This time, I will not fail.

PART THREE

The Selkie

14.

MORGANA

Darkness enveloped me. Its swirling presence was like unseen hands pulling me into a dance. Red eyes stared unblinkingly into the void. There was the familiar whistling noise and my blood in the water again—someone cried out, but the oppressive blackness obscured my vision.

Sweat drenched my body. I was awake and in my grandparents' attic, not my grimy little cabin deep under the ocean.

I threw my quilt to the floor, heart racing. I didn't remember falling asleep. It was like I had jet lag from the difference between this world and the murky depths of the sea. It was the same dream I always had, yet it didn't frighten me as much. This time, the engulfing darkness reminded me of the ocean's sway, and I felt as if I were back there.

Two days—only two days had passed here, meaning time in the Kingdom of the Deep operated somewhat similarly. I felt like I had completely lost sense of it. The dead weren't counting anymore because they had nothing to count up to.

Yesterday had gone better than expected. I told my grandfather I'd been with Finn for two days. He grumbled but accepted my story. After a hot bath, I raced down to Bayside to see Skye, and I told her I had been sick. She cried and hugged me, admitting she had started to suspect Finn. I knew I was weaving a fragile web of lies that could easily unravel in a small town, but it was all I had to work with.

Barry's son, Jamie, had been covering my shifts at Celtic Keepsakes and had begrudgingly offered me my job back. Words of acceptance tumbled out of my mouth before I could stop them. Did I even want it?

The guilt that flooded me when I said yes told me I didn't, but I wasn't sure if I wanted to return to the world of the Drowned either. I wasn't sure I even knew how.

The only thing I knew for certain was that I needed to understand what a "Selkie" was, and what this had to do with me.

"What's for breakfast?" I slid onto one of the wooden chairs across from my grandfather.

The kitchen exuded a warm, inviting ambiance compared to the ocean's gloomy emerald depths. The sun's rays filtered in through the small window above the sink, lighting the room in soft shades.

"Fresh fish on toast," he said, popping a piece of bread slathered in oily mackerel into his mouth. His hands were marked with scars and calluses, the result of a lifelong dedication to the seas.

His fish breakfasts usually repulsed me, but something about their smell had changed. Now, I desired them.

"Ugh." I feigned disgust, opting for cornflakes.

"Shouldn't you be at work?" He glanced at the wooden grandfather clock in the corner of the room—9:35 a.m.

"I have the day off."

I shoveled cereal into my mouth. It tasted foreign, and I was hungrily eyeing Granddad's toast. I'd told Jamie I wouldn't be back until the next day because I needed to "recover," but really I needed time for research.

"I don't want any more complaints from Barry. I was embarrassed to call Officer Wilson and tell him you were back, and that it was a false alarm." He chewed his fish slowly, mashing it between his fragile gums. I could sense his anger, but also a genuine concern.

"Yes, Granddad." I smiled at him, forcing down some more cornflakes. His anger faltered, replaced with a sliver of happiness.

He coughed, as if trying to master a stern tone. "First he carries you in here unconscious, and then you disappear with him for two days." He shook his head. "I think this lad is bad news, Morgana. There are strange folk in this old port town. You hear stories..."

"Are you going fishing today?" I raised my eyebrows at him, guiltily changing the subject.

He nodded and glanced out the window. "Your mother called while you were asleep. She wonders when you are planning on going to college." He ran a hand through his hair and sighed.

"I don't think I want to go back... and who would stay with you?" I muttered, toying with my soggy breakfast.

Granddad huffed. "Your mom won't like that, and don't worry about me."

"I can make my own choices now," I grumbled.

"And what choices are those? Disappearing with strange lads... She calls me every bloody hour." He rubbed the gray stubble on his jaw.

"Granddad, I am sorry for leaving you." I avoided his eyes, but when I looked up, his face softened.

"You remind me of her, you know." His grief washed over me.

"Thank you," I said gently.

We sat in silence for a while. Granddad was lost in his memories, his sadness decorating the room.

"D-do you know of any bookstores nearby? Maybe one with books on local history." I met his brown eyes.

When I transformed into an underwater being, my mobile phone, jeans, and T-shirt had been lost, and Granddad didn't have a computer, so I would have to do my research the old-fashioned way.

"I'm not much o' a reader." He waved off the question.

I returned to my cornflakes, the aroma of his fish toast still hanging in the air.

"There's one a few streets back from here," he finally said. "Your grandmother used to go there sometimes."

An idea struck me. My grandfather had lived here all his life . . .

"Um, Granddad, maybe *you* can help me. Could you tell me about Selkies?"

The toast fell from his hand, his eyes narrowing suspiciously. I sensed a wave of defensiveness and something else: guilt. I watched him apprehensively, convinced he *must* know something.

"You can't believe what people in this town say," he said gruffly, pushing out his chair.

"But what *are* they?" I pressed.

"I've never heard o' them, and don't ask me again," he growled, pulling his jacket from the hook beside the back door and hobbling out. He slammed it in his wake and then opened it again. "And, please let me know if you spend any more nights at this lad's place." He shook his head as he retreated.

This area of the town had certainly not been revamped for tourism. To my right, a worn corner store caught my eye—a good start. I headed down the lane beside it, which was named Saltmarsh Row. Rounding a corner, I passed a dilapidated dry cleaner and a closed takeout diner. The next building was a pub that looked like a stone house. The paint was peeling from its white walls, and the faded sign read, "The Port House." An old coil of rope, its bends now blackened, had been artfully positioned beside a carved wooden fish at the entrance. Beside it was the bookstore. It was a small—also whitewashed stone—building. I would have passed straight by if not for the crooked "BOOKS" sign in the grimy window. The shop seemed to lack a proper name.

When I opened the door, a bell tinkled somewhere, but I couldn't see any staff, so I began to browse. The scent of aging paper and leather bindings enveloped me. Shelves, haphazardly packed with books, reached ambitiously toward the rafters. Some volumes were neatly aligned, while others were piled in teetering stacks that looked like they hadn't been disturbed in years. I made my way through the narrow aisles until I found a factual section. Flipping through town history books, I saw no mention of Selkies.

"H-herm."

The cough made me jump, and I dropped *Wild and Wonderful Sea Life of the Atlantic*. It sent dust particles flying as it hit the wooden floor.

"Can I help you?"

I turned to see a little gray-haired woman standing behind me. She had dark skin and many smile lines around her eyes.

"I was looking for a book on Selkies." I rocked back and forth on the balls of my feet, and the dusty floorboards creaked.

"Selkies," the woman repeated, reaching down to retrieve the open book I had dropped. "You're in the wrong section. It's fiction you'll be wanting." She shuffled toward an aisle at the back of the store.

"No, no, I don't think so. I'm looking for an animal that lives in *these* waters," I called after her, remaining in the nonfiction section.

"Aye, but you asked for Selkies, if I heard you right. So, you'll be wanting this." She held up a dusty black book. "But there's no Selkies in these waters, lass." She shuffled back toward me, holding the hardcover. The title was embossed in golden lettering: *Mythical Creatures of the Water*.

The old woman opened it and pointed to chapter six in the index.

I took the book from her, hands trembling. I waited until she shuffled back to the counter at the furthest point of the store before I flicked the book to "Chapter Six: Selkies" and dragged my finger to the first line of text. "Selkies are fantastical creatures from Celtic and Icelandic folklore. The Selkie Legend of Orkney . . ."

"You may also want this book." The voice startled me, and I turned to see the young man from my grandmother's funeral rising from a threadbare armchair in a dark corner. I took in his brown skin, dark hair, and amber eyes. He was wearing a plain black T-shirt, knee-length gray shorts, and a lanyard.

"Don't mind my aunty." He grinned as he ran his fingers across the titles I had initially been browsing in the nonfiction section. "She looks after this store while my mom is away and hates every minute of it." He gestured at the old lady behind the counter, grumbling as she straightened books. His gentle caress stopped on a green-spined title, and he held it out to me: *Myths & Legends of Ruadán's Port*.

"Is it fiction?" I asked, running my hands over the cover, which depicted an artist's impression of Merrow Rocks jutting into the ocean.

"It depends on who you're talking to. I keep it in the nonfiction section." He smiled again, flashing his perfectly white teeth.

"Do you think some things people *think* are mythology could be real?" I lowered my voice as his aunty hobbled to the glowing entrance of a room at the back of the shop, disappearing behind a dark wooden door. I knew this was an overly philosophical question to ask someone you'd just met, but something about his presence made me feel at ease.

"The myths had to come from somewhere." He leaned on the dusty shelf and surveyed me with his brown eyes. "You're Iona's granddaughter." His voice was as soft as the caramel of his skin. I sensed a warmth and gentleness in him. This was a welcome change from the things I usually sensed in men.

"Yes, I remember you from the funeral."

"I'm Aranare Williamson." He wiped the dust from his palms on his shorts and held out his hand.

"How did you know my grandmother?" I asked, pulling the books into my left arm to shake it.

"She visited the store sometimes to see my mother. They traveled together. Why are you so interested in learning about the mythology of the ocean?" Aranare's topaz eyes gleamed as they swept over me.

I spluttered the first thing that came into my head. "I, uh, I'm writing a book!"

"Where is it set?" he asked, straightening some of the volumes on the shelf beside us. I didn't know why he bothered when the rest of the shop seemed in disarray, but I couldn't help but notice his forearms. They were muscular but not overly so, like the arms of a swimmer.

"Well . . . here," I said, continuing with my half-truth, half-lie.

"In that case, you better take both books. You can't write about Ruadán's Port without understanding the local legends. This has been a port town for hundreds of years—many strange things used to pass through these shores."

His book straightening had led him closer to me. He was tall. Looking straight ahead, my eyeline came to the top of his chest.

"How much do I owe you?" I laughed.

"Twenty-six pounds." A grin tugged at the corners of his mouth.

We made our way to the counter. Nestled at the very back of the store, its surface was almost entirely obscured by a miscellany of objects. Beside the register, stacks of books leaned precariously, awaiting purchase or return to the shelves.

"There's an EFTPOS machine here somewhere, don't worry." Aranare ducked under the counter. The wall space around it was lined with shelves crammed with rare-looking books. "Here you go." He shoved the clutter aside and offered me a modern machine.

As I tapped my card, I felt the radiating warmth from his palms. For a moment, I was tempted to linger, savoring the heat. Instead, I thanked him and slid the books into my satchel.

"Oh, and Morgana." Aranare's amber eyes softened. "I was sorry about your father."

The ground seemed to slide out from beneath me. I swallowed. "My father . . . You knew him?" The blood was pumping so loudly in my ears that I wondered if I would be able to hear Aranare's response.

"I was fourteen when he died, but I knew Rory and your mother, Anna, too. The port is a very small place." His eyes had a pained look, and his emotions washed over me. *Sympathy.*

Suddenly, I didn't care about the books or the underwater world. *My father. Rory.* For the first time in my life, he had a name.

"How did he die?" A knot formed in my throat as I said the words. I tried to busy myself by buckling my satchel, but my hands were trembling.

"You don't know?" Aranare's brows furrowed in confusion as he stepped from behind the counter and touched my back.

I shook my head, scared tears would burst from me if I spoke.

"Aranare!" His aunt appeared, carrying a stack of books. "Are you going to help me get these out to customers or stand chatting all day?"

I brushed his hand off and stepped away from the counter.

"I have to help my aunty, but Mom's back tomorrow. Why don't you meet me for lunch at Bayside? My uncle owns the café under the Ferris wheel. Do you know it?"

I nodded.

Aranare's aunty turned her dark eyes on me. "I was sorry to hear about your father and your gran as well, lass. The sea takes and it gives. Your grandfather stole from the sea, so it took back. Run along, and Aranare will fill you in on the morn."

15.

MORGANA

My father was called Rory, and he was dead.

The pub next door was virtually empty. I ordered a dark beer and took a deep gulp. My hands were shaking. Aranare was going to tell me everything tomorrow.

For now, I needed a distraction.

I slipped into a booth at the back of the venue, pulled the book on Selkies from my satchel, and set it on the table. The cover was a dark canvas, and its title was embossed in gold Celtic font: *Mythical Creatures of the Water*.

I scanned the contents.

1. SIRENS
2. GRINDYLOW
3. MER
4. KORRIGANS
5. ST. ELMO'S FIRE
6. SELKIES
7. KELPIE

8. *MORGEN*
9. *NYMPHS*
10. *BLUE MEN OF THE MINCH*
11. *FINFOLK*
12. *SEA SNAKES & MONSTERS*
13. *RUSALKI*
14. *THE KRAKEN*

My grandmother had told me stories of some of these creatures, but not Selkies.

Never Selkies.

Could all these other mythical beings also exist if Mer, Selkies, and the Drowned were real? I flicked through the pages and found myself stopped at chapter three.

> *A mermaid or merman is a legendary aquatic creature that combines a human's upper body with a fish's tail.*

Yes, yes, I knew all of this. I skimmed further.

> *The Mer's tale has been told for centuries; sightings mainly occur around small isles and deserted beaches. Sailors often associate the Mer with storms and bad weather. They have beautiful voices that are treacherous to human ears and have lured many sailors to their death.*

The book then documented images of Mer in Scotland, Ireland, Europe, Asia, and Africa. Each culture had a slightly different representation and name for the creatures, but their mythology shared striking similarities. I skipped forward to a chapter that caught my eye:

> *Powers of the Mer:*
> *Throughout folklore, Mer are described as dangerous and possessing various magical powers. Most tales tell of the Mer being beautiful and charming, but their charms can become deadly when they lure humans out to sea or into captivity. The Mer are immensely beautiful, yet*

grotesquely fierce when aggravated. There are tales of humans receiving gifts from Mer, but these often come with watery curses.

It sounded like the Mer had used their powers against humans for centuries. But what about the Drowned? There was no chapter on them. Who knew what sins they had committed? Edward had mentioned "four great battles."

I skimmed the following paragraph, and disappointment flooded me. This text said nothing about the seven houses or their unique powers drawn from the different oceans. If I wanted to learn more about the House of Neptūnus and the other Mer houses, that would mean returning to the deep.

My heart quickened as I flipped to chapter six.

Selkies live as seals in the sea and transform into humans on land. These shape-shifters can only transform at dawn or dusk, when they are most powerful.

Seals! The little dark heads I had seen bobbing above the water and sunning themselves on the rocks swam into my mind.

In Gaelic lore, Selkies are often called "maighdean-mhara," meaning "maidens of the sea."

According to the text, Selkies originated from the Celts. Granddad had grown up in this town, and my grandmother said her family came from Orkney. Could I be a Selkie? My hands trembled against the open page as the thought washed over me. But wait, I couldn't be. This text said they turned into seals. I'd just been . . . furry. I needed to know more. I needed to go down to the water and look for some seals.

"May I join you?" The voice startled me, and I instinctively scooped the book up to my chest.

Finn. I'd been so preoccupied I hadn't noticed his approach. Now, he was in front of me, and I was struggling to breathe again.

He didn't wait for an answer before sliding into the booth across from me. His black hair was slicked to one side, accentuating his dark brows and eyes. The dim shaft of light from the small nearby window barely touched his face, now shadowed by the pub's walls, but I felt his gaze on me. The vulgar tunes of the slot machines chimed somewhere behind us.

"Your jacket . . . I'll bring it to work."

Finn gestured dismissively, as if he couldn't care less about me still having his expensive woolen coat. "What are you doing in this pub, drinking beer? You are unusual." His eyes lingered on me for a quiet moment.

I had forgotten my beer and took a little sip. *Shit.* I put it down again quickly, remembering the whisky.

"I'm just exploring my local area. Is that *okay* with you? Wait a minute, what are *you* doing here?"

He smiled playfully. His smile differed from the boy's at the bookstore. Finn's was darkness, and Aranare's had been light.

"I came here looking for *you*. I was coming to see you at your place, but then I saw you wandering up here."

The way he emphasized the word made me feel light-headed. The thoughts he stirred in me were wrong, yet temptation kept clawing at my resolve.

Why does he keep seeking me out when he has a fiancé?

"You didn't yell out, just followed behind? That's not creepy at all." I rolled my eyes, slinging my satchel over my shoulder.

"I saw you go into the bookstore, and I could see you talking to Aranare."

"You know him?"

"I know of him." A flicker of annoyance passed Finn's face.

"Of course, the small town thing." I began shuffling out of the booth. "But wait, you only just moved here . . ."

"We've had the pawnshop here for years. It's impossible *not* to know the Williamsons when they own half the town. I don't know why you care so much." His shoulders twitched.

"I was just about to go down to the beach. You don't happen to know where the best spot to see seals would be?" I mumbled, fidgeting with my hair.

"Seals?" His eyes flickered with something. "I'll show you." A grin curled the corners of his mouth as he gestured to the door.

It was chilly outside, and a light rain tickled our faces. Finn walked close to me as we trailed down the hill toward the bay. I sensed his proximity—quiet, dark, and broody. He'd worn his green jacket again today, and I peeked at him from the corner of my eye. He really was attractive. I found it hard not to watch him, but his charisma came more from how he carried himself.

"Where is your fiancé anyway?" I bit the words out before I could stop myself. Skye and I had tried to find Finn on Instagram, but he didn't seem to have an account, and there was no sign of anyone living with him in his clifftop fortress.

"She lives on the . . . estate." He waved a hand as if trying to brush off the question.

"How did you meet?" I asked, even though I wasn't sure I wanted to know.

"Oh, you know, it was just like one of those romance movies you love." He shrugged.

Sarcasm. Another mask. It was better than arrogance or ice, but it was still a mask.

He stopped at the top of the dark rocks that led to the sand and turned to face me.

"So, was it love at first sight?" I pressed him.

His brows narrowed as I said the word *love*, shadows flickering in his eyes. "In my family, we don't have the luxury of such trivial things. It's not about what I want . . . it's about what's expected."

We descended the rocks in silence as I scanned the beach for seals. The salty sea air caressed me, and I searched for those familiar smells and rushing sensations, but I felt nothing. I hadn't felt that pull since I returned.

Finn jumped onto the sand at the bottom of the rocks and turned to face me. "I'm sorry for being short with you." He let out a weary breath, running a hand through his hair. "You're asking too many questions about things you won't understand."

Something was eating away at the sense of self-confidence he'd shown that night at his house. He looked out to sea and sighed. "Have you ever wanted to just . . . leave everything behind and go somewhere you can be yourself without all the pressure?"

"Yes." I jumped the final cluster of rocks, landing on the sand beside him. "That's why I came here."

He smiled sadly, taking in my face before continuing toward the bay's curve. Slick black pebbles were imprinted in the sand beneath his lace-up army boots as he led the way.

"I guess the life I lead numbs you in a way, so I never really think about it or who I might be without the confines . . ." He shook his head, looking out over the ocean again.

"Working in the pawnshop can't be that difficult."

He let out a low chuckle, waving off my comment. We walked in silence for a moment.

"You're not wearing your signature fur jacket today." He turned and looked me up and down. The Finn I had just glimpsed had disappeared, replaced by a steely mask, but there was a hunger in his eyes as he surveyed my body.

"Glad you are so interested in my fashion choices. I will wear it just for you next time." I batted my eyelashes at him in mock flirtation.

He ran a hand through his dark curls, and heat warmed the space below my navel. *Shit*. His salty scent, that deep, silken voice—each word he spoke ignited a fire inside me. And those damned dark eyes, flickering with things I couldn't decipher. It was as if my traitorous body didn't care that he was moody or engaged. I pressed my thighs together and turned to the gray ocean, searching for a distraction. These feelings were so confusing. These feelings were so *wrong*.

The weather blurred the distant horizon, and I hoped Granddad had returned safely from his fishing trip. With my newfound understanding of the Drowned, my worries had somewhat abated—he would probably relish sharing rum with gnarly sailors in Davy Jones's Tavern.

A buoy tinkled in the fog, and a gull left tracks across the granite sand. Finn led us toward Merrow Rocks, the outcrop that made up the bay's left fist—the same one the two kids had disappeared from, the ones who now lived under the sea with the Drowned.

Mist veiled the bay. I glanced back, spotting the rocks we had climbed near my jetty, but the harbor and its moored boats had faded into the haze.

"The Cailleach is holding us in her old wintery fingers today." Finn turned to me, the fog curling about his leather boots.

My grandmother had told me stories of the Callieach, a divine hag associated with storms and winter.

Unfazed by the growing mist, Finn hopped onto the first rock and offered me his hand, my feet sliding as he helped me up. We navigated the haze, guided by the sound of waves crashing against the distant edge. Despite myself, I was glad to have his company in this weather.

As we neared the point where the rocky arm met the open sea, the stones ahead seemed to shift and move. *Seals.* They hauled themselves over the edge and into the ocean as we approached. If they were connected to the world I'd discovered, perhaps I could communicate with them for answers. Only three of the animals lingered.

"Hello..." I looked intently through the fog into the largest creature's big black eyes.

The seals were silent. They continued to hasten into the water, disappearing one after the other.

Finn erupted in laughter at my side. "Were you just trying to talk to them?"

I glared at him.

He grasped my cold free hand and spun me around to face him, studying me curiously. His hair was damp with mist and sea spray. I tried to pull myself from his gaze, but he didn't let go. He took a step, and then another, until we were close enough for his warm breath to caress my cheek.

"It's killing me that I can't figure you out." His fingers softly tangled in the hair framing my face before gliding down to rest on my shoulders. His eyes narrowed and flitted back and forth, searching mine. I let them. Perhaps he would read my mind and discover all my secrets. Then I wouldn't have to carry them alone. My father. The underwater world. *My father.* I couldn't bring myself to talk with Finn about what I had discovered—at least not yet. Not until I knew more.

I locked on to his obsidian gaze as his hands glided from my shoulders to my waist. With one tug, he could pull me against him. Then I would feel *all* of him.

Drops of water decorated his cheeks, dark brows, and lips, and I couldn't stop staring at them. My body began heating up, filling with things I didn't usually feel.

What is he doing?

I willed myself to push him away. Placing my hand against his torso, I felt the definition of his stomach beneath his sweater.

"You know, I've never met anyone like you." Finn's voice had dropped, now rough and gravelly. He lifted his hand from my hip, tracing his lower lip with his thumb as he studied me.

Heat expanded within me, throbbing below my navel. It was so nice not to be nauseated by his *feelings*. Only my hand on his chest kept our bodies apart. My fingers were curling at the cloth of his sweater. One tug—that's all it would take to pull him into me.

No, no, no. This was not okay. I unfurled my fingers and shook myself free of him. Exhaling, I moved toward the rock's edge and let the sea spray pepper my face.

This was too far. I had let myself get too close. The urge to be near him was consuming every rational thought. He needed to stop doing this confusing stuff.

My eyes scanned the area where the seals had been for skins or some sign. Perhaps they hadn't responded because I was with Finn. Maybe I should read the rest of the book and return here tomorrow evening.

"What do you know about Selkies?" I asked, seating myself on a damp rock.

"So *that's* why you tried to talk to the seals. Selkies are seal shape-shifters." Finn crouched beside me, a flicker of a smile haunting his lips.

"So, you've heard of them then?" My eyes widened with excitement.

"Selkies are an old myth. Now I'm curious. What makes you want to learn about them?"

I swallowed as a warning flared, my instincts urging me to keep this from Finn.

"I-I just came across a book about them." I shrugged.

"Which book?" His eyes pinned me in place.

Mist coiled around us as Finn inclined his head, slow, assessing, like a predator studying its prey.

"It doesn't matter. It was a stupid question." I rose to my feet and turned away.

"If you believe in them, then why not Mer?" Finn stood also, folding his arms across his chest.

"Maybe I believe in both, and more." I pouted, my cheeks warming.

"If you believe in Mer, you should be afraid, because local legends say that this is a spot from which many innocents have been lured to their death by their song." He gestured at the mist-encircled rock pools around us.

He was teasing me again, but he had no idea how much truth might be in those tales. Goosebumps spread across my skin, and I pulled the hood up on my coat.

The fog had thickened, hemming us in like a hungry crowd. Mer aside, it was easy to imagine how many had unknowingly wandered to their deaths in haze like this.

Mist curled about our feet, its tendrils crawling across the water, pooling in the crevices of the rocks, reminding me of the creeping darkness that enveloped my dreams.

"Let's go back," I grumbled. The seals had provided no answers, and I couldn't stay here any longer alone with Finn, battling this electric current between us, drawing me into him . . . making me want to . . .

No! I shook my head.

A chill enveloped me as I splashed back through the rock pools. It wasn't just from the wetness of the surrounding mist, but from something more intangible, a sensation I couldn't entirely attribute to the environment. A sensation that gave me the creeps.

I looked for Finn, but I couldn't see him.

"Finn?" I peered into the mist. *That's strange.* I was sure he had been right behind me a moment ago.

"*Finn!*" I called his name louder. Had he been beside, behind, or in front of me? I wasn't sure now.

Slinging my satchel across my back to shield my precious books, I navigated the slick rocks, crawling when the terrain demanded it. My hands were red and numb from the cold. Each splash of ocean spray sent a flicker of fear through me—I was close to where the shore met the sea. I turned in circles, hoping to see the top of the old stone lighthouse, but the fog was too thick—*too close.* It was reaching for me, hemming me in.

"Finn!" I called his name again. No answer.

How far had we walked? Surely no more than a couple of feet onto the rocks.

Then I saw the eyes. They appeared in the mist like two crimson coals in an ashy fireplace. My pulse thudded so loudly that it drowned out the ocean's sighs. I shook my head, but they didn't disappear. They blinked.

I let out a strangled cry, splashing into waist-deep freezing water that had pooled between the rocks. I clambered out, and the eyes were still there. A body slowly materialized around them—the traces of a sharp jawline and a man's muscular torso. I knew those red eyes. They were the ones from my dreams.

Join me, amica mea.

The words echoed as a whisper in my mind, and the mouth that emerged from the mist curled into a smile.

I didn't stick around to see the rest of the red-eyed man come into being. I sprinted in what I believed to be the direction of the mainland. I stumbled and fell—another rock pool. I was soaked from head to toe, but I pulled myself up, gasping for breath as a stitch shot through me.

Suddenly, the red eyes were in front of me again, like two rubies rimmed with long dark lashes. *Shit.* I pivoted. My wet hair clung to my face, obscuring my vision. Icy water seared my waist—I'd tumbled back into the cold pool. I was going around in circles.

I clambered out, reaching for the navigational instincts I'd developed beneath the waves. *Nothing.* Perhaps they didn't work on land. I was almost ready to give up and offer myself to the strange man, but then the music began. The black pupils within the red eyes flicked back and forth as if they had caught the song before vanishing into a swirl of mist.

The tune caressed me softly, then swelled until it surrounded me. I wasn't just listening to it; it was inside me. Was it the Drowned calling me back? Perhaps the seals had opened a portal for me to return.

Oh wow. I am thinking like a crazy person.

The music grew louder, but it wasn't the music of the Drowned. The call of the dead had been haunting and melancholic. This was eerily beautiful, but it wasn't mournful. The notes weaved around me, cold and ancient, like swell moving through an underwater cavern. As the tune caressed my being, it became bright and tantalizing, like starlight glittering on the waves. I had never heard such beautiful music. *Mer!*

I clamped my hands over my ears and hunched over, stumbling in the direction I imagined the safety of the shore was.

I slid and stumbled over the wet rocks as the music filled me with longing—I *had* to walk in the direction it was taking me. I knew this was some malicious Mer leading me toward my death, but I couldn't stop myself. I closed my eyes and let the beautiful melody draw me forward. I no longer stumbled but walked sure-footedly along with the tune.

Soon, the jagged rocks gave way to grass and concrete. The old lighthouse stood before me, and when I turned, I could make out the harbor and the bobbing shapes of boats beyond.

The fog was thinning, and the song began to fade. I tried to hold on to the melody, but it slipped away. Soon, all that was left was the sound of the waves breaking on the rocks behind me. So far behind me. I hadn't been led to death, but to safety.

But where was Finn?

I was soaked from rock pools, sea spray, and dew. My long hair clung to my face like moist red vines, and my eyes stung from the salt. I turned on the spot, but I couldn't see him. Had he been lured out to sea by the song or climbed too close to the edge and fallen?

"Finn!" I cried. "*Finnnnn!*" But my screams were smothered as the gathering wind put its fingers in my mouth.

Help. I'd have to go for help.

I started jogging back to the boardwalk; I'd made it all but a few meters when I saw him sitting on a park bench, watching me.

"You're okay!" I flung my arms around him without thinking. I let go when I realized he was dry.

"I think it should be me rejoicing, by the looks of you." He tilted his head as I threw myself onto the bench beside him.

"Where did you go?" I tried to smooth my wet hair, but the wind made it wild. I looked like a drowned rat, and irritation flared within me when I saw how put together he was.

"I was just in front of you." He took my cold hands in his and attempted to rub them warm.

"That's strange. I thought I was in front of you. I called out to you. Didn't you hear?" I pulled my hands away.

"No, I guess the wind drowned it out." He shrugged.

"Or something else."

He looked at me, puzzled.

"You said yourself those rocks were haunted." I raised my brows at him and whispered, "*Mer*," as if worried they might hear me.

Finn burst into laughter, his eyes sparkling. "Those are the tales of a superstitious town."

"B-but didn't you hear the song? I think they saved me." I squinted at the gray ocean, half expecting to see one waving.

"Saved you from what?" He was still laughing.

"The fog . . . and . . . It doesn't matter." I stopped before saying, *Red eyes that have haunted my dreams my entire life.*

"Are you sure it wasn't the seals?" He let out a few last chuckles. "Come on, let's get you warm." Taking off his dry jacket, he threw it over my quivering shoulders. "Do you want to come up to mine?" He motioned toward his sleek designer home perched on the opposite arm of the bay.

"I don't think it would be appropriate." I shoved his coat back, my jaw tightening.

A look flickered in his eyes. *Shock.*

16.

MORGANA

Thunder cracked and storm clouds churned the sky as Finn tucked his jacket back under his arm.

Jeez, the Cailleach was having some fun today! As if the old hag had heard me, the sky split open above our bench. A clap of thunder rumbled, and rain came pouring down.

"Over here!" Finn rose, and motioned toward the lighthouse.

I glanced back toward the path leading to the boardwalk and my grandfather's house, but rain blurred the way as lightning split the sky, so I let Finn guide me, clutching my books. I had to keep them dry.

Rain streamed down our faces as he threw his shoulder into the dark wood door, and I pulled my satchel under my jacket.

"There's a trick to it," he grumbled when it refused to budge.

The door finally creaked in admittance when Finn heaved his shoulder against it for the third time, and we stepped inside.

My teeth chattered, and I wrapped my arms around myself as I took in the space. There wasn't much to see: a dusty stone floor that met thick brick walls. The room was damp and dim, and there wasn't any furniture save for an old thatch broom that rested in one of the corners.

"Look up." Finn grinned. His dark hair was plastered to his forehead, but he didn't seem to be trembling with cold like I was.

I cast my eyes to the ceiling, and my breath caught in my throat. A spiral staircase wound up from the edge of the building to the top of the tower, where a sliver of light leaked through.

"Come on." Finn beckoned me to follow him.

As we ascended the steps, the only sound was our damp shoes squeaking against the stone, mingling with rain and the tossing waves outside. At the top was a glass tower, and light flooded in from the windows that spanned the circumference of the building. It wasn't a huge lighthouse—perhaps 90 feet—but it looked taller from the outside because it was perched on elevated rocks.

Outside, waves crashed against the stones, leaving saltwater embellishments on the tower's windows. Lightning streaked across the sky in erratic, jagged bolts before striking the ocean.

"Morgana." Finn's voice was gentle. He had started a small fire from some old wood littering the dusty stone floor. Strange. I hadn't even noticed him move or heard him flick a lighter.

I sat across from him on the cold floor, the flames flickering between us. Their warmth was a welcome comfort.

"It's beautiful, isn't it." Finn rested his elbows on his knees, tipping his head back as he took in the space.

I nodded.

"I come here sometimes to watch the sunrise after gathering rubbish."

"Why do you do it? The rubbish pickups."

He rubbed his neck and then met my stare. "Have you ever seen a fish stuck in six-pack rings? Or a dolphin caught in a fishing net?"

I shook my head.

"If you had," he breathed, "then you wouldn't have to ask." His jaw was hard as he turned back to the windows.

"I get it." I shrugged. "It's just surprising because you seem so . . . unfeeling."

"I find it easier to care for animals than people." His face remained drawn as lightning skittered across the sky.

We were quiet for a moment, captivated by the storm's rage.

"These storms are becoming more frequent." Finn's brow creased.

"This one reminds me of my life right now." I laughed as another flash illuminated our faces. My last few days had been . . . Well, there was no describing my last few days.

"Out of a storm's chaos, something new can grow." Finn leaned back on one arm, resting the other on his cocked knees. "Kind of like life, I guess." He looked at me, and the angry sky was reflected in his dark eyes.

"I wonder if people are destined for certain lives or if they create their paths." I thought about the path I had been catapulted onto. With the tempest outside, what else could we do but talk? As the words escaped my lips, I realized I needed to speak with someone.

"Maybe destiny gives us choices, and what we choose defines us," Finn said, brushing his damp hair from his forehead as he watched the rain beat against the glass. "But in *my* life, the choices are few." He sighed. I thought I heard sadness in it, but I couldn't be sure.

"It's strange . . . I can't sense your emotions like I can feel others." I had never told anyone about my "condition" before, but with him here now, the words just came tumbling out.

"You can detect people's feelings?" His eyes were on me, raging with curiosity.

"Yes." I blew out a breath. "But never with you. It's like there's a wall around you."

"Maybe I'm just good at hiding." His mouth twitched at the corners, as if he was about to smile but then thought better of it.

"It's more than that. It's like you're shielded." I surveyed his face. "I'm so used to understanding people, to knowing what they're feeling to the extent that it's suffocating. With you, I . . . I can't feel a thing."

"Does it bother you that much?" The hint of a smile curled into something wicked.

"It's like a breath of fresh air." I exhaled. "But it makes me feel like I don't know you as well as I know some people I've never met."

"Do you *want* to know me, Morgana?" His dark eyes stripped me bare.

"Yes." I squeezed my thighs together to extinguish the throbbing his playful grin had evoked, biting my lip to hold back a smile. I *did* want to know him. We were playing a dangerous game, but I couldn't pull myself from it.

Finn looked away, and the cockiness he had previously exhibited faltered. "Maybe some things are better left unknown."

"Why would you say that?" My eyes bored into the side of his angular cheek, searching for any emotion. *Nothing.*

He was silent momentarily, still looking away from me at the turbulent sky.

"Because if you could sense my feelings . . ." He brought his dark eyes back to mine. "I'm not sure you'd like what you'd find."

"Why don't you let me be the judge of that? What are you protecting yourself from, anyway?"

"Emotions are for the weak." His eyebrows drew apart, and his mouth tightened

The rain had stopped, and patches of blue sky appeared between the racing clouds. Still, we continued to sit in silence as the waves sighed outside.

Finally, Finn rubbed a hand down his face. "Do you want to know what you would feel if you could sense my emotions?"

"Yes," I whispered, taking him in.

"Loneliness." He released a deep breath, and it was like a layer of the protective shield he had around him melted off. I could see it clearly on his face. It hung around his eyes like shadows—he was the loneliest person I'd ever seen. Something in my heart fluttered as I looked at him. It was a feeling I knew only too well. I was sure it had hung around me the same way my entire life.

"Living my whole life consumed by the emotions of others, I found safety in loneliness, but being with you, without sensing your feelings, gives me hope . . . and hope is a dangerous thing." I chewed on my lip.

"It is." He sighed.

"Maybe that's why we're drawn to each other. Two broken pieces trying to fit together," I mused, spilling more of my treacherous thoughts out loud.

"You don't feel broken to me." He surveyed me with dark eyes. "You feel . . . *real*."

"When I looked at your tattoo that day in the store—" The words were halfway out of my mouth when I regretted them.

"Say it—what you're thinking." The loneliness evaporated from his expression, replaced by ice.

"I . . . I noticed scars. What happened?" I let the words cascade from my lips. There was no going back now.

Finn was silent beside me, his throat working. A muscle ticked in his cheek, and his lips were pursed as he turned to face me.

"I like hanging out with you. I do. And I want to continue to hang out with you more than I think you realize . . ." His voice was quiet as his inky eyes took in my face. "But don't ever bring up my scars again."

I swallowed, a little too loudly. "I've got to go." I had lost myself in whatever *this* was today.

"I'm sorry." His voice had softened, but it didn't matter.

I shot to my feet, snatching up my satchel, the books inside jostling as I turned to leave.

"Morgana . . ."

I paused on the stairs as he said my name but didn't turn back.

※

I needed to think without . . . *distractions*. I had said too much today. I let myself feel too much. The evening was closing in as I stomped back up the darkening hill. What was it about this man?

I thought back to the look in Finn's eyes when my fingers were curled in his sweatshirt; the feral glint had made me want to throw caution to the wind and kiss those lips. I needed to end whatever held me captive under his spell. His dark eyes and salty scent scrambled my thoughts.

After my past experiences, I had all but sworn off men, but something about him was tearing the cage around my heart open. We seemed drawn to one another, as if some inexplicable force was pulling us into a dangerous dance with destiny. My body responded to him as if it had its own will, and my heart seemed to beat solely for him.

No!

I pushed the thoughts aside. Finn was engaged, and I needed to focus on uncovering everything I could about Selkies—what I'd learned so far wasn't enough.

I knew that they were seal shapeshifters, but I didn't know what this had to do with me. I ran my fingers over my arms, where the fur had been. It had been sleek like a seal's; could that be some key?

I'd heard the Mer singing. I was sure of it. As Aranare had said, these folk tales always stem from some truth, and today, they had sung for me. The memory of their song produced a ripple of sensation that swept over my arms, coaxing goosebumps from my skin. I could not remember the tune, but I knew it had been beautiful and cold, summoned from the deepest ocean caverns. Finn hadn't heard it, though.

The small print on my left shoulder was my one confirmation that I wasn't completely mad. The Symbol of the Ocean was still burned in black on my skin. Perhaps that was why I heard the Mer's song and Finn did not.

Granddad had gone to bed by the time I arrived home, but he'd left me a bowl of fresh fish and microwaved vegetables on the kitchen table. I wolfed it down like a creature of the deep. I hadn't realized how hungry I was. Grabbing a muesli bar and hot tea, I showered and holed up in bed to read more.

Legend of the Selkie

Selkies are literal skin changers. The shedding of their skin makes them human, and the re-dressing turns them back into seals. However, if the Selkie's skin is lost or stolen, it cannot transform back into a seal. The transformed Selkies are beautiful, thus causing many humans to fall for their spells and attempt to obtain their skins. Legend says that if a human steals a Selkie's skin, the Selkie will be forced to marry them.

Sometimes, the Selkies have children with their human partners. Selkie and human children are not always born Selkies. However, some possess strange powers. Sometimes, these abilities can skip a generation and return stronger or mutate in distant relatives. In Selkie folklore, Selkie women, known for their peaceful nature, are more likely to be trapped in marriage. The males are renowned for using their good looks to lure women to sea.

Typical. I rolled my eyes.

Like seals, Selkies store oxygen in their blood and muscles. Unlike seals, which need to surface every one to two hours, Selkies can stay under for much longer, sometimes days, without coming up for air.

If Selkies and Mer exist, beware all the good-looking people in this town. I laughed as my mind slipped to Finn—and then Aranare. He was beautiful too.

I still couldn't grasp how my link to the Selkies had plunged me into the depths of the ocean and then pulled me back out again. Maybe I was descended from one, but exhaustion weighed heavy on my eyelids. I shut the book and tucked it safely beneath my bed.

17.

MORGANA

I was running late, but what did it matter? I might be magical—a *Selkie*. That made everyday life seem trivial, especially Celtic Keepsakes and tourist souvenirs.

But I planned on working today—if only to access Google and meet Aranare for lunch—which meant adhering to nine-to-five hours.

Finn and Skye were hanging outside the store when I got there. Skye was wiping tears from beneath her brown eyes. Her sleek raven hair framed her face, and her bright red pumps shone in the morning sun.

"I was just telling Finn about the McMillan boys. They lived on my parents' street." She sniffed.

"What happened?" My brow furrowed as I glanced between them.

"Their boat turned over in yesterday's storm, and their bodies haven't been found. This town is no stranger to drownings, but this coming just after we lost those wee kids." Skye shook her head, wiping mascara-filled droplets from her cheeks with a dainty hand.

A chill caressed my arms. Were these McMillan boys now deep beneath the Atlantic on SS *Jones's Lady*?

I patted Skye on the back, her sadness washing over me, but she sniffed back her tears, mouth curving into a perfectly whitened smile as she looked between me and Finn.

He was watching me, onyx eyes glittering. He was wearing a black hand-cut T-shirt, and I could see his tattoos—see the scars. How he wasn't freezing, I didn't know. After his mood swings yesterday, I tried not to look at him—*at them*.

"I have to get to work," I said, flipping my hair over my shoulder, but I stopped at the door and glanced back at Finn. "Don't you have anything better to do than follow me around this town?"

"Morgana." His voice cracked.

My key stuck in the lock. Barry really needed to get this door fixed. I jiggled it furiously until I felt Finn's cold hand atop mine. I froze as his salty scent washed over me. Turning my head, I let my eyes find his. He was so close. His breath warmed my face, and his body . . . *his body* was pressed against my back. His heart was hammering just as fast as mine, and my stomach fluttered.

"I'm so sorry about yesterday," he whispered against my cheek. His lips brushed my skin, and the hairs on my neck prickled.

"I—" The words I wanted to say wouldn't come out. I didn't even know what those words were. I didn't know how to deal with these feelings—the ones making me want to punch Finn and run my fingers through his dark hair simultaneously. If I could just open this damn store!

"Trouble in paradise?" Skye's coo reminded me of her presence, and her glee washed over me. Finn removed his hand from mine and stepped back. I jiggled the key again, and the lock finally gave way.

"Have lunch with me?" Finn's silken voice asked the question of my back.

"I've already made plans." I didn't turn around.

"With who?" His tone sharpened, but I ignored him. I let out a long exhale before marching inside.

☙❧

The center was quiet, but after glancing at the clear sky, I decided to do my research now, just in case the impossible happened and customers showed up.

The computer at the counter had internet access, so I opened Google Images and typed "Selkie." Hundreds of artists' paintings of perfectly formed naked women shedding their skin appeared. They seemed to have curves in all the right places. I looked down at my own body; I had small breasts and could have been described as lanky. I didn't look anything like these women. They all had dark hair, and mine was red.

I shrugged and typed "seals." Images of the animals filled the screen—some basking on rocks, others peeking up from the waves. Their large, black eyes had a human quality, reminding me of Finn's. I studied photos of seals sleeping on land and in water. If I was part Selkie, maybe that's why I slept when the Drowned didn't.

I continued scrolling. Most pictures were of fluffy white seal pups, which were cute but didn't offer me any more clues. Then, an image caught my eye. Something about this seal's mottled gray coloring seemed strangely familiar.

I froze, scared to believe I might have found an answer.

☙❧

"You're *actually* meeting someone!" Skye exclaimed, noticing I was grabbing my keys from under the counter.

I shrugged as I headed for the door.

"I thought you made that up to annoy Finn. He totally likes you."

"He's *engaged*, remember?" I shook my head, hanging up the "BACK SOON" sign on the glass.

She trotted behind me. "Have you seen her?" She craned her neck around the center as if she expected to see Finn and his fiancée somewhere, sharing a hot drink.

I shook my head.

"I still think he likes you." Skye chewed on her cheek, following me up the lane of shops. I guess she was coming to lunch.

When we arrived at the café, it was humming with the muted sounds of the few other diners and the occasional clink of cutlery. I scanned the tables for Aranare, but he hadn't arrived yet.

The air was filled with the aroma of freshly battered fish, chips, and coffee. I let myself take it in. If my theory was correct, this could be my last day on land for a while. Skye and I ordered salads with calamari. The salty, slick squid brought my meals under the sea to mind as it slid down my throat.

Skye had done the inevitable and moved in with Parker, and he had done the predictable and was spending most nights out in Campbeltown without calling.

"You know, Parker's got a great job. What do I have? I work at a tartan store." Skye pushed her salad around her plate and sighed.

I didn't reply. My heart was thundering. Soon, I would learn more about my father. And then later . . .

"I think he'll grow out of it," she continued. "He might do it for the first couple of years, but in the end, I win out over other girls because I have the house and the security."

"I suppose," I tried to agree as I scanned the other diners for any sign of Aranare.

"You came," a voice said from behind me.

Aranare was carrying an open cooler filled with silvery fish. Their smell washed over me, and I clasped the edges of the table to stop myself from grabbing one.

"I wasn't sure if you would show up, but I'm glad you did." He set the cooler beside us, grinning as the muscles in his bronzed arms flexed. Skye was watching him, too.

"Don't tell me *this* is who you're meeting?" She tilted her head to take him in.

So not subtle!

"I'm Aranare." He held out his hand to her. "My uncle owns this café."

"I hear your family owns this whole town." I laughed, but my knuckles were white against the table as I battled against the delicious aroma of fresh fish.

"Aye, pretty much." He shrugged. "Calamari salad. Nice choice." He plucked an uneaten piece from Skye's bowl, and she threw him a red-lipped smile. Aranare's brow furrowed as he surveyed her. "Where are your people from?"

"Here." She simpered, looking up at him from under her lashes.

"Really?" He looked surprised, which I thought was odd. Maybe he was wondering why he'd never met her before.

Skye didn't seem to notice; she was busy adjusting her sleek tresses. "Morgana is meeting cute boys everywhere she goes these days." She tilted her head, toying with a strand of hair.

"Way to make me feel special." Aranare winked at me.

I flushed but found myself looking over my shoulder at the pawnshop. Finn was leaning against the doorway, watching us, a look of cool disdain on his face.

"Morgana and Finn have a *thing*," Skye crooned.

Aranare glanced over and caught Finn's eye, nodding curtly. Finn didn't return it. He simply strode inside.

"Do you know each other?" I searched Aranare's brown eyes.

"Aye, I know him." His words were clipped, and he ran a hand through his chestnut curls.

"He's *always* hanging around Morgana." Skye chirped.

I shot her a warning glare.

Aranare gazed at me. "He's not right for you, Morgana."

"And why's that?" Skye's eyes widened with glee.

"Our families have known each other for years." He paused, as if carefully choosing his next words. "He's a troubled person . . . you won't be able to change him." He sighed.

"Firstly, you only met me yesterday, so you can't say who is or isn't right for me. Secondly, I thought you were going to tell me about my father?" I grumbled, pushing my empty bowl aside.

"Aye." Aranare's eyes softened. "We are going to the library. First, let me drop off these fish." He hoisted the cooler back up.

Skye leaned into my space as soon as he'd retreated. "Where did you find *him*?"

"At the bookstore," I muttered, watching him help the serving lady pack the fish away.

"It almost makes me want to take up reading." She giggled. "I'm coming with you. I've had like one customer today."

We followed Aranare back to the entrance of the outdoor complex and toward the public library. Skye was prattling on about something, but I wasn't listening. The blood was thrumming in my ears again.

"What's in the library?" I asked suddenly. I couldn't take it anymore. Aranare halted, and Skye's burbling trailed off.

"Well, the local news archives." He shrugged. "I *could* tell you what

I remember about your father's death from when I was fourteen, but I thought it would be better to get the paper from that day."

"Oh." My stomach curdled.

Aranare and Skye kept walking, but I remained frozen. The mild midday sun suddenly felt like it was blaring down on the back of my neck. I didn't move. I *couldn't* move.

"Morgana?" Aranare turned to me.

Skye glanced between us.

"Just tell me what happened. I need to know." My voice sounded raspy. Why was my throat so dry?

"He drowned," Aranare said matter-of-factly, as if there was no easier way to divulge it.

Drowned. I swallowed. *Is that why I awoke in the Kingdom of the Drowned? Is my father somewhere on that great ship?*

"I want to see the paper."

I marched past them toward the sliding glass doors leading into the refurbished stone library, whipping my head left and right as the artificial heating hit me. There were rows and rows of books. Where were the archives?

"This way." Aranare nodded at the shelves to our right. There were stacks and stacks of newspapers—a pile for each year. Some were freshly printed, and others bronzed with age. The pages had been piled by date and looped together with pieces of string through punched holes.

I kneeled on the scratchy carpet and rifled frantically through one of the piles on the lower shelf. There was no method to my madness.

Aranare put a warm hand on my shoulder. I shook him off.

1989, 1997, 2001 . . . What year did he even die? I didn't know. My mom hadn't told me *anything*. Hot tears burned my cheeks.

"It would have been in 2005," Aranare said softly, as if he had read my mind.

2005, the year I was born, was the year we left Ruadán's Port. This... this had to be the reason—my father's death.

"I've found the year," Skye said, her voice quiet as she pulled a stack of pages from one of the piles. She laid it gently in front of me with her perfectly manicured hands.

Ruadán's Port News. I ran my trembling hands over the issue on the top of the stack but couldn't bring myself to search further.

Aranare knelt beside me and gently took the heap from me. Skye crouched on my other side and put one of her dainty hands on the small of my back.

I drew in a short sob as Aranare started flipping through the papers. My heart was pounding, and tears blurred my vision as he drew out the issue he sought. He flicked through the pages until he stopped, and my breath caught in my chest as I read the headline: "Local Man Drowns While Intoxicated."

There beneath the headline was his picture. Though the paper was golden with age, I could make out his red hair and green eyes. He had copper stubble on his cheeks and a pleasant face. He was smiling, and the lines bunched at the sides of his eyes made him look kind.

"I can't." I shoved the paper away.

Aranare began reading. "A fisherman from Ruadán's Port has drowned while acutely intoxicated . . ." He paused. I could feel his eyes on me. I nodded for him to continue.

"Rory Balfour, 28, was walking home from The Port House on the evening of October 6, 2005."

The Port House. The pub I'd sat in only yesterday. My father could have sat in that same booth.

"Witnesses reported him leaving the establishment at around 9 p.m. He had been drinking heavily, celebrating the purchase of an expensive engagement ring. His body has not been found, but the ring was discovered on the shore near Merrow Rocks."

He was going to propose to her. The ugly antique ring my mother wore around her neck, the one she was always touching—tarnished silver with a deep-blue stone. My chest ached. It was no wonder she didn't want to come back to this place, where she would search every face for Rory's. It was no wonder she had become so hardened, so untrusting.

"But why didn't she just tell me?" I asked aloud.

"Perhaps it was too hard," Skye said gently, her hand still on the small of my back.

"There's something else . . ." Aranare's throat bobbed as he surveyed me.

"What?" My voice was sharp as my eyes flicked to his.

"I was helping my uncle bring in a catch the night he died." Aranare paused. "At what must have been a similar time to your dad's departure from the pub, we heard music, beautiful music, and there was a strange light. It illuminated the ocean and sky, and then it was gone. Something about that night has stayed with me all these years."

Beautiful music. My heart thundered in my ears. *Mer*. Could the Mer have had something to do with my father's death?

18.

Finn

I slammed my fist into the dusty counter.

Why was I so agitated?

The veins in my arms were pronounced as I curled my fingers. It was day three, and I always got unsettled on day three. I needed to return to the water. I could feel it singing to me as it lapped against the distant cliffs—a siren call. I blew out a long breath.

Why should I care if she had lunch with Aranare?

Still, even as I dispelled the thought, something coiled, as if a beast slumbering deep inside me had been prodded, and I found myself pacing between the shelves of odds and ends cluttering this junkyard.

I peered through the dusty window, but they had left the café.

What was this—this gnawing, ugly thing slithering through my chest?

I raked a hand through my hair, swallowing the heat that crept up my throat. It was not anger, not possessiveness. No, this was something else, something dangerous.

My fists curled again as I remembered how she had leaned forward, listening to him, her green eyes reflecting the sunlight. My fingers twitched with a sudden, reckless urge to find them and drag her away, to remind her where she truly belonged.

But where was that?

With me?

I let out a long, slow breath as my jaw tightened. No. I couldn't think like this. I had spent a lifetime fortifying my walls, keeping my heart out of reach of foolish things like longing. But then she came, crashing into my world like a rogue wave, tearing through every carefully built defense.

And now I was left drowning.

I was drowning in the way she tilted her head, the curve of her lips as she spoke, and the way she had goddamn looked at me as we sat in that lighthouse and she let down her walls.

Maybe that's why we're drawn to each other—two broken pieces trying to fit together. Her words caressed my mind, reminding me that hope is the most beautiful and simultaneously painful word in the English language.

I should turn away.

I should let this be.

She wasn't broken, but I was, and I was afraid if she let me too close, I'd hurt her. After all, I'd already tried.

I didn't deserve her.

What would I have done if my gifts had worked at my house or on those treacherous misty rocks I led her onto? I would have found out everything my father wanted and never let myself get this close.

My pulse hammered like the ocean against the jagged cliffs adorning this wild coastline. I exhaled and stretched. This was probably just the usual day-three sickness.

There was a presence behind me, and I whipped around.

Inegar.

He was looking at me from under those bushy brows in a way that tested my patience. His eyes traveled from my furrowed brow to the veins now protruding from my forearms as I clenched and unclenched my fists.

"Your father would tell you you're a fool for showing such weakness, and your mother the same if she were still around." He had the nerve to look sympathetic, as if he were saying this because he cared and not because he was meddlesome.

My father was the reason I'd learned to hide my feelings. I suspected this was why my emotional shields worked on the girl when my other mind magic didn't. My song had reached her too—she must love music. Books and melodies. I was gathering pieces of her, tucking them away like rare treasures, hoarding every detail as if they were jewels meant only for me.

"It's day three," I ground out, focusing on breathing and controlling the untamable beast that had awoken inside me, making me want to smash the pawnshop to pieces, the same way she'd broken the walls inside me down.

"Yes, perhaps a visit home to your *fiancé* would help."

At the way Inegar emphasized that word, I was overcome with the urge to kick something. I needed a drink or to hurt someone. I needed to do what I usually did to feel nothing.

He didn't reply, simply began rifling through some of the worthless crap stacked on the dusty shelves behind the counter.

My breathing began to steady, and the veins in my arms retreated.

"Why do you and my father insist on keeping this junkyard anyway?" I cast my eyes over the shelves surrounding us, filled with piles of garbage from a consumer society, now covered in dust.

Inegar flicked a speck of dirt from an old compass, his eyes shifting with something unreadable. "Junk, you call it?" He sighed. "Perhaps. But something is waiting to be found among the rusted trinkets and forgotten relics. Something that was lost long before you or I took our first breath."

Oh, for fuck's sake. It was another one of my father's quests, no doubt. At least he hadn't seen fit to involve me in this charade.

Inegar met my gaze. "Just don't forget your duty, boy. You were born privileged, and with that comes responsibilities."

A muscle ticked in my jaw; this old man was getting on my last nerve today.

I could curse day three and lay the blame at Inegar's feet, but deep down, I knew the truth. This pain, this unchecked fury clawing at my insides—it was all because of *her*.

19.

MORGANA

The grocery store was devoid of customers. I grabbed a basket and strolled the neon aisles, wondering what Granddad would need while I was away: milk, bread, vegetables . . .

My father, a man I had known nothing about my entire life, suddenly had a face and a story—a story in which he loved my mother, and perhaps me, too. Was he somewhere in the Kingdom of the Drowned? Maybe I had passed him already without realizing it. These thoughts only deepened my resolve.

"Morgana—"

I froze, my fingers resting on a can of spaghetti. I knew that deep voice and the turmoil it created inside me. *Finn.*

"Following me again?" I muttered, shaking off the feelings and tossing the can into my basket.

He didn't reply. His chest was heaving beneath his black coat, and his hair was astray. He rubbed a hand over his forehead and then released it. It looked as if he was going to say something, but then he turned away from me, his lace-up army-style boots squeaking on the vinyl shop floor.

"Finn," I put my mood aside and spoke his name gently.

"Why were you having lunch with *him*?" He turned back to me, his face blanched. I couldn't sense his feelings, but the disturbance in his mind was evident in his drawn brows.

"Who I have lunch with is none of your business." A surge of anger flared through me.

I brushed past him down the household aisle, tossing laundry detergent into my basket. Finn followed me. Did I need anything else? Oh, right, toilet paper. My cheeks flushed. Granddad could get that.

Finn blocked my path as I headed for the counter, leaning one arm on a wooden crate stacked with vegetables and brushing his dark hair from his face. His chest was still heaving, and the neon lights made him look paler than usual.

"I am not good at this." He ground the words out as if it were my fault he had to come here and say them.

I was frozen between his taut body and the shop counter. A muscle in the side of his jaw worked as he rubbed his forehead again.

I didn't know what to make of this, but I smiled encouragingly, because he looked so . . . broken.

"Amor perdot nos." Finn muttered the words almost to himself.

"What?" I looked at him in utter confusion.

"Just something my mother used to say." He ran another hand through his hair.

"I . . ." he started, then spun on his heel to turn away from me as if he'd thought better of it. When he turned back, his face was a cold mask. "Don't worry about it. Sorry for taking up your time." His expression was wholly unmoved by any feeling as he strode toward the store's glass doors.

Was this all because I'd had lunch with Aranare? No, it couldn't be.

As I stepped out into the cool autumn air, clutching my groceries in a paper bag, part of me wondered if I should go after him, but I didn't have time. I had a sunset to meet.

※

I took the stairs two at a time. Barging into my bedroom, I threw on my grandmother's long fur coat. I'd been wearing it the day I fell deep into the sea, and it was the only thing that returned with me.

Heading downstairs, I stopped at the entrance to the living area. "I am staying at Finn's for a couple of nights," I yelled, continuing to the door so I didn't have to face Granddad, who was reading the paper by the fire. He grumbled, but I was shutting the door behind me before he could protest.

My lie would only buy me a few days. What then? Would he call Officer Wilson or my mother?

I couldn't think about the consequences now.

I had a few questions for Granddad, but they could wait until another day. I had to test my theory, and time was running out.

The bay was deserted, and the sky darkened as angry clouds moved in to oppress it—another storm. I let the sounds and smells wash over me, searching for the sensations I'd experienced the last time. Nothing.

As the last light faded, I discarded my shoes at the bottom of the rocks and ran barefoot across the sand. The black clouds obscured the setting sun. Was I too late?

My entire body was alert, searching for the roaring wind, the music of the Drowned, and *oblivion*. But still, I felt nothing.

The surf crashed against the hem of my coat, but everything remained the same.

Selkies can only transform at dawn or dusk; in these in-between times, they are at their most powerful.

Perhaps I was mistaken, and this coat was not the key to the underwater realm. *No.* I shook these thoughts away. I *had* to be correct.

The water was biting cold, but I didn't care; the pain matched my disappointment.

Perhaps the gateway was only open during Samhain, and it will be a year before I can return.

I swallowed.

I didn't want to give up. The wet fur flapped listlessly in the water at my sides as I recited the passage from the book that I suspected confirmed my theory: "Selkies and human children are not always born Selkies. Sometimes, these powers can skip a generation, returning stronger or mutating in distant relatives."

I stiffened. *The wind.* It was once again yanking at my hair like it had hands. A roaring filled my ears, and my control slipped away as the tide crashed over me.

Come ye drunken sailors to the bottom of the sea.

This time, I did not fear. My father was singing for me.

Then everything faded into nothing.

20.

Finn

Two Mer guards flanked the castle's entrance. Their battle-scarred tails flicked idly as they stood watch, eyes scanning the waters for any sign of intrusion.

"Welcome home, Prince Aigéan." Alga made a sweeping bow, his seaweed crest rippling in the swell, but his spear remained raised.

The castle's entrance yawned like the mouth of a leviathan, its towering archway crafted from granite sand.

I gave Alga a tight-lipped smile as guilt twisted inside me like a poisoned blade. I hadn't stopped the storms—more of our people were turning up dead, and *his* power was only growing.

Alga stepped away from the glowing doorway, his stern silhouette fading into the shadows. My gaze swept over the castle's towering spires—one day, all of this would be mine. It should have felt like home, yet somehow, it felt like a gilded cage.

"Your Highness." Alga's silver breastplate clinked as he turned toward me. "The king has requested your presence in the war room."

A wrinkle deepened between my brows. *Of course, he has.*

He probably wanted to berate me for my lack of progress with the storms, or perhaps he wanted to interrogate me about the girl.

Morgana.

A tightness coiled around my chest as I allowed her name into my mind.

What had I planned to say when I confronted her in the grocery store? I wasn't even sure. Seeing her with Aranare had awakened something in me, a fire like none I'd ever felt—a *danger*.

I had tried to push these feelings away, but she lingered in me like salt in the sea, undeniable and inescapable.

I couldn't tell her anything, because it would mean admitting *everything*.

"There's been another storm . . . ten drowned." My father waved a hand dismissively as he glided in, his magnificent golden tail catching the light.

Pisceon and I had been waiting in the war room for over an hour—typical of my father. I wasn't sure if he did it deliberately. He didn't need to flex. He was already the most powerful merman in the Seven Kingdoms.

"I am aware." I ran a hand through my hair as he regarded me with cold disappointment.

Behind him, two guards sealed the grand wooden doors shut. My father snapped his head toward them, eyes narrowing. "I don't trust Alga."

"He's our most loyal guard. I would charge him with my life," I breathed.

My father stroked his chin, his slitted eyes distant, until his expression slackened as if the conversation had already slipped from his mind.

In these moments, I wished I never had to sit in this frigid stone room, waiting on this cold man again. I wished I could simply exist as

Finn—the man who took the pretty girl from the souvenir shop on dates and didn't bear the weight of a kingdom on his shoulders. But Finn was just a construct, like all the others.

"I'll trade places with you if you like, cousin. You know how I love human delicacies—coffee, among other things . . ." Pisceon smirked at me from across the limestone table, the room's centerpiece. Colors from the stained-glass window behind him gently caressed his chiseled cheeks.

"The future of my kingdom lies in the hands of amateurs." My father moved to the head of the table and pressed his palms into it, glancing between us before a manic laugh tore from his throat.

My face fell into a scowl—it was not like he did any of his own dirty work—but as his eyes fell upon me, his glare cut right to my gut and twisted in the way that only he could.

He waited until he knew I felt it to speak again. "And the human girl . . ."

"Who's he torturing this time?" Pisceon rolled his muscular shoulders in a bored manner. He could brush off my father's erratic behavior in a way I never could.

"Torturing?" My father ran a hand through his long dark hair and had the nerve to raise his eyebrows, which were covered in tattoos—runes, but they were faded now—like it wasn't always torture with him. "I want to know if she's a human or a shifter," he growled, turning his dark eyes on me.

"So far, I have seen nothing to suggest she is a shifter." Lies. Even though it was rare for a Selkie descendant to inherit shifter abilities, I was almost certain there was something more to the girl. Selkies were skilled in mind magic, which could be why she was able to resist my gifts. She had also tried to communicate with the seals. I almost huffed a laugh at the memory but curbed it when I caught my father's narrowed eyes.

Rage roiled in my belly as he glared at me, awaiting an answer, and my fist clenched on the table.

"You want him to torture her?" Pisceon sniggered.

I kept my face neutral, but I loved having my cousin here. When he lost his parents, he became our ward. Before that, when it was just me and father, things were so . . . dark. Believe it or not, when you're the only son and muscle of a mad king who loves torture, it's much easier to have someone to laugh about it with.

"No. What is it with you morons and torture?" My father's voice rumbled through the room, and a skitter of lightning charged the walls. I was worried he might shatter the windows. He'd been in a foul mood these past few months—actually, he'd been in a foul mood since my mother died, so that would be over fifty years now.

"I want you to let me know if you see *anything*." My father's black eyes flashed as he looked at me, the flickerings of a madman. I couldn't help but notice how much they resembled mine.

"Why do you care so much about a weak little human?" I stretched in my chair, my tail curling around its side in what I imagined to be a bored manner.

My father ignored me, lips pressing into a thin line as he raked his webbed fingers through his hair.

"Would you like me to give him a hand, uncle?" Pisceon looked hopefully at my father again, and his tattooed chest rippled.

My father whipped his head at him. "I've heard of the antics you two indulge in on land. This girl is no human plaything for you fools to toy with." His brows narrowed, and his eyes drifted off somewhere else, as they often did, until he was no longer in the room with Pisecon and me.

Not all Mer could walk on land—only those with royal blood—and we had to return to the sea every three days, but Pisceon and I only rose when my father willed it.

Getting information from a human should have been easy. Humans are naturally drawn to us; once they get close enough to look into our eyes, we can hypnotize them. They will tell us anything we need to know and do anything we need them to do.

I wondered if I should tell my father about the presence I'd sensed in the mist on Merrow Rocks. No, he would likely fly into an uncontrollable rage. I glanced at him as he glided back and forth along the length of the stone table, his golden tail shimmering behind him.

Was this it? Had he finally lost his mind? He turned his dark eyes on me, and my stomach tightened. I hated that he could still make me feel this way with just a look after all these years.

"Don't fuck this up, Aigéan." My father's lip curled as he turned from me, his mouth moving in an incoherent whisper as if finishing a thought meant only for himself.

There was irony in his harsh words. It was him the other kingdoms were whispering about. They were questioning whether he could still wield the trident, the one that made him the most powerful merman in the Seven Kingdoms—even if that power was stunted like the rest of ours.

I didn't doubt his ability to wield it, but I wondered about his ability to use it for what was best for our people. I might not care about humans, but I did care about my people. My mother had taught me the importance of that while she was still around.

I sighed and pulled myself from the stone chair, my emerald tail beating against the water as I approached the door.

"Aigéan," Pisceon called after me. "What name are you using this time? I think Bruce would suit you. Don't you think he looks like a Bruce?" He nodded at my father, whose eyes were still flashing.

"I've called myself Finn."

"Ah . . . after the dark race from Finfolkaheem, who regularly lure humans into their oceanic home. You're twisted, cousin. I like it."

I shut the wooden doors on Pisceon's devilish grin, gliding back up the dimly lit sandstone passage. It was time to check on my wife-to-be. What mood would she be in?

Guilt tightened in my chest. I had lied to my father regarding my suspicions about the girl. He might be a tyrant, but some dark recess of me still craved his approval.

But *her*. I swallowed hard as the thought of Morgana sent heat rushing to the sensitive spots on my tail. The way her lips curved in subtle pouts, the fire in her green eyes . . . she was unraveling me.

She would make a madman out of me, and then I'd be just like my father.

21.

Morgana

My ancient mattress groaned beneath me, and the unnatural quiet of the deep pressed in. I smiled as my little room swam into view. I knew how to get out of this world, and now, I knew how to get back in.

I was sure it was my father's drowning that had caused me to wake up here. I didn't think it would be the same when a full-blooded Selkie transformed. The book on mythical creatures did not mention the Kingdom of the Drowned.

Mobile shadows danced over the games room's high walls as the anglerfish chandelier swayed with the ocean's tides. Tables lay smashed around the roulette wheel where fights had broken out. The young boy spinning the wheel looked apprehensive, probably praying that it would favor his most menacing players.

I scanned the room for the face I had seen in the yellowed paper—the face of Rory Balfour, *my father*. But no one resembled him.

Edward was tucked away, reading at a wooden table pressed against one of the stained walls. I observed him from the fragmented doorway—he was undeniably handsome. His hair, neatly combed to one side beneath his maroon cap, framed his full lips and blue eyes. Sensing my gaze, he glanced up and smiled.

"Where have you been?" he demanded as I slid into the seat across from him.

"I went home for a bit," I muttered.

"You can do that?" His eyes filled with a yearning that broke my heart.

"Do you know . . ." My throat tightened. "Do you know a Rory Balfour?" I scanned the room again for the face of my father.

"Hmm, no. It doesn't ring a bell. But I have been here for 111 years, and the Drowned migrate from portal to portal. It is hard to keep track of names." Edward folded over the page, marking a place in his book. He must have used preservation potion to protect it, because it was unscathed by the ocean's decay.

"Oh." The hope building in my chest deflated. "My father drowned. I . . . I thought he might be here somewhere."

"Your father *drowned*!" Edward choked on his rum, eyes darting about the room.

"He had red hair. There are no redheads here aside from us. I already checked." I bit back my disappointment.

I couldn't help but examine the room again. Teachie, the man with the black mustache from Port Royal, was at the roulette wheel. Next to him was the tattooed Rackham, whose beaded braids were tied up in a bun. Rackham drew a small knife from behind his ear to pick at his rotting teeth—a pirate flex, no doubt.

There were men playing poker at a long table to the right of the roulette wheel, and treasures were exchanged. A pirate handed over a glittering necklace, its pearls glowing faintly, to a naval officer in return for a small neon fish that swam lazily in a glass bowl. None of them had the face I'd seen in the newspaper.

"It's bollocks how people suck up to them." I was surprised by the contempt in Edward's voice. His eyes were narrowed on a modern-day boy wearing ripped jeans and sneakers, who looked like he had more biceps than brains.

"So Donahue and Jackie got themselves some muscle." I rolled my eyes as the boy got up from their table to the left of the roulette wheel, ran to the bar, and re-emerged with fresh rum bottles. Jackie bared his gums in a sneer of a thank you, but Donahue ignored the kid completely. His shoulder-length dark hair hid his expression.

"He drowned less than twelve hours ago, and he's already doing their bidding," Edward spat.

"They look *more* drowned," I whispered.

Donahue's sallow cheeks were sunken, and Jackie's teeth, which I could have sworn had just been yellow, looked missing. Bits of his scalp showed where his blonde hair had come away.

"We *are* Drowned!" Edward gestured around the room sarcastically.

"No, I mean more decayed. Can't you see it?"

"Donahue has been here for centuries," Edward hissed. "Although we are immortal, in the way we heal and age, the ocean begins to have its way with us eventually." He picked at a barnacle on his neck.

I was still watching Donahue. Bits of the skin on his cheek were hanging off, but he was letting his dark curls fall over them. He looked up, catching my gaze and grabbing his crotch in a mock gesture.

Edward turned bright red. He was glaring at Donahue, knuckles white from the force with which he was gripping the table.

"So, I think I know what I am now." I gestured to my furry bodysuit in a bid to distract Edward from the man's lewd gesture.

"Don't tell me you're actually a Selkie!" he hissed, glancing over his shoulder as if worried the Drowned girls at the table closest to us might be listening.

"I'm descended from a Selkie, so I only half morph from my human form. Do you know of them?"

"You're not a relative of Siana Selich by any chance?" Edward glanced over his shoulder again.

"I don't think so. My family name is Scott."

"Shhh." Edward motioned for me to keep my voice down, eyes sharp with fear.

"Who is Siana Selich?" I scrunched up my face. There was nothing about her in the book on Selkies.

"Well, she's more of a folktale than an actual person—the wife of Manannán, God of the Drowned." Edward pulled his tatty velvet-backed chair toward the table.

"What?" My mouth popped open.

"Yes, but Morgana, it is rumored that only a descendant of Siana Selich can end the curse." His eyes flitted around the venue.

"The three-thousand-year-old curse on the Drowned and the Mer?" I raised my brows in incredulity.

"*Yes*." His nostrils flared.

I snorted, and rum came out of my nose. "Surely it's not me."

"But that's the thing. There aren't any Selkies left! So whatever you do, don't tell *anyone* what you are," Edward gritted out.

"Y-you're serious, aren't you? If it's a folktale, then why are you so worried?" I looked around the rowdy bar, and no one seemed concerned by anything other than gambling and drinking.

"Because even though the Mer and Drowned have suffered under the curse for thousands of years, many still hang on to the hope of the prophecy that can break it." Edward rubbed the skin on his freckled neck.

"How exactly did this curse come about?" I leaned into his space and let my eyes widen in a way that I hoped flattered his intelligence.

"Well, I am not sure I know the full tale, because I can only rely on translations from the Runes of the Ocean." Edward straightened his shoulders and looked pleased. "But once upon a time, the ocean clans were united. This was over three thousand years ago, in the Days of Gods. Back then, the five gods of the ocean and its creatures lived harmoniously, as did the humans of the time." He raised his eyebrows as if anticipating my disbelief, but I waited eagerly for him to continue. "Legend has it that Manannán—who was, at the time, the God of the Drowned—fell in love with a beautiful and powerful Selkie woman called Siana Selich."

"Wait a minute," I interrupted. "You said there were five Gods?"

"Yes, yes." He furrowed his brow. "There was a god for each clan: Manannán, known by many names. Naútēs Diábolos, or the modern-day Davy Jones, was the God of the Drowned. Siochain, a Selkie and mother to Siana, was the God of Peace and Wisdom. Poseidon, a merman, was the God of the Seas and Skies, while Cetus, a sea monster, ruled over beasts and sea life. Lastly, Agápē, a Siren, was the God of Love."

The five images from the insignia! I nodded and bade him continue.

"Now, where was I? Oh yes, Manannán fell in love with the Selkie, Siana, and she loved him back. For a while, they were the perfect match. He collected dead souls, and she could offer them peace using her magic." Edward sighed. "They say that before Siana, Manannán never offered the Drowned Mourning, but when he fell in love with her, his heart softened, and he allowed us to say goodbye."

I remembered the love I had seen shining in even the most ferocious-looking pirates' eyes as we rose to the surface with the glowing balls.

"But she was wild and free, and he was jealous." Edward's eyes darkened as he gestured around the rowdy bar. It was as if I could feel Manannán's resentment permeating the space. The sensation crept across my arms, leaving a field of tiny goosebumps in its wake.

Edward noticed his tale's effect and continued more enthusiastically, "As Manannán watched a friendship blossom between Siana and Mer Prince Kyano of the House of Ătlanticus, he grew increasingly angry."

"Ătlanticus, like Atlantis?" My eyes widened.

"Yes, yes, we will get to that." Edward waved a hand. "Manannán saw how Kyano looked at Siana, and one day, he confronted the merman. A fight broke out, and they each returned to their kingdoms to raise an army. The Sirens joined the Mer, and the sea beasts joined the Drowned. The armies collided in the Battle of Caeruleus Templum—Blue Temple." He swallowed. "Siana hastened to the battlefield, bellowing for peace. Before she could call upon her magic, she was struck by two arrows, one from the Mer army and one from the Drowned. She died right there on the field. Her blood streamed into the water, but the two armies were so bent on destroying one another that none of them noticed."

I folded my webbed hands in my lap, eyes wide as I listened. The gaming of the Drowned had faded into the background as Edward's tale transported me back in time.

"The rest of the gods were angry as many members of all their houses had been unnecessarily lost. They cursed the Mer and the Drowned. Manannán was stripped of his title as the Drowned God, and seven Protectors were installed in his place." Edward glanced at the Captain, and I followed his gaze.

"He's a Protector?" I hissed. The red-eyed sea snake in the man's eye socket popped its head out and curled around to look at me as if it had heard. Its eyes glowed faintly in the underwater gloom, casting a crimson shadow on the Captain's weathered cheek.

Edward nodded.

"But what happened to Manannán?"

He fell quiet, as if considering this. "Well, he couldn't die, as all our souls feed his spirit." He gestured across the room. "Instead, he was destined to walk in shadows for an eternity, never to return to his godly form."

I could have sworn the anglerfish illuminating the room flickered.

"And then, of course, there is the Garden of Mortimer." Edward shuddered.

"The place where evil Drowned souls are kept?" My question came out in a whisper.

He took a long swig of his rum. "Yes. Legend says the gods created it to help the Protectors control the Drowned. Nothing like concern about a place in the Garden to ensure the most vicious of us obey the Protectors."

I glanced at the Captain again. He was sharing a rum with Evelyn, and his remaining amber eye was fixed on her. "So, can *he* send you to the Garden?"

"Yes. But I have only seen him do it once, when he found a pirate raping a teenage girl." Edward's face hardened at the memory.

My throat worked as I glanced at the menacing pirates at the roulette wheel. Teachie's pile of treasure had shrunk, and he was glaring at the boy spinning the wheel as if he were to blame.

"What does the prophecy say? *How* is this descendant of Siana supposed to end the curse?" I leaned forward on the slimy table, eyeing Edward curiously.

"That's just it. Only the first half of the prophecy is known." His eyes glazed over as he recited: "Evil begets evil. Sin begets sin. All love will be lost, and you'll know no peace. In shadowed depths where silence reigns, a curse was cast, eternal chains. The spirits of Manannán and Siana must return, for only then shall the clans truly learn."

I ran my hands over my arms, but the goosebumps refused to fade.

"The second half of the prophecy detailed how the curse could be broken, but it was lost in the fall of Ătlanticus," Edward whispered, his eyes darting around the faces in the room. "Both the Mer and the Drowned believe whichever clan finds a way to enact the prophecy will reign supreme. Of course, this just fuels the fire."

"Come on. The spirit of Siana Selich. Really?" I raised my brows at him.

"As I said, it's the stuff of myths and legends." Edward rubbed his chin. "But I wouldn't tell this lot you're a Selkie." He jerked his head at the Drowned. "It is whispered that before the curse, the Drowned lived in castles like the Mer. Some still sit around fantasizing about what life could be like if they caught a Selkie related to Siana and ended the curse . . . But they would be looking for a seal, of course."

A fight broke out over the roulette wheel, and Teachie threw a man in a naval uniform across the room. He skidded across the floor, then picked himself up, muttering as he straightened his clothes and returned to the game.

"What about the Mer? You mentioned they were also cursed." I swallowed.

"As arrows from *both* armies caused Siana's fatal blow. The gods stripped the Mer of most of their powers—it is said the magic they have now is but a husk of what it was in the Days of Gods."

What would a "husk" of the Atlantic's power produce?

22.

Morgana

"Kill the mer. Reclaim drowned glory."

The blood was shimmering across the tavern wall, and a group of Drowned stood around it, leering. The letters glowed with the same eerie light as the words Edward and I had discovered in the room with the broken chandelier.

Edward had promised to take me to the Taberna when the storm globe showed clear weather. I had slept in my little cabin that night—for how long, I didn't know—but a nagging feeling had awoken me. I'd found him in the bar, standing frozen as he surveyed the blood.

The writing shone against the stained wall behind the piano under the light of the anglerfish nets. Whoever was behind the graffiti was growing bolder—and they most likely resided on this boat.

"Reclaim the Drowned's glory!" A fisherman in a battered blue sweater and faded slacks tucked into gumboots raised his rum bottle.

"Hear! Hear!" shouted a Drowned woman wearing a ripped full-skirted dress.

"I don't know about you, but I'm not risking the wrath of the Mer Prince," a naval officer cried. "Don't you remember what he did to José?"

"Gulliver was never the same after his run-in with the Mer!" a woman in modern clothes added, shaking her head at the bloody graffiti.

The Drowned looked at each other and began muttering in agreement. I glanced sideways at Edward. He was straightening the lapels of his porter's uniform, his eyes moving from one person to the next as if he didn't know what to make of it.

"Yes, kill the scoundrels that sunk our city." Teachie and Rackham had appeared in the tavern behind us.

"Sunk our city?" I raised my brows at Edward.

"Legend says the Seven Mer Kingdoms combined their powers to sink the debaucherous city, though no one knows for sure. The newly Drowned took this as a call to arms, igniting the final great war—the Battle of Port Royal. Neither side triumphed, and now the Mer avoid those waters, known as the Wild West of the Ocean," Edward muttered.

This support from the two most ferocious pirates on SS *Jones's Lady* emboldened the Drowned.

"Kill the Mer. Reclaim Drowned glory!" the fisherman cried.

The tavern reverberated as the others joined in. They raised their rum bottles, eyes wild. "Kill the Mer. Reclaim Drowned—"

The rhythmic clomp of a wooden leg silenced the cries as the Captain entered the room.

"If you want to remain in *my* bar and drink *my* rum, there will be no killing anybody," he snarled. His face looked younger as his brown eyes narrowed on each chanting Drowned—*the Protector*.

With a wave of his fist, the shimmering graffiti disappeared.

My mouth was agape, and Edward emitted a noise of wonder at my side. We stood staring at the stained wall as the Captain moved to the piano and took a seat. He began to play an upbeat jig.

The Drowned looked disgruntled, but slowly, they dispersed and found tables. Teachie and Rackham were the last ones to obey. They were still standing there bristling, eyes narrowed on the Captain, when Edward and I exited through the saloon doors.

"Do you know how abhorrent you look?" Edward grimaced.

A half-eaten fish was hanging from one of my webbed hands. I snatched another from the silvery school of them weaving around us.

The eerie war chat of the Drowned stayed with me as we followed the looming pillars of the stalagmite forest, climbing upward until we reached the warmer water. The heat vents shivered like nervous companions at our side, but we didn't venture in.

Edward didn't have webs, so I walked beside him. This made traveling considerably slower, but I was grateful to have him with me. Much to his disgust, I was using my aquatic speed and vision to capture and gorge on fish. There was more variety here, unlike the terrifying glowing creatures that hung around the tavern.

"How come you're so sophisticated?" I wobbled a fish skeleton in his face before letting it float away.

"Whatever do you mean?" Edward mumbled, swatting the debris out of his path.

"How come you're not like the other Drowned?" I used my webs to scoot in front of him and block his path. "I haven't seen you lecherously drunk, I haven't seen you having sex, and you don't shun me like the others."

The desolate rocky expanses of the deep had softened; we had passed a trembling kelp forest and a few sunken boats, and now, oceanic greenery was beginning to sprout from every corner.

"I've been here for over a hundred years, remember, and you only know me now." His mouth thinned as he pushed past me through a rocky cavern.

"But you said you hadn't—"

As we cleared the rock face, color in the form of vegetation manifested in every corner. I looked around in wonder as I breast-stroked to catch up with Edward again.

"I learned from an error." His teeth were gritted.

"So you *have* slept with someone?" I pulled my finger from an anemone and gave him my full attention.

"When I first arrived here, I was confused and miserable, so like the others, I turned to the rum to diffuse my pain. In my vulnerable state, I had but one slipup. Afterward, I was riddled with guilt and thoughts of my living lover. I vowed never to do it again, and I haven't." His tone was icy. I could tell he wanted me to drop it, even without sensing his feelings.

"Are they still here, this person?" Another school of fish parted as we strolled through them.

"I've already shared more than I ought." Edward batted the fish out of his path.

"Okay, but I swear I won't—"

"Stop!" He grabbed me by the elbow and pulled me behind a large coral-encrusted mound streaming with clumps of seaweed.

"What are you doing?" I pulled away from him.

"Shhh, look."

He parted the wavering fronds, and there they were: the Mer. Edward emitted a noise of condemnation, and I elbowed him. There were two of them gliding silently through the emerald water. The female's hair was a white blonde. It snaked around her shoulder blades and down her back, thriving in the water.

"That's Princess Glacies of the House of Niveus," Edward whispered.

Princess Glacies's slim torso was tinged blue and complemented by a tail of glittering black, its scales creeping up her torso to adorn parts of her breasts.

"She's beautiful." I swallowed.

Edward's eyes followed her companion. I took in the strong-built merman swimming beside the princess. His skin was darker than her ivory sheen and had a green tinge rather than blue.

"That's King Neptūnus V's nephew. I don't know his name. I've heard of the princess because there have been rumors that they are merging the kingdoms by marriage."

The Mer's skin shone in harmony with their surroundings, and they moved with a grace that was beyond human. They approached us quickly. Their large tails beat against the water, propelling them faster than my webs could have. Never in my life could I have imagined such wondrous beings existed. I stepped out from behind the mound as they glided above us, looking up at them in a trance.

"Morgana!" Edward hissed, lunging for my arm, but his fingers slipped against my sleek fur.

I raised my gaze to meet theirs, and the Mer stared down at me as they swam over. Princess Glacies had pale blue eyes—the color of icy seas—and the merman's irises were an amber brown. I was on the verge of attempting communication when the muscular merman turned and spat right at me.

"Drowned scum!" The princess's eyes flashed. Like with the Drowned, only bubbles left her mouth, but I heard her in my mind, her voice clear and cold as ice.

"Hey!" I called out, but they continued swimming. "Why did they do that?" My voice broke as I brushed the merman's saliva from my arm. It shimmered silver on my fingertips.

"What did I tell you? The Mer hate us, and so it has been for thousands of years." Edward rolled his eyes. "Not to mention that someone has been using their blood for paint! I'm surprised they didn't attack us. They are dangerous . . . beautiful, yet terrible." He stepped out from behind the seaweed-clad rock, where he had been crouching.

"And you think it all started with this Selkie, Siana, and Prince Kyano?" I asked, looking at the Mer's glimmering tales as they sped away.

"Legend has it that there's always been unrest between the Mer and Drowned, and the altercation between Manannán and Prince Kyano gave both parties the ammunition they needed." He pointed. "Look, there's Prince Aigéan! He's supposed to be the cruelest of the lot."

A third merman had joined the retreating Princess Glacies and her muscular comrade. The prince must have been about the same age as me, or so it looked from this distance. I couldn't make out his features, but he had a tail of deep emerald, which melted into an inky crimson tip. His dark hair seemed to hold a seaweed crown—or perhaps I was imagining it because I knew he was the prince.

"There's his dolphin, Pháos." Edward's eyes were wide in wonder, and I followed his gaze.

The dolphin's nose and back were black but melted into gray, which became white on the creature's belly. The prince stopped and turned to pat it as it floated by his side, and it let out a series of playful clicks.

"Holy shit," I whispered as the dolphin zoomed around to his other side and looked right at me.

The prince turned, too. He had an angular jawline and dark hair billowing in the swell. His chest and right arm were covered in tattoos. I thought about the trembling pirate, José. I had seen him twitching in fear in the games room and the tavern whenever a fight broke out. He hadn't quite recovered from whatever this prince had done to him.

23.

Finn

"I can't bear the sight of them," Glacies spat.

Pisceon glared at the two Drowned, his fists balled. "They are lucky we don't assault them like they've done to our people!"

Pháos clicked in my ear, and I squinted into the murky green.

No, it couldn't be.

Long, flowing red hair, a slender frame covered in what seemed to be fur . . . and those aquamarine eyes. Even from this distance, they were like two emeralds peering at me from the gloom.

What is she? I suspected a seal, but not this. And why is she keeping company with the Drowned?

The thing growing in my chest swelled like an unsettled beast raising its head and asking to be petted. I shoved it back down.

"Why are you looking at them?" Glacies angled her head high, eyes narrowed.

I nodded at Pháos, and the dolphin chirped in understanding. *Follow her.*

So, she possessed shifter abilities yet remained trapped between forms. Interesting.

I rubbed my chin as Pháos disappeared into the green. I would be goddamned if I told my father about this. Not until I knew more about his plans for her.

The girl's face stayed with me as we moved away. My whole life, I'd been married to duty. Now, she'd awakened something inside me—a constant presence in my subconscious. I was either searching for ways to think of her or trying to push her out of my mind.

"I don't see why they couldn't build the Sanitatem in our kingdom." Glacies straightened, and color stained her cheeks.

She was in one of her moods. She knew why the Sanitatem healing quarters were not on Mer territory—it had to be accessible to all sea creatures.

Her mood swings were becoming more frequent, alternating between icy detachment and unnecessary cruelty. I understood. She despised this arranged marriage as much as I did, but watching it consume her was unbearable. And somehow, I couldn't shake the feeling that it was my fault.

We glided over a sunken galleon, its skeletal remains half-buried in the sand. Two Drowned men were rifling through a massive metal safe wedged between a piece of wreckage and the ship's hull. Looking for treasure as always, like that piece of shit, José. At least this wasn't Mer territory.

One of the men dragged a barnacle-crusted painting from the ship's remains. Its colors had faded after years in the sea. The other pried open a wooden chest, its contents spilling into the water.

The Drowned men peered up at us as we passed overhead, and their irises glowed. My jaw tightened as I dived down for a closer look. *Silver.* It gleamed in their hollow eyes and spread beneath their skin like cobwebs.

My fingers curled around the hilt of the dagger strapped to my back as rage roiled inside of me. "They've been using Mer blood," I growled, my tail flicking sharply.

Pisceon exhaled, blocking my path with a firm arm. "Leave it, cousin. This is neutral ground."

I let out a long, steady breath. Pisceon had always been my anchor, the steady hand against the storm, keeping me from being swallowed whole by the rage that often threatened to devour me.

Glacies scoffed, crossing her arms. "Neutral ground? They would have killed *our* people to get that blood."

Blood addicts were nothing new. Our blood granted the Drowned access to the Mer's power, a fleeting taste of invincibility, but prolonged use rotted them from inside until they crumbled into nothing. Then, the Garden of Mortimer would claim them—no less than they deserved! Still, their numbers were growing. Once, they relied on peddlers who siphoned blood from the naturally deceased, selling their spoils in shadowy markets like the Sunken Bazaar. Now, Mer were turning up dead, their wrists punctured where the Drowned had drained them.

"We could use some *royal* blood." The Drowned man's lips curled back, and the whites of his eyes shone silver.

"Holy shit, they've turned rabid," Pisceon breathed.

I barely had time to brace myself before one of the Drowned men leaped for me, his hands cold as death as they grabbed the tip of my tail. I twisted and dived, driving my dagger into his gut; the man cried as the blade slid through his flesh.

I watched the cut I had carved begin to heal as the Drowned man grinned, silver veins pulsing.

"Worthless scum!" Glacies hissed as we lowered ourselves further, ready to fight.

Pisceon rolled his shoulders, slicing his dagger across the Drowned's arm. The wound sealed over almost instantly, the silver in his veins glowing brighter.

The Drowned man let out a guttural laugh. "You can't kill us."

That was the problem, and the only leverage they had. We had extended lifespans, but a death blow could still kill us. The damned curse had stripped us of our full powers, so the Drowned had immortality on their side.

The Drowned wouldn't die until they'd served their sentence to the gods of the sea. So, they could kill us, but it was harder for us to kill them. There hadn't been a war in hundreds of years because the Drowned were cowards who drew strength from numbers, so without mass drownings, they didn't go to war.

"They are going to be a nuisance." Pisceon flexed his biceps.

"They won't have long until Mortimer claims their souls. Let's contain them." My gaze flicked to the rusted safe they'd been plundering, wedged precariously against the ship's splintered hull.

"He is coming!" One of the Drowned men roared and lunged for Glacies, who dodged his grasp.

"Cousin." I jerked my head at the safe.

Pisceon's eyes lit up in wicked delight, and he twisted through the water, his tail a cobalt blur. "You want some of this?" He licked his tattooed bicep, inciting the rabid blood-hungry scum while dodging their frenzied swipes.

I dug my hands beneath the safe, muscles burning as I conjured the force of a crashing wave. I unleashed the wave's fury as Pisceon led the Drowned beneath it.

The safe groaned as it gave way, crashing down with a deafening boom, stirring up a thick cloud of sand and debris. The Drowned shrieked as the weight crushed them against the wreck, pinning them beneath its immovable mass.

Silence followed, save for the distant sound of the ocean shifting.

Glacies flicked a strand of hair from her face, exhaling. "Well, that was unpleasant."

Pisceon nudged me, smirking. "Neutral ground, huh?"

24.

MORGANA

Stone eyes peered at me from a bust half-submerged in the sand. Strands of carved hair, now eroded, disappeared beneath the soft grains.

"What is this place?" I stopped, running my finger across the woman's forehead above one of her vacant eyes.

The vegetation had thinned, giving way to soft sand and scattered rocks. Stone arches rose along our path, draped in swaying strands of seaweed, while the remnants of carved monoliths stretched endlessly into the murky expanse.

"This is Archōn Agorá. It was once a magical place," Edward said from beside me.

"Once?" I raised my eyebrows at him. "Let me guess—in the Days of Gods."

He nodded, surveying the statue. "This was Agápē, the Siren God of Love."

"What happened to the other clans—the Sirens and sea monsters?" I wondered aloud, still thinking about the beautiful Mer.

"Fearing the gods' wrath, the other clans chose to remain neutral in the feud."

Edward's mood had darkened after our run-in with the Mer, but he perked up as he began to recount another tale. "But after the gods retreated from the earth, they had a new foe, one you will be familiar with—pollution. They started to die out. I have been here over one hundred years and have never seen a sea monster; the Sirens are few. Selkies, like yourself, were said to be extinct. The Mer call it 'the Shadow' or 'Skia.'"

"B-but they're still magical. Can't they just fight it?" I ran my finger through the little dots of algae that swirled around us.

"Selkies and Sirens wield mind magic, unlike the Mer, who once dominated the clans with sheer might. Had the Mer's powers not been stripped, they might have fought the Shadow, saved the other clans, and perhaps ruled sea and land over humans." Edward blew out a breath, and bubbles were emitted from his mouth.

Barnacles and coral had claimed Agápē's skin, creeping along the curves of her cheeks and across her forehead like a crown of decay. The sand buried her shoulders and torso, leaving only hints of her outstretched arms, which now seemed frozen in a mournful reach toward the surface.

"That's so . . . sad," I said, my throat burning as I thought of all the oil spills I had seen on the news as we moved away from Agápē's vacant stare.

"Of course, they blame us for this new sickness, so the cycle continues," Edward grumbled, ducking around a long-tendrilled jellyfish as it meandered past.

The ruins stretched before us, the crumbled rocks deliberately placed to form circles. I stopped beside one of the pillars, half-submerged in sand. There was writing on it, but it had faded from years in the deep.

"It's the Runes of the Ocean," Edward breathed.

I ran my fingers along the soft grooves in the stone—a spiral rune.

"Once, statues of all the gods were displayed here, but most have now been lost to the sea," Edward said, looking at the pillars surrounding us with wonder.

We passed another crumbled stone circle, and I could sense it—the ancient magic that still emanated from this place. A massive cavern loomed between the scattered boulders. Behind it and to our left, sand stretched into distant dunes, and on our right, the tumbled rocky terrain of Archōn Agorá stretched into blue as far as the eye could see.

"It's the worst part but the quickest route to the Taberna." Edward gestured at the cavern. Darkness was festering inside it. "It will take us half the time compared to my boots on that soft sand."

"I'm game if you are."

There were faint markings over the rough entrance: more runes. Once inside, a rocky mass leered up on either side of us, but we followed the gash of jade above. Even with my improved aquatic vision, I couldn't see far ahead.

Occasionally, we passed under a shelf, and it felt like soft fingers were caressing my head, like the persuasive touch of a deadly lover. It's just seaweed, I reassured myself.

"Why do you shun the Mer like the rest of the Drowned, yet spend time with me when the others won't?" I asked Edward. The seaweed had brought the prince and his crown to mind.

"The Mer are rude—you saw them. I've seen nothing from them except arrogance and contempt. You're not like them," Edward muttered into the darkness at my side.

"But what gave you the courage to find that out? I'm not like you either. I'm living like them." I glanced at him to see if I had hurt his feelings, but the darkness consumed his features.

"The Captain suggested that I would find a friend in you, and he's the kind of man you listen to." Edward grabbed my hand to guide me underneath more sluggish seaweed that hung from a jutting rock shelf above us.

"That's right, the *Protector*. It's good to know you didn't do it of your own accord." I scoffed. "Do you think he can see the future?" I kept my grip on Edward's hand in the darkness.

"No one knows much about the Protectors. It is rumored they have ancient powers, but they are dormant unless activated by the need to defend. Some say they alone can still communicate with the gods of old, but who knows if that's true. The Captain has been here longer than any of us. I suspect he may have had several bodies."

"What do you mean?" I ran my fingers along the slimy cavern wall, thinking about how the Captain had made the graffiti disappear.

"I think he looks Drowned, but he is a spirit, perhaps," Edward explained.

"If you got to know the Mer as you have me, do you think you could befriend them?"

"No, and I wouldn't want to. Would you drop it already?" His tone was icy, and he let go of my hand.

"Why do you hate them so much? You've read enough books to see that it's pointless to hate based on nothing more than an ancient grudge!"

"I saw them when I was drowning." Edward stopped as if trying to obtain a memory the years had obscured. "I had a large gash in my stomach, and I was struggling to stay conscious." He gestured to the tear in his uniform. We were nearing the edge of the ravine, its walls tapering off into sand as blue light enveloped us.

"As I rose and fell beneath the waves, they watched me with unfeeling eyes. I cried out to them for help, but they just looked on. At first, I thought I was hallucinating from blood loss and exhaustion. However, once I awoke and came to terms with this new existence, I knew they had been there. It would have taken them one moment to save me, but they did nothing." There was resentment mingled with grief on his face.

I understood why the Mer hadn't saved Edward. They were wild creatures of the sea, and he'd been succumbing to his fate, but I decided to keep this to myself. I also got the impression that Edward wanted to be accepted by the Mer more than anything, manifesting in his obsession with the history of the ocean. Perhaps that was the real reason he'd befriended me.

25.

Morgana

"The Taberna is down here." Edward jumped into a crater to our right. Cut out of the rock face before him was a round opening. Strings of shells hung across it, jingling as we parted them.

"You can swim down, but I must use this." He grabbed a knotted rope fastened beside the entrance and began edging down into the darkness. I hesitated briefly as he vanished into the gloom before diving down after him.

I swam through shadows until lights appeared, revealing a rounded cave. I snapped my head from side to side, taking in everything as I plunged past Edward, who drifted leisurely down the rope. There were shelves carved into the rock at regular intervals, which were lined with bottles, trinkets, and paraphernalia and illuminated by glowing lights. I shot past more and more of them until I reached the sandy shop floor of the cavern shaft.

"Hurry up, would you?" I sniggered as Edward swayed precariously on the rope above.

"They do this on purpose, you know," he huffed. "We have to debase ourselves just to get a few books."

On the floor stood two large chests, overflowing with treasures and jewels. A heap of swords lay stacked beside a pile of shields and spears in one corner. Beneath a glass counter, pistols were neatly arranged, while the stone ledges above it displayed an eclectic mix of clocks, compasses, and radios. I even spotted an old microwave.

I could use my webs to propel myself upward and explore the towering shelves. Edward's Drowned abilities meant that—unless he used the rope—he was confined to the sandy floor or the few lower-level shelves he could tread water to peer at.

I surveyed some of the higher shelves. Above the clutter on the lower levels, books of all colors, shapes, and sizes lined the upper rockface. Surely, there was something on Selkies here. Edward remained on the cavern floor, as if he didn't want to degrade himself further by treading water.

"Not more rum." I landed on the seabed beside him and leaned over his shoulder.

"Preservation potion," he said, selecting a green glass bottle from the rack. "I suspect this whole cave has a preservation spell cast over it. However, we magically inept Drowned must purchase it in bottled form." He grabbed a second bottle and handed it to me. "You should get some."

"I don't have any money." I ran my fingers over the delicate blue glass. It sparkled, and I could sense its magic. It was stopped with a small cork.

Edward reached into his tattered pocket and produced a handful of coins. "Here." He tipped them into my palm. "These will get you started, but I suggest you start winning at chess if you want more."

My retort caught in my throat as I spotted an old merman behind the counter. How long had he been watching us?

His eyebrows were overgrown, but not enough to hide his piercing amber gaze. His skin hung limp and wrinkled about his chest, and whiskers pushed from his ears and cheeks. Unlike the prince and his companions' vibrant-colored ones, this merman's tail was a faded copper. Scales were missing in places, and here and there, a spattering of barnacles clung to it.

I followed Edward to the counter, clutching my little blue bottle.

"Do you have any books on Selkies or the—what did you call it?" I turned to Edward. "Prophecy of the Blue Temple."

The old man's amber eyes narrowed, and he started laughing.

"*I told you* it was lost," Edward hissed at my side.

I continued to look at the old man expectantly.

"No, we don't have any books on the prophecy. *If* such a thing existed, it was lost thousands of years ago." He pressed his long, thin fingers together and surveyed me over the top of them.

"W-well, what about Selkies . . . or the legend of Manannán and Siana Selich?"

"Can you read Tartessian or Ogham?" The merman raised a bushy white brow at me.

"Well, no." Heat rose in my cheeks.

"Latin?" His mouth curved into a malicious grin. "Or Ancient Greek?"

"No," I admitted, crestfallen.

"How about the Runes of the Ocean?"

I shook my head. He was mocking me.

"I thought not."

"I—I can." Edward bristled at my side.

"You can now, can you?" The merman turned his glistening eyes on Edward, raising both brows this time.

"W-well, Latin, and I've taught myself some Ancient Greek." Edward flushed under his gaze.

"You two are very curious. The Drowned rarely ask me for books. Treasure maps, on the other hand . . ." He chuckled.

"Firstly, I'm *not* Drowned." I gestured to my furry bodysuit. Edward shoved me and issued a look of warning. "Secondly, surely you have something that's been translated into English."

"Not Drowned?" The old merman looked me up and down. "Well, that explains it. Let me see." He shot from behind the counter and glided toward the shelves wrapped around the cave ceiling. From below, I took in the full extent of his glimmering tail as he ran a sinewy arm along his beloved books.

"Ah," he exclaimed as he plucked a thin title from the rows before him. "This should cater to your intellectual abilities." He sailed back down and settled behind the glass counter before holding it out to me, his mouth curving into another grin.

"It's a kids' picture book!"

Slime coated the cover in a thin film, but one swipe from my webbed palm revealed an artist's impression of a swirling sea. Around its edges were cartoon-like characters; sea snakes writhed in the bottom left corner, and above them, a beautiful woman sunned herself on some rocks. In the bottom right corner, a human, presumably Drowned, was brandishing a sword, and a merman and seal twirled above him. The title was written in the Runes of the Ocean.

"What does it say?" I asked, running my hands over the letters.

"*Myths of the Clans and Gods*," the merman purred. Then he cackled as he added, "For *little* Mer children. You can start with the basics." His pale chest heaved, and the loose pockets of skin around each of his nipples jiggled in unison.

"Can you buy me this as well?" I shoved the book at Edward.

He rolled his eyes but took it from me.

"That will be three silvers for each potion, and I'll throw in the book for free." The merman howled again.

As Edward rifled in his pocket, a shadow passed over his face. Was it my imagination? No, the darkness remained. Something—or someone—was blocking the azure light that had previously filtered through the rock opening high above us.

A chill swept the back of my neck as a thud sent the strands of shells tinkling and echoed down to the bottom of the cavern. My eyes narrowed on the old merman behind the counter. Was he about to take revenge for the graffiti in the bar? But he wasn't looking malicious. His eyes were also fixed on the doorway above, wide with concern.

Before I could second-guess myself, instinct took over. I surged upward, weaving past the cluttered shelves and darting out of the cavern's mouth. Outside, the water seemed darker than before as an icy wave brushed my skin. Sensing movement on the sandy expanse above, I pushed off the rock shelf, surging upward.

Before me, there was a stain upon the darkness. No, not a stain—a cloaked figure.

"Who's there?" I yelled as another burst of adrenaline spread through me.

The figure stopped and slowly turned to face me, and the hem of its cloak spilled into the water like ink. My heart beat so fast that I was barely drawing oxygen. Under the hood, there was only darkness and a glint of gold—a mask.

A withered hand emerged from the folds of the cloak, pale skin stretched taut over bone, and streaks of silver shimmered faintly across long claw-like fingers, which curled as if grasping something unseen.

My insides coiled like a spring wound too tight. I knew I needed to act—to move—but my body pulled further away from the scene. I was back at the base of the Ferris wheel with Skye. Something about this figure stirred a familiar unease, reminding me of the strange man we had encountered.

I stumbled backward. The silhouette stood motionless, its cloak rippling in the swell before it vanished into the same dark cavern from which Edward and I had emerged earlier.

A stream of debris clouded the water around me. I sniffed, and my stomach rumbled as I spun around.

What the fuck?

A disembodied tail hacked from a giant fish had been daggered into the coral growing above the Taberna's circular doorway. Its insides were streaming into the water around me. Below it, the word "DIE" was scrawled in the same silvery substance I had seen in the tavern—Mer blood.

"I think you guys should come and see this," I called as bits of flesh and scales danced irritatingly around my face like flies on land.

Edward appeared in the shop's entrance, looking panicky and flushed from climbing back up the rope. The old merman followed calmly behind him. Edward dry-heaved when he saw the giant fishtail. I wasn't disgusted by the sight; in fact, it was making me hungry.

"Who do you think did this, and why?" I turned to the old merman.

"Bored, brainless, Drowned thugs," he spat.

"Well, *excuse* me," Edward hmphed.

"A knifed fishtail, and 'Kill the Mer' graffiti. You would think these were guerrilla messages meaning the same thing," I mused aloud as I pulled out the dagger. The fishtail floated forlornly into the blue gloom. I resisted the urge to snack on it.

"Seeing as we are apparently dying, let's leave the investigation to our kind." The merman offered a cold smile, but his fists were balled.

I was still holding the dagger. Its blade was made of plain copper, and the edges were bitten by decay, but faint runes were visible in the metal.

The hilt was roughly constructed, but two red stones shone brightly from either side of an irregular carving. It wasn't a picture, just swirling lines. It reminded me of my nightmares.

26.

MORGANA

"Are you truly intending to wear that?" Edward nodded to the blade now hanging at my hip.

We'd been about to leave the Taberna when the old merman called me back. He pushed a small scabbard into my hands. It perfectly fitted the dagger I had retrieved.

"This is a gift—I may have underestimated you. I hope that I have." His tone was finite, so I accepted the sheath and slung it across my hips. I was acutely aware of its presence at my side. I couldn't believe my life had changed from a sad art house film into a Hollywood blockbuster. I kept expecting the blue screen to lift away and stagehands to rush in to change the props.

"Not all of us have *webs*, you know!" Edward muttered, his boots sinking into the soft sand of the dunes.

"Sorry, I forgot!" I floated in mock repose, beating against the water with my webbed feet as Edward struggled toward me.

Neither of us felt like going back through the tunnel, which meant crossing the dunes. I watched in awe as my footprints dissolved behind me. It was like traipsing across a blue moon. No wonder NASA had chosen to study the ocean before taking their chances with Mars.

"You can carry your own belongings if you wish," Edward grumbled, gesturing to my preservation potion and the children's book tucked inside his maroon uniform. As if relieving himself of these two items would speed him up.

Behind him, the dunes undulated like the back of some great, slumbering beast. They stretched in torrents beneath me, rising and falling like a desert beneath the waves.

"I do wonder how . . . old . . . that merman truly is," Edward panted as he made it to my side. The sand from the giant dunes swirled around him with each step. "Surely, he would have seen some of the great battles."

"You think?" I asked, rubbing stray specks of sand from my eyes.

"The Mer have an extended lifespan, so to be that aged, he must be thousands of years old. He's been running the Taberna for as long as I've been among the Drowned, yet I've never dared to speak to him until today."

Archōn Agorá stretched into the blue waters beyond a light haze around the scattered boulders marked with runes. Edward was right—this had once been a magical place, and it was old. I could feel it in my bones.

Cold leached through me as I thought about the cloaked figure that had slipped into the cavern; there had been an otherness about it. I could sense it in the same way that I could feel the primeval power of this place.

"Although we harbor resentment for the Mer, I'd wager few among us would trade our manhood for a tail." Edward chuckled as he watched a large fish with a tail reminiscent of the Mer's nibble at a bushel of seaweed nestled between the ruins.

"So Mer don't have sex, then?" I forgot about the cloaked figure, stumbling over a clump of coral in my curiosity.

"Do you suppose engaging in humanlike intimacy with a tail is possible?" Edward raised his brows.

"But how do they reproduce?"

"Much like fish, naturally. The female lays her eggs, which the male fertilizes afterward."

"You're kidding!"

"I've heard they possess certain erogenous zones, enabling them to experience the same pleasures as humans—maybe greater."

The ruins were giving way to sandy plains, interspersed with rocky outcrops and lumps of coral. I couldn't help but wonder what it would be like to embrace one of those beautiful creatures. The prince's dark hair and muscular arms covered with ink caressed my mind. How would they feel around me?

A kelp forest swayed to our right as the sand became increasingly rocky and began to slope downward. I recognized these waters—soon, the ground would dip further, taking us to the outskirts of the hydrothermal vents.

Hunger overcame me as schools of fish darted in and out between the fronds. Dark shapes were gliding among the leaves. *A pod of seals*. Could they know the answer to why I had found myself in this strange underwater world? Could one of them be a Selkie?

"I'll meet you back at the tavern." I motioned toward the dark shapes among the fronds.

"Are you sure?" Edward glanced over his shoulder as if to make sure the cloaked figure hadn't followed us.

"I'm going to see if I can find anything out from them."

"Suit yourself." He shrugged.

The seals surrounded me. Their fur shone in the sways of the ocean, and my fur bodysuit shimmered the same way, but my long red hair made me an outsider as it snaked around my shoulders. One of the seals turned its dark eyes upon me, and my heart beat faster.

"Hello," I said, the sea language leaving my lips in bubbles.

The seal eyed me carefully for a second, then returned to its comrades and its food.

Of course they weren't Selkie seals! Edward had said that they were extinct. But perhaps I could communicate with ordinary seals without Edward or Finn nearby. I let my surroundings wash over me. I couldn't read the seals' emotions, but their wildness, serenity, and pure love for the ocean radiated from them. It was comforting.

I sensed more prey nearby and sped toward the scent. The pod did the same, and with my webbed feet and hands, I kept up easily.

They accepted me as a silent red-haired feeding companion in a tattered version of their own skin. Together, we swam through the kelp forest, aiming for the lighter water, where the fish swarmed.

Kelp strands wound around my ankles in a gentle caress, releasing me as I kicked forward. Soon, the water grew brighter, and the vines around me became dark outlines against an aqua background.

I swam and ate with the pod for what seemed like miles, the pearly scales of the fish I consumed escaping the corners of my mouth and dancing between the kelp fronds.

When the seals popped their heads above the waves to replenish air, I went with them. I reached out gingerly to pat one. It didn't dash away, and its coat was sleek beneath my fingers.

The water grew darker again, signaling our return to deeper territory. I wondered how far the kelp forest stretched. By my estimate, it must have been miles.

A golden fish shimmied before me, I snatched it and bit into its still-wriggling body. When I emerged, my seal companions had vanished.

I sensed the seal pod was gone—they had returned to the shallower water. And there was something else, something that made the fur on my arms rise. Suddenly, I craved the warm glow of the tavern and the jostling Drowned.

I headed in the direction my senses told me SS *Jones's Lady* lay, and soon, the kelp fronds began to shrink, replaced by coral-encrusted rocks and soft sand. The ocean floor spread out beneath me as I swam. Long sandy turrets stretched between the rocks, and coral blossomed below me in dark fan-like structures and little skeletal trees.

A patch of shining coral caught my eye, and I dived to examine it as my hair billowed around me in the swell. First, it shimmered pearly pink and then transitioned into a twinkling aqua. *Strange.* The green rocks before me were also covered in this coral, glimmering alluringly.

But wait—it wasn't just on the rocks. It also covered bits of the sandy sea floor, and the patches were becoming broader and thicker.

"It's not coral," I said aloud, reaching for the substance. It stuck to my finger and glimmered as it dripped down its side.

Mer blood! A gasp escaped my lips, and I shook the liquid from my finger. I careened forward, glancing over my shoulder and simultaneously colliding with something.

The glistening blood was all over me. I shook it off frantically, stepping backward to get my bearings. I had struck something anchored and looming large—a driftwood pole with a wooden crossbar, a mermaid's form attached to it.

Blood spilled from slashes on the mermaid's belly and wrists. Her wrists had been shot through with arrows, attaching her crudely to the driftwood cross.

She was young and beautiful—at least she would have been before her face was marked by death. Indigo shadows hung around her eyes and mouth, her skin was sallow, and her tail had faded to a lifeless gray. Her long red hair drifted mournfully behind her, the strands brushing against her torn wrists as if trying to offer comfort.

The water around me seemed to be getting thicker and heavier, pressing against me with the invisible weight of fear, and my whole body went rigid as every muscle switched into alert mode. I couldn't move even though my instincts were screaming for me to *run . . . hide . . . get help.*

Although they had the tails of fish, the Mer still felt acutely human.

I staggered backward, and a sob escaped my lips as I took in the girl's limp body again. There was no help to be had. She was dead and had been for hours, by the looks of things.

This was pure evil.

I slid the arrows from her limp wrists, removed the ropes, and shut her eyes. Her red hair snaked around her torso as she floated from my arms, and she looked like one of the wooden figureheads I had seen on depictions of ships. The current lifted her, and soon, her body was swallowed by blue.

Why murder then display the body in this manner? Perhaps the killers had been trying to make a statement.

I was desperate to return to SS *Jones's Lady*. Even if the culprit was there somewhere celebrating, so were Edward and the Captain. I needed a friendly face. I needed a face that could replace the dead mergirl's, now burned into my subconscious.

I moved away, but as I did so, little fronds of the pale treelike seaweed that littered the rocks followed me. I lunged forward, but they reached for me.

What the fuck?

I dived to examine the seaweed, holding my hand above it as if to say *sit* to a dog. The seaweed stilled.

I moved my hand back and forth, and it followed.

I twirled my hand in a circle, and the seaweed circled alongside it.

A twinkling caught my eye—the blood of the dead mergirl was still on my skin. Edward's words echoed in my mind. *Mer blood is powerful, but its powers come at a price.* I let out a bubbly shriek, wiping the shimmering substance from my arms, legs, and torso.

◈

My muscles ached, but I kept going. I couldn't stop. Not now. The blood graffiti, a fishtail, and now a dead mergirl.

Who was doing this, and why?

There was something meditative in this endless swimming. Time began to lose meaning as I replayed the images in my mind. There was an ancient grudge between the Mer and the Drowned, but Edward said he had never seen anything like this in his hundred years. The last battle had been the Battle of Port Royal.

Could the attacks be related to a war that ended over three hundred years ago?

Bubbling pillars rose beneath me, marking the edge of the stalagmite forest, and the water around me grew dimmer, cloaking the landscape in shadows. I found myself glancing over my shoulder as if the murderer might appear with the darkening of the environment.

Edward and I had stuck to the sandy track that ran alongside the heat vents, but now I swam across them. Shimmering water cascaded below me, and the darkness weighed upon me. I peered ahead, hoping to glimpse the glowing pillar corals that marked the tavern's entrance. Now and then,

I rushed forward, thinking I'd spied them, but finding only a deep-sea creature's bioluminescence. They danced before me, teasing and taunting, before skittering away and leaving murky darkness in their wake.

A whisper cut through the eerie silence. Was it behind me or in my mind?

Siana, the voice purred.

I spun around. Where had it come from?

Darkness undulated around me. It seemed to move, shadows creeping from the spaces between the gnarled pillars.

Where were the fish? Usually they crowded the heat vents, nibbling away at an assortment of pale shrimp, but there were no animals here now. Even one of the aliens of the deep would have been comforting in this darkness.

Wait. There was something in the shadows—slits of red. *Eyes.* The slits blinked, and I froze. I knew in my bones this was not a hallucination.

I remembered the dagger at my hip and unsheathed it. With the blade in front of me, I began to swim.

Somnus Siana, somnus. That voice, again, hissing in my subconscious. Siana, it called me.

27.

Finn

Glacies let out a trembling cry as we arrived at the Sanitatem, the healing quarters deep within the kelp forest. She rushed ahead of us, pushing through the slimy strands, which created walls like shredded curtains moving gently with the currents. Dappled sunlight from somewhere high above filtered through the canopy, and the constant motion of the seaweed gave the space a living, breathing quality. The healers leveraged the ancient powers of the forest in the mending process.

To the untrained eye, this may have looked like a thick patch of kelp, but if you knew where to part its strands, leafy beds hung between the fronds, each cradling a sick Mer or other oceanic creature. Bioluminescent globes were woven among them, lighting the hospital and creating soft shadows that danced across the swell.

Glacies's sobs drifted from the greenery, and I found her at her cousin Íss's bedside. Her long blonde hair heaved against her back as she held her cousin's limp hand.

Íss smiled bravely, but her eyes were sunken, surrounded by dark rings, and her lips were white. Once a beauty like Glacies, the girl's light hair was limp, and the telltale black veins of the Shadow crept across her neck and down her arms. She didn't have long.

I shut the curtain and stepped away, my fists balled. The disease was insidious. It crept inside us, eating away at our core while we remained unaware. Once the veins appeared, it was too late.

"Prince Aigéan." A gentle touch on my tail caused me to spin around. A young merboy, no more than four or five, was floating behind me. The veins hadn't yet spread over his body in the same way they'd consumed Íss, but there was a tiny spidery web on the side of his neck.

"Hello, little one." I grinned, but my heart was weighed by darkness as I took in the shadows under his eyes and his hopeful expression.

"Healer Airmed says one day the Mer will get their powers back, and there will no longer be any Shadow. Is this true?"

"Yes." My heart clenched as I lied to him.

The Mer had been unable to break the curse for thousands of years. I doubted it would be broken in this boy's lifetime, and the pollution in the water was only growing.

"Healer Airmed also says that my parents are playing a game of hide-and-seek, and soon I will find them again."

The child's words dragged me from my thoughts, and I leaned over to look him straight in the eye. "You are lucky to have parents who play games with you." I ruffled his hair, and he let out a cough.

My brow furrowed as I parted the seaweed at the entrance to the healer's quarter, where kelp trunks hemmed in a sandy glade. Coral shelves were woven into the strands, housing jars of remedies, balms, and shells filled with medicines for the sick. Tiny cleaner fish darted between the shelves, tending to algae growth or sanitizing the spaces like devoted assistants.

A pool of bubbling, mineral-rich water in one corner was used for restorative soaks. Its healing properties were drawn from nearby geothermal vents.

Healer Airmed was draped in flowing strands of iridescent seaweed and glided from patient to patient in the heated pool. Her hands glowed faintly with magic as she administered care.

Spotting me, she touched the man she was tending to gently on the brow and glided across the room with a flick of her tail. Like all Mer born with healing powers, she had long dark hair and pale eyes.

"Your Highness." She made a little bow, and it reminded me of how much I loved being Finn in a world where no one bowed to me.

My thoughts drifted to Morgana—how she rolled her eyes and flicked her hair when I tested her patience in a way none of my kind would dare to. The tilt of her head, the curve of those petulant lips . . . a challenge, a lure, a storm I longed to chase. I rolled my shoulders, dispelling the thoughts.

"The boy thinks the Mer will get their powers back." An angry breath shot out of me.

Airmed's eyes were filled with sadness, and she shook her head. "Do not underestimate the potency of hope, Your Highness. It is a powerful thing."

A powerful, dangerous thing, I thought as I made my way out of the Sanitatem.

Pisceon was waiting outside, arms folded across his chest and his jaw stiff. He refused to come in whenever we visited. I didn't blame him. The Shadow wasn't contagious; it was contracted by coming into contact with polluted waters or eating too many contaminated fish. But Pisceon had watched his parents be consumed by the same black spidery veins that were creeping across Íss's body and the young boy's neck.

Glacies appeared behind us, drawing a shuddering sob, and I moved to comfort her.

"Don't touch me!" She glared at me through tear-stained eyes as she pushed me away.

I threw up my hands in apology.

"I am going to the Kingdom of Okeanós. I will be back before the Blood Moon Ball," she sniffed.

I nodded.

Pisceon put a hand on my shoulder. "Is it wise? If the king finds out you let her go, he will be livid at you both."

I shrugged him off and smiled at Glacies. "Go," I told her softly.

Who was I to deny her the comfort of a loved one in these times?

Perhaps it's *her*—the girl who's undone me. When I met that merboy's purple-stained eyes, I thought only of Morgana, my tortuous obsession.

A rush of water pulsed to my left, and Pháos circled frantically. He squeaked and gestured with his flipper.

The girl. Morgana. She was in trouble.

28.

MORGANA

I wheeled around, dagger raised, but my limbs were weak.

The eyes were still there, and the shadows around them were building . . . building.

I wanted to look away, to run, but my body was heavy. Why was it so heavy?

The darkness swirled around the eyes and thickened. A man's torso and a glittering white tail appeared—a merman. Was I hallucinating?

The shadows built a face about the eyes, a beautiful yet terrible face framed by pale shoulder-length hair and with high chiseled cheekbones. Dark lashes and brows rimmed the red irises and black pupils I knew so well.

Siana, said the gentle murmur in my mind. Strong arms closed around me from behind.

The red-eyed merman's pupils flared and then narrowed on my new assailant. His mouth curved into a malicious grin, and the grip around me stiffened. Cold scales pressed against my back—another merman had wrapped me in his muscled embrace.

A slick, slicing sound cut through the darkness, and a bubbly cry escaped my lips. The arms that held me had grown claws.

The red-eyed merman let out a long, slow laugh—I heard it in my head—and then disappeared into swirling shadows.

I wriggled, and my new attacker tensed. I thrashed, scratching and shrieking, as whoever it was began to swim with me held in their clawed fists.

The merman was carrying me through the water faster than I could ever go. Its arms were cold, and the claws . . . *the claws.* They were razor-sharp and glistened green, held together by slimy thick webs. I tried to free myself again, but the harder I struggled, the feebler my attempts became. My body relaxed, and my mind clouded with a pleasant calm. I let the dagger drift from my hands, and the darkness claimed it.

No, I tried to protest—*someone help.*

But my body had gone limp in my assailant's arms.

"Morgana?"

I opened my eyes, and yellow light filtered in.

"Morgana?" the voice said again. It was familiar—but how could it be? Surely, I had been captured and was in some foul dungeon somewhere. It took a few blinks to clear my contracting vision.

"Where am I?" I asked as the coral pillars marking the front of the tavern came into view. The Captain was crouching beside me. I peeled my torso from the sandy seabed and scanned the dark waters for any sign of the clawed attacker or the red eyes. Had they been working together? It hadn't seemed that way, but now I wasn't sure.

"D-did you rescue me?" I asked the Captain, bringing a hand to my throbbing temple as it registered the familiar piano music and Drowned's squabbling emanating from the doorway beside me.

"No, child, that was the merman." The Captain's amber eye was kind as he surveyed me.

"The merman?" Pulling myself to my feet, I stared into the darkness. I blinked and blinked, willing the world to come back into focus. Instead, my legs gave way, and a wave of nausea washed over me. I reached for one of the glowing coral pillars to steady myself.

"The one with a pure white tail . . ." I thought about the beautiful red-eyed merman who had disappeared in a cloud of shadows. The one who had called me Siana and whose whispers had made me sleepy. "B-but he cast a spell over me?"

"No, child, this merman did not have a white tail." The Captain blew out a long breath before standing and wrapping an arm around my back to steady me. "He even had the nerve to scold me for letting you wander alone."

What? I had been brought here by a different merman!

I thought back to the strong arms that had been clasped around me.

"B-but he had claws." I looked at my own hands. I too had webs, but mine were delicate, and the merman's had been thick.

"Yes." The Captain smiled at me. "The Mer are fierce when aggravated. In this instance, I imagine he grew them to protect you."

I was in the arms of a merman. By the sounds of it, I had also been put into a bewitched sleep by the merman with the red eyes and white tail.

"But what was he protecting me *from*?" I was still blinking the stupor away.

"You shouldn't venture too deep into the forest. They call it Therme Skótos." He gestured to the pillars, still spewing out heat. "The Forest of

Heat and Darkness. It is an ancient place. They say life itself came from within its depth."

"I think I saw a merman built from shadows with . . . red eyes. He called me Siana." I spilled my thoughts out loud. If the Captain were a Protector, perhaps he would know something.

He stiffened, and something flickered in his eye—fear and sadness. But he said, "You've had quite the ordeal. Let's get you some rum."

I continued to hold on to the pillar for support as the world faded in and out of focus. The sheath on my hip reminded me of the dagger I had lost, and I reached for it. To my surprise, I felt the hilt of the blade. My merman rescuer must have retrieved it when it fell.

"You were right. I am a descendant of a Selkie . . . Why didn't you just tell me?" My throat bobbed as I surveyed the Captain's lined face for answers.

He smiled, and his eye was understanding. "Would you have stayed and learned about our world if I had?"

"I don't know." My eyes fluttered with another wave of dizziness.

"Few visit this world from above and live to see it again. I say it's a gift. Discover it carefully, and use it wisely, because you are likely here for a reason."

29.

MORGANA

A hush settled over the tavern as I pushed open the swinging doors. Where were the brawling pirates? Where were the giggling girls? Even the piano stood silent. The naval officer who had previously been caressing its keys was staring at me. They were all staring at me. No, not staring—*scowling*.

"There's the mermaid lover!" hissed Teachie, his scars illuminated in the anglerfish light, and the rest of his table sniggered.

A clomping alerted me to the Captain's return to my side. "Drink this." He thrust a rum bottle into my hands. Another snigger sliced through the room, but a glance from the Captain quieted them. The silence was worse.

I lifted the bottle to my lips, and as the warm liquid entered my body, I felt my strength return.

"Don't mind them." The Captain motioned to the gaping Drowned. "It's been hundreds of years since a merman came this close to the tavern. They're in shock." He chuckled, and his little sea snake grinned gleefully in unison.

I began to make my way warily forward, sighing in relief when I saw Edward sitting at our usual table adjacent to the big wooden doors.

"Why don't you return to where you came from?" a man spat. He had beady rat eyes and straw-like hair. "You are no longer welcome here."

Another hiss followed. "Mer-loving seal slut—your time is coming!" It was Jackie. He was hunched over next to Donahue and the new muscly Drowned boy.

Seal slut. They'd called me that before. He knew what I was. *They* knew what I was. Did that mean I was in danger? I searched for Donahue's scornful gaze, but his eyes weren't on me—they were fixed over his shoulder, on Edward.

I kept moving, ignoring the slurs—one step, then another. The glow from the anglerfish jars on the tables created eerie patterns that danced across the faces of the scowling patrons.

Only when I slid onto the wooden stool across from Edward did the whispers morph into conversations again. The Captain was handing out bottles of rum in my wake. A haunting tune swept through the bar as a woman with long dark hair and sad eyes took the naval officer's place at the grand piano.

Edward wasn't looking at me. It was as if he was trying to pretend I wasn't there.

I grabbed a chessboard from one of the overflowing chests that lined the stained wall and started setting up the pieces. We began to play, but twenty minutes into the game, his mood had worsened.

"Would you focus, or else you'll never be able to beat me!" Edward banged his fist on the table, sending the pieces bouncing.

"What is your problem? I thought chess would cheer you up."

"Cheer me up? And *why*, pray tell, would I need such a thing?" His pale blue eyes had become slits.

"I—well, I just thought you were feeling a little depressed." I immediately regretted my words as I watched his face darken.

"I don't need your pity!" His lips became a single inky line. "You just *had* to befriend them, didn't you? You may as well take up residence in the castle with your Mer friends and slander me as you swim past." He folded his arms across the big red gash in his maroon uniform, and his little red hat toppled off.

"You're acting just like the rest of the Drowned!" I gestured across the bar as anger ignited my senses.

Heat stained Edward's cheeks. "I *am* like the rest of them. I *am* Drowned scum with no powers and no means to walk upon the land!" He was shaking now, his nostrils flaring with each breath. "I told you what they did to me. I *told* you they left me for dead."

"I didn't ask the merman to rescue me!" A lump was forming in my throat.

Edward bowed his head, as if embarrassed to be associated with me. I took a long swig of my rum, banging the bottle back onto the table as loudly as possible. He didn't look up.

"Seriously, screw this." I kicked my stool aside as the lump in my throat expanded.

"Go." Edward's voice had softened, but he kept his eyes fixed on the slimy table. "I don't see why the devil you want to hang out with the Mer in the first place," he yelled after me, but I ignored him. "Oh, and checkmate!" I heard him finish angrily as I pushed the large wooden doors open, rage and hurt eddying inside me.

I descended the decayed steps to the lower decks, my legs unsteady. Perhaps some of the red-eyed merman's magic was still clinging to me. Red eyes, a dead mergirl, and a knifed fishtail—were these just coincidences, or was there a connection between the events? A connection to me? I knew those red eyes. They had haunted my dreams since I was a child, and he had called me *Siana* . . .

I passed through the room that had once been a swimming pool and was now a botanical garden for the Drowned. Somehow, I found myself back in the murky hallway, ascending the stairs to the room with the crashed chandelier where we had first found the Mer blood graffiti. The fur-covered skin on my forearms pebbled at the memory of the shimmering writing. I ran my hands over the dark, mottled surface where the words had been, searching for any trace as to their origin. But there was nothing—only darkness.

What was I doing, acting like I was Sherlock Holmes and could solve the Mer murders . . . I shook my head. The sadness in the mermaid's eyes when her body drifted from my arms had planted something within me—a desperate need to act.

I left the dark room behind, making my way up another set of partially decayed stairs. After a few steps, my foot slipped through one of the planks. *They should put their preservation potion to good use and fix this boat.* I continued forward, but soon fell through another stair. *Lazy, selfish, Drowned!*

The room the stairs led to had probably once been a men's cigar room or perhaps a first-class cabin. A fireplace ornamented the back wall, but it was orange with rust.

Suddenly, I longed for heat, the feeling of the sun on my face, or the warmth of a hearth. It was so cold down here, like the eyes of the Drowned had been. The remains of a few armchairs were scattered about the room. I made myself comfortable in one, thankful I didn't fall through it.

Someone was killing Mer and sending hate messages. But who would do this, and why?

They want to start a war.

The words swam into my head as I thought about the endless wars waged on land, fueled by nothing but ancient grudges or greed. But why would the Drowned want to pick a fight with such fearsome creatures? Surely they would lose. Human wars were primarily economic, religious, or political. Perhaps the Drowned wanted to rule the ocean—

"Well, well. What do we have here?"

I stiffened. I had been so lost in thought I hadn't noticed dark figures encircling me.

Pirates. I gulped. They must have followed me from the bar.

My mind darted to the dagger at my waist. My fingers twitched, ready to grab it.

The speaker shuffled into the light—it was Teachie. The tattoos on his chest were visible through his waistcoat, and his long dark hair with its gray streaks was tied back in a ponytail.

"The Mer sank our home, and we don't take kindly to their allies." His awful smile grew.

Port Royal. The Wild West of the Ocean. Swallowing a gulp, I met Teachie's stare.

"There was never a city so perfect. The gambling was wicked, the whores were dirty, and the treasure . . . oh, the treasure." He sighed, and his eyes filled with something that looked like sadness. Then they narrowed. "The Mer didn't like that we had more wealth than they did—so they sank us, they did." He leaned over me, and his breath was foul with rum.

I recognized his accomplice, Rackham. There were only two of them. *Only two.* This emboldened me. The dagger hummed at my side, like it was calling to me with its ancient magic. I reached for the hilt.

"We don't get many girls down here with warm twats," Teachie cackled, and Rackham joined in his slobbery mirth.

"Back the fuck off," I cried, whipping the blade from its sheath and holding it in front of me. It gleamed in the emerald light. I prayed they believed I knew how to use it. I prayed they couldn't see it had been half eaten by rust.

"Rackham," Teachie barked at his sniggering companion.

Rackham began advancing on my right. I twisted in the chair to face him, the blade shining between us.

White lights danced behind my eyes, and I tasted metal—blood—from the inside of my cheek. Teachie had struck me with his ring-covered hand while my attention was fixed on Rackham.

I whirled to face Teachie, waving my knife angrily as pain rippled through me. The lump had returned to my throat. *I will not cry.*

White lights flashed again, and I was blinded by pain.

Cowards!

Teachie grabbed my limp knife arm and twisted it behind my back. "You're only making this harder on yourself," he growled.

"Get your fucking hands off me!" My voice broke with the pain shooting up my wrist.

Teachie cackled, his body heaving against mine, and he used his free hand to pull my head back with my hair.

Rackham approached me. He was skinny, and if possible, he was missing even more teeth than last time I saw him. He pressed his groin against my cheek, and its hardness hurt my bruised face—this was arousing him. I swung my left arm wildly, connecting with Rackham's side, but he only laughed.

This was *not* how I would lose my virginity. I tried to tug my knife arm free, but Teachie held it tight.

"And I thought I'd never be with a living woman again." Rackham laughed, stepping back from me. "Although I wouldn't call you a *real* woman—"

Terror knotted my stomach as he began untying the tattered red sash at his waist and pulling his shirt out from his trousers.

"Please," I tried to beseech Teachie, who seemed to be the leader. He let go of my hair and answered me with another smack across the cheek.

Lights flickered in my eyes again, and when my vision returned, blood from my lip was spilling into the water.

I lashed out at Teachie, but he wrenched both my arms behind my back.

"Shut up, mermaid lover. No pretty boys here to save you now," Rackham growled as he unbuttoned his baggy black pants.

"I'll take this." Teachie plucked the dagger from my hand and tossed it into the darkness. "I might as well take the scabbard too."

Rackham approached, his pants now gaping, and held me against the chair as Teachie sauntered around to stand before me. I threw my shoulders into Rackham's grip, but it was too firm. Too strong.

Teachie folded his tattooed arms across his chest, eyes gleaming as they traveled to the scabbard at my waist. They flitted back and forth, searching the fur between my legs for what I knew was still there. The pirate let out a low growl as he leaned over me, and nausea churned in my stomach as his meaty hands found the curves of my ass, pulling my body toward him.

Foul breath laced with rum washed over me in a scattering of bubbles as he undid the buckle, his breathing growing increasingly ragged against my ear as he slid the belt off me. The sheath whipped from my body and landed somewhere on the floor with a thump.

Rackham was still holding me from behind as Teachie pulled away from my body so we were eye to eye. His scar wound its way from the bottom of his chin across the side of his mouth and around the back of his cheek. My heart was hammering. I was powerless, completely powerless.

This is it—

My stomach twisted from the nausea.

No, this is not it. This is not how I will lose my virginity.

"Don't worry, I'm not going to kill you," Teachie said as his mouth morphed into a malicious grin. "We're just going to have some fun so you can run along and tell your mermaid friends."

Teachie ran a scarred, tattooed hand along my leg. I kicked upward. My webbed foot found matter, and he yelped in pain. I writhed, trying to take this opportunity to escape, but Rackham still held me against the chair.

"I wouldn't have done that if I were you." Teachie surveyed my body, anger and lust flickering in his yellow eyes. "Why don't we see what we have here?" the pirate rasped as he gripped my knees and tried to pull my legs apart. I fought him—with every inch of my being, I fought him. But he was slowly prying them open . . .

This is not how I will lose my virginity.

I steadied my breathing and leaned further back into Rackham, grimacing as his thick fingers dug into my collarbone. The chair groaned beneath me, its decayed fabric exposing rough metal that dug into my spine.

Teachie's malicious grin slackened when he saw what lay between my legs, and panic surged through me, but I harnessed it, channeling it into my limbs. I went still for a moment—deceivingly inviting in a way that made my stomach twist—then flung my weight back with a sharp gasp, slamming into the backrest.

Rackham adjusted instinctively, leaning in to tighten his grip. A devious grin spread across my lips because that was exactly what I wanted. I whipped forward with all my strength and then came slamming back, smashing my skull into his chin. His grip faltered, and I surged upward, twisting free as the chair toppled and splintered against the floor, sending Teachie sprawling to all fours.

"You little wench," Rackham growled, wiping blood from his split lip.

I was already moving, webs slicing through the water as I dove through the doorway and swam down the dark stairs. My throat burned from holding back tears, and my whole body trembled as I surged through a gash in the boat's hull and into the murky waters beyond.

30.

Finn

I shouldn't have left her at the tavern with the Drowned, not with that kind of evil lurking so close, but I couldn't take her to the castle either, to my father.

I paced back and forth in my clifftop fortress. She would be safe with the Captain, yet the nagging feeling lingered. I should have taken her to the surface with me. My restless gaze kept returning to the waves, glimmering in the moonlight.

Had I brought her here, she might have woken and seen me for what I truly was, shattering whatever fragile thing existed between us. Then she would no longer treat me like a human, and she might never forgive me for what I've done.

Selfish. It was selfish of me to leave her there rather than risk revealing myself.

I poured myself a Lagavulin and lit a cigarette. I should be investigating the storms, not obsessing over a girl.

Fuck it, the storms could wait.

I grabbed the glass decanter and headed out the front door, perching myself on the cliff's edge to watch the jetty. Her jetty. Our jetty. Hoping that she would emerge.

But the girl didn't come.

I stood up and paced the cliff face. The grass was soft beneath my bare feet. The sleepy, whitewashed town spread out beneath me, and the waters of the bay rippled under the moonlight. It looked like something from a fucking fairy tale.

What is this girl doing to me?

She was the starlight reflected on the waves, the mist that sometimes coated the isles, wrapping around my thoughts and drawing me into her.

I sat back down, rested my forearms on my knees, and swirled my whisky glass with one hand.

My thoughts wandered to her fur bodysuit and the shape of her breasts when they'd been pressed against my arms. A swell of pain throbbed in my groin as I imagined burying my cock inside her and feeling every inch of her body underneath that damn fur.

She told me that she'd never been with a man. And to think she'd offered all of herself to me. Her body could have been mine to have first, mine to kiss first, mine to adore first.

I would tear her body apart and then worship every piece of it as it broke for me. Then, I'd take the pieces and rebuild a temple in her honor with my tongue.

More blood surged to my dick, and it pressed hungrily at my jeans. I unbuckled them, letting it spring free, and ran my hand down its length, hissing.

One pump, two pumps. I threw my head back.

Everything around me reminded me of her. The ocean breeze in my hair was her hands, the soft sighing of the waves, the noise her full lips would make when they parted and whimpered just for me. But nothing rivaled her eyes—two priceless emeralds. I would spill blood just to ensure they looked only at me.

She didn't just haunt my thoughts; she owned them. She had anchored my soul, and I never wanted to be free.

My body stiffened as more blood shot to my cock, and I pumped harder.

No! This was wrong. I brushed my dark hair from my forehead with one hand, the other still on my cock.

Think of anything but her . . . anyone.

I tried to conjure some of the other human girls I'd been with, but she consumed my mind.

Fuck!

I stuffed my still-hard cock back into my jeans and threw my empty glass against the concrete docks far below. I needed a cure for this ridiculous obsession. To focus.

She deserved better than me. The things I'd done . . . I would only cause her pain.

There was something in the looks she gave me that quieted the monsters inside me, and I would fight every battle, break every rule, just to feel it again.

I had to tell her everything. I raked my hand through my hair as I paced the clifftop. The first rays of the sun were on the distant horizon, and a woman was swimming toward the shore.

31.

MORGANA

The memory of the attack, of the pirates' bloodshot eyes and rough hands, clung to me like seaweed, wrapping around my thoughts and suffocating me as I fought my way toward the shore.

The anti-Mer propaganda, the dead mermaid with her purple features, those red eyes, and the shadows surrounding them—I no longer cared if these horrors were connected. I just wanted to put them behind me. To forget.

Something seethed through my blood and boiled around my bones. I didn't know if I wanted to be sick or if I wanted to smash something to pieces—perhaps both. My eyes burned, and my jaw remained clenched. Rage, nausea, and shame twisted within me like ribbons coiling around my organs, leaving me drained.

Clouds hung low in the sky like hammocks holding too much weight, and the water was dark, but the milky glow of dawn on the horizon comforted me. I suspected I'd only been away a night or two, but I couldn't be sure.

My grandmother's fur coat flapped around my now-human body, and the cold water clashed against my hips as I dragged myself toward the beach.

A silhouette emerged on the boardwalk and quickly descended the rocks.

Shit, it's headed for me.

The waves were just above my knees now, crashing against me like a desperate lover begging me to stay, and my wet coat was heavy on my back.

The figure was almost upon me. Their feet splashed my face with water as they approached, and there was nowhere to run.

I cried out, stumbling forward. At the same time, strong arms wrapped around me. Images of Teachie and Rackham flooded my mind, and I tried to push the attacker off, but my body was still weak from my transition into human form.

I fell, and my would-be attacker lifted me back up. Their touch was gentle, and they pulled my wet fur over my body. So, not a pirate. Not a danger.

The murky shades of dawn illuminated dark features. *Finn.*

I let out a gargle of relief. How welcome his familiar face was at this moment.

His gaze searched mine, and the absurdity hit me. How on earth was I going to explain this?

"I-I, um . . . swimming—again." My teeth were chattering.

Finn's black eyes glistened in the half-light, and I waited for him to pepper me with questions, but he said nothing. Keeping one hand on my back, he used the other to cup my chin, and his eyes darkened as he took in the places where the pirates had beaten me.

"What happened here?" He ran his fingers gently over the skin under my right eye.

I flinched at his touch, the memory of the attack flashing through my mind, and he quickly withdrew his hand.

"I must have hit my head on some rocks," I lied. Badly.

His other hand, still on my back, curled into a fist. "This is all my fault," he breathed.

Tears threatened to spill from my eyes, and all I could do was shake my head.

His black jeans were soaked, and his white T-shirt, which had become wet from my coat, was sticking to his chest. Yet he wasn't trembling with cold like I was. He pressed his body close to mine, and I thought about how many times I had imagined this—imagined my hands on him, digging my nails into his chest.

"This is not your fault," I exhaled. The nauseating thoughts of the pirate's rough hands eddied from my mind as he looked at me.

An inner turmoil seemed to plague his features as his eyes fell upon my lips.

"What are you fucking doing to me?" He sighed, removing his hand from my cheek to rake it through his hair.

"Make me forget . . ." The words slipped from my mouth before I could stop them, and as Finn turned back to me, his features were shadowed by something carnal, but then he looked away again, biting his knuckle as if fighting a battle in his mind.

Before I could second-guess myself, I dragged his face back to mine and kissed him. He stiffened in surprise, but then his tongue swept into my mouth, and I whimpered.

Finn's movements became driven by need as he grabbed my hair, intensifying the kiss. My split lips cried out in protest, but I didn't want to stop. The faces of Teachie, Rackham, and the dead mermaid faded from my mind with his touch.

His lips found my neck, and he pressed his open mouth into it. His intoxicating scent washed over me—a blend of sea salt, cologne, and the smoky trace of whisky, as if he'd tossed back a glass before rushing to meet me.

The water lapped at our ankles, as persistent as the heat building between us, and his lips met mine once more. Our tongues slid against each other, wet, warm, and salty. So this was what it felt like to enjoy a kiss? There was loneliness and pain on his tongue as it searched my mouth, desperate for release. I had never been kissed like this before.

It had been clumsy and rough with other boys, their emotions a nauseating mess. But this . . . this was something else. This was dangerous—the kind of kiss that lingers in your bones, haunting your thoughts for a lifetime.

Finn's hands skimmed my hips and then closed around the fur coat covering my ass as he felt the shape of me. An image of the pirate's grasping hands flickered through my mind. I flinched. Finn noticed and released his grip.

No, this was my choice. I would not let the pirates take this away from me. I arched into him and met a stiffness beneath his jeans. I trembled as an image of Rackham's crotch pressed against my face made it through the throbbing pleasure. Trying to forget it, I ran my hand down Finn's front and cupped the hardness growing there.

"*Fuck*," he rasped into my neck. My hands lingered between his thighs, feeling the length of him pressing against the wet denim of his jeans—but Rackham's rotten grin crawled back into my subconscious.

Reality washed over me in the absence of pleasure.

"Wait, stop!" I pulled myself from Finn's embrace. "You have a fiancée!" As the words came tumbling from my mouth, my heart ached with the weight of the truth.

Finn turned from me, looking out over the ocean. His arms were still at my waist, and part of me wanted to pull him back into me. I chewed on my lips—they tasted of him.

"Forgive me." He let his arms fall from my sides. The wind was in his dark hair, and his white shirt, now soaked, was adhering to him, outlining the muscles in his torso. When he turned back to face me, his impenetrable mask had returned.

"I've tried to fight this because you deserve . . . better. But that's also why I couldn't stay away. " Rubbing the back of his neck, he dragged his gaze from mine.

No, no, *no*. That was not what I wanted him to say. I wanted him to say that it was over with his fiancée and that he was free. Free to kiss me, free to let me run my hands over every inch of his body, free to run his hands over mine. Free to take me here and make me forget about it all . . .

How could I have been so stupid? Perhaps it was because I was still half in my water-world mentality, where anything seemed possible. My heart raced—it was no longer pounding from Finn's touch but from boiling rage that bubbled up somewhere deep within.

"Why are you here, and why now?" Color bloomed on my cheeks. The wind was in my hair, too, and it had begun to pluck at its strands. Like Medusa calling her many snakes to action.

Finn looked bashful for once in his life. "I, ah—intuition," he muttered.

"Why do you continue to seek me out when you have a fiancée? *Why?*"

"I . . . " His face looked pained, as if finding the words he needed to say was a struggle. "I'm sorry," he finally managed. "I'm not a good person or someone you should be around." He hung his head, and the wind toyed with his curls.

"You're the one who's come here and found me!" I cried. Oh no, the lump in my chest was back.

He raised his eyes to meet mine, his expression cold as ice. "It was wrong. Everything I have done with you has been wrong."

Everything I have done with you has been wrong. His words impaled my chest.

A burning line of anger slithered through my being.

Seriously, fuck him.

How was he able to be so cold, so composed, when my emotions were tearing my body to shreds?

"I never want to see you or your split personalities again. Just leave me alone!" My voice broke, as I pulled my wet coat around me. As tears burned my cheeks, I marched out of the surf and onto the damp sand.

I will not let him see me cry.

"Morgana, I've got to talk to you! I can explain," he called after me, still standing in the crashing waves.

I disregarded his cries and clambered up the slick black rocks. As I left the concrete docks behind, the horizon was bleeding into a golden hue. I didn't look back. I didn't want to see Finn standing there.

It dawned on me how crazy I must look striding up this sleepy street in the early morning hours, tears streaming down my bruised cheeks, my red hair wild and wet, wearing nothing but a long fur coat.

The panic of being trapped by the pirates still clung to me. But Finn's kiss had made me forget them. His kiss had made me forget *everything*.

My anger dissipated slightly. What had he wanted to tell me?

Wrong, he said that we were wrong.

32.

MORGANA

It was time Granddad answered some questions.

I hurried up the slick street, past the other stone buildings, their whitewashed walls tinted indigo in the early morning light. The lights were on in my grandfather's house. Good, he was awake.

"Morgana?" he croaked as I burst through the door.

In the dim light of dawn, the hallway seemed to stretch longer than usual.

He emerged from the living room and blocked my path. "Why are you . . . wet?" His eyes fell on the droplets welling at my feet on the wooden floor.

"How long have I been gone?" I scanned his face, searching for any recognition of what I might have been through.

"What—you don't know?" Fear clouded his eyes.

"No, I don't. How long?" I glared at him. My shoulders squared, tension rippling through my muscles.

"It's been two days. Barry said you've not been at work. He's given your job to someone else. What happened to your face?" Questions were exploding from him, but first, he needed to answer mine.

"Tell me about Iona." My voice wavered, but I straightened to my full height.

"I'm glad you're safe. I'm going out." Granddad reached for his jacket, which was hanging on the rack beside me.

I put my hand on top of his and remained in his path.

"Where did this coat come from?" I gestured to the sopping-wet fur.

"I told you, it belonged to your grandmother." He sighed, and his guilt washed over me.

I was right.

"But she didn't get to wear it much, did she?" I rounded on him. "In fact, I'm pretty sure you never let her wear it *at all!*"

"I-I don't know what you're talking about," Granddad stammered, but he walked away from me, back through the living room, toward the kitchen's light. I pursued him to make sure he didn't slip out the back door but found him sitting at the dining table. He was crying.

"I'm sorry. I know you loved her," I said more gently, sliding onto one of the wooden chairs beside him. "I know she had a magic that bewitched you in a way I can never understand. Please tell me how you met her. It's important." I took his calloused hand in mine. The big wooden clock ticked away on the wall behind us.

"I've never spoken o' this to anyone before, not even your mother," he croaked, shaking his head.

"I think it's best that you keep it that way, but I need to know," I whispered, leaning toward him.

Dawn was pervading the kitchen now, making the yellow glow from the light above us obsolete. I wondered if my grandmother was watching as we sat in the very room in which she had lost her life.

Granddad sighed and stared at his tough hands, which lay on the faded white tablecloth. "I first saw Iona when I was naught but seventeen. I wasn't popular as a lad and often went fishing alone on the islands. I remember the day I first saw her like yesterday: a cold autumn morning like this one." He waved a weather-beaten hand. "My father had been yelling at me about chores the night before, and I went out early to avoid him. The sun had not yet risen as I rowed away from the shore. It was blowing a gale, and my fingers were stiff from its iciness. Still, it beat cleaning my room or helping my father gut fish. The sun's rays were only breaching the horizon as I hauled my boat onto the rocky shore o' my favorite island." He ran a hand through his gray hair, his eyes returning to the floor beside the sink where he had found my grandmother's body.

"I began clattering around with my tackle, and there she was, the bonniest lass I had ever seen. She stood waist-deep in the sea, watching me.

"At first, I was frozen. I couldn't take my eyes off her large brown ones. Her long black hair was half-wet and falling across her body, but I could still make out her naked breasts and dark nipples." Embarrassed, he glanced at me, but I bid him to continue. I knew the desire my grandmother had inspired was necessary for the tale.

"Then I realized that she could die out there, naked in the icy water, so I rushed out to save her. But when I reached her, she stood there, not shivering, watching me with those big dark eyes."

I had seen pictures of Granddad as a youth in his cotton shirt and overalls. He'd been handsome back then. That was how I pictured him, splashing through the water toward my grandmother.

"I led her to the shore and gave her my jacket. She sat on the wet sand and watched me, so I told her my name and asked for her own. She managed *Iona*, but no other conversation could be had with her. She was fascinated by me; she touched my clothes and sat close to me. I remember seeing the wee dark heads o' seals watching us from the waves. She smiled at them, but I paid them no mind. I only saw *her*.

"When it was time for me to return home, I begged her to come with me and tried to pull her into the boat. She resisted, so I had no choice but to let her go and leave for home.

"She was in my dreams that night, and I returned to the island the next day, looking for her, but she wasn't there. I asked the neighbors, the grocer, and about the pub, but no one knew her. I recall one old man saying, 'You're in love with a Selkie, lad. It's best to leave it alone.'

"I didn't believe in such things, but still, I didn't see Iona for another month. One evening, as I was about to push my wee boat out, I saw the strangest sight. A group o' seals were resting on the nearby rocks; I could see their silhouettes against the darkening sky. Then, one o' them grew. Its skin seemed to peel away. Where there had been simply rock and sky and the wee dumpy shapes o' seals, there was now the profile of a woman. I knew it was her.

"I ran clumsily toward her, calling her name. She looked up and saw me. This time, alarm filled those inky eyes. She grabbed her skin and dived into the water. The other seals shuffled off the rocks at my approach. I was left alone, searching the darkening horizon.

"On my return home, I decided to find out all I could about Selkies. It was only a matter of time before I discovered that stealing her skin would bind her to me, making her unable to return to the sea.

"I didn't see her again until I was nineteen and fishing on the same isle. This time, I was careful. I kept myself hidden. She'd left her seal skin unguarded and was dancing on the sand, her dark hair moving with her. Now and then, she would dip and trace her fingers along the tide's edge. It was easy for me to creep up behind her and wrap the soft folds of her skin into my chest. I stowed it in my cool box.

"She came home with me that evening, and that year, we were married. I taught her English and made her a home. Folk wondered at my outlandish bride, but I never cared for gossip. After fifteen years, she fell pregnant with your mother."

He sighed. I could see how this tale brought him back to life yet simultaneously broke his heart.

"On our sixteenth wedding anniversary, I made her skin into a coat for her. She had your mother and seemed happy with me. She'd developed a passion for traveling the world, which appeared to bring her joy. I was going to give her the coat as a surprise. She didn't age the same way I did, and I thought if I were to die first, at least let her have the sea.

"On the night o' the anniversary, I remembered the old tales of Selkie wives leaving everything to return to the sea, never to be seen again. I got cold feet. I took the coat and locked it back away in storage. I wish now that I had never seen her. As I got older, I began to notice her sadness. She would sing softly o' the sea to your mother while staring out the window. I knew I had done her wrong but couldn't let her go."

He was crying again. I reached for his leathery hand and held it tight. "I have seen her world," I whispered.

He looked up and smiled, like a wet piece of paper crinkling up. "She would have liked that."

We sat silently for a moment, the milky glow of dawn softening our faces, and then I asked the next question that had been churning within me.

"My father, did you know him?"

"Aye, I knew him," Granddad exhaled.

I chewed on my lip, staring out the kitchen window.

"Rory was a good man, and he loved your mother and you, even though he was taken before he got to know you," he continued, as if he could read my thoughts.

I nodded, unable to speak as tears stung the corners of my eyes.

PART FOUR

Iona

33.

MORGANA

Boxes towered to the attic's ceiling, papers littered the floor, and broken furniture was scattered among dusty statues and rolled-up carpets. My grandmother's old dresser—the twin of the one in my room—stood among the clutter.

A single small window struggled to illuminate the gloom, its light swallowed by stacks of boxes. Dust motes swirled in the sliver of sun, and I needed artificial light even though it was daytime.

It had been a week since I left the watery realm behind, but I found it hard to forget. Every morning, I awoke in a sweat from dreams of deep darkness.

Thoughts of Finn and our kiss plagued my mind, but I would make myself so busy doing chores for Granddad to escape them. I had scrubbed every inch of the house to keep my mind off the deep—and Finn's salty embrace—but now, the attic awaited me.

I felt so many things when we kissed—anger, confusion, guilt—but mostly, I wanted him in a way I'd never felt before.

Sometimes, images of Teachie and Rackham and what they'd done filled my mind, making my heart clamor as if trying to escape my body, just as I had wanted to escape them. My thoughts were a tangle of fear the pirates had instilled and new desires Finn had awoken within me.

I had started thinking of Finn in the early mornings and before falling asleep: how he'd pulled me into him, the hardness of his cock pressed between our bodies—a desire that I had wanted to evoke in him, unlike the pirates.

As I slid my hand between my legs and felt wetness there, I clung to these images for fleeting relief, but that's all they could ever be. After my desires faded, searing anger took its place. Finn was engaged, so even kissing him was wrong. He knew it, too. He had said I was wrong, and *we* were wrong.

Shaking away the rage that had flared at the thought of Finn, I drew a deep breath, and pried open the top box from one of the stacks. Photographs spilled out, and a black-and-white picture of my grandparents' wedding caught my eye. Granddad wore a kilt, smiling as he held my grandmother's arm.

Granddad and I still didn't talk much, but our relationship had deepened. Our silences were no longer awkward; we understood each other. The morning after he told me the story of my grandmother's fur coat, we'd had breakfast in the little kitchen.

"I'm not going back," I told him. Though my words were quiet, my tone was firm.

He only nodded and surveyed the purple bruises the pirates had left on my cheeks.

My grandmother stood taller than him in the photograph, even in flats, and her thick, dark hair was swept into a bun. She was smiling too, but her gaze had a vacant sadness. I wondered why I hadn't noticed it before; her grin was wide, but her eyes were distant. They were off somewhere else, not at this wedding, accompanying her smile.

I shuffled through the rest of the pile. The pictures were all like this. The look in her large brown eyes was absent even when she cuddled her daughter or laughed. Had she borne the same shoulder marking as I had now?

So many questions bubbled up, ones I wished I could have asked her.

"I have seen what you've seen and chose to come back," I whispered, running my finger across the photo's shiny surface.

I stacked the pictures neatly and placed them in a new box labeled "KEEP."

Memories of my grandmother drew my attention to her dresser. Its three expansive mirrors were now covered in dust. I picked my way across the cluttered floor and reached for a drawer. The handle detached when I pulled it, so I set it aside and pried the drawer open from beneath. It was filled with jewelry—an Aztec cuff, little bell earrings that looked like they were from India, and pearls of all different colors and sizes.

The beaded strands were tangled, and as I lifted their mass, I noticed something underneath—a small leather-bound book. "Diary" was embossed on the cover in gilded lettering.

Excitement clawed its way up my throat, but I pushed it down as I carefully retrieved the book. I flicked through the pages. *There is writing!*

There wasn't much, though. I flicked further, but the diary was mostly unused. I opened it to the first entry. The handwriting was messy and childish, but legible.

July 3, 1970

Robbie is sweet, caring, and everything the women in town say I am supposed to marry. I know he feels guilty about what he did—I can see it in his eyes whenever I talk to him. But his love overpowers his guilt, and he will never be able to let me go.

I maintain my powers of intuition, even in human form. Sometimes, I still have predictions, which makes me happy and sad. These skills seem meaningless here. I don't want to sense what time the mailman will be arriving or that the lady next door is having an affair. I want to feel the current change when a storm is brewing or know what Abalone is feeling so I can counsel her. I wonder if I will begin to miss it less, but I don't think that will ever happen. The smell will always drift in through the windows, and the waves whisper in my ear as I sleep, calling me home. It's been a year now, and I miss Abalone the most. Despite knowing it is unsafe for me to return, I have searched high and low for my skin, but Robbie has hidden it well, as I suspected he would.

I put the book down and stared at the dust swirling in the sliver of light from the window. What did she mean, "I suspected he would"? The diary's soft leather was warm in my clammy hands, and I could remember my grandmother's voice again. It was gentle yet musical, like the sighing of the sea.

July 7, 1970

Robbie gave me this book. He said humans use them to write what they feel or what has happened in their day. He said it would help with my English. I only seem to write memories; the things I do nowadays aren't beautiful. They are dreary and not worth writing.

Without my skin, I am aging like a human—I notice fine lines under my eyes that weren't there before.

Robbie taught me how to read and write and brought me beautiful books on the sea, but these gifts do not ease the pain.

When I think of what to write, Abalone comes to mind again. She was from the Kingdom of Thálassa-the smallest of the Mer clans and the closest descendants to Ătlanticus. After the last of my family succumbed to the Shadow, they embraced me as one of their own. Abalone became like a daughter to me, so I accompanied her to the House of Neptūnus when she was sent to unite the kingdoms through marriage.

Today, I smell the salt in the air, and I remember . . . I can see Abalone so clearly. No mermaid could surpass her beauty. Her long purple hair billowed in the swell, and her tail was a glistening green, but it shined fuchsia as she moved in the emerald water.

Sometimes, Abalone and I would walk on land together. When she was with me, we ventured further than the shore. We hid in the hills, watching the women in town in their stifling dresses and pitying them. It's funny and sad, because now I wear dresses like those women.

I enjoyed going ashore and taking my human form. Under the sea, I was a seal, but ashore, I was a seductive woman. I liked how men like Robbie stumbled when they saw me. The first day I met Robbie, he had a lust in his eyes that I knew he couldn't control. This scared me until I needed to use it.

August 8, 1970

Today, I remember how Taranis, King Merrik Neptūnus V's half-brother, used to watch Abalone. Taranis was always a timid merman. He had the Neptūnus family's dark lashes and brows, but his hair was sandy. His tail was opal white, almost transparent. He was a fearsome and sickly beauty.

King Merrik's father, Aalto Neptūnus, was slain in the Battle of Port Royal. Afterward, Queen Vaiana Neptūnus is said to have taken a lover-a knight from another kingdom-before succumbing to the Shadow.

With their mother gone, King Merrik never let Taranis forget he was only his half-brother. He constantly sent him off on errands, as if punishing him for his late mother's indiscretions.

Then, King Merrik sent Taranis away on official business. When he returned, he was different. At times, he was still the timid man I remembered, but other times, a darkness clung to him. Whispers spread that he had learned powerful magic during his time away. Occasionally, he would watch Abalone like before, but other times, his gaze seemed filled with hatred.

On the day that Abalone set her wedding date with King Merrik, I found her crying. As she sobbed, flashes of Taranis kept appearing to me. It wasn't just him wanting her. I saw a scene in which they embraced:

"Amor perdot nos," he whispered as he held her. "Love destroys us."

Abalone stroked his pale face and looked bravely into his red-rimmed eyes. "You will get through this," she whispered.

I couldn't read the thoughts of the other Mer; their magic shielded them from me. With Abalone, it was different-I could glimpse her thoughts when she let her guard down, likely because of how close we were.

A reverberating clang dragged me from my grandmother's world. As the house jolted, I dropped the diary. An echo accompanied it, then silence. Dread pooled in my stomach.

Peering through the dusty window, I saw the sky was clear. But something wasn't right; it was too loud, *too close*. I hesitated, looking at the unfinished diary, then scrambled down the attic's narrow stairs and out the front door.

A few people had emerged on my grandparents' street, drawn by the same sound, their faces etched with concern. They shielded their eyes, gazing toward the cliff where Bayside stood above the docks. *Shit.*

I started jogging toward Bayside, toward Skye and Finn. More people had come out from their houses and were standing there, staring. Cars with flashing sirens rushed past me. A stitch prodded my side.

Don't stop. Keep going.

I sprinted up the winding concrete path, its steep incline pulling at my breath as the pain in my side refused to relent. When I reached the center, I was breathless and heaving, wiping sweat from my brow.

The lane leading to the eateries was filled with people. The shop assistants must have rushed out to investigate the noise. I pushed my way through them, looking for Skye and Finn. The restaurant owned by Aranare's family was closed, cordoned off by red-and-white tape. A dark-haired man stood beneath the carriage-less Ferris wheel, looking up at it. I recognized his khaki-colored jacket, black jeans, and lace-up boots. *Finn.*

What was he doing?

"Morgana!" I heard Skye's squeal before I saw her.

I turned as she emerged from the crowd, teetering in knee-high black boots, arms open for an embrace.

"What happened?" I turned back to the wheel. Some men in yellow hard hats rushed past, and Finn was gone.

"No one knows. It was like a mini earthquake over there or something." She let go of me. "Oh, Morgana. I thought you had gone back to America without saying goodbye. But Finn said you'd be back." She took my hands in hers. Her nails were pearly acrylics with little diamantes on them.

Finn said I would be back, did he? A flicker of anger reignited inside me. It was time I stopped avoiding the situation.

"I miss having lunch with you." Skye sighed. Her hair was still shiny and perfect, but I noticed a hint of purple under her right eye.

"Did you get hurt?" I reached out to touch the bruise.

"No one was hurt. The ground just trembled." She brushed me away.

"But what happened to your face?" I pressed, realizing the bruise was old. She had tried to cover it with foundation.

"It hasn't been easy living with Parker . . ." There was a heaviness behind her reflective eyes, and I sensed the sadness in her. I hadn't noticed it before amid the heightened emotions of the many onlookers. "It's nothing." She picked at her nails, avoiding my gaze.

"Parker did this to you? That fucker!" I balled my fists, thinking of Rackham and Teachie.

"Don't, Morgana . . ." She lifted her eyes to meet mine again.

"Do you want to come and stay at mine for a while?" My throat ached as her sadness washed over me.

"He was just stressed from work. It won't happen again. I'd been out shopping all day and forgot to clean the house. It was my fault." She hung her head.

"Oh, Skye." I sighed, reaching for her hands again. "This was *not* your fault." Although my bruises had faded, I knew what it was like to be bullied by someone stronger.

"Don't start with me, please!" Skye's voice broke; it was high-pitched and desperate. Once, I had sensed that she was unaware of her sadness. Now, it consumed her. It overpowered me, and I faltered under its weight.

"Are you okay?" She leaned forward and looked at me with sincerity.

I pulled myself together. "If you ever need a place to stay—"

"I'm fine." She pulled her sweaty palm out of my grasp, her voice pleading with me to drop it. "I saw Aranare earlier—he was shirtless, fixing something on the roof. The muscles on that guy!" A flicker of happiness permeated her despair.

"Someone's got a bit of a crush."

"Speaking of love, you should try to catch Finn before he leaves." She winked at me.

"What do you mean leaves? I just saw him." I looked toward the wheel again, but there was no sign of him. Fluorescent-shirted workmen were checking it over like flies on a carcass, but its skeletal circle seemed unscathed by the tremor.

"He told me this morning he was returning home for a while. Something about his father. Honestly, the way that guy talks . . ."

"Oh." My heart sank to the soles of my feet. That must have been what he was trying to tell me.

"Go." She nudged me.

◦⁓🐚⁓◦

There was no one in the pawnshop, so I feigned browsing, running my finger across the nearest ornament on the dusty counter—a silver box with Celtic designs carved on the lid. It contained a variety of trinkets: green glass beads, heart-shaped lockets, and rings in multiple colors. Draped over the edge, necklaces jostled for space. One piece drew my attention—a silver chain featuring a detailed key pendant. Its head was embellished with raised spirals, caressing a heart crafted from a plain stone.

Voices were coming from the back room, and I let the key fall from my fingers.

"It couldn't be done. I'm going to tell my father," Finn's voice said.

I battled the warmth that bloomed within me at hearing his familiar tone.

"Your uncle will know it was us, so stay vigilant," Mr. Inegar growled.

"I am nothing if not vigilant." Finn scoffed.

"The girl. I fear you're getting reckless . . ." I could hear Mr. Inegar's sneer.

I stiffened. Were they speaking about his fiancée?

"Watch yourself, old man."

The voices went silent, and Mr. Inegar appeared behind the glass counter, Finn on his heels.

"Can I help you?" Mr. Inegar leered at me from under bushy brows.

"I—" I locked eyes with Finn, but his face fell into a mask colder than any I'd seen him wear.

Mr. Inegar glanced between us, his eyes narrowing suspiciously. I couldn't sense his feelings. I never had. I just hadn't noticed, because he made no effort to hide them.

"Can we talk?" I tried to smile at Finn, but his face remained stony.

Mr. Inegar continued to scowl.

"I can't talk to you right now. I'm busy." Finn's words were flat and cutting. His expression didn't falter as he turned away from me and marched out the back of the shop.

Mr. Inegar continued to glower at me, and I remembered the coins. I scanned the dusty counter, but the bowl had disappeared.

"Where are the coins that were here?" I searched the jumbled contents beneath the glass.

"Must have sold 'em." The man's sharp eyes were tracking my every movement.

"You told me they weren't for sale!" I dragged my gaze across the shelves behind him, but they were nowhere to be seen.

"Well, that was you, wasn't it?" Mr. Inegar began placing items under the glass as if worried I might reach for them next.

I turned on my heel and slammed the door in my wake, my hands curling into fists. I had pondered Finn's possible reactions to our kiss, but this . . . this was worse than anything I had imagined.

34.

Finn

The kiss had stayed with me—sucking on those pouty, salty lips of hers as she devoured mine. I stood at the edge of the grassy cliff, the wind tearing through my clothes as the sea raged against the black rocks far below.

I had planned to tell her everything when I met her in the waves, but it was better to stay away. She despised me for what I'd said, and I'd let her. Better she hated me for this than for the things I couldn't bear her to know. *I would only bring her pain.*

Taking a deep breath, I dove.

As the water engulfed my body, my clothes shredded, dissolving into the depths as if they'd never existed. Slits tore open along the sides of my neck, flesh parting like the petals of a Venus flytrap. The gills flared, sucking hungrily at the water as if tasting the ocean for the first time. A shimmer rippled across my legs as they fused, bones shifting and stretching. Scales blossomed like emeralds across my skin as my feet melded into a powerful crimson-tipped tail fin. I rose to the surface, my torso breaking the water, and I brushed my wet hair from my forehead, my tail now easily keeping me afloat in the swell.

Inegar suspected something was going on between us, that I might be withholding information from my reports. I couldn't let him see how she affected me.

Yet the heartbreak in her eyes when I'd turned her away cut deep, even as it stirred a dangerous flicker of hope. Perhaps she felt the same.

No, she couldn't . . . The feelings churning inside of me were all-consuming. She was the undercurrent pulling me in, the force I could not fight. Even if I could break free, I wouldn't want to. She was in my bones, my blood, the spaces between every breath. No force in the sea or sky could pull her from my thoughts.

She'd told me to leave her alone, and that's what I would do—even if it meant breaking her heart. My focus had to be on saving my people and redirecting my father's curious eyes.

She hadn't returned to the Kingdom of the Deep. I'd been watching from afar. Maybe the Drowned had driven her away for good. But if she ever chose to come back, I would make sure they never touched her again.

35.

MORGANA

I was sitting against the attic wall, under the only window, using the shards of light it relinquished to peruse the rest of my grandmother's diary.

November 30, 1982

I often think about the day I followed Abalone to Taranis's chambers.

Queen Abalone and King Merrik had been married for some time and had a son-Prince Aigéan. Abalone had done her duty to the realm. Taranis hadn't attended the wedding. He'd disappeared from the Neptūnus Kingdom that day, and many years had passed before he returned.

I should not have trailed Abalone, but I sensed something terrible might happen. I could see her and Taranis arguing through the strands of beaded seaweed that shrouded the door to the bedroom within his chamber.

"Please, Abalone, meet me in the garden tonight like we used to," he begged her. His shaky voice reminded me of the Taranis I had once known.

Abalone let out a choked cry, and I swam further into Taranis's chambers. They were hewn of dark sand, and there was clutter everywhere. Contraptions, papers, and maps were strewn all around-things he must have gathered on his travels.

I parted the seaweed strands with my flipper.

"You know this is what my family wants . . . and I have my son now." Abalone was looking into his red-rimmed eyes.

Taranis's face was gentle for a moment, then it was as though a shadow passed across it, and his eyes glimmered. "I can give you a kingdom, if that's what you want."

"This is not you. You can fight it," she whispered pleadingly.

It was then that a piece of parchment caught my eye. It was tacked to the rock wall, scribbled in the Runes of the Ocean.

"Only with blood that need not be taken is the curse shaken."

The words made my heart beat faster, and then I read the scrawled text above it: "The Prophecy of Cerulean Templum."

All Selkies knew of the prophecy and the story of the Drowned and Mer's feud, which started with a Selkie, Siana Selich, my great ancestor.

Could Taranis have found part of the second half of the prophecy? The part that was lost . . .

I was overcome with a terrifying sense of dread as a vision washed over me. I would die at the hands of a merman.

Abalone's sob from the next room brought my body back to life. I scooted from the chambers and ducked behind a cluster of seaweed just in time to see her racing from the place.

Taranis appeared in the doorway of his cavern. He whispered, "Amor perdot nos," after the disappearing tail of the mermaid he'd once loved.

As I swam through the courts, I wondered if anyone else had seen the parchment. I glanced at the Mer guards. They were holding spears, their torsos rippled and eyes fierce. The legends blamed all Mer misfortune on this "prophecy." Which one would do the deed? My visions were barely ever wrong.

Fearing for my safety, I sped to the surface and presented myself to Robbie for a third time. As I expected, he stole my skin. We rowed across the dark waters back to Ruadán's Port, his home, which would now be mine.

The seals I swam with watched us from the waves. Tears streamed down my cheeks as I looked into their beautiful, dark eyes. I would never swim with them again. The Mer would find me eventually, but this would buy me time. I vowed to spend my time on land searching for the rest of the prophecy. I suspected what Taranis had found on that parchment could not be the whole story. I would travel to all the museums and ancient sites until I found what had been lost in Ãtlanticus.

January 1, 1984

Robbie never complains when I book yet another ticket to a foreign country. It eases his guilt. Sometimes, I take my only friend in this town, Louisa Williamson, with me. She is a young historian passionate about ancient civilizations.

I am with child, and some days, I feel so exhausted that I sleep all day. When I sleep, I dream of the sea; it's always been the sea. The child means I have had to stop my travels for a while. Sadness has taken hold of me.

July 24, 1988

My daughter, Anna, is four now. My heart worries, knowing that she, too, will be a descendant of Siana. Would they come for her? I let Robbie name her. Anna means "favored by God," he says. I hope the gods will favor her.

December 12, 1988

We found something: a stone tablet in the Mediterranean with a poem about the prophecy. It was partially destroyed, but we could translate more of the text. I am not the one of whom the prophecy speaks. I cannot write more here in case it falls into the wrong hands. Some things might be better lost . . .

I barely noticed my trembling body or fractured breaths as I let the diary fall to the dusty floor. Had the attic grown colder? I folded my arms around myself and leaned my head against the wall.

Siana Selich. I was a relative of Siana Selich.

The blood was pounding in my ears in unison with my heart. The prophecy—after trying and failing to find any books on the subject under the sea in the Taberna, I couldn't believe I had read these words on land and in my grandmother's diary. Had my grandmother's death been a murder?

36.

MORGANA

Aranare looked up from the paperback he was reading as I burst through the bookshop's front door, the sweat on my brow turning to droplets. I doubled over, drawing shuddering breaths.

Could this Taranis character have been in my grandparents' house? In the kitchen, I ate in each day? I pushed past my heaving chest, winding my way through the narrow aisles to the counter at the back of the store.

"Are you okay?" Aranare's amber eyes flooded with concern as he took in the state of me.

"I . . . I need to . . . speak with Louisa," I gasped, still struggling to breathe after my jog up the hill.

Aranare shut his book and glanced toward the back room. The older woman from my grandmother's funeral appeared in the doorway, her body a silhouette against the yellow glow inside.

"Morgana, it is a pleasure to see you again."

She moved into the store's dim light. Her short gray hair was sleek and straight, and she wore a sweater with the same loose brown slacks I'd seen her in before.

Louisa, the historian. Louisa, the woman who had been friends with my grandmother. The woman who might know something about the prophecy. Aranare's mother. I glanced between them.

"Tell me what you know about my grandmother—about . . . the prophecy." I was still panting. I cursed my lungs, wiping perspiration from my forehead.

"Shall we sit down?" Louisa gestured to the back room. I sensed gentleness from her, and a flicker of something: fear. The same fear I'd felt that day on the beach when she'd observed me.

I didn't move, but Aranare was at my back, and his touch was warm as he escorted me. I shook him off but continued toward the table and chairs in the back.

"Tell me what you found out about the prophecy," I demanded again, eyes narrowed on Louisa as I slid into one of the seats.

"Hush." She motioned to her lips. "It is not wise to yell about such things."

"Well . . ." I continued to stare at her.

She moved to a small kitchenette, filling a stainless steel kettle with water. Only when its boiling whistle filled the room did she turn to me.

"After your mother moved you to the middle of America, as far away from the ocean as possible, we thought you'd be safe. We didn't think it would come to this." Louisa sighed.

"Come to what?" I ground out.

"'One of both Drowned and Selkie lines is the answer, the curse's sign.'" She recited the words in a whisper over the kettle's brewing. "We were initially relieved when we found more of the prophecy. It did not name Iona or Anna; perhaps there were other relatives of Siana Selich in hiding."

"But then my father drowned . . ." The kettle reached a piercing peak as the realization washed over me. The prophecy named me. Unlike my grandmother, who'd transformed into a seal, I transformed into something else—the fur that covered my body was ragged and sparse. My human form was still visible underneath. I was not a true Selkie—I was half Drowned.

"So you know about . . . me being . . . a shifter?" I looked from Louisa to Aranare. The words felt so strange to say out loud on land. Aranare's eyes were wide, and I sensed his surprise, but Louisa's face remained passive. I sensed sadness.

"I knew Iona was a shifter. I didn't know you would be." Her brow creased. "After your father's death, we wondered if you might have inherited powers—the powers of the Selichs. We wondered if we should train you, raise you to embrace those powers and fulfill the prophecy. To fight the evil we knew would seek you. But your mother was devastated by your father's death. She bundled you up and moved you far away from the ocean that broke her heart."

"B-but my grandmother visited me in America. She never mentioned my father's drowning. I never knew." My voice was cracking.

"She thought that knowledge might draw you back here. We saw your mother's reaction to your father's passing as a blessing; perhaps you could escape the prophecy."

Anger bubbled within me. "A blessing!" My words were sharp as a blade, but tears appeared on my cheeks. "Do you have any idea what I've been through?" I thought about the pirate's rough hands, the dead mergirl, and the red eyes—always watching me.

I glared between the two of them.

"I'm sorry," Louisa whispered.

"D-do you think Taranis killed my grandmother?" I asked, swallowing the lump in my throat.

Louisa's eyes widened, as if she hadn't been expecting me to know so much. She glanced at Aranare and nodded. He slipped from the room. I could hear him rifling around on the wall behind the counter. The wall that held the rare books. He returned with a dark leather-bound volume. It had no title and was fraying in places.

"Taranis is no longer himself." Aranare's throat bobbed as he set the book on the table before me.

"What is this?" My head whipped between him and his mother.

"It's my research." Louisa's tone was grave. "After your grandmother's death, I started piecing together the things she had told me about the Mer kingdoms and Taranis . . . How he had changed."

She leaned over me and flipped the book open to a marked page. The pencil sketch made my blood chill. It was a horse, but its eyes were glistening chasms on either side of its skull. Its black mane draped from its bony body like wet vines as it emerged from the ocean. A cold shiver ran down my spine. Its eyes contained a glimmer of red.

"Wh-what is it?" My voice shook.

"There is a story written in Gaelic. It tells of death's shadow taking the form of a horse. It would wander by the waters and lure people onto its back, then gallop into the water and drown them. Each-uisce, they called it," Louisa said gravely, flicking forward a few pages to another drawing. This time, the horse was underwater, and it had the glistening tail of a fish.

"The people of Crete described this to me." She ran her fingers over the new sketch. "They said death took the form of a Hippocampus horse. With each drowning, he collected more souls and grew stronger. Kelpies, water horses, kappas . . . throughout mythology across the world, there have been stories of animals drowning humans." She sighed.

"Manannán," I whispered, a shiver rippling through me.

Louisa nodded. "He appeared throughout different folklore, and each narration chilled me further as I remembered what Iona had told me. Manannán was stripped of his godly form after the battle of Cerulean

Templum, but he's been attaching himself to animals for centuries, no doubt hoping to return to power. I now believe the spirit of Manannán found Taranis on his travels."

"So you think it was Taranis possessed by Manannán who killed my grandmother." Winter had seeped into my bones. *Red eyes and shadows.* I thought of the merman I had seen in the Therme Skótos forest and my dreams. *He called me Siana.*

Louisa nodded.

"'The spirits of Siana and Manannán must return, for only then shall the clans truly learn . . . only with blood that need not be taken.'" I whispered the other parts of the prophecy we knew. "So you're saying my blood could end the feud . . ."

"*No!* We have no idea what that sentence about blood relates to. So much is still missing. All we know is that you have a role to play. I have to find the rest." Louisa's eyes were stern, and she crossed her arms.

"What do you think Taranis plans to do?" My hands were trembling.

"My guess would be to overthrow the Mer and regain his power." Aranare's tone was grave.

The Mer strung up on crosses.

"You knew all this!" I rounded on him.

"I didn't know about the prophecy or your family's connection to this, but I have been helping Mom research Manannán. Our family has a vested interest in the feud," he said, eyes narrowing on Louisa.

She looked at her son, and pain shadowed her features. "I didn't tell you or anybody about the prophecy because I wanted to keep you safe. Knowledge of the prophecy is power." I felt her agony as she said this. "But now you know, and like Morgana, you are in danger."

Anger coursed through me. My grandmother and Louisa had kept all of this from me, and now, coming here and asking about it, I had unwittingly put Aranare in danger.

"You saw me at the funeral! You could have pulled me aside and said something." My balled fists were shaking.

"I was scared. I thought maybe it was best to leave it alone . . . But it's not too late," Louisa whispered.

Aranare had moved to my side. He put his hand on my shoulder.

"Don't . . ." I shook him off, pushing out of my chair.

My heart was thundering as my thoughts spiraled. My grandmother had been murdered, and whoever did it could be looking for me. From the sound of it, my presence alone could be putting Louisa and Aranare at risk—and maybe even my granddad, Finn, and Skye. The dingy bookshop's confined space began to feel suffocating. This was all too much. I needed to get out. To think.

I stumbled back toward the entrance and the gray afternoon light, but I turned in the doorway to hear Louisa call my name.

"Power comes from in here." She tapped her heart.

I shoved the door shut, and the little crooked "BOOKS" sign tinkled behind me.

The ocean's sighing calmed my pattering heart as I walked back toward the bay. My grandmother had kept this from me my whole life, and now I had to face it alone—to discover it on my own.

My grandmother had known her blood wouldn't work because she was not of Selkie *and* Drowned. She could have told Taranis when he came for her, but she didn't; she died to keep the prophecy's secrets. She died to save me. My stomach turned as the realization washed over me.

I swallowed but couldn't bring myself to move.

She died to save me.

The Mer blood graffiti, the knifed fishtail, and the young mermaid drifting away from me, her one good eye wide and unblinking—were these occurrences all related to a prophecy that I have something to do with?

How many more people might die because Louisa and my grandmother had allowed me to be sent away? They hadn't given me a choice, but I had one now.

The rest of the prophecy had to be found. No doubt Taranis was searching for it if my grandmother's blood hadn't worked, but finding it could take years, and I had no idea where to start. In the meantime, I had to try and do something . . . *anything*.

I held my hands out in front of me; they were trembling.

When I got home, Granddad wasn't there. Perhaps he was still at sea or in the pub with his friends. I ripped out the first pages of my grandmother's diary, which revealed she'd wanted to be trapped. Then I wrote a quick note and left them underneath it on the kitchen table.

I'm going back. I think she would have wanted it, and I think she would have wanted you to have this.

It was time Granddad knew the truth about her skin. It was time he found some peace.

As I walked toward the beach, the sky was clear over the bay, my hands nestled in my grandmother's fur coat pockets. The waters were a deep blue as the last light danced on the ridges of the swell. I strode into the waves until they were about my waist. Then, as the sun's dying rays glimmered on the skyline, I dived.

Come ye drunken sailors to the bottom of the sea . . . the sea . . .

PART FIVE

The Kingdom of Neptūnus

37.

MORGANA

The bar was unusually quiet. A group of Drowned men were sitting at a long table, loudly exchanging stories about the women they'd seen naked in their lifetimes.

"I once saw a woman with pubes as red as a sunrise!" a man in a 1950s suit and hat who resembled Humphry Bogart slurred.

"Tssss, that's nothing," a dark-skinned man said, leering. "I once had a woman with two great melons. She let me suckle at her teats like a babe." The group guffawed, and they all continued to speak over one another, slamming their rum bottles down whenever one told of a particularly exciting encounter.

I couldn't see Teachie's scarred face anywhere, nor Rackham and his beaded braids. I breathed a sigh of relief but then sucked it back through my teeth—they could be out committing more villainies.

I couldn't stop my eyes from searching the bar, seeking traces of Rory in every face, but my father wasn't there. Edward said there were Drowned boats all over the world's oceans. I supposed he could be in any of these.

Perhaps he had awoken here and then migrated elsewhere, like some other Drowned had.

The Captain was polishing tumblers behind the bar, and he smiled as I approached.

"I've been doing some reading..." I ran my finger along the slime-covered surface of the counter, choosing my words carefully. "I read about Manannán. Is—is it possible he could come back here?"

"Manannán was banished three thousand years ago. This is my ship now."

A feral gleam was in the Captain's good eye. Then he softened, a grin tugging at his lips as he filled a brown glass bottle from the rum tap. He handed it to me, and I took a swig, warmth spreading through me as the rich spiced liquid burned down my throat.

I exhaled in relief. We should be safe here—but what about out there? My gaze shifted to the dark portholes.

The Captain reached under the bar and rose again stiffly, holding my dagger and scabbard. "I think this is yours."

"Thank you." Tears peeked at the corners of my eyes as I remembered how I'd lost it. I swallowed, tucking it under my arm.

<hr />

I found Edward in the games room, seated on one of the high-backed couches, engrossed in a chess match with Daniel, the good-looking man in military uniform.

"Checkmate." Daniel smiled. His white teeth had not yet succumbed to the ocean's decay.

"Now, observe—*this* is how one plays chess. Next time I'll beat you, old sport." Edward gestured to the board.

"In your dreams." Daniel brushed his brown fringe from his face and winked at me before wandering off to join some elderly ladies playing cards at a table nearby.

"I'm sorry I ran off on you," I told Edward, toying with the bottle in my hands.

"It is I who should apologize." Edward's eyes had changed—softened, or maybe saddened. "I've been chastising myself over the way I spoke to you. The Drowned curse of envy got the better of me." He sighed and fiddled with a white pawn. "Since you've been gone, I've realized I am a total prat!"

"It's okay. I know you didn't mean it." I leaned into his space. "I've got to talk to you about something important."

His expression fell into a frown as I recounted everything that had happened since I'd left him.

"That's why I need you to take me to the Mer kingdom immediately," I finished, gripping the table with both hands and peering hopefully into his blue eyes. I'd go alone if I had to, but I would prefer to go with Edward.

He was silent; he looked as though he was taking in everything I had said bit by bit. I watched him impatiently as he chewed on his lip.

"Don't you think Queen Abalone needs to know that it could be her ex-lover killing her people?" I pressed.

"I saw Abalone but once . . . She was indeed beautiful." Edward inhaled a slow breath and then let it out with a sigh. "But Morgana, Abalone is dead."

"*How?*" I gasped.

"It is said she died at the hands of an enemy to the crown." Edward propped his chin on his freckled wrist in thought.

"My grandmother's diary said there was a prince—Prince Aigéan. I think we need to speak with him." I blinked at Edward, thinking about the dark-haired merman and his white-bellied dolphin.

"But the prince is reputed to be the cruelest of them all." Edward's jaw tightened.

"What about the murders? We need to warn them! Perhaps no one knows about *Taranis*." I whispered the last part, as if saying his name might make the beautiful pale merman possessed by the God of the Drowned materialize behind me.

"I don't think we should risk our lives for the Mer. What have they ever done for us?" Edward fiddled with the pawn and avoided my gaze.

"There's something else." I hesitated, and my cheeks warmed. "My grandmother believed a child descended of both Drowned and Selkie could end the feud and be the key to fulfilling the prophecy. She believed that child to be me." I cast my eyes to the floor. It felt so crazy to say it out loud. To even think that I could be unique—the chosen one. I didn't say anything about the possibility I might have inherited the Selich's powers, because that was just way too much.

"You're related to Siana?" Edward hissed, glancing about the room again, but no one was watching us. "I knew it . . . I just knew it." He shook his head.

"My grandmother spent her whole life searching for the prophecy, and I think this Taranis character—possessed by Manannán—killed her for her blood, and I think he killed Abalone also. Now he's using Teachie and Rackham to murder Mer."

Edward's face paled, and he looked at me like I had gone insane.

"I can still see that dead mergirl's face when I close my eyes. I have to see if I can do . . . something." I sat back in my chair and stared at him.

"But the Mer hate us." Edward looked exasperated.

"Yet one saved my life." I folded my arms and continued to pierce him with my stare.

Edward said nothing. His brows were furrowed as he chewed on his cheek.

"This could be your chance to experience the history you're passionate about firsthand. Don't you want more than this existence?" I gestured around the games room.

As if on cue, a round-bellied chef let out a loud burp, muttering, "Don't mind if I do" before tipping his head back and letting more rum pour into his gullet, turning his uniform brown.

I chose my next words carefully. "My friends are in danger because of me, and I could be next. I would rather get to the bottom of it now than sit here waiting for those red eyes. Don't you want to see if we could end this feud?" I clasped my hands together as I surveyed Edward. Even as I said the words, they felt ridiculous. How could I end a three-thousand-year-old dispute? But I had to try. I had to warn the prince, at least.

A heaviness built around Edward's eyes, and defeat pervaded his freckled face.

"Very well"—he sighed—"but I shall only get as close to them as absolutely necessary."

38.

MORGANA

The ocean shadows felt darker now that I knew the God of the Drowned was somewhere searching for me. The tavern's glow illuminated the debris strewn around the ship—twisted metal jutting out, coins scattered like forgotten relics, their value meaningless in this other world.

It didn't feel like I had the powers of Siana Selich. What would my life have been like if my grandmother and Louisa had trained me in the ocean's ancient magic instead of letting me be taken away?

"Wait," Edward called as I stepped out of the last sliver of the ship's light. He was looking at the blade I'd rehung from my side. "You are going to need some of this." He plucked a blue bottle from his maroon uniform—the preservation potion we'd bought at the Taberna.

I laid the dagger and sheath on the sand between us and knelt beside Edward to observe. The blade's surface was marred by patches of greenish rust, its once-sharp edge dulled by time. The rune patterns were faint beneath the corroded surface, but the two red stones gleamed from either side of the swirling engraving. Though tarnished, it seemed to emanate an ancient magic—I sensed it. What battles had it witnessed?

Edward handed me the bottle. It was filled with a clear, luminous liquid. Uncorking it, I sprinkled a few drops onto the metal. I sucked in a breath as the rust started to dissolve. It was as if it were being erased by an invisible hand as the potion worked its way into every crevice, revealing the blade's proper form. The copper began to gleam with a renewed luster, its intricate engravings becoming more pronounced.

Holy shit! I held it to the jade light and pressed my finger to its edge. *Ouch.* A drop of blood seeped from the cut before the ocean licked it clean.

"I thought you'd appreciate that." A grin split Edward's face. "Even though I was mad at you, I kept this bottle safe, and your silly children's book is in my cabin."

After enduring Edward's many sighs and grumbles about his aching bones, we reached the emerald waters, and I knew we were getting close to the Taberna.

We followed a sandy path through a towering ravine. Colors were bursting from every crevice, and the surface felt almost carpeted as I ran my hands along the edges. Delicate grass fans swayed gently with the ocean's ebb while red and yellow coral clusters nestled in cracks.

Soon, the water brightened further, revealing small kelp forests undulating in the current. Schools of fish darted in shimmering waves, weaving through rocky outcroppings.

"I know where we are!" I exclaimed as we passed under a stone arch bearing the remnants of runes. *Archōn Agorá.*

The tumbled ruins sprawled before us, flecks of debris swirling in the pale blue water like glittering mist. The dark cavern appeared, and our surroundings felt suddenly colder as I remembered the hooded creature vanishing into its depths. We were beyond the Captain's protection now.

"We'll take the path across the dunes," Edward said, as though sensing my apprehension. He veered left through the tumbled boulders.

Edward traveled even slower here, constantly stopping to empty sand from his leather boots. Despite the urgency in my chest to speak with the Mer and their prince, I was glad to have him by my side. As we scaled one of the towering dunes, I realized how small we must appear. The dark cerulean water enveloped us, its color staining the ground beneath our feet.

From the crest of the largest dune, rolling sand hills spread into the distance, dotted with occasional patches of algae and scattered rocks. An isolated structure caught my eye. At first, I thought it might be a watchtower—until it began to move.

"What is that?" I pulled Edward to a halt by the sleeve of his uniform.

"That's strange. I don't remember it being there before." He followed my gaze, rubbing the copper stubble on his jaw.

"It's Drowned," I hissed. The shapes ahead were vague, yet unmistakably human.

"No, I think it's Mer. I can see a silver tail."

Fear knotted my stomach as I dragged Edward onto the sand beside me. There were three Mer. They hung still and suspended with their backs to us, their arms outstretched across three wooden crosses. The one in the middle had a silver tail. What moved were the black-clad figures around them. There were also three of them, and they were binding the final mermaid's wrists to one of the poles.

My webbed hands clenched into tight fists, nails pressing into my palms. I couldn't discern the villains' features, only the outlines of their cloaks and hoods silhouetted against the aquamarine backdrop.

"We have to do something." My throat constricted as I surveyed the scene.

"We can't!" Edward spluttered.

Who was up there beneath the cloaks? Was it Teachie and Rackham—or was it Taranis? *A plan. We needed a plan.*

"I'm not risking my life for the Mer. They didn't save me when I was dying—and we *can* still feel pain, you know," Edward muttered, refusing to look at me.

"Fine! I hope you enjoy watching comfortably from up here."

I took a deep breath. *Stay calm.*

None of the Mer seemed to be struggling. I peered at their limp bodies, and fear gripped my insides with frosty hands. A silvery substance was floating in the water—Mer blood.

I had to act *now*.

I inched forward along the dune's crest, mimicking the cadets crawling in those army movies I'd always found boring. What would Tom Cruise do? I regretted not paying more attention to them now.

"Okay, I'll assist with this madness." Edward's breathless whisper at my side brought my commando roll to a halt. There was determination on his pale face, and the inklings of a plan came to me. It was a terrible one, but it was all I had to work with.

"So let me get this straight: you want me to dance around in front of what could be the spirit of Manannán." Edward's eyes widened when he heard what I was thinking.

"Do you have a better idea?"

Edward shook his head, gulping down his fear.

"Good luck." I slid my hand over and squeezed his cold one.

Sand flew around me as I skidded toward the bottom of the dune, where the crossbars stood. I could no longer see Edward. I scrambled upward; dust clouded my vision, but I used the tops of the crosses as guideposts.

A cry rang out, and I froze. They had Edward.

All their backs would be turned now, focusing on the intruder. This was my shot.

I was at the top of the dune before I was ready. The crosses towered above me, their shadows spreading eerily across the sand. They were crudely fashioned out of thick driftwood planks. The Mer were large, too; there was the blonde girl I had seen the hooded figures tying up. The merman in the middle had graying hair and a silver tail, and the young boy on the end had a cobalt tail.

Edward's cry drew my attention back toward him. He was stooped on the ground as the cloaked figures surrounded him. They were only nine feet away, in the shadow of the crosses. I could only hope Edward kept them distracted long enough for me to free the Mer.

"P-please. I was merely walking and happened upon you," he stuttered.

My gut twisted. Perhaps I had been wrong to force him to help me. If anything happened to him, it would be all my fault. I wanted to come to his defense—my whole being yearned for it—but foolish or not, we were here now, and I had to use this time wisely. I approached the young boy first. His body hung listlessly. Was he dead, or drugged, or both? I couldn't tell.

My hands were shaking as I withdrew my dagger and began to cut the ropes at his wrists. I could barely reach them and had to stand on tiptoes. Luckily, his heavy, floppy tail was long enough to hide behind.

"What shall we do with him?" The shortest cloaked figure gestured to Edward.

"Kill him," one of the taller figures hissed. He had an Irish accent.

That's strange. I didn't remember Teachie or Rackham having Irish accents.

The other tall man put his hand against his comrade's chest. "If he is indeed here spying, we ought to find out how much he knows." He had an eloquent English accent like Edward's.

"I'm no spy," Edward persisted. "And I can't even see your faces."

They were wearing masks under their hoods. Cowards.

One of the merboy's wrists slipped free, falling limp at his side. I turned my attention to his other hand when I caught sight of a familiar shimmer in the water—blood. Where was it coming from?

My fingers searched his waist for splits, finding only the smooth contours of his abs. I returned to slicing at the final knot.

"A solitary stroll—how very unlike you, Edward. We know your time is spent with that Mer-loving wench." The English man kicked Edward in the stomach, and he convulsed.

They know his name!

My stomach felt like someone was wringing a sheet out inside it. The ropes binding the Mer boy's wrist suddenly gave way, and horror gripped me as his unconscious body drifted forward into the crowd gathered around Edward.

Shit!

The men spun around, and I raised my dagger, hands trembling.

"Well, if it isn't the little wench herself," said the masked man with an aristocratic drawl.

"Seize her," his tall Irish companion muttered.

The shorter, bulky man rounded on me. His mask's gold coloring had tarnished. Its two eyes were shut, but underneath them, carved slits allowed the wearer to look out, and its mouth curved downward.

The man continued circling me, rounding his shoulders and grunting. I spun to face him as he moved, keeping the dagger between us.

Something whistled past me, followed by a heavy thud. I didn't dare take my eyes off my assailant, but a knot of fear tightened in my chest—I could only hope Edward was unharmed.

The sound came again, this time closer, and something grazed my cheek—an arrow had missed my head by inches.

"I'm getting fed up waiting for this idiot to do his job," said the shooter—the man with the Irish accent. He was pointing a crossbow at me. "Drop your dagger, or the next one won't miss."

The bulky man retreated with his head bowed.

With the crossbow pointed at me, I let my dagger fall. Suddenly, I remembered where I'd heard the men's voices. "Jackie?" I yelled, "And Donahue?"

I glanced at Edward to see if he too had recognized them. His pale face had turned crimson, and shock widened his eyes.

Jackie pulled at the front of his golden mask, revealing his sallow face. His dirty-blonde hair billowed from inside his cloak, and his cheekbones protruded where bits of skin had peeled away.

Donahue also removed his mask and tossed it onto the sand. His dark-featured face, which I'd once thought handsome, looked foul, with eyes sunken and locks of hair falling away from his scalp.

Silver stained the hollows of both their faces.

Then it hit me. I had seen Donahue somewhere before—not down here, but on land! His long cloak rippled in the current, mottled patches of his skin peeling away. Veins ran like molten rivers beneath its ruined surface, glimmering with silvery streaks. Donahue was the man Skye and I had seen at the base of the Ferris wheel. But how was that possible?

"I demand you release these poor Mer at once, or I will go to their king and disclose you." My voice trembled. What the hell was I doing?

Edward shook his head vigorously at me, still crouching on the ground.

"That will be hard when you're dead." Jackie let out an awful laugh, again cocking his crossbow at my head.

I glanced at the suspended Mer. Was it too late for this chivalry?

Then I saw the source of the blood. Their wrists weren't just bound—they were pinned to the wood by arrows. Shimmering liquid seeped from the puncture wounds, dripping into small vials fastened to the crosses.

They are collecting Mer blood! A surge of rage burned through me.

"You can't stand that the Mer are more powerful than you'll ever be! You even had to drug them before you could apprehend them, didn't you?" I glared between Jackie and Donahue. "What was it, poisoned arrows? Where is the authority in that?"

Donahue laughed. "The Mer Kingdoms falter, beset by the Shadow. Too long have I witnessed them idly bask within their grand castles while we plead for a draft of preservation potion. Once, I was a nobleman. When the Mer Kingdoms fall, the Drowned shall reclaim their nobility."

"And how do you plan to overthrow the Mer? You have no powers." I had to keep them talking, *bragging*.

"He that we serve has powers drawn forth from the souls of each of us—even yours, Edward." Donahue jerked his chin at my friend, still kneeling on the sand. "Now, he commands an army."

Taranis. They must be working for Taranis.

"An army of the Drowned couldn't match the Mer's powers," I spat.

"Even now, the pirates of Port Royal gather their strength. With them and our other Drowned brethren, we number thirty thousand strong. Let them dare to challenge us." Donahue cackled.

"Enough! Let's kill them and be done with this." Jackie moved the crossbow from my head to my heart. His skeletal fingers flexed unnaturally around the weapon, glimmering silver.

"No!" Donahue cried. "He wants her alive once this is finished. She's made our job easier by coming to us. Seize her properly this time—she is unarmed," he told the short assistant.

Their servant, who had also removed his mask, turned out to be the new puffed-up Drowned boy. He rolled his shoulders, but I barreled straight at him. He swung his bulbous fists at my head, but somehow, I managed to duck beneath them and charge his legs. I wrapped my arms around them and heaved. He didn't budge. *Shit.* I tried again, but he scooped me up in his meaty fists and held me against his chest. I struggled, thrashing and clawing against him, but his grip was rock hard.

"Good work, Bron." Jackie sniggered.

"How could you do something like this?" The outburst had come from Edward. He glared up at Donahue.

"It was rather easy—we conjured storms to swell the ranks of the Drowned. We sowed whispers of the merfolk's misdeeds, and then we created hate crimes to embolden the angry Drowned and rally them to our cause." Donahue sneered from behind his sunken cheekbones. "We sent emissaries from Port Royal to every Drowned ship across the seas, gathering more to join our cause. I believe you had the . . . pleasure of meeting Teachie and Rackham." His top lip curled as he turned his eyes on me.

"Wait, *you* are creating the storms?" A white-hot rage flared inside me.

"Yes. The Mer tried to stop us, and they failed. With every storm, our army grows, and the more Drowned, the greater *his* power." Donahue's eyes glittered.

"You're despicable," Edward spat.

"We've lingered too long. We'll bring the seal girl to him—kill the Drowned boy if you can, and the Mer." Jackie yawned.

"No!" I cried, struggling with all my might against Bron's muscly arms.

Please. I cast my eyes to the watery green above us, trying desperately to call upon my so-called "powers," but I felt nothing.

"Perhaps we ought to bring him too?" Donahue jerked his head at Edward.

Jackie turned sharply on him. "Why would we do that? He won't fight against the Mer—he's a traitor."

"Do *not* kill him." Donahue's words were sharp. He ran a hand through his dark hair, and more disappeared.

"Have you gone soft, Donny boy?" Jackie cackled. He let his golden mask fall to the ground before bringing both hands to his crossbow and pointing it at Edward's trembling body.

Edward wasn't looking at Jackie. Even with the crossbow now pointed at his head, Edward's eyes were on Donahue, burning with a plea for mercy.

Jackie's mouth curled into a wicked smile as his fingers squeezed the trigger. Sand and silver fragments of Mer blood swirled around him. His cloaked arm shuddered as the weapon released its fury.

"Stop, you cowards!" I cried. Hot tears burst from my eyes as I struggled against Bron. I turned inward, searching for anything—any spark of power. I thought I felt something flicker, but then it was gone. Perhaps I'd imagined it.

A hiss alerted me as the arrow had whittled past, heading straight for Edward's head.

I pummeled the arms that gripped me—my eyes were half-shut. I didn't want to witness the scene unfolding if I could do nothing to change it. It was all my fault.

It was all my fault.

The arms that held me relaxed, and I fell to the sand as Bron's cloaked figure rushed away from me toward the bodies writhing on the ground.

Edward!

Snatching up my dagger and diving forward, I sunk the blade into Bron's large upper thigh. His skin popped, and I raked the knife down as the flesh shredded. Down and down I kept going, until he let out a guttural shriek.

I couldn't help but feel good about the pain I'd caused as I withdrew the blade, and Bron rolled aside to nurse the wound.

Edward was now slumped over, cloaked in black. One of the other men was on top of him, finishing the job. Grabbing his bony shoulders, I threw him off Edward, who was recoiling underneath. My eyes darted across him, searching for an arrow wound, but I couldn't see one. He was crying.

I spun around, bracing for Jackie's attack, only to find him sprawled lifeless on the sand. His wicked smile was frozen in time, and his pale eyes were wide. A blade jutted from the center of his forehead, the skin split where it had pierced the bone.

I brandished my dagger as Jackie's body jerked upward. His limbs thrashed outward, and his dirty-blonde hair spiked in disarray as his wicked grin twisted into a bloodcurdling shriek.

Was he casting a spell? No—the Drowned had no powers.

Bron was scuttling away from the scene into the murky gloom; his thigh must have already begun to heal.

Jackie shrieked again, and I braced myself for an attack, but his eyes were not filled with malice. They were rolling back in his head as he continued to cry out in what sounded like . . . pain.

I remained frozen as his body lifted from the ground, and his head swung in circles like something out of an '80s horror movie. All the while, he screamed. I needed to do something—move, at least—but I couldn't look away.

The two older Mer hung immobile on their crosses, faces peaceful, oblivious to the silvery blood leaking from their wrists and to Jackie's unearthly cries, and the merboy I had released drifted face down nearby. *Please don't be dead.* I whispered a silent prayer.

Jackie's features began contorting and shrinking at a tremendous speed, and still, he screamed. A light ignited where his heart had been and spread to his fingertips, encompassing him in a radiant glow.

Why couldn't I take my eyes off him? There were things I needed to do—people I needed to save.

The light enveloped Jackie completely, his writhing body shrinking into a small luminescent ball.

My gosh, it is beautiful.

I no longer thought of it as Jackie. No, this was the most precious light I had ever seen. I looked around aggressively; no one would take this treasure from me! I was ready to fight for it.

Edward was kneeling where Donahue had fallen, his gaze fixed longingly on the light. It was mine—I'd seen it first. Spinning back around, I lunged for the glowing orb, but it darted just out of reach, teasing me. I glared at Edward, but he remained motionless, making no move to follow.

Fixing my gaze on the sphere, I began to walk toward it. Everything else faded away—Edward, Donahue, the three Mer—leaving only the beautiful, entrancing glow. I leaped for it again, my fingers nearly grazing its surface, and it let out a final, bloodcurdling wail and vanished into nothingness.

I felt as if I had been released from a trance. I'd almost followed the light back down the bank. For a moment, I'd forgotten why I was here on this wasteland of dunes, but then I saw the crosses atop the hill.

Jackie had been taken to the Garden of Mortimer, and if I had grasped that light, I would have gone with him. I shuddered.

Returning to Edward, I saw he had been holding a body all this time. Donahue.

I rushed to his side. How could I have been so foolish, chasing after a light when my friend had been under attack?

But Donahue was not attacking Edward; he was dying. His pale head lay in Edward's lap, his half-open eyes fluttering as he took ragged inhales. There was an arrow embedded in his chest.

Where was the Donahue I had seen moments ago, sneering at us from the dune top? He was clutching Edward's hand now, and Edward was using the other one to smooth what was left of Donahue's curls over his lap. Edward seemed completely unharmed.

"We have to go." I grasped his shoulder, but he shook me off and continued patting Donahue.

"*Edward*," I said, "he's going to come back to life and kill us both! We need to get those Mer out of here."

"No—no, I can't." He shouldered me away while scooping Donahue's head protectively into his chest.

"Did you kill Jackie? I don't understand." I blinked at him. I didn't remember him ever saying he had a weapon.

"No." Edward sniffed. He could barely speak through his tears.

"Did you do this?" I gestured to Donahue's wilted body. Trust Edward to feel the need to comfort the villain after he killed them.

"No, I didn't kill him either." He leaned further over the man and drew in a shuddering sob. "He—he saved me. Jumped in front of me and threw a dagger at Jackie's head just as Jackie released the arrow." Edward choked, peering up at me with bloodshot eyes.

This was all too confusing.

"Why would you do that?" I crouched down, addressing Donahue. He was in bad shape.

"I-I had to," he croaked. He was not looking at me but at Edward. "Can you ever forgive me?"

"Yes," Edward whispered, brushing the man's dark hair from his forehead again. "Thank you."

Heat rose in my cheeks, and I turned away. This was an intimate moment I didn't understand. But then a horrible thought struck me: what if it was all an act? Donahue might pull the arrow out and stab Edward with it at any minute. I spun around, but he didn't look like he had the strength to attack. His eyes snapped open as he departed.

I stepped back, waiting for the same display of shrieking Jackie had demonstrated, making a mental note to look away when the light began. But a sigh of relief escaped Donahue's lips as he relaxed in Edward's arms, eyes closing softly as his form grew weightless, drifting gently into the current. He floated above us for a moment and, with another long moan of release, disintegrated into the watery surroundings as tiny foam bubbles danced around us, singing the same song of freedom.

Edward fell forward, sobbing. I knelt beside him in the sand and put my arm around his shoulders. I wasn't quite sure what to say. I wasn't sure I even understood what had just happened.

"I think he's at peace now." I patted his heaving back. We had just witnessed both versions of what happened when the Drowned died and didn't return.

"I know," Edward wailed, "because he died to save me while I cowered like a fool." His little red cap was discarded nearby, and his usually immaculate quaff was a mess.

"You were brave. You put your prejudice aside to save the Mer when there was almost no chance we could have won, but we did." I stood up, giving him a sad smile.

He looked up at me with red-rimmed eyes. "H-he must have loved me."

Yes, I thought. That was it.

"Did you love him?" I asked gently.

"I vowed to remain faithful to the man I had given myself to before I set sail. He was everything I could have dreamed of loving. On the other hand, Donahue was handsome, yet dark and tormented. But now I realize I m-may have loved him as well. B-but I never told him . . . I never gave him a chance!" Edward broke off into another wail, clasping his face in his hands.

"Edward, was he—was he the person . . ."

He looked up at me and nodded.

"But it only happened once? And you think he loved you for all these years?" I took his hand and drew him up from the seabed.

"Yes, though I never would have imagined it until now. When I first drowned, we read books together, and he helped me polish my pianoforte. Then, one night, it simply happened. Afterward, I grew distant toward him, believing I had sullied the memory of my true love on land. From that moment, we were cold to one another. I thought him heartless; if I had known, I could have saved him . . . and stopped this. Perhaps I might have found happiness here." He stifled a gut-wrenching sob.

"You couldn't have stopped this. Taranis would have found other Drowned cronies to do his bidding." I patted his back. "But I think you *did* save Donahue by allowing him to die for you and find peace. Now we are going to save three more people." I gestured to the crosses looming above us.

39.

MORGANA

It was easier to cut through the cords binding the old merman with the silver tail now that my hands weren't shaking. I withdrew the arrows that had pierced his wrists, but blood was spilling from the gashes they had left. My hands were coated and sticky, shimmering in the gloom. The merman drifted free from the wooden cross as I sliced the final bond, and a prickle caressed the back of my neck. *Mer.*

They had silently surrounded Edward, the Mer on the crossbars, and me.

These Mer were not like the ones I was trying to untie. Their tails were not made of assorted colors; they were a unanimous pearl. They all had muscular, green-tinged torsos and wore the same tarnished silver breastplates, finely carved, with thin spiraling lines. The plates covered only the upper halves of their chests and backs, leaving their rippling abs exposed.

The Mer guards—I assumed that was what they were—all had different faces. Some were lined and old, and others were young, yet the helmets made them uniform. Hewn from the same fine silver, they showed most of the men's faces but reached a point in the middle of their foreheads. There was a crest, but where old-fashioned knights might have sported feathers, these guards had fronds of green seaweed that floated eerily above them in the current. Little silver cloaks, almost transparent, danced about their shoulders. Some had small holes and frays, suggesting they had seen many wars. If Mer could live for thousands of years, had some of these older guards seen one of the four great battles?

I was staring, as was Edward. His mouth was hanging open in the same way I imagined mine was. The guards pressed around us, their faces drawn in fierce yet inhumanly beautiful stares.

My gaze darted from the vials attached to the crossbars to the blood on our hands. *They think we did this!*

The guards moved closer, hemming us in. Some raised round silver shields, all identical. They bore the Symbol of the Ocean in their middle. These must be the guards of King Neptūnus V, ruler of the Atlantic Mer.

I looked for Jackie's and Donahue's bodies to point out the real criminals, and my stomach sank. They had both disappeared.

Glancing from one guard's fierce, unyielding face to the next, I dropped my dagger and raised my hands in what I felt would surely translate to "I come in peace," even in this world. Edward did the same. My gut twisted. Our outstretched palms glistened with Mer blood.

"W-we didn't do this. We were trying to help," I stammered, turning on the spot to offer a pleading look to as many of the guards as I could. One of them grabbed Edward under his armpits, and his companion drew a sword to his throat. Edward let out a noise of terror.

"Please, you've got to listen to us. We tried to save them!" I cried.

"You will come with us to the palace, and King Neptūnus will decide what to do with you murdering Drowned scum." The bubbles from the guard's mouth translated into English in my mind. His armor was decorated with blue gems instead of pearls, and his seaweed crest was fuller than his companions'. He must be the leader.

The merman's fist closed around my upper arm, and he set his sword's pointy edge against my throat. I didn't wince. Somehow, I felt the Mer would respect strength.

"P-please," I began again.

"Utter another word, and it will be your last, *Drowned scum*." His face flickered, his beautiful green eyes momentarily transforming into pale globes and his mouth revealing rows of razor-sharp teeth. I thought about the claws the merman who'd carried me out of Therme Skótos had grown. Would this guard grow those same claws if I pushed him too far?

"Alga, stay here with your men and release our kin from their degrading bonds." My captor nodded to a strongly built merman on his right. "Then, take them to the Sanitatem and ensure they are seen. I will take the scum to the dungeons to await the king's judgment."

"Yes, Sir Korul." The guard called Alga bowed his head to his leader, then moved toward the crosses with a flick of his pale tail.

Korul gave my hand a sharp twist, and a cry rose in my throat, but I swallowed it.

"Walk, *scum*!" he commanded, moving his sword from my throat to my back.

I had no choice but to stumble forward at the blade's authority. I glanced to my left and saw Edward suffering the same treatment. It looked like we would make it to the castle after all, but not in the way we had expected.

The guards escorted us out of the dunes. The soft sand was replaced by jagged rocks, causing me to stumble, but I kept walking. A sudden stop could thrust Korul's sword through my back.

The merman glided silently behind me on his tail of white pearl. Once, I tried to twist around to plead my case again, but he punished me with a stiff jab and a cold stare. There was blood on my back now; I could feel its sticky warmth every so often before the water claimed it.

Edward was faring worse than I was. He had fallen over four or five times, only to be grabbed roughly back up by his assailant and commanded to "Keep walking, *scum*."

I suspected they had set this pace deliberately, taking pleasure in our struggle. I could have kept up if I'd been allowed to swim using my webs, but Korul's blade forced me to walk.

When the scenery began changing again, I knew we must be approaching the castle. Things started to look groomed and purposeful. We proceeded down a sandy track, where long beds of colorful coral bloomed on either side and small circles of black pebbles hemmed in patches of seaweed.

The garden path guided us to a stone archway encrusted with barnacles and dotted with patches of fungi. On either side stood chipped statues resembling our guards, their stone-cold eyes glaring at me with the same resentment as my living captors'. Their carved tails coiled around the pillars, and above us, Runes of the Ocean etched a message into the archway. Beyond it stretched a bridge, also hewn from dark stone.

Korul hustled me onto the bridge. It was slippery with algae, so I tried to step carefully. This didn't bother the guards, who glided gracefully an inch above the slimy surface, forcing me to continue at their pace. The ravine stretched into the blackness below us. It was so deep that I couldn't see the bottom—only darkness. I gulped. If I had to, I could use my webs to propel myself out of its depth, but Edward would fall to the bottom.

The dark chasm faded from my mind as the castle came into view. It rose above us in a magnificent mass of towers and glowing lights, seemingly sculpted from countless particles of sand. Some sparkled silver in the aquamarine light, making the entire structure shimmer as if it were alive with glitter.

I counted eight turrets. They spiraled naturally from different ledges at the castle's sides, their points standing black against the jade surrounds. Little glowing windows were scattered here and there on the walls.

The bridge led us into the castle's shadow, and the walkway was now crowded with small, sandy mounds—houses, I realized, as Mer slipped outside to watch us pass. So this was where the lesser folk lived.

The Mer eyed us coolly as we passed. One or two spat at us. Some had created sea gardens around their dwellings, and others used delicate seaweed to keep fish in nets. One house had a giant brown lobster tied to a leash at its front door.

Despite all this, my gaze returned to the dark castle. It was the most beautiful yet terrifying structure I had ever seen.

The mounds of the Mer village gradually thinned as we started up a winding track leading to the castle's base. Perched atop a rocky mass, it loomed above us. Clumps of seaweed clung to the craggy edges as we twisted ever upward.

My legs were tired, and my back ached from where Korul's sword continually poked at me. I was glad when we reached the entrance, even though it meant facing King Neptūnus and Prince Aigéan.

Above us was another archway, with Runes of the Ocean etched on its walls. On it, a bearded face with a large open mouth and eyes was carved. The arch led us to a final path, and a yellow glow emanated from a door at its end. Two guards in the same armor as the ones escorting us flanked it.

Korul grunted, urging me forward with his blade, and a fresh trickle of blood oozed from my back before it dissipated into the current. We marched past the guards, who ignored us and continued to stare out to sea. Long spears were clasped at their chests, and their seaweed clefts swayed in the water.

Upon entering the castle, I barely had time to look around. The floor was a polished gray stone, and two stairwells stretched in opposite directions, leading to multiple stories above. There were blown glass bulbs in different shapes and sizes along the walls. Above us, a giant chandelier twinkled.

That was all I saw before Korul growled, "To the dungeons," and ushered us to a dark passage to the left of the entrance. We were escorted down slippery stone steps into the shadows. Edward was taking shaky breaths in the darkness behind me.

I twisted my neck to face Korul. I could barely see him in the gloom, but his pearl tail shone luminously. It made me think of my grandmother's description of Taranis.

"Please," I began again. I knew it was risky, but the alternative was getting locked away in this darkness.

"You will not talk to me," he snarled, prodding my back.

"Aren't you supposed to be magic? You should *know* that we are innocent. If it weren't for us, your Mer friends might be dead!"

"How dare you talk about my friends! I have seen the faces of others you brutish Drowned have murdered." The words rumbled into the darkness behind me.

"I'm *not* Drowned," I bit back.

"You are going to pay nevertheless!" He gave me another prod. I winced, but I didn't cry out.

"I—I know Abalone. She was my grandmother's friend! We came to warn you," I shrieked in desperation as the darkness festered around us.

"Do not speak of our queen!" Korul quaked, and I heard a slick slicing sound.

Claws. His claws had extended.

"Now, quiet before my blade slips." His voice was icy.

I fell silent. Perhaps he had been romantically tied to one of the victims. The thought made me pity him, but that pity would not help me now.

There was light at the bottom of the stairwell, but my relief quickly disintegrated when I saw what it illuminated. The cells were dark and cut roughly into the rock. Broad metal bars thick with barnacles and algae shut off the enclosures. They creaked as Korul slid open the nearest ones by the stairs.

I stopped.

No, no, I can't go in there.

If I could channel any of Siana Selich's ancient power, now was the time. But how?

I scrunched up my eyes and upturned my wrists, making my hands into claws the way witches did in movies. *Nothing.*

I tried again, sensing a faint flicker of something deep within me, but it was beyond my grasp.

"Walk forward, scum," Korul growled.

I remained paralyzed in the doorway.

Come on, come on, come on.

I closed my eyes and looked inward—something was there, flickering silver.

What the fuck do I do now?

I scrunched up my face again, clutching for whatever was slumbering within me, but doubt slithered in.

I can't be magic. This is crazy.

If only my grandmother had trained me. I should have stayed on land and sought Louisa's counsel before returning.

A jab from the sword at my back forced me into the dark cell. I fell onto the cold ground on all fours, and Edward tumbled in beside me. We quickly scrambled together and clung to each other in the darkness. The faint glimmer I'd felt within had vanished. I closed my eyes, searching for it, but whatever had briefly ignited was gone.

"Do you still wish to save the Mer?" Edward asked coolly from the gloom. He had been quiet for the entire journey.

"We will explain everything when we see the king." I forced a smile, but I knew uncertainty permeated my voice. After the way the guards had treated us, I wasn't sure what would happen.

I wondered if Edward was right and the Mer were best left to their own devices. How long would it be before they took us to the king? Edward would survive the wait, but I would need to surface to replenish my air at some point.

40.

Morgana

The darkness was playing tricks on me. It festered in the corners and moved across the walls. Now and then, I cried out, convinced something was creeping through the gloom, only to find it was just shadows flickering against the rocks. They sometimes felt almost *gentle*, brushing my cheeks like the phantom touch of a long-lost lover.

Perhaps I was losing my mind.

It was cold in the cell. We must have been deep below the rock face supporting the castle. Had we been imprisoned for hours or days? Maybe it was weeks—no, it couldn't be. I would have died from lack of oxygen already.

Eventually, I found the courage to inch toward the back of the enclosure. Relief and disappointment warred within me—it only stretched thirty feet. Had it gone on endlessly, escape might have felt possible. Deep holes pockmarked the walls, some large enough to swallow my entire arm. I forced myself not to wonder what might slither from them as Edward and I rested. Who knew what lurked in these black corners of the ocean? Even the ever-probing humans hadn't uncovered all its secrets.

The cell was large enough to offer permanent unease about potential unwanted company, and there was also a sense of something ancient down here—something nameless and timeless that permeated the darkness, something that made the hairs on the back of my neck stand up. We huddled in the meager pool of light against the wall nearest the bars and tried to speak of other things.

"You told me that you believe the Drowned are souls who have been wicked in some way or another. When you spoke of your sin, what were you referring to?" I asked.

The anxious tightness had begun in my chest. This time, I knew what it meant. Soon, I would need to breathe. I might as well pry. After all, what else could we do down here but talk? It distracted me from the images of the pirates' hands on my body, the dead mergirl's face, and Donahue's silver veins that crept into my mind from the darkness whenever I let my guard down—not to mention the throb of hunger that was gnawing out my insides.

"Supposedly Manannán claims all souls because no one is free of sin, but no one really knows the truth. Perhaps it is a myth." I could see a hint of Edward's sad smile as he leaned his head back.

"But what's the worst thing you ever did when you were alive?" I urged, tracing lines on the algae-covered floor.

He breathed into the darkness at my side. "When I was younger, I lived with my parents in a grand manor in Belgravia," he said, leaning further into the slimy wall.

"You lived in a manor? I assumed you were poor." I gestured to his porter's uniform.

"Who said I was finished?" Edward's tone darkened, and I could tell he had returned to his past.

"My lover's name was Peter. He was a handsome boy who delivered our paper each day. I would watch him with my nose pressed against the window, admiring his curly hair and beautiful brown eyes.

"One day, he looked up and saw me at the window. I quickly ducked down and hid. The next day, I watched him again. This time, he waved and beckoned me to join him. After that, we wandered the streets together and grew into our teenage years, though my parents disapproved, as he came from a different class. Thus, we began meeting in secret. As time went on, we realized our desire for one another.

"When I was sixteen, my father caught us embracing. He told us we were sinners and would be punished by the Lord, and then he beat us both something ghastly. He banished me from the manor, so Peter and I moved into a poor neighborhood. At first, times were tough"—Edward sighed, and I found his cold hand—"but during the early 1900s, tourist travel proliferated, calling forth a new wave of construction on passenger liners. This was interrupted by World War I, but right before the outbreak, I got a job on a boat headed for New York as a porter. The plan was to sail to America on SS *Jones's Lady* and look for more work. After I had enough money, I would return, and we would move to the country together." He shifted uncomfortably.

"Peter made me vow that I would return. He gazed at me with those beautiful eyes of his. Even now, I can still see them—flecked with amber and framed by dark lashes. Time and again, he made me promise. I looked into those eyes and swore that I would." Edward rubbed his jaw and looked at me. His gaze was filled with anguish in the half-light.

"As you know, SS *Jones's Lady* never reached New York. Not only did I break my promise by drowning, but my father's words had begun to eat at me, and I had made up my mind that I would never return for Peter. I was planning to start a new life in America alone."

He shook his head and stared into the darkness before continuing.

"You see, Peter may have discovered, or at least assumed, that I drowned, and he would have believed that was why I failed to keep my promise. Yet I must bear the knowledge that I intended to betray him . . . I shall carry that burden for all eternity." He turned to me, and I saw his eyes were dry. He had no tears for his self-hatred.

"Edward," I whispered, my throat tight as I said the words that had been haunting me the whole way to the Mer's castle. "I am sorry for bringing you on this quest, and I am sorry for guilt-tripping you into helping me on the dune top."

"It's okay," he murmured.

"After reading my grandmother's diary, I started to believe that, just maybe, I could end this war somehow. That maybe I was the chosen one . . . but it all feels so stupid now." I blew out a breath.

"At least we tried." He turned to me in the darkness. "I don't regret it, Morgana."

"There's something else," I muttered. "I didn't tell you because I was embarrassed."

"Whatever is it?" He tilted his head.

"Louisa said I might have powers. Ancient powers. The powers of Siana Selich. I guess I thought we would be . . . protected or something." I swallowed.

"Well, *do* you?" Edward's eyes widened with hope.

I shifted on the damp floor. "I thought I sensed something stirring within me, but now I'm not so sure—unless you think sensing emotions or finding a juicy fish might help us."

He chuckled.

"It's strange," I continued, "but I think I have been dreaming of Siana and Manannán my whole life."

"What the devil do you mean?" Edward's brows drew together in the dim light.

"Well, you said she died on the battlefield from arrows, and for as long as I can remember, I have had these dreams of swirling darkness, blood in the water, and a rushing sound. I never knew what it was until Jackie tried to kill you with his crossbow, and I realized it was the sound of an arrow being released." I exhaled slowly, sending a stream of bubbles swirling between us. It felt good to tell Edward what had been weighing on me.

"I just wish my grandmother were alive so I could speak to her." I shook my head slowly.

"I'm still thinking about Donahue and what might have been." Edward sighed.

"I'm sorry about him," I whispered, trying to meet my friend's eyes in the gloom.

He was silent, gazing into the darkness.

"Did you notice how Jackie's and Donahue's faces had decayed?" I wondered aloud, staring into the black as if I would find an answer there.

He nodded slowly. "Donahue's face was always handsome, but he looked sick."

"This is going to sound strange, but I think I saw Donahue on land before all this happened." I thought again about the cloaked figure by the Ferris wheel.

"B-but that's impossible," Edward spluttered.

"I know." I said, running a hand through my matted locks.

I shuddered, and Edward put his arm around me. He pulled my head into his shoulder and stroked my hair. His wonky badge dug into my cheek, and I could feel the damp patches of decay on his coat, but I didn't mind. I didn't tell him about the tightness that had begun in my chest and that I didn't know how long I had until I would need to surface.

41.

Finn

Teachie screamed as I raked my webbed claw through his flesh. Drops of sweat tried to pool across his red and furrowed brow, but the water immediately claimed them.

It hadn't been hard to track him down. The Captain had told me who'd given Morgana the bruises; he'd heard the pair bragging about it, and I waited in the shadows of the ship until I found him dragging another woman into the vessel's dark bowels against her will.

I might not be able to kill the pirate, but I could ensure that, once I was done with him, he would never touch Morgana again.

I couldn't kiss her, couldn't claim her the way I ached to, but at least I could give her this. I also needed information, so I'd kill two birds with one stone.

"Where is his fortress? Don't make me ask you again," I whispered icily.

"I'm telling you, I don't know," Teachie snarled. His eyes darted about the slick, dark chambers, searching for a way out, but there would be no escape for him.

Beneath the Neptūnus castle sprawled a labyrinth of tunnels and dungeons. Hewn from dark rock, they twisted like the skeletal remains of some long-forgotten sea beast. The tunnels had been built thousands of years earlier and stretched in all directions, some narrowing into corridors, others opening into vast chambers where the ruins of old prisons remained. Iron-barred cells encrusted with barnacles, their gates long rusted shut and shackles dangling from stone walls, held remnants of those who'd once suffered here. Deeper within, the tunnels grew more treacherous. Chasms split the pathways. Some had caved in, and others had become shrouded in the ink-black abyss, where the gods knew what lurked just out of sight.

The castle dungeons comprised part of this network, but the central dungeon was at the heart of the labyrinth, and that's where my interrogation chambers were. Some said the tunnels stretched beyond the castle's domain, linking to secret caves and trenches where the ocean's darkest secrets slumbered. But those tales were likely the ravings of the Drowned men I'd sent on their way, mad with fear after what I'd put them through.

Teachie grunted in pain as I raked my clawed finger down the flesh on his right leg, splitting the material of his tattered pants. Wicked delight surged through me as a gaping wound appeared. Had Morgana screamed when he had his big, calloused hands on her? The thought made me dig deeper.

"Are you ready to talk?" The words came out a hiss and my gills flared.

"Never." Teachie's top lip curled under his mustache.

I chuckled and shook my head, dragging my claw down Teachie's left leg and watching his skin open for me again. His thick calf jolted with the pain, and his many-ringed hands curled into fists in their rusted shackles. *Good.*

The water down here was heavy, pressing with an unnatural stillness, disturbed only by the occasional echo of a distant, unseen current.

Strangely, I had always found solace in these dark, silent tunnels. After my mother's death, it was here I would come to read or seek an escape from my father's sporadic rages, but it was also here that I had carried out all the heinous tasks he demanded of me.

I dragged my eyes across the shelves lining the space, filled with books, maps, and artifacts I'd collected over the years.

Teachie's eyes rolled back in his head, and he slumped onto the stone table. My lips curled into a grin. The pain had rendered him unconscious. He wasn't getting out of here until I broke him or he died. It might take weeks, but I was patient.

I cleared my instruments off the second stone table. The guards had apprehended two more Drowned caught stringing up Mer and filling vials with their blood on the dune tops. I ran my hand over the now-empty benchtop, unlocking the rusted manacles. I was looking forward to dragging these new prisoners in and breaking them alongside Teachie.

I settled into a carved chair beside the unconscious Teachie. Leaning back, I poured myself a glass of whisky and waited patiently from the shadows as his flesh knitted itself back together and his eyes flew open.

"Fucking Mer scum!" He snarled, eyes narrowed as he struggled against the shackles that held him.

Morgana must have begged him to let her go, but he didn't. He bruised her beautiful face with his rough hands.

Exhaling, I leaned forward and rested my elbows on my tail. "If you tell me where his fortress is, perhaps I'll be lenient . . ."

"I'd rather stay here until I die," Teachie spat.

"That can be arranged." I smiled and stretched back in my chair again, my tail curling up one side.

"Your Highness."

There was a presence in the doorway—one of the guards.

"What is it, Percival?" An angry breath shot out of me. I didn't like my sessions being interrupted.

"It's the new prisoners, sir. The king has called them to the throne room for a trial." The man hung his head, and his seaweed cleft billowed.

"I see."

"And another thing." He averted his gaze. "The merboy we retrieved from the dunes didn't make it. I know he was your valet."

I curled my fists. "Take me to the throne room."

Knocking my chair away with my tail, I focused my attention back on Teachie on the table, grating my claw through his abdomen before turning and following Percival out. Teachie's screams ricocheted through the dark tunnel as I made my way back to the castle.

I will make them all pay.

42.

MORGANA

There was a presence on the stairwell. Two of the gem-tailed guards had arrived, both holding long spears. Their fine silver cloaks billowed softly behind them, juxtaposed against their stiff shoulders and stern expressions. I recognized their faces as they glided into the lamplight: Alga and Korul.

Alga slid forward and unlocked the heavy gate. The echoing clang was a welcome contrast to the silence. Edward and I crawled forward at their command, our knees skidding on the mucky floor. Korul produced ropes of thick, slippery seaweed and bound both our wrists, and then we were steered back up the dark steps.

I felt faint when we finally reached the polished floors of the entrance hall. The stairs had exhausted me. I needed to surface, and I needed to surface soon.

The glow from the twinkling chandelier was overpowering after spending so long in the dark, but the guards didn't give us time to rest; they pushed us toward one of the two stairwells.

"Why do Mer even have stairs?" I grumbled.

"Perhaps they built them when they had alliances with the Drowned," Edward whispered.

This earned me a shove from the blunt end of Korul's spear, sending me to all fours.

Once we'd ascended, we met another polished stone floor hemmed by railings fashioned from sand—they would have been white if not for the green algae covering them. The polished stones stretched all the way around to the opposite side of the large space, but we were stopped at two double doors at the front of the pair of stairs.

The wooden doors glistened, their crevices dark with blackened slime. Carved into the surface was the same insignia I'd seen on my grandmother's box—a wave encircled by runes flanked by five figures. Now, I recognized them: a Mer, Selkie, sea beast, a Drowned skull, and a Siren.

I glanced sideways at Edward. "I'll do the talking. I got us into this; the least I can do is try to get us out," I hissed through gritted teeth.

This earned me another shove from my captor.

Edward nodded. His face was pale, and his red hair was a mess. He had lost his porter's hat on the hilltop.

A buzzing sound met our ears as the doors slid open, and the guards pushed us inside. We had been escorted into a vast hall with an arching ceiling. Marble pillars met carved beams that stretched across its roof, flanking a polished marble walkway. Hundreds of Mer of all shapes and colors crowded the space, and they were all whispering.

They had all come to see us sentenced.

My breath caught in my throat when I saw the dais and the thrones. There were six of them, but only three were occupied. The largest ones were in the middle; they must have been for the king and queen of the Neptūnus Kingdom. One was vacant. *Abalone.*

I felt like I had been paralyzed when my gaze found the sea king—King Neptūnus V. He looked a million years old, yet somehow young and strong. His hair was long and fell over his shoulders down to his chest. Like his eyes, it was black but sprinkled with gray. His face was handsome, but every one of his beautiful attributes was pulled into a fierce stare. His torso was tinged green, aged yet still muscular, and his tale glittered pale gold, curling up around the side of his large throne, which was carved from sand and set with hundreds of shells and stones.

A shove from the spear at my back reminded me I was supposed to be walking. Despite the Mer whispering on either side of me, I only had eyes for the king. He continued glaring at us as we approached the dais. The Symbol of the Ocean was drawn in the center of his forehead, runes were tattooed across his eyebrows, and thick ink bands circled his arms.

Dragging my eyes from him, I recognized the Mer at his sides. The muscular merman who'd spat at me sat two seats to his right, and the pale blonde Princess Glacies, who'd called us "scum," was on his left. Her long black tail glittered as it slithered around the side of her throne and slowly fanned her from behind.

Alga and Korul retreated when we reached the foot of the dais, leaving Edward and me standing in front of the imposing Mer. Edward trembled beside me as he looked up at them.

A grizzled merman floated out from a door behind the dais. His skin was a tanned brown, his tail faded lilac, and his gray hair floated around his shoulders as he drew out a parchment to read from.

"You have been brought before the court, convicted of torturing and murdering our people. We do not believe that Drowned vermin like yourselves would have the brains to be behind this." The Mer in the room snickered, and the herald paused before continuing. "If you can provide us with suitable information, your fate will be decided quickly and painlessly.

If we are unhappy with what you have given, you will wish you had helped us before the end." He shuffled his papers and peered over the top at us. "You are standing before the great King Merrik Neptūnus V. To his right sits his nephew Pisceon Neptūnus, and to his left sits Princess Glacies Niveus of the Niveus Ice Kingdom. You will bow before royalty, *Drowned!*" A scornful spit in our direction emphasized the last word as the old man retreated to the sidelines.

I watched him go, a nagging sense of familiarity tugging at me. Before I could dwell on it, Edward hastily dipped into a clumsy bow beside me. I followed suit.

"You may rise." King Neptūnus had spoken. His voice was as cold as the ocean's depths.

Edward and I lifted our heads, our bound hands clasped before us.

"Twenty-four dead Mer and two who are recovering in the Sanitatem." The king's eyes narrowed as he peered at us.

Twenty-four dead? Gods, no wonder they were angry. But wait, only two recovering—that meant one of the three we rescued had died.

My stomach hollowed out.

"Now tell me . . ." The king's mouth curved into an awful smile. "Tell me where my brother is—for I know that the sniveling, powerless Drowned couldn't be responsible for all these deaths."

Did he just say his brother? He already knows about Taranis.

"Please, Your Majesty, we didn't kill your people," I pleaded. My throat was burning. I cursed my tears. I would choke on them before I let them fall.

The king's eyes bored into mine. I tried to sense his feelings, but there was nothing. I remembered my grandmother's diary saying that the Mer's magic prevented her from sensing their emotions.

"My guards only saw you, and you were covered in our people's blood." The king arched a dark brow, and the runes tattooed above it rose.

"One Drowned escaped, and the bodies of the others disappeared. One we believe found peace in saving Edward's life." I waved a hand at my friend, and he nodded in confirmation. "The other looked like he ended up in a worse place, Your Majesty."

He must believe me. He has to.

"Ah, yes. That is convenient." The king threw back his head and laughed, his dark hair shaking against his shoulders. He stopped abruptly, his eyes snapping to mine with a sharp gleam as if he'd forgotten why he was laughing in the first place.

My whole body was trembling, and my chest was being squeezed. I recognized the feeling—I needed to surface for air, *now*.

"So you refuse to tell me of my brother's whereabouts?" The king tilted his head, laughter still dancing around his eyes.

"I told you. It wasn't us! We do not know where Taranis is." I didn't have time for this. From the corner of my eye, I saw Edward shaking his head furiously at me.

I spun around and scanned the angry crowd, searching for any faces showing sympathy—perhaps the merman who'd rescued me was among them—but they all remained fierce.

"And yet you know my brother's name when I have not spoken it?" Venom seeped into the king's smile as his lip curled back from his teeth.

"We were on our way to speak to you." My voice became high-pitched—talking was taking all my precious air. "My gr—" I paused. Perhaps it was better not to enlighten the court of Mer that I was not Drowned, but a Selkie. My grandmother had feared for her life in this very court. "We have information that concerns your wife, Queen Abalone. We believe that Taranis killed her, and we believe that he is, in fact, Manannán."

A hush fell over the courtroom. I took a moment to double over and suck in what oxygen I could from my watery surroundings.

Edward looked at me sideways, concern knitting his brows.

The king's eyes flashed, and the shadow of a globe-eyed beast flickered on his face. "We already know that my half-brother is harnessing the powers of the Drowned God—he was always a pitiful thing. Without Manannán, he would be *nothing*." The rumbling words filled the hall, and King Neptūnus's eyes glittered in black amusement.

Fuck. He's mental.

"Guards! Hand them over to my son and see that they are tortured before they're executed!"

"No, wait—" There was a ringing in my ears, and the room was fading in and out of focus. I grasped at any last fragments of oxygen.

"Your Majesty, is it wise to give the prisoners to Aigéan? You know how easily he loses control during interrogation, he might kill them before they get a chance to talk." Pisceon, the muscular, dark-skinned merman to the king's right, had spoken.

"Who cares! Let him have them. It's no less than they deserve," hissed Princess Glacies.

The king didn't answer. He just continued laughing, an icy sound, and the rest of the congregation joined in.

"The young merman who died from blood loss was my valet, and he had dreams of being a guard." A cold, clear voice rang out from the back of the room, and another whisper rippled through the crowd.

Edward admitted a frightened exhale at my side. "It's Prince Aigéan."

The ringing in my ears intensified, and I could no longer see the congregation before me. The granite floor was coming closer, *closer* . . . Now it was at eye level.

I knew I must have fallen.

My long red hair splayed softly over my face, spilling in all directions. A second later, a hand pulled my head back. One of the guards had drawn me from the floor using my hair as a rope.

How was I going to answer questions when I couldn't talk? My chest was too tight, and the room was fading in and out. In and out.

The guard, most likely Korul, continued to hold my head back, presenting me to someone—to the prince. A swish told me a sword had been unsheathed. Cold steel was at my throat.

"Morgana?" The question sounded gentle, but firm hands still held my hair.

I knew that voice and how it made my body feel. Finn.

I must be hallucinating, but what a pleasant hallucination it is.

"Let her go," said Finn's voice, and it seemed like the guard released me.

If I'm dying and this vision of Finn leads my path to the afterlife, I will go willingly.

Metal flashed, and the shackles that bound my hands were released. Through my contracting vision, I could see the prince before me, his green tail shimmering in the light of the glass bulbs above.

"Bring the boy back to me," he demanded. I tried to squint up at him. He had dark hair, eyes, and tattoos on his right arm. He had Finn's strong torso as well, but he had the tail of a merman. The white lights began to dance in front of my eyes again. I was losing consciousness. *This was it.*

"What's wrong with her?" I heard him say.

"She needs oxygen," Edward's voice answered. It was urgent and fearful.

"I see. Korul, make sure this young man is treated well in my absence."

"Yes, Your Highness."

"Aigéan, what is the meaning of this?" the king's voice boomed. He was no longer laughing.

"Do not harm him, Father. This is *the girl*. I will explain everything."

"She's a shifter. When were you going to fill us in on *that* piece of information, Aigéan?"

That was the last thing I heard as I felt strong arms tighten around me.

I fell into them, thinking of Finn's voice and seeing his torso on the prince's tail. Water was rushing on all sides of my body, and I was traveling faster than I'd ever swum before, but I was barely conscious. The ringing in my ears was overwhelming, and I gasped for breath. I didn't want to give up, but the harder I tried, the less oxygen I seemed to receive. The ringing became deafening, and darkness consumed me.

# PART SIX

The Prince

43.

MORGANA

Wind bit at my cheeks, its vicious howl cutting through the air. Slowly, its oxygen was revitalizing me.

My seal fur corset was still stretched across my breasts and down my arms. I tried to swim forward, but I couldn't move—there were strong arms around my waist.

I thrashed out, peering over my shoulder, and found myself face-to-face with Finn. His dark hair was wet and messy, curling in the breeze, and his black eyelashes were encrusted with salt.

"You're okay," he breathed.

I turned away from him, taking in my surroundings. We were in the middle of a gray sea, but a spec of land was on the horizon. Out here, there were no crashing waves; there was only swell, and our bodies were rising and falling in unison.

Finn, or the merman who looked like him, held me tight against his muscled torso. I recognized his tattoos. The cuffs around his right wrist had that same strange lettering I couldn't read—runes. They were the Runes of the Ocean. He had the same scars hidden underneath them as well.

My fur-covered breasts, nipples peaking with the cold, pressed into his arms as we bobbed in the swell, and my body betrayed me as the heat rose between my legs. I pulled myself from his embrace, needing to take him in fully and get a grasp on what the fuck was going on.

On Finn's left pectoral, I saw a crescent moon tossed over a stormy sea—the Symbol of the Ocean. I hadn't seen him shirtless before, so I had never noticed it.

Am I dreaming?

Finn dragged his gaze across my furry corset, which I knew outlined every curve of my body, and color burned my cheeks. His eyes found mine, and he held my gaze so hard my chest constricted. I looked away to gather my thoughts.

The prince had been about to kill me, and then Finn was there, and he had saved me. I turned back to face him as the reality of the situation dawned on me.

Grinning, he pushed his wet hair from his forehead. It was as if he enjoyed seeing the cogs in my mind working overtime.

My heart hammered, and I pulled my gaze beneath the waves. There, protruding from Finn's torso, was the glittering green tail of Prince Aigéan. Its crimson tips flapped gracefully to keep him afloat.

"Y-you're *the prince*?" I stammered.

"Are you the only one allowed to have secrets?" He raised a dark brow.

"You've been like this all along and didn't tell me? You laughed at me when I said I heard the Mer's song!"

"I wanted to tell you." His tone was strained as he moved closer, reaching beneath the waves. His hand grazed my waist, but I slipped from his grasp—I couldn't think when he was touching me.

"It was *you* who sang on the rocks." I used my fingers to comb my sopping hair from my face.

His black eyes twinkled in the afternoon light. "We were not alone that day." A shadow passed over his face.

"And it was you who saved me in the Therme Skótos forest. Wait, a minute—what did you mean 'this is the girl'?" I pulled further away from him.

A pained expression flickered in Finn's eyes, as though he could see the mistrust taking shape on my face.

"My father is obsessed with finding the lost prophecy. When he heard Iona, the last of the ancient Selkies, was dead, but her granddaughter had come to Ruadán's Port, he sent me to observe you and report back." His eyes seemed to be pleading with me to understand.

"That's why you came to Ruadán's Port . . . for me?" My thoughts spiraled as I replayed that night at his house. He had been intent on finding out about my family. Were any of the things he'd said even real? The probing questions I thought meant he wanted to know me better had just been him gathering intel. I was struggling to breathe again.

"No, you were secondary. I was running another errand for my father." Finn's voice turned cold as he spoke of the king.

"Is that all you do in life? Run errands for Daddy?" My eyes narrowed on his muscular torso, which flexed with every flick of his magnificent tail.

"Yeah, I guess so." The gills along his neck flared.

He was silent. I'd hit a nerve. *Good*.

Finally, he sighed, and the shadow that had passed over his face was gone. "I tried to tell you, Morgana, in the grocery store, and that morning after we kissed in the waves—"

"When you said everything about us was *wrong*?" The clouds thickened into mist above us, and rain beat against my furrowed brow.

"I'll admit, at first I intended to get close to you to gather information."

He held my gaze, unflinching. Drops of water clung to his bottom lip, and I couldn't stop staring at them.

"So you only invited me to your house on your father's orders." I inclined my head in challenge.

"Yes, but then . . . then I started to *want* to be around you. I was going to tell you, but I couldn't find the words for these feelings, as they are not something I'm accustomed to." His expression changed, and sadness seeped into the waves. "I thought if you knew who I was—*what* I was—things would change between us."

"No shit." Heat rose in my face, and I hooked my wet hair behind my ear.

Finn's gaze dipped, rain tracing paths down his creased brow.

"You're still engaged?" I batted my lashes against the drizzle.

"Yes."

"On land or in the sea?"

"In the sea—well, both, I guess. But it's not what you think." He exhaled slowly, his expression filled with many things. "I've never had a choice. It's the kingdom . . . my duty. I'm trapped."

Princess Glacies. Of course!

I moved away from him, but his webbed fingers closed around my arm. "Morgana, I can't fucking breathe without you. I may wear a crown beneath the waves, but before you, I am only a man—unraveled and undone."

My heart thudded, but I shook myself free of his hand and dragged myself further from him in the swell.

I glanced at the sky. It was late in the day, but the evening was still a few hours away. The sea splashed clumsily at my mouth, and Finn wouldn't keep his eyes off me. He was making me feel aware of every stray hair.

"Where are we?" I asked coolly.

"We are close to home." He gestured toward the faint sliver of land barely visible through the rain-streaked horizon, his tail keeping him afloat easily.

I pulled my gaze from his and began to move toward the shore.

"A thank you for saving your life *twice* might be nice." Finn caught up with me, and we were now swimming alongside one another.

"First of all, you were only able to save me because you were stalking me, and secondly, an hour ago, you wanted to torture and kill me mercilessly." I shook my head. *Typical.*

"Technically, *I* wasn't stalking you. I asked Pháos to do that, and luckily I did, because my uncle almost pulled you into his clutches." Finn's fists were clenched beneath the waves. "He took my mother from me. I won't let him take you, too."

So the fierce, beautiful merman in Therme Skótos *had* been Taranis.

If Finn was Prince Aigéan, then the purple-haired Abalone, who I had found so mysterious, must have been his mother. So much had happened that I had completely forgotten he was the one we had set out to see.

"So you had your pet follow me." I thought of the white-bellied dolphin I had seen clicking in his ear.

"Pháos is no pet." Finn's angular jaw was stiff. "He is a wild animal of the sea. He chose me."

The gray clouds were still hanging low overhead, and the rain continued stinging our skin as we swam in silence. I glanced sideways at Finn, and he met my gaze.

I wanted to punch him in his smug face. But I also wanted to kiss him again.

Oh, gods, I wanted to kiss him.

I can't fucking breathe without you. His words wrapped around my thoughts, and my cheeks flamed. *Okay, let's stick to punching.*

He had lied to me . . . He had been sent to follow me! I cast another side-look at him, taking in his dark brows, angular jaw, and the dripping wet hair he had just pushed from his forehead. Damn him. Despite it all, the desire was still there. When he was near, he consumed my every thought. Maybe it was just the enticement of the forbidden? No, it was something deeper, something pulling us together. And that's what terrified me. If only I could sense his feelings, I'd know if he was telling the truth. But wasn't that exactly why I wanted him—because I couldn't?

Rain had obscured the horizon, and the ocean tossed about us as the wind picked up. Finn slid in front of me. I moved to slip past him, but he was quicker and blocked my path. His gaze locked on to mine, and unwanted heat curled within me, but I didn't look away. I stared at the droplets running off every inch of his beautiful face.

"Wh-where's Edward?" I asked, suddenly realizing we had left him behind.

"He is safe and will be treated well." Finn waved a hand. "Now, tell me what you know of my mother."

"I read about her in—" I was interrupted by an engine whirring, and a small motorboat pulled up beside us.

"Morgana?" A voice called from its deck.

Great. I don't have the powers of invisibility.

I clasped my hands over my fur-covered chest.

I glanced at the sky again. The sun was hidden behind clouds, but based on my seal's intuition, it was still about twenty minutes until sunset, and someone on that boat knew who I was.

"Who's there?" I spluttered as the idling engine doused our faces with seawater.

"It's Barry. Your granddad is on board. What on earth are you doing out here? I'll pull you up and take you straight to the hospital. It's all going to be okay."

A hand reached toward me in the water, but I hesitated. My fingers and toes still had webs, and my body was half-coated in sleek fur.

"Morgana?" Barry's pinched face peered out of the rain. I continued to hover in the swell, ignoring his outstretched hand.

"Barry, is it? Thank goodness you guys found us." It was Finn's voice. He had scrambled over the other side of the boat and transformed into his human self, covering his nakedness with a blanket that must have been on board. He couldn't have pulled off that maneuver without some Mer magic. I rolled my eyes. He was saving my ass again, and he wouldn't let me forget it.

Sure enough, I looked up to find him grinning at me. He was holding his hand out from beneath the blanket. I scrambled into the boat and wrapped the throw Finn had waiting around my deformity while Barry hovered at the wheel. Granddad sat bundled up in the hull but gave me a smile and a little wink. Barry didn't notice, as he was now busy shoving buckets of dead fish and tackle out of the way to make room for us.

Barry and Granddad were wearing jackets and beanies. This made our situation look even more ludicrous.

Finn sat down beside me. I glanced to where his emerald tail had been to see bare legs protruding from beneath the rough wool fabric. I moved my eyes up to his torso. Now that my fear of Barry seeing my Selkie skin had passed, I was acutely aware that Finn was naked under that covering. I chewed on my lip and cast my eyes to the space between his legs, wondering what was there now that his tail was gone.

He lowered his voice and grinned. "Yes, when we take human form, we come with the whole package."

I swallowed, and my cheeks burned.

"Robbie," Barry growled. I had been so preoccupied with Finn's crotch that I hadn't noticed his narrowed eyes on us. "Aren't you going to ask your granddaughter what she was doing this far out at sea and why *he* is naked?" He nodded at Finn. He must have mistaken my fur for clothes.

Shit. How were we going to explain this?

My granddad was chewing his gums nervously, as if wondering the same thing.

"You could have been killed! What if we hadn't found you?" Even through the drizzle, I caught the flush in Barry's sallow cheeks, his narrowed eyes set deep in his weather-beaten face. "How did you even get out here? Did he try to have it on with you, Morgana? Tell us now, and we'll chuck him overboard." His face turned almost gleeful as he jerked a thumb at the swollen waves.

"Okay, that's quite enough," interjected Finn. He stared hard at Barry, and the man met his gaze.

I only knew Barry a little, but he was a stern old guy, and Finn wasn't scaring him. Yet, to my surprise, his expression softened. He continued to stare at Finn, but his eyes became full. His tight jaw slackened.

"We came out fishing with you," Finn continued, his voice like silk. "We've been in the boat the whole time. Morgana caught that large one right there." He gestured to a big brown-skinned fish in the bucket by my feet. "We are wet and cold from the rain but will be fine."

Barry's hardened face came back to life when Finn stopped talking. His dark eyes narrowed momentarily, but then his face split into a grin. "You caught a beauty today, Morgana!" he croaked, squinting against the spit of the rain.

"Erm, thanks," I mumbled, looking at Finn in disbelief.

What the fuck was that? My stomach knotted itself.

Finn turned his gaze to Granddad, but I grabbed his arm

"It's okay. He knows," I whispered.

Finn shrugged and settled in next to me.

"That night at your place, when you looked into my eyes and asked about my family, that's what you were doing? You were trying to hypnotize me?"

"Well, yes." Finn looked bashful and reached for my hand. "But Morgana, it didn't work on you, which fascinated me. At first, it seemed like my powers of allure still worked, but then I realized they weren't affecting you either, or you overcame them. By that point, I was hooked. I *had* to know more."

Powers of allure? Asshole!

"But we *can* read heightened emotions, so you should probably learn to hide those." Finn spread his legs under the blanket, and his thigh pressed against mine. "Anger, sadness . . . arousal." He raised his eyebrows.

That's just great. Usually, I can read emotions; now he can read mine, and I'm blind to his.

The wavelike structure intertwined with Celtic patterns adorning the right-hand side of Finn's chest protruded from the blanket. On the left side, I now knew he had the same inky symbol as me. I hated being so curious about the rest of him . . . I wanted to slide my hand underneath the fabric and feel all of him. I glanced sideways, and he was grinning again.

Damn it. I needed to keep my emotions in check.

"How can you read my emotions but not hypnotize me?" I leaned forward, letting myself eye him curiously.

"Like the fact that you're wondering what's under this blanket?" He raised his brows.

Shit. I flushed and focused on the swirling sea.

"I was joking. I can't sense your emotions, Morgana. They are written on your face. After years of interrogating Drowned and humans, I have learned how to read people." He slid his knee across so it found mine again.

Smug bastard. I rolled my eyes.

"If you... If you are naked when you take human form..." I allowed myself to bring my eyes back to him and willed my traitorous cheeks not to burn. "Then how do you not draw attention to yourself when you acquire clothes?"

The rain had eased, and the lights of Ruadán's Port twinkled in the distance, and I pictured a nude Finn, strolling casually out of the sea, waving to people as he sauntered down the boardwalk.

He snorted a laugh, and his whole face lit up. It was nice seeing him like this. He had been so stern since we'd emerged from the castle. From his father.

"We can make ourselves invisible to humans"—he choked the words, still laughing—"but if I weren't with you, I would probably go up the front of the cliff."

I fought the corners of my mouth from tugging upward. "It would have been nice if my Selich ancestors had granted me that invisibility magic."

"All the Houses of the Ocean have unique magic. Think of it like genetics. We grow into the magic we need or that our ancestors acquired through some dealing with the gods." Finn tilted his head. "Selkies never needed invisibility from humans because, under the sea, you look like a seal, whereas we Mer with our magnificent tails and opulent castles..." He smirked. "We *really* need it."

Prick.

"As for walking on land, Mer royalty acquired that skill thousands of years ago thanks to Eríkos and Angeliki... but that is a story for another time."

⁘

Stars twinkled above us as we pulled the motorboat into Ruadán's Port. My human form had returned. Glancing down the front of my rug, I saw I was fully naked apart from my fur coat.

My bare feet were stiff and cold, wedged between the tackle and buckets of dead fish. Granddad had been silent for most of the trip. Perhaps he was too old to go out in such a small boat in this weather, but I knew he'd rather die than be deprived of the open water. On the other hand, Barry had been jubilant since Finn had had his way with him. He'd chattered aimlessly about the day's catch, the weather, and rumors he'd heard at the pub.

The boat's engine jogged to a stop, and we all climbed out. Finn took my hand, and Barry helped Granddad.

"What a night! Just look at these stars." Barry caressed the skies with his hand. "Shall we go to the pub? I feel like I might get lucky on the slots tonight." He nudged Granddad, who nodded his assent.

Granddad looked like he needed a drink. I didn't blame him. He had seen his granddaughter in a seal costume swimming with a naked man and watched his best friend be hypnotized, all in one night. At least now, he would have read the diary pages I left behind and let go of the guilt he harbored for trapping my grandmother.

"You two want a lift?" Barry jerked his thumb at the white truck parked by the boardwalk.

I looked sideways at Finn. We still had things to talk about.

"Did you want to come to mine?" I asked in a would-be casual voice.

Amusement danced in his eyes. "What, to watch Netflix?"

44.

MORGANA

"Wine?" I smiled nervously, wondering why I was suddenly so awkward as I escorted Finn into our small kitchen. I was acutely aware of the vulgar mustard linoleum floor and stained white walls. This guy lived in a palace.

Granddad had left the fire burning, and the place was toasty. Finn searched the cupboards for glasses as I opened a dusty bottle of pinot noir my grandmother had bought in France. The blanket was still wrapped around his shoulders, and I watched him move, part of me hoping it would slip. I busied myself with the cork as he turned around and placed two glass goblets on the table.

Once the wine was poured, Finn's dark eyes were on me again. They were serious, and I forgot all about my shabby kitchen when I met his gaze.

"So tell me what you know of my mother," he said as he slid into one of the rickety wooden chairs beside me. "Iona left our kingdom just before her death. I've always wondered if she knew something."

He turned his chair to face me, and the closeness of our knees sent a ripple through me. The wool throw still covered most of him, but I could see the tattoos adorning his chest between its folds. Heat rose in my cheeks, and I focused on the patterns at the lacy edge of the tablecloth as I began telling him about what I'd read in the diary.

As I recounted my grandmother's story, my eyes returned to the space on the floor where I knew they had found her. What would she think if she could see me now, in her kitchen with Abalone's son? I omitted the part where she'd found more of the prophecy and its connection to me. She hadn't been sure she could trust the Mer, and now I wasn't sure I could trust Finn.

When I finished, I eyed him keenly, waiting for a response, but he seemed lost in contemplation. So I continued telling him about Jackie and Donahue reporting to Taranis, who had an army of thirty thousand Drowned men.

Finally, Finn spoke. "Yes, I knew the Drowned were rallying for Taranis, and that he possessed the powers of Manannán's shadow." He rubbed his chin thoughtfully. "I also knew someone was creating unearthly storms, which I suspected was being used as a tool for building an army. What is new to me is the love affair between my mother and Taranis. I don't think it would be wise to tell my father this . . ." His eyebrows were knotted in thought.

"Donahue said the Mer tried to stop the storms. That was *you*?" My chair creaked as I leaned my elbows on the table and searched Finn's face. My blanket had fallen from my shoulders, my nakedness now only covered by the damp fur coat.

"Why do you think I was on land? No, I didn't just come here to watch you, although it has been enjoyable." His eyes sparkled. "I did my research and tortured my suspects." He paused, mouth twitching. "It led me to believe Taranis was using an on-land device to create the storms, something large enough to carry magic and distribute it across the sea. Do you see where I'm headed?"

"The Ferris wheel!" I'd seen Finn at its base the day the ground around it trembled.

"It's positioned perfectly on the cliff face. I suspect it's been an object of his since it stopped working three years ago, but with the curse, my magic wasn't strong enough to destroy it." He rubbed the back of his neck, and the blanket slipped entirely from his right side, bunching around his hips.

I choked on my wine as heat licked the space between my thighs. What was wrong with me? This man was in my veins, consuming my body like wildfire. The corner of Finn's mouth twitched upward, and I busied myself smoothing the hem of the tablecloth.

Focus, Morgana.

"I don't understand. Edward said the Drowned can't return to land. If that's the case, how are they moving the wheel?" My brow furrowed as I continued to survey Finn.

"They are using Mer blood—from the murders with royal lineage. It allows them to walk on land and harness the ocean's might with the wheel." The muscles in Finn's tattooed chest flexed.

"The silver markings on the wheel, you think that was blood?" A chill skittered its way down my spine, and I pulled the folds of my damp fur coat tighter.

So that was why Donahue and Jackie had been decaying. They were paying the price for using the Mer blood. The kitchen seemed suddenly darker.

"What would have happened to Donahue and Jackie if they hadn't been killed and kept using the blood?" I wrapped my arms around myself to keep from shivering. I knew I should change into warm clothes, but I was hooked on Finn's tale.

"They would have turned rabid and decayed until, eventually, the Garden would have claimed them." Finn's black brows were rigid, and his shoulders hunched.

"What I don't understand is why Taranis needed Donahue and Jackie. Couldn't he turn the wheel on his own if he's got the powers of the Mer *and* Manannán?" I tilted my head in thought.

"He will be able to soon. Taranis was always weak." Finn blew out a long breath. "He needs more drownings to help him regain Manannán's full power—a strength sucked from their souls."

I shuddered. "The wheel . . . we need to stop him before more people die." My grandfather was no longer safe at sea.

"I might need my father's help, but the thought of asking him fills me with loathing." Finn exhaled, swilling his wine and gazing out the dark window, his features etched with concern. "Both times we saw my uncle, he was in Manannán's bodiless form—a shadow drawn from the ocean's darkness. Wait till I see him in the flesh." His hands balled into fists, and I remembered his beastly form, which had held me in Therme Skótos.

A longing consumed me to take his bunched fists and uncurl them, finger by finger. I shook the thoughts from my mind.

Finn took a sip of wine and leaned back in his chair. Then he sighed. "You may have noticed that my father . . ." He paused as if the words were hard to utter. "My father . . . is not quite himself."

I thought about the king's manic laugh and ferocious eyes.

"He is set on breaking the ancient curse before Manannán or another one of the Drowned does. My family has been bent on it for generations, searching for the lost part of the prophecy and a way to break the spell cast over our people." Finn ran a hand through his dark curls. He looked tired. "He sent his own half-brother to search the deepest, darkest parts of the ocean, where the shadow of Manannán found him. Manannán has been trying to come back for years, grasping on to the bodies of animals, but none could sustain such power for long. Then, he found Taranis. My father's fruitless search created his worst enemy. Now he has to live with that."

A shiver ran down my spine as I recalled the shadow taking the shape of a horse sketched in Louisa's book.

"So you don't believe there is a prophecy, then?" I observed him, thinking about the part of my grandmother's story I had kept to myself—the part where she had found more of the prophecy and believed it to name me.

"I like to stick to the facts, and the facts are that if there ever was a second half to the prophecy, my father and his father before him have never found it," Finn said, taking another sip of wine. His eyes met mine, and his expression was earnest.

So he doesn't know Taranis discovered more—or he's hiding it.

"Prophecy or no, that doesn't change the fact that Taranis killed my mother, and now he's got an army," he continued. His face fell into a frown.

"I—I think Taranis might have killed my grandmother as well." My throat bobbed, and I looked at the space on the floor where they'd found her.

Finn leaned forward and tucked a strand of hair behind my ear. "I'm sorry," he whispered.

The searing droplets of hot water felt so good as they cascaded over my body. I was glad to have discarded the coat and be washing away the bone-chilling cold of the deep in the steaming shower. There was only one at my grandparents' house, and it was downstairs, so Finn was in the living room, awaiting his turn.

Mer Prince Aigéan was in the living room.

I shook my head at the sheer craziness of it all and ran my hands over my face and furless body. I was enjoying every moment of being human.

Even away from him, I couldn't shake Finn from my mind. He wrapped himself around my thoughts like a silk ribbon from which I didn't want to be released.

I pictured him shirtless, his torso glistening with sea spray, tattoos sprawling across his chest and right arm, and his dark eyes devouring me, leaving me breathless.

He had said he wanted me, that he couldn't breathe without me. The thought caused me to dip my hand between my legs; the space there was already slippery. I couldn't have him, and I wasn't entirely sure if I could trust him, but I *could* have this.

I allowed myself to imagine what was underneath that blanket, where the V-line of his hips led to his emerald tail. I thought about what he would look like above me, propped up on those inked arms, and what expression he would wear as he slid inside.

I can't fucking breathe without you. I bit my lip to keep my emotions in check as I slid my fingers in deep, gathering the wetness I found there and bringing them back out to caress just the right spot.

Let's see what we have here . . . Teachie's rasp as he'd plied apart my legs made it through my pleasure, and the building heat turned to nausea. *No!* I shook the images of the pirates from my head and thought again of Finn, his hands on my body. I let out a little gasp as I brought myself to a conclusion. My eyes rolled back in my head to images of him, and the pirates' faces faded from my subconscious, replaced with oblivion.

"Good shower?" Finn smirked as I entered the living room.

He had stoked the fire, the wall heater was blaring, and the room was toasty. One of his arms was draped over the back of the tan leather couch. Chest now fully bare, he'd slung the blanket around his waist like a towel.

Did he hear me?

No, he couldn't have—the bathroom was on the other side of the house. But it was so quiet. I could perceive the gentle hum of the heater. Did Mer have preternatural hearing like the faeries and vampires I'd read about in books?

He was still grinning as I combed my fingers through my wet hair. When I got dressed, I'd had two choices of pajamas: lacy or pink cotton. I'd gone with the cotton.

"If your hypnosis doesn't work on me, how come you can shield me from your emotions?" I wondered aloud.

"I've been trained my entire life not to feel emotion." Finn's mouth thinned, and his gaze traveled somewhere else.

"Your turn." I threw a fresh towel at his face, wanting to pull him back from whatever was haunting him. "I've put some of Granddad's old pajamas out."

He headed off to the shower, and a little while later, I was fluffing the pillows for Finn's bed on the couch when he emerged in Granddad's old nightgown.

"Seriously?" He raised his dark eyebrows at me.

The cotton nightgown fell to his ankles, making his feet look overly skinny. I could still see the faint blue and white stripes it had once been adorned with. The fabric was loose even on Finn's broad frame, and the sleeves were wide.

I choked. There would be no more wondering what's under *that*.

Finn brushed his damp hair from his face, and a spray of droplets found the shoulders of the nightgown.

"I can't..." I laughed so hard I had to sit down on the couch.

He took a seat beside me in the ridiculous gown. Leaning forward, he let his fingers graze the top of my hand. We exchanged a stare for what felt like minutes as I bit back my sniggers. His eyes traced a path from my feet on the carpet to my ankles resting against the base of the leather couch, finally landing on my pink-cotton-pajama-clad body. The nightgown had bunched, revealing the bits of uneven skin at his wrist, but the tattoos cleverly covered each scar. I wanted to let him touch me like I'd just touched myself, to touch him back and find out who'd given him those terrible scars, but instead, I pulled my hand away.

"What about Princess Glacies?" I looked away from him, studying the wooden coffee table.

"We are a dying breed, you know." His voice was quiet.

My gaze returned to his, finding a pained expression in his eyes as he stared past me. "We used to be great, long ago when we had access to our full power, but our people are dwindling."

"B-but you're immortal." My brows furrowed as I surveyed his beautiful face, wondering how old he was.

"We have an extended lifespan, if we stay out of danger... But we can still die, and we still age—it just takes us much longer than humans. Our people cannot handle the pollution spreading through the water." He shifted on the couch but kept his dark eyes on me. "My ancestors used to live for thousands of years were they not killed, but now the lesser folk are lucky if they make it to five hundred. Soon, there may not be any of us left. I have been promised to Princess Glacies all my life to unite the race and protect the realm."

There was sadness etched into his features. It took all my strength not to cup his face in my hands and kiss him, but I couldn't kiss him—I still wasn't sure if I could trust him. And duty or not, he was still engaged.

"Then my father tasked me with learning about you. I am no stranger to magic, but you . . . you bewitched me."

I swallowed. The leather couch was heating up beneath my thighs as his words cascaded over my body.

"Did your father tell you *why* he had you follow me?" My gaze sharpened on his face.

"He wanted to know whether or not you were a shifter. I wasn't going to tell him anything, but I guess he knows now." Finn's expression shifted, his features tightening.

I searched his eyes, and I could only see sincerity. Perhaps he was telling the truth. Maybe he and his father didn't know about the parts of the prophecy Taranis had found.

"How old are you really?" I eyed him thoughtfully.

His face split into a grin. "I guess you could say in human terms, I am 116 years old."

"Seriously? You're an old man!" I threw back my head and laughed.

Finn laughed, too. His black eyes crinkled at the sides, lips curling up to show his straight teeth. "You're going to look this age for the next hundred years or so as well," he said, curbing his laughter to devour my body with his gaze.

The heat rose in my cheeks and ears. "I'm sure you've met many girls in your hundred years. What is it about me? Midlife crisis?" I raised my brows.

"These days, we Mer have our midlife crises at around two hundred years of age." He grinned, then was silent momentarily, as if pondering what to say. "I've lived a lonely life doing what duty requires of me . . . sometimes on land, and sometimes under the sea. Don't get me wrong, I've been with humans." A faint smirk curved his lips at that. "But you're not like anyone I've ever met. Normally, when I desire humans, I just . . . take them." He shrugged, and his eyes met mine.

"You hypnotize them?" I narrowed my eyes.

"No, but I don't need to. They are drawn to me. Everything about me is alluring to humans—how I look, my voice, even my smell. This pull drags them in, their eyes turning glassy. But not with you. You remained unaffected." He made a small, indifferent gesture.

"What about Glacies?"

"We have an understanding." He raked a hand through his hair. "Trust me when I say she has no attraction to me. She prefers women, and her heart is with a mermaid in the Kingdom of Okeanós, but she too has been bred to do her duty to the realm."

I swallowed. "If you'd been able to hypnotize me that day at your house, would you have extracted the information, and then slept with me when I offered myself to you?" I shifted on the couch and pulled at the front of my pajama top. It was suddenly uncomfortably hot in this room.

"I might have." His eyes glimmered.

"You're a pig." I rolled my eyes to hide the anxiety that clutched at my chest.

"I am just adhering to my nature." He gave a nonchalant shrug. "In the Days of Gods, we bred with humans, even married them after we were granted the ability to walk on land. But the feud and the Shadow has made man our enemy . . . and it just so happens that this enemy goes weak for my face." He angled his jawline toward me, a smirk playing on his lips.

"That's why you've been so awkward and moody around me—because you have no idea how to court a human without hypnosis or allure, do you?" I huffed a laugh.

"I— Well, I think I'm doing alright." He reached for my hand.

I withdrew mine, and he sighed. "I have spent my life torturing people on behalf of my kingdom. " His dark eyes burned into mine. "I find myself haunted by their cries, their pleas for mercy. Now *you* live in my mind, torturing me the same way I tortured all those poor fools. I beg you for mercy, but you won't let me be." He shook his head slowly.

The fire made a faint crackling noise beside us, and I couldn't sense his feelings.

I couldn't sense his feelings.

45.

Morgana

Thunder cracked with a force that rattled the house. I sat upright in bed as Finn burst through my door, still in my granddad's robe, hair tousled from sleep.

"The Ferris wheel!" I cried.

"I need to try and stop it. There's no time to go to my father." Finn had a dark look in his jet-black eyes.

Rage exploded within me, and I tossed my blanket aside.

"What are the chances you would stay here if I asked you to?" Finn raised a brow.

I replied with a laugh, pulling on boyfriend jeans over my pajama pants and grabbing a jacket.

As we raced down the hill, the storm roared into the bay. Rain pelted the whitewashed stone houses on my grandparents' street, and swollen, dark waves towered four feet or more in height before unleashing their fury across my jetty.

I whipped my head toward the Ferris wheel, dread knotting my gut.

It loomed like a skeletal giant, its carriage-less circle spinning against the dark sky. I could feel something in the air—magic, perhaps—crackling with electricity. This storm was different from the others.

We skidded to a halt in the middle of Bayside shopping center, hair plastered to our faces from the rain. The wheel loomed ahead, its bone-like frame creaking under the weight of the gale.

Finn pulled me behind the outdoor furniture of Aranare's uncle's closed diner. We crouched behind the blue retro chairs, our breaths coming in sharp bursts as the droplets lashed our faces.

"They know we're onto them, so they're risking a larger storm," Finn yelled.

"What does that mean?" My heart pounded as I peered through the misty veil at the wheel. It wasn't just spinning—it was alive. A glow emanated from its center, illuminating the rain with an unnatural light.

"I don't know, but it can't be good . . ."

Panic began clawing at my core. I swallowed, thinking about the rising swell we had seen on our way up. Would they raise the waves to engulf the town and take Granddad, Skye, and Aranare? No. We had to do something.

"Looks like Manannán's powers have returned. I think Taranis is using *his* blood this time." Finn's brows were drawn as he squinted through the rain at the wheel.

A cold emptiness spread through my gut. "He's a coward hiding behind shadows and letting the Drowned do his dirty work," I said through gritted teeth.

"They've fortified it too." Finn pointed to the wheel's base, where two hooded figures were standing motionless—the Drowned. "I shouldn't have brought you. It's too dangerous." He shook his head.

"But that wheel—it's not turning because of them. Something's powering it from the center." I tore my gaze from the figures to look at Finn.

"Mer blood at its apex." His jaw tightened as he watched it spin. "It's amplifying Taranis's magic. This storm is going to be lethal."

I shivered but clenched my fists, nails digging into my palms. "Then we need to go for the source."

A lightning bolt struck the sea just beyond the wheel, illuminating its frame. The glow at its core pulsed brighter, almost like a heartbeat.

"We'll have to split up," I yelled over the rain. "You distract the Drowned at the base. I'll find a way to the center and stop it."

"No! It's too dangerous." Finn's grip tightened around my wrist, a flicker of fear in his eyes.

"It's the only way," I said, letting my gaze lock with his. "If you do your job right, I'll be fine . . . or don't you think you can handle them?" I arched a brow, challenging him.

Finn chuckled. "Let's see what you've got, shifter." He trailed his cold hand from my wrist to interlock his fingers with mine. Then he crept into the darkness, leaving me alone. I stood in the lashing rain, feeling suddenly foolish.

I crept across the grassy area. The wheel loomed above me like a titan, its rusted beams slick with rain and sea spray. I had no idea how to stop its powerful apex, but I had to try. A cry rang out from its other side, and magic flared. Now was my chance.

As I reached for the first rung, the smell of rotting fish filled my nostrils. A prickle spread across my neck, and I spun around. There were three dark figures behind me. Men—*Drowned* men.

My heart clamored as I looked between them. It was Bron and two others I did not recognize. Their eyes were sunken, and their skin hung off their bones in places, but they had covered their deterioration with black cloaks. Silver lined their faces—Mer blood.

The largest of the three cocked his head at me, and his hood slipped from his face. His long, dark hair dripped over his shoulders like rain-soaked vines, and his pale, hollow eyes locked on to mine.

Adrenaline speared through me, and I leaped for the first rung of the wheel, but cold fingers wrapped around my ankle, sharp nails dug into my skin as the long-haired leader yanked me down. My jacket bunched, and my pink pajama top slid up as he pulled me across the wet grass.

No, I thought. *No, this is not how I will die!* I'd escaped the Drowned before, and Taranis in the flesh twice. His cronies would not kill me. My voice returned, and I screamed, a blood-curdling wail that would have matched the Mourning Drowned.

The Drowned corpse had me in both his hands now. I thrashed, kicking at him, but he held me tight. He let his hands wander as he pressed my soaked, trembling body against his. His right hand found my breast beneath the thin cotton of my top and then moved lower. *No!*

"Careful," Bron croaked from beneath his hood. "He will punish you if you touch her."

The Drowned leader who was holding me just laughed, and the scent of rotting flesh burned my nostrils as his body heaved against me. He turned from the wheel, clutching me against him like a prize.

No, no, no! I screamed and thrashed again. I had to harness whatever powers I was supposed to have, but how could I when my mind was scattered by fear? The arms that held me stiffened.

Finn was standing before us, eyes flashing. His dark hair was plastered to his face, and he was still in my granddad's old nightgown, wet and rippling in the wind.

"Put her down," he growled, and a surge of something traveled through him.

"Well, well, well, if it isn't the little princeling. Two birds with one stone." The Drowned man let out an awful laugh, and his decaying body heaved against me again. He slid his right hand back up toward my breast while his other arm kept me firmly pressed against his skeletal frame.

Finn's dark eyes simmered with lightning, and he slung his arm, palm facing upward, at us. I fell to the wet ground as the Drowned leader was flung against the base of the wheel with the force of a cold gust, like wind blowing across the waves.

His eyes widened with shock as he hit the wheel's support tower. His neck cracked in a way that said it was broken, but he snapped it back and pulled himself from the ground, a wicked smile stretching his lips.

Bron and the other Drowned man were advancing on Finn now, their cloaks flapping in the roaring wind. Finn stood his ground and stared them down, his eyes glinting obsidian.

Bron's meaty fist connected with Finn's face, sending his head flying back. I gasped, but Finn quickly steadied himself. A split lip left blood trickling down his chin, but he wiped it away with the back of his hand, grinning in a way that was positively wicked.

The other Drowned man landed a blow, and Finn took it with another smirk, as though enjoying the pain.

"Look out!" I yelled as Bron drew a sword from inside his cloak. Neither Finn nor I had any weapons. We really hadn't thought this through. Bron's small, watery eyes flickered with delight when he realized it too.

My mouth fell open as Finn looked between the two men, and storm clouds raced across his dark eyes. *The power of the Atlantic . . .*

The men continued to advance, and Finn smiled almost lazily, flicking his eyes between them. Bron looked at his comrade, shock plastered across his face, as the Drowned man started writhing.

An invisible force tore through him, his tattered clothes whipping around his decayed frame. His pale eyes bulged as if trying to escape their sockets; his mouth opened in a soundless scream.

I swallowed. Finn was . . . drowning him internally.

Silver streaks glimmered in the man's veins, pulsing frantically beneath the paper-thin skin stretched over his bones, resisting the force consuming him. Finn upturned his wrist and let the force of wind join the water. He looked like a wizard from a picture book in the long nightgown. I might have found it funny if the situation hadn't been so dire.

The Drowned man began to shriek and shrivel in the same way Jackie had. Soon, he was floating above us, his body being claimed by the Garden. Light illuminated our faces as he became one of the beautiful orbs, but I didn't look up.

Finn's wind and water hadn't fazed Bron, who simply shook it off with a cackle. Finn unleashed another torrent, but the man kept advancing. Meanwhile, the leader had risen from where he'd been slammed against the wheel's base and was now closing in on Finn from his other side.

Finn shot more wind at them, but this time, they were prepared and held their ground.

"They can fight my magic because they're drawing strength from the Mer blood in the wheel's core!" Finn roared as the two men approached.

I was sitting on the wet grass where I had been dropped, gaping at the scene and doing nothing. I needed to harness my powers, but I couldn't. I didn't know how.

I'd have to do things the old-fashioned way.

I grabbed a crumpled can from the grass beside me and tossed it at Bron. It clattered against his bulky shoulder, then fell to the ground. He didn't even notice it, but Finn looked at me and snorted.

"Really?" He raised his brows.

I rolled my eyes and then my shoulders.

Finn was using a sword formed from water particles to parry both Drowned men now, but they were two against one, and the Mer blood propelled them. I had to do something—anything.

Please, I beseeched the power within me. I was on my knees in the wet grass, the rain streaming down my face as I turned my eyes to the sky.

I looked inward, frantically scanning my mind, hoping to access what I knew was stored in my subconscious. Then I saw it—a glowing silver ball flickering just out of my grasp. It was the same light I had seen inside me in the dungeons, but how could I access it?

Finn gave a low growl as the leader's blade found his shoulder.

"Finn," I cried through a mist of tears as silver-tinged scarlet blood spilled from his wound.

A cold hollow expanded in my chest; the Drowned were fighting Finn's magic, and now he was injured.

I didn't know how to get past that wall within me that said this was impossible—that magic wasn't real, and there was no way I could have powers.

Power comes from here. I remembered Louisa tapping her heart.

Finn let out another grunt, grasping at his shoulder, where blood stained my granddad's robe.

I exhaled, letting my internal walls crumble. I let myself feel everything—the wonder that this new world existed and that I was a part of it, that after feeling like an outsider my whole life, I had a place here. I let these thoughts course through me and swell my heart. That love and utter belief merged into a mental space where anything was possible, where any power could be drawn. It was the sphere of birth and death, the before and after, the always—the timeless and all-connected plane.

There was the flickering silver, within easy grasp.

Exhaling a long breath, I let it fill me until it simmered through every inch of my body, as though my heart had pumped it into my veins. Finn's eyes widened when he looked at me, confirming that the power I felt inside was also burning in my eyes.

I had no idea how to wield it, but I turned my flaming eyes on the Drowned and gave them a death wish as I extended my palm in their direction like Finn had done. The group before me froze in time.

Bron's steel was locked in battle with Finn's water sword. At the same time, the Drowned leader aimed his blade at Finn's gut as Finn stared at me in shock and awe. When this frozen scene came back to life, Finn would be stabbed—a death blow. A wicked smile curved the corners of the leader's silver-stained mouth as if he knew it.

Power comes from the heart.

"No!" I cried. I slung my wrists at the frozen scene and twisted, letting whatever ancient power was writhing inside me hit its mark.

Finn and the Drowned came back to life momentarily, but as the two men moved into Finn, their bodies disintegrated into the rain in a cloud of silver dust. With a sweep of my fist, the ocean breeze claimed it.

What the fuck?

I slumped on the grass beside Finn. Whatever I had just done had exhausted me.

He brushed his wet hair from his forehead. "I haven't seen power like that in . . . Well, I've never seen power like that." He shook his head.

I looked at my hands, which had been wielding something a moment ago. They seemed so normal now—just plain, wet, grass-stained, trembling human hands.

Lightning skittered over the wheel above us, a reminder that this was not over yet.

Finn held out his hand, pulling me up. "You've got this. Just throw another can at it . . ."

With that he grabbed the blade, still coated with his blood, from where it was lying on the ground and jogged into the darkness. His magic flared. He was again distracting the Drowned guarding the wheel's base.

This was my shot.

My hands trembled as I grabbed the first rung, and my fingers slipped before I found a firmer hold. I pulled myself up, wrapping my legs around, clinging to it like a sloth in the rain.

I was now inside one of the many skeletal prongs, and the wheel was turning. I crawled upward toward the apex.

Don't look down. Just don't look down.

I looked down.

Below, the storm raged. The roar of the wind and waves mingled with the clash of steel as Finn fought the other Drowned guards.

"Morgana, go!" he shouted, his voice cutting through the chaos. I glanced down to see him dodge a spear thrust. The Drowned guards seemed to be advancing relentlessly; their weapons glowed faintly with corrupted magic.

Taking a deep breath, I turned my attention to the climb. The wheel groaned underneath me, its creaks amplified by the storm. Each step up felt like a battle against gravity and the unyielding pull of the wind. Rain lashed my face, and my soaked clothes clung to my skin, making every movement heavier.

Lightning flashed, casting the cliff in a blinding glow. Another shout from below drew my gaze downward again. Finn drove his blade through one of the Drowned, pinning him against the wheel's base, but another closed in.

"Keep climbing!" he yelled as if he sensed my gaze, pulling his sword free and narrowly dodging another attack.

My heart raced as I forced myself upward. I'd never make it. This was crazy—

My hands slipped on the wet metal, panic shooting through me when my foot missed a rung. I clung to the wheel, gasping, as it continued to turn. The structure groaned as if alive.

As I climbed higher, the storm intensified, wind howling through the spokes. I could feel the pulse of magic, a tangible force pressing against my chest. The glow from the wheel's core grew brighter, casting eerie shadows across the rusted beams.

Just keep going...

Before I was ready, the apex was before me, a swirling vortex of light and energy. I hesitated, my breath hitching as the sheer intensity of the magic washed over me. I let out a slow exhale and crawled the final runs toward the core.

Sparks of raw energy arced outward, searing the metal around me. My powers stirred in response, an ancient, untapped force rising within me—Siana's power. She was from a time long ago, the same time as Manannán. Perhaps her power could match his. But I had no idea what to do...

Below, Finn's battle raged on. He grunted in pain as one of the Drowned landed a blow.

Clinging to the beams, I looked down at the cliff face and ocean stretching before me. My blood went cold—a massive wall of water was rising from the sea. Lightning illuminated its size as the bay stretched below, helpless and exposed.

I had to act now.

Without thinking, I placed both hands on the wheel's apex. I was met with white oblivion. My arms trembled with whatever power was snaking through them, but I held firm. I had to do this. It felt like this storm was my fault somehow, like if I had never been sent away and fulfilled my destiny, none of this would have happened. If I didn't break whatever was at this wheel's core, everyone in Ruadán's Port might die.

Heat traveled through me in waves as I propelled whatever power had awakened within me into the metal. I let the anger I felt at my grandmother for keeping this from me and the guilt I bore for her death course through me to the apex. The kids in high school calling me Mad Morgana, and my "condition" causing me to believe that there was something wrong with me—it had all been for this. The Drowned pirates pawing at me in places I did not permit them to touch . . . Anger rippled through me. It had all been for *this*.

Then, the world cracked.

The wind stopped howling, the sky cleared, and stars twinkled above me. Everything was still as the wheel broke.

I was falling through the crisp night sky as pieces of white metal cascaded to the ground around me. One of them smashed against the ground below. I would hit the rocks and crumple just like it, but at least I'd stopped the storms. Perhaps this was it—this was what I'd been supposed to do as the "chosen one"—to end the curse or whatever. I tried to reach for my power and stop my fall, but I could no longer see it. I was exhausted—so exhausted.

Whatever I had just done had sucked the life out of me. Another beam crashed into splinters below, and the earth was coming closer.

I collided with something, but it wasn't the ground. It was Finn. He held me gently in his arms as the world faded into darkness.

46.

FINN

The moonlight draped her in silver. Her face was pale, her brow clammy against my chest as her arms wrapped gently around my neck.

My shoulder throbbed where the sword had struck, blood seeping into the ridiculous robe I was wearing, but none of that mattered—only her.

The cool autumn air ruffled my hair, and stars scattered the now-clear night sky. The atmosphere remained charged with magic, but it was beginning to fade.

I'd tried to stay away, convincing myself it was for her own good, but fate brought her back to me, and I was glad it had. Distance was a coward's choice, and I would no longer be a coward. No, I would stay by her side. If she needed me, I would tear the world apart for her. If she asked, I would burn it to its bones.

She was far more powerful than I'd ever be. It terrified me, because it made her a target. Taranis and my father had both set their sights on her, which meant one thing: I had to stay close.

I had fought storms, faced monsters, and bled for a throne I did not want, but nothing had unraveled me like this girl in my arms.

When we reached her grandparents' street, she stirred against my chest. Her warmth was the only real thing in this night of ghosts and shadows. I would gladly have walked that hill forever if it meant holding her a little longer.

My brave beauty.

I blew out a breath as I pushed open the front door to her grandparents' place. Lucky I was magic, or the crooked stairs to her attic bedroom would have been a pain. The corners of my mouth twitched into a grin as I remembered the first time I'd brought her back here.

She was home, and she was safe.

I laid her on the bed and removed her damp clothes. The way my cock pushed against the fabric of her grandfather's robe felt wrong. She was unconscious, but it had a mind of its own.

I averted my gaze as I pulled fresh pajamas over her hips, catching a glimpse of lace panties. Clenching my fist, I forced myself to look away before carefully adjusting the waistband into place.

I padded downstairs to the dark kitchen. Grabbing a washcloth, I exhaled and let the inappropriate arousal leave my body.

Returning to her side, I dabbed her clammy forehead with the moist cloth. She'd depleted herself and needed rest. You couldn't fix a magic drainage with more magic.

"Where am I?" she asked groggily as her eyes fluttered open.

"Your room." I smoothed the hair from her face as those ocean eyes looked up at me.

"I am so tired." Her lids dropped, and she tried to blink through her contracted vision.

"You are not yet trained to wield such magic. It's exhausted you." I moved to the open window and shut it, running my palms over the walls, whispering in the old tongue of the sea.

"What are you doing?" She yawned, her lashes fluttering as she struggled to open her eyes.

"I am warding your room. Taranis will be angry."

"Your arm!" She tried to sit up again, but exhaustion pulled her back. "There's a first aid kit in the kitchen under the sink," she managed, before sinking back into the pillow.

"It's just a scratch." I grinned and gently pulled the patchwork quilt over her, but her hand shot out, catching my forearm.

"Stay with me for a moment?" she asked, withdrawing her arm and patting the space beside her.

I swallowed hard, then climbed onto the bed, staying above the covers as I draped an arm around her.

I drifted off to the sound of her soft, steady breaths and her chest's gentle rise and fall pressed to mine.

I woke to a searing ache in my arm, the nightgown stiff with dried blood where the wound had set.

One of my arms was draped protectively over Morgana, her red hair fanned across the pillow, her body tucked beneath the patchwork quilt that rose and fell with each breath. Some of my blood had spread onto the quilt where my shoulder had rested.

Moonlight filtered through the window, painting silvery patterns across Morgana's bare shoulder. I shifted carefully, muscles tightening as I tried to free my arm without disturbing her. As I eased my body from hers, my erection revealed itself. *Shit.* I swallowed.

She stirred, letting out a soft, sleepy moan. The movement pressed her quit-covered ass against my stiff cock, causing a tremor of new arousal.

I froze, breath held, my heart caught between guilt and the ache of wanting to stay and press myself deeper into her. She moaned again and nestled her ass further into my erection. My rigid cock prodded at her as images of the lacy panties she had been wearing flooded my mind.

I almost groaned as need coiled through me, and it took all my strength not to thrust my hips forward. I imagined her rolling toward me, her hands finding the aching parts of me. My cock nudged forward again, and she let out another sleepy sigh. A tingling sensation enveloped the space between my legs. My blood thrummed, and I stiffened further.

I exhaled and clenched my fist, peeling myself from the bed.

I glanced back at the sleeping girl. Strands of auburn spilled across the pillow like molten fire, a river of embers—a dangerous beauty.

"Goodnight, little shifter, and thank you," I murmured into the darkness as I closed the door.

I sank onto the couch downstairs, poured myself a drink to expel the desire, and got to work stitching up my arm.

47.

MORGANA

Someone was standing over me. My breath hitched in my chest, but it was only Finn.

How long had he been watching me?

I wiped a drool patch from my mouth and moved my elbow to cover its shadow on the pillow. Finn had replaced his nightgown with more of Granddad's old clothes from the downstairs closet—an oversized knitted jumper and loose jeans. He'd tucked the jeans into a pair of Granddad's old boots.

"I have to warn my father that Manannán's powers have returned and his army is thirty thousand strong." Finn's tone was firm, but his voice remained quiet. "If we don't go now, we'll miss the dawn."

I blinked at him through bleary eyes—I was still so tired.

"I understand if you need to rest." He sat at the end of my bed. "My father has always suspected Taranis would attack. My whole life, he has ensured that I would be ready . . ." His face darkened. "But his plans are becoming more erratic. He has often put me in dangerous situations where

I have just escaped death, and he doesn't seem to care. I am worried about my people." Finn gazed out the dark window, his features carved with worry.

I didn't feel like putting my Selkie coat on. I felt like doing normal human stuff, like lazing around in front of the TV all day and eating chocolate. I felt like catching up on the latest reality dating show or gossiping with Skye, but Finn looked anxious, and Edward was still in the Neptūnus castle, so I got up, casting a longing glance at my unmade bed.

"Really?" I raised my brows at Finn, noticing the lacy pajamas I was wearing.

"Your other ones were damp." The corners of his mouth twitched.

I shuddered as the events of the night came flooding back. The Drowned man's cold, dead hands grasping at my body . . . the power that had ignited inside of me . . . and the massive black wave which had come this close to engulfing the town. The wheel shattering around me, and falling . . . falling into Finn's arms.

It wasn't over yet; Taranis was still out there, and he had an army.

I threw the fur coat over my shoulders but didn't bother changing my clothes. As we reached the hallway, a loud rap on the front door saw me jump out of my skin. I glanced at Granddad's bedroom, but his door was still shut. Barry had dropped him off late last night, and I doubted they would be up early to fish today.

Finn tensed beside me before striding to the door and throwing it open.

Pisceon was standing outside, holding a gas station takeaway coffee. *A coffee!*

He was wearing human clothes—jeans and a white T-shirt. Was that all these Mer wore when they were on land?

"Cousin." Finn's voice was curt but flickered with amusement.

"I went to the house first, but your father suggested I might find you here." Pisceon ran a hand through his dark hair.

Wait, the king knows where I live?

"I see the interrogation is going well." He smirked as he took in my pajamas and sleepy eyes.

"We were just leaving." Finn pushed past him through the door.

I followed. It was still dark outside.

"Let me guess . . ." Finn blew out a breath and surveyed his cousin. "Father sent you to make sure I came back and explained myself."

"That's the gist of it, and as you know, what Daddy Neptūnus says goes." Pisceon winked at me and slapped Finn's back, and the material of his tight shirt was strained across his muscular biceps.

I couldn't believe this was the same Pisceon from the throne room. He was acting so normal—so human. I half expected him to ask Finn if they would catch the game later.

"You needn't have bothered. We're on our way." Finn strode onto the dewy street. The streetlamps were still on, and their yellow light pooled around him.

"But then I wouldn't have had a chance to come up here, would I, cousin?" He took another sip of his takeaway coffee and smacked his lips. "Ah, I love this drink!" He grinned at me.

"So does this mean you believe me now?" I narrowed my eyes on Pisceon, remembering how he had spat at me.

"I trust my cousin." He surveyed me thoughtfully, his voice quieter. "If you had killed our people, there's no way you'd still be standing here. This man is a *beast*." He slapped Finn's back again. Finn threw his arm off, rolling his eyes.

"You never know with this guy." Pisceon was chuckling now. "Ah, the messes we've had to clean up . . . the blood . . ." He drew his chiseled face into a mock grimace.

"That's enough." Finn's tone was a warning, but remained warm.

Together, we made our way down the hill toward the ocean. No one was about, only a cool fog. The waves were crashing against the faces of the distant cliffs. The clifftop looked empty without the Ferris wheel. Construction workers and police would undoubtedly be investigating the wreckage soon.

"I see you finally broke the wheel." Pisceon quirked a brow. "Took you long enough." He pulled a silver cigarette case from his pocket and offered Finn one.

"We fought Taranis's Drowned last night. They were able to withstand my powers." Finn looked at his cousin, his face grave.

"We?" Pisceon's eyes widened.

"She did most of the work." Finn placed the cigarette between his lips and smirked.

"What are you?" Pisceon peered at me in the morning light. I ignored him. It was a question I had been asking myself—what the hell was I? And what the fuck happened last night? When I didn't answer, he turned back to Finn. "Do you think they were channeling Manannán's necromancy?"

"Either that or his Mer blood, but some powerful force fueled them." Finn's cheeks caved as he drew on the cigarette.

"Should you be doing that with the Shadow and everything?" My brows kicked up.

"It's been a rough night." Finn blew out a cloud of smoke. "And we only contract the Shadow from polluted water, not human indulgences, but I am glad you're so worried about me."

I rolled my eyes, pulling the folds of my fur tighter as we reached the dark rocks at the top of the bay. The sky was still a deep shade of indigo, so I knew we hadn't missed the dawn.

Pisceon started clambering over the rocks, and Finn followed, tossing the butt from his smoke into a bin on the boardwalk.

I hesitated. I couldn't control my transformation. Finn turned and met my eyes. Noticing my reluctance, he said, "We will meet you there, cousin."

"Suit yourself." Pisceon shrugged as he stepped onto the slick sand. "I came up on Pháos anyway. I hope you don't mind." He gestured toward the white-bellied dolphin frolicking in the dark waves before striding into the surf. Aside from his back being too broad for his shirt, he looked the epitome of humanness. I couldn't believe he was about to ride a dolphin back to his Mer castle!

What the actual fuck.

I almost chuckled out loud at the absurdity.

As he strode into the ocean, the faint glow on the horizon made his torso a dark silhouette. When the waves reached his waist, he dived. A moment later, he emerged further out, shirtless and grasping Pháos's fin. He waved a muscular arm at us before the pair disappeared into the depths.

I looked at Finn in disbelief. "What happens to your clothes when you transform?" I scrambled down the remaining rocks to join him on the sand.

"Same thing as yours, I imagine. They disappear." His dark curls had dried in a windswept look about his face. "You seem fascinated by our clothes . . . or lack of them." The corners of his mouth twitched in amusement.

My cheeks burned.

"When I transform, I will wake up on SS *Jones's Lady*." I searched his face for any sign of recognition of the prophecy and what that might mean about my father, but I saw nothing.

"That explains why you decided to live there, with the Drowned." Finn scoffed.

I pushed past him, but he grabbed my hand, and his touch warmed my cold fingers.

"Do you know how fucking beautiful you look in the early morning light?" He stepped back, still holding on to me, as if he wanted to take me in fully.

"You can't say these things to me." I pulled my hand away, thinking of Princess Glacies and her tail of peridotite. But he'd said they had an understanding—that she had another lover.

He stepped toward me again, his eyes flickering with something predatory.

I took a step backward.

"When you fell last night, I didn't know if I would reach you in time. I cursed myself for not saying everything I wanted to say or *doing* everything I wanted to do. " A wrinkle deepened between his brows.

"When you were stabbed, I felt something similar," I mumbled, examining the line of light glimmering on the distant horizon.

Finn moved toward me, his boots leaving imprints in the sand with each step until our bodies were inches apart.

"What if we took this moment to say them?" He ran his hand down my shoulder, drawing me to face him.

Silence enveloped us, and the intensity deepened the longer we swam in each other's gaze. Even the crashing waves seemed softer.

Finally, I said, "You promise never to speak to me like this again if I tell you how I feel?" I lifted my chin to meet his dark eyes.

"I promise." He exhaled the words. "I know I don't deserve you—deserve *this*. I have tried to fight it, to focus on my duty, but you haunt me all the time, like the most beautiful fucking ghost."

My thoughts were racing against the symphony of sighs from the crashing waves.

"You and Glacies?" My voice was quiet.

"I have never kissed her. She's beautiful, yes, but I will not be a part of forcing her to go against her nature for our archaic traditions. When I succeed my father, I will set her free." He thumbed my jaw, his expression now soft and with traces of a smile. "Even if this is all we ever have, I need to know how you feel."

I chewed on my lip as my racing thoughts consumed me. I wanted to brush his dark hair from his forehead, to chase away the shadows that sometimes haunted his face. I longed to kiss the scars I knew lay hidden beneath his tattoos and uncover everything he kept behind those walls. But it was those very walls that frightened me. Now that I knew he'd been sent to follow me, how could I trust who the real Finn was?

He put his hand on my hip, and the distance between us seemed to tighten. He was so close, and yet I sensed nothing. *Nothing.*

The sea's sighs became louder and louder as I studied his face.

Shimmering particles of sea spray and morning mist had formed ribbons across the bay, which sparkled with hues of soft pink in the faint morning light. The index finger on Finn's free hand was ever so cocked, moving slowly from side to side; as it did, the glimmering droplets moved too. He was conducting them.

No thinking, just feeling.

I dragged my fingers through his hair, closing the space between us. His mouth found mine. The kiss was ferocious and salty as he pushed his body against me, tearing at my hair and my coat. His hands traveled to my waist, and he pulled me to him. The movement was rough and desperate as he whispered, "*Fuck.*"

I let myself be drawn, putting one leg on either side of his; I ground myself against the hardness growing there.

The ribbons of mist he had been holding encircled us, drifting gracefully around our tangled bodies. It felt like we were embracing in a whirlpool of glitter made from nature's beauty.

He pulled back from me ever so slightly to let his fingers caress the front of my pajama shorts. His mouth was still atop mine, but he withheld his tongue so he could hear my breathing . . . so he could hear the gasp I made when the circles he was making brushed just the right spot.

"I do want to fuck you, Morgana," he whispered against my ear. "But I want you to know that I removed my allure, just in case that human part of you was still drawn to it. So if anything happened between us, I would be sure it was your choice."

My choice. My knees turned to jelly. Oh, gods, I hadn't known my body could feel these things.

How many humans had he been with? He certainly knew what he was doing.

There I go, thinking again. I should hate him because he'd lied to me and was engaged—but I didn't . . . I *couldn't* hate him, not after last night.

I loved the way his body was pressing against mine, the heat of his kiss, and his hands, which were now back at my waist, sliding against the bare skin under my lacy pajama top. He found my peaked nipple and gently caressed it before moving his calloused palm lower to cup my breast.

"Do you know how much I've wanted to do this since I saw you in your seal's attire?" His voice was like gravel.

I responded with a whimper as his lips made their way to my neck, and his hand left my breast, traveling back to the space between my legs where the heat was building, begging for his touch. I might explode if I didn't get it.

His breath warmed my skin, and suddenly I was back in the dark room as Rackham held me down and Teachie tried to pull open my legs. I grasped at my chest as anxiety washed over me, removing myself from Finn's arms.

"Are you okay?" Concern flooded his dark eyes as he stepped back from me.

"I want you to do it," I whispered. I needed a reprieve from my mind. The faces of the pirates, the sunken eyes of the Drowned, the wheel, the falling, and whatever ancient power I had awoken within myself were gnawing at the back of my subconscious.

"What are you saying?" he breathed.

"Do it. Fuck me," I rasped out the words.

The mauve light suggested that the sun wouldn't rise for another half hour, so we had time. I wanted to erase the experience of Rackham and Teachie from my mind—to replace it with this. My choice. *This was my choice.*

Sweeping me into his arms, Finn gently laid me on the sand, but my back was comfortable against my coat's lining.

Propped on his elbows, he hovered above me, wincing slightly from the cut on his left shoulder. His sculpted chest was visible beneath the loose neckline of his sweater, and I could see where he must have stitched himself up last night.

I dragged my hands through his hair, pulling him to me, and his lips crashed against mine. My heart pounded against my rib cage as he lowered himself slowly, gently onto me without breaking the kiss. His hard cock was pressed between us, and I arched my back to grind into him.

"Fuck, you have no idea how much I've dreamed of this," he growled, and the words coaxed heat from me until it was dripping onto my thighs.

Plucking at the elastic waist of my shorts, he slid a hand between my legs.

"Look how fucking wet you are for me." The roughness in his voice only made me wetter.

"I want you now," I whispered as his fingers teased me, and something began to build inside of me.

"Are you sure you want this? Once we do this, it can't be undone." His eyes roved my face while one hand continued to stroke between my thighs.

I nodded, but he withdrew his touch, propping himself up on his forearms to survey me.

"I am not a good person. I've done terrible things. You don't know the real me..." His dark eyes bored into mine.

"Let me see," I exhaled. "Let down your shields."

His eyes flared with fear, still locked on mine.

"Let me see it all, and then I will decide if I want this or not," I said, gentler this time, reaching up and cupping his jaw.

He bowed his head, and a gush of wind rushed over me as his shields evaporated.

Darkness. I was consumed by darkness. I could no longer see Finn above me, only the swirling black. His loneliness reached out to me from the shadows with long, bony fingers, and then his pain shook the bars of the blackness like it had been suppressed for too long. I started drawing quick breaths. I couldn't see. I couldn't get out.

"Morgana?" Finn's voice said my name, but I was stuck in the dark void of his emotions. As he said it, a flicker of light ignited, a soft flame of gentleness, fighting against the swirling darkness to stay lit.

"Morgana?" He repeated my name, and the light flared.

Then, the shadows were gone. They were sucked away in another gust of wind. The world returned, and Finn's handsome face swam back into view, his shields in place again.

His eyes searched mine, and they were filled with fear and sadness as he pulled his body away, leaning on one arm. "I understand if you don't want anything to do with me now that you've seen what I am at my core."

I reached for him, pulling him back on top of me.

The darkness in him had been terrifying, but I had seen the light, too—a flicker that ignited when he thought of me.

"I want you," I breathed, looking into his silver-flecked black eyes. "I want *all* of you."

I had come this close to losing my virginity against my will to the pirates. I wanted this—needed this—and I wanted it to be *my* decision. Finn had shown me everything that he was, and I *chose* him. I'd chosen him from the moment I met him.

The glittering mist cocooned us now, and I could no longer see the beach, so I assumed that meant people couldn't see us.

He kissed me deeply; it was gentler than his earlier kisses, but he grew hard against me.

I moaned into the kiss, and he pressed his hardness deeper.

"I want you," I said again, shuffling my pajama shorts to reveal lacy panties, and his eyes flared. It was as if no one had ever said these words to him and truly meant it.

He held my gaze as he bent down to press his lips against my thigh, sending a shudder coursing through me. Brushing his dark hair from his forehead, he surveyed the space between my legs with an expression that said he liked what he saw before tearing my underwear to one side and feasting on me. My back arched, hips rocking against his face, as I presented myself greedily, hungrily to him until my eyes rolled back and the mist above me blurred into a shimmering haze.

Oh, gods!

No one had ever done this to me—or made me feel this way. This . . . *this* was what it was like to enjoy foreplay.

Just as I was about to shatter for him, I tangled my fingers in his dark hair, dragging him from between my thighs and guiding his lips back to mine.

Our eyes met as he pulled back from the kiss, and I saw the question there.

"Do it, *please*," I breathed in assent, reaching for his jeans and unbuckling them.

His cock sprung free, and he took hold of it, running his hand up and down as he surveyed the space between my legs.

"You're so fucking beautiful." His eyes had turned pure onyx with hunger.

Heat pounded between my thighs as I watched him stroke himself, and I wriggled my underwear off, letting my knees fall apart and presenting myself to him the way I'd seen women do in movies.

"Fucking hell." A guttural noise rumbled from him, storm clouds racing across his jet-black eyes.

I linked my arms around his neck, pulling him onto me. He teased the tip of his length at my entrance, coating it with my wetness before he thrust forward in one long, slow movement. My body tensed from the burst of pain that rippled through me, but then it was gone, replaced with growing pleasure as he rolled his hips into me.

Slowly, he was going so slowly. I pulled at his hips, grinding on him, a silent plea for him to go harder. He chuckled into my ear before he obeyed. The world disappeared, and there was only us—breathing, clawing, and panting at one another.

He consumed me like a wave crashing against the shore, devouring my body, running over every inch of me. The power that rippled in his veins moved inside of me. The darkness was there too, but it was only a whisper, because he kept his shields in place. I let myself drown in him. Something deep inside warned me this would end in pain, but I didn't care. I wanted him—I needed this.

One deep thrust had me breaking into pieces for him.

"Oh, gods, Finn!" I cried out his name as the world around me blurred into nothingness.

Finn's hips slammed into me, and he let out a low growl. A final thrust saw his groan morph into a roar of release as he came too, showing me he was falling apart like I had.

It left me breathless—the intensity of it, of my pleasure. It was as if I had died, experienced nirvana, and been reborn, all in ten seconds.

As Finn sank onto my chest, the glittering mist remained around us like a cocoon, and our shattered pieces joined together to become whole.

We stayed like this for minutes until, in the absence of pleasure, my thoughts began to creep back in. I slipped out from under him and stood, brushing the sand from the back of my coat, and pulled my shorts back on. Finn's eyes followed my every move.

"Should we . . . should we have used a condom?" My face blanched.

"It is highly unlikely that a Mer would get a different species pregnant—don't worry. We may be able to walk on land, but our genetics haven't progressed that far yet." Finn chuckled, standing up.

His dark hair fell across his face as he buckled his jeans. When his eyes found mine again, they were sad, as if he knew what I was about to say.

Stepping backward, I kept my eyes locked on his. "This will never happen again—you promised. We've had this moment, and now, should anything happen, we will have no regrets." I swallowed.

He nodded. "Never again, unless you ask for it." His chest was heaving.

The heat inside me was crying out in protest, willing to sell its soul to have more of his touch, but I ignored it.

He brushed his hair from his forehead, stepping closer to me so our faces were inches apart. His breath was warm on my cheeks in the cold morning air. He leaned forward, and as he did, the shimmering mist of sea spray enveloped us again. Pressing his mouth against my forehead, he kissed me softly. Then, he rested his head against mine.

"Thank you," he said quietly.

"What for?"

He exhaled sadly as I pulled away, and the magical mist disappeared. "For allowing me this moment, where I forgot the world existed and only saw you."

I strode into the water, nibbling on my lip to stop myself from smiling. I was no longer a virgin, and it had been my choice.

I could still taste him on my lips—feel his hands on me. I shook the thoughts away. *Never again.* We'd had this moment, and I didn't regret it, but a moment was all it could be.

"You won't get a warm welcome," I warned as my toes met the surf. The cold water was a good distraction from the heat lingering on my cheeks and the residue between my legs.

"The Drowned don't scare me," Finn spat as he dashed after me.

We were both waist-deep in water now. Its chilly arms clenched my hips as the sun appeared above the horizon. Finn hadn't transformed yet; he was looking at me, intrigued.

Great. He is going to watch me shift. I had no idea what I looked like when I changed, but it probably wasn't graceful.

The glow on the horizon was spreading. Finn moved behind me as if waiting for the showdown. I glanced over my shoulder at him—the legs of his jeans were soaking, and the wind plucked at his sweater, but he showed no sign of cold.

Please let me control the way I morph.

I had the powers of Siana Selich. They had turned two Drowned men to dust and split the Ferris wheel. Surely, I could control this.

I concentrated on the glow pervading the horizon. I tried to block SS *Jones's Lady* out of my mind and imagined being free to fall into the open sea. The wind picked up around me, and I felt the familiar rushing sensation. I fought to hold on to my clarity, but consciousness was slipping away from me. Glancing down, I saw I had transformed. The waves still lapped at my waist, the sea stretching out before me.

I did it!

I spun around to Finn. In that moment of weakness, the transformation overtook me. I doubled over, retching as vertigo swept through me. The sound of music confirmed what I already feared—I had failed.

Come ye sunken traitors to the bottom of the sea.

The hollow voices of the dead heralded my arrival.

The Drowned in the bar were silent; there was no fighting or sloshing of cups. They sat at the crowded wood benches and round tables, all glowering in the same direction.

Finn lounged at the bar, his crimson-tipped tail keeping him casually afloat. He was conversing with the Captain and ignoring the menacing scowls of the Drowned.

I picked my way through the tables toward him. Some of the muttering became louder as I passed. Amusement flickered in Finn's eyes when he saw me.

"What?" I asked sharply as I reached his side.

"Nice transformation." He continued to laugh, leaning both elbows on the bar as he surveyed me.

I glared at him.

"You transformed and seemed fine, but then you fell face-first into the water and disappeared. Boy am I glad I stuck around to see that." He chuckled, shaking his head as he reached his tattooed arm around for the bottle of rum the Captain had filled for him.

"I see Prince Aigéan has found you," the Captain said, his amber eye sparkling. His little sea snake came out and bobbed its head.

"You knew it was the prince who'd rescued me, but you didn't say anything?" I rounded on him.

"I know many things that I do not say." He shrugged and placed a second bottle of rum on the slimy counter for me.

No shit!

"I look forward to making you my bitch, Prince Aigéan!" The cry came from one of the tables of Drowned. A ripple of supportive hisses passed through the bar.

"Say that to my face, I dare you." The muscles in Finn's tattooed pectorals rippled as he glared across the room. The breath whooshed from my chest as his image faltered, and razor-sharp, jagged teeth, and hollow, pale eyes flashed across his face. His hands became the webbed claws that had held me in Therme Skótos.

The Drowned went silent.

A gnarly fisherman let out a loud hiccup, then clamped his fist across his mouth, terror sweeping his face as Finn turned his now globe-like eyes on him. Then his monstrous features were gone, and the handsome dark-haired merman returned as his body relaxed, but his black eyes still simmered with the inklings of something beast-like.

The heat rose between my legs again. What the fuck was wrong with me?

48.

MORGANA

I couldn't wrap my head around the fact that this merman was Finn from Bayside. *My* Finn. Here he was, now gliding beside me on a tail of emerald scales. They weren't just one color either; they were every shade of the green spectrum, and they changed hues with each flick or twist of his muscular torso. The torso that I was trying not to look at, but somehow couldn't take my eyes off.

With him by my side, the Mer castle felt less intimidating. But as we approached its looming shadow, my throat tightened, memories of the dungeons flooding back.

We were passing through the village now. Again, the merfolk came out of their sandy mounds to watch us. This time, they didn't scowl or spit; instead, they lowered their eyes and bowed. Finn was different, too. He had drawn himself up taller. He turned both ways and acknowledged the merfolk paying him homage.

"I can't believe people bow to you," I muttered as a young Mer couple holding a child slipped out of their dwelling and dipped their heads.

"And why's that?" He raised a black brow.

"Because you're Finn, the mysterious boy who works in a dusty pawnshop."

"*Prince* Finn, who works in a dusty pawnshop," he corrected me.

I laughed and saw two Mer tending their seaweed garden, eyeing me curiously. Well, curiosity was better than spite.

"Are you and your cousin close?" I asked, thinking of the bromance I had witnessed earlier.

"When Pisceon's father died eleven years ago, he became our ward. My father has always been . . ." He paused, and a muscle in his jaw ticked. ". . . tough on me, but he eased off after we took Pisceon in. I am forever grateful to Pisceon for that, even if he did it unintentionally."

"I bet you have some fun on land together." I fought a grin as I imagined those beautiful men walking into a bar.

"We only go to land when the king wills it." Finn's mouth thinned.

"But surely you would want to engage in human pleasure while you're up there?" I pressed, glancing at his magnificent tail. I was still thinking about his hands on me . . . his lips. *No!*

"Don't get me wrong—human pleasure is nice . . ." Finn's lips tugged into a grin. "But once you've been with me as a Mer, you'll never scream a mortal man's name again."

Gods. I swallowed.

"Has your father always been this way?" I asked to distract myself from these damned feelings.

"There are moments I can almost remember him being . . . kind." Finn stopped flicking his tail, floating stationary while staring into the green. "But that was before my mother's death. It's like losing her broke him. But instead of shutting down, he became . . . something else."

"I know what it's like to live with someone haunted by the past," I said gently, thinking of my mother.

"It's funny, isn't it? How we can feel so alone even when we have someone left." He turned to me, his dark hair drifting in the swell.

"Can't you just tell your father no when he asks you to do things?" I stared at Finn thoughtfully, wondering if there was a way out of his engagement.

"The leader of each Mer kingdom controls a trident." He ran a hand through his dark hair. "Not a physical trident like the ones you've seen in movies, but a three-pronged combination of powers. My father's trident channels lightning, stormy weather, and the current. This makes him the most powerful merman in the seven kingdoms—and he's losing his mind, which only makes him more dangerous."

My stomach tightened as I remembered the king's wild black eyes.

"My power will never match his until I succeed him. Even with the curse, his lightning trident could stop a heartbeat with one prod." The shadows had returned to Finn's face.

The ascent to the glittering sandstone castle seemed to go slower than it had last time, even though Finn and I were swimming. Perhaps it was because I wasn't going toward certain doom this time, but I wasn't sure about this venture either.

Finn followed my gaze. "If you think this is grand, wait until I show you our gardens. Every color of coral imaginable—" He motioned toward the shadowy waters behind the castle, where a faint glow shimmered.

"For some reason, when I think about your castle, the dark dungeons have been imprinted on my mind. I wonder why that is?"

He let out a low chuckle. "We will have to rectify that impression, won't we?"

As we reached the stone passageway leading to the grand entrance, I glanced up at the open-mouthed figurine carved on the arch above us, recognizing the Runes of the Ocean on either side of it. The same ones that decorated Finn's wrists.

We made our way toward the yellow glow ahead. Finn glided on his magnificent tail, and I kicked beside him on my webbed feet. My webbed fingers were splayed before me as I parted the water with them. There were guards in the doorway. Their pearl tails glistened in the sapphire light, and their identities were shrouded by tarnished silver armor.

Finn moved closer, and his shoulder brushed against mine. "While we are down here, I have to be . . . a prince." He let the soft crimson tips of his tail caress the back of my thigh.

"What do you mean?" I whispered as the fierce stares of the Mer guards found us.

He didn't answer, but his fingers furled with mine quickly. He let go as we reached the doorway.

"Your Highness." The men bowed their heads, and the seaweed crests atop their helmets rippled in the swell.

"I need an audience with the king. Send word to prepare the war room and request he meet me there," Finn commanded. His voice, which had been soft with me, had become deep and authoritative.

My mouth was agape as I watched him, straight-backed and confident, barking out orders while keeping himself afloat on that magnificent tail.

"H-herm," I coughed at Finn's side, and one of the guards turned his wild eyes on me. "I would also like my dagger back, please." I lifted my chin in a manner that matched Finn's.

The man eyed me coolly before turning to Finn.

"Yes, yes, retrieve the girl's dagger from the armory." There was a grin in his voice as he nodded in assent.

One of the guards bowed and then retreated into the castle. Finn and I followed. This time, I was not immediately shoved down the dark passageway leading to the dungeons, and I could look around.

Sparkling granite staircases rose on either side of me, converging at the intricately carved double doors of the throne room. Above the doors, countless levels towered endlessly into the distance. A ribbon wound down between them, attached somewhere high above. Lights glimmered on either side of it until it blossomed above us in a glittering chandelier.

Once the guards had disappeared, Finn retook my hand and led me into what looked like a waiting room. It was smaller than the vast hallways—a Mer architectural attempt at cozy. The ceiling was lower, and couch-like masses had been constructed out of sea sponge. I bounced up and down on one, and it made a squelching sound.

Finn rolled his eyes, furrowed his brow, and sat with his elbows on his tail.

This room was also made of glittering sandstone and had a polished stone floor. A pretty shell mural had been embedded in the wall. There was a small table before us, and on it, a glass vase held sprigs of seaweed. Next to it, a giant clam lay open, holding small pieces of raw fish that had been cut up and wrapped delicately in seaweed, available to ease guests' appetites. I took one hungrily. So, the Mer had discovered sushi—or maybe they'd invented it.

"Want one?" I offered the fish to Finn, but he raised his hand in rejection.

He's nervous.

"The king says he will debrief with you after the Blood Moon Ball." The pearly-tailed guard's voice in the doorway made me choke on my sushi. His cloak ballooned in the swell at his back.

"This is important." Finn floated up from his sponge chair and puffed his chest out again.

"He says it can wait until tomorrow. He knows you don't care for balls, but it's important to show our people united strength in uncertain times. Your friend will be treated as a guest of honor." The guard turned his eyes to me.

"I forgot about the darn ball—foolish frivolities," Finn growled, his eyes darkening.

"The Blood Moon Ball?" I raised my eyebrows.

"The tides are higher and the currents stronger when there's a blood moon; it's something our people celebrate." Finn waved a hand, his brow still furrowed in frustration.

"Your dagger," the guard said, pulling a sponge cushion from behind his back, on which the blade lay.

I took it and fastened it around my waist. As its shape found the side of my thigh, it emanated something tender: love. No, it couldn't be.

Finn waited until the guard disappeared before glancing sideways at me. "I like the new look," he snorted, but his eyes flared hungrily as they traveled over my hips.

"Say one more smug word, and it will be at your throat." I threw my hair over my shoulder, grinning.

49.

Finn

The heart of the graveyard was the Hall of Kings and Queens. The dead eyes of stone statues of long-forgotten rulers peered at me as I made my way between the sarcophagi of those who had gone before me, some half-submerged in sand, others decorated with sea life.

I ran my hand over my mother's coffin, and it came away coated in slime. A stone likeness of her face was chiseled at its center. Her expression was serene, eyes closed in eternal rest and lips barely parted, as if caught between the last breath of life and the first sight of the afterworld.

I placed my scarred hand on her forehead and whispered the apology I made every time I came to see her. "I'm sorry I let this happen to you and didn't protect you from him."

If what Morgana had read in Iona's diary was true, Taranis had loved my mother. It didn't make sense. How could you kill something that you loved? I would kill for Morgana, but I would sooner take a blade to my own throat than to hers.

The graveyard was bathed in the ocean's perpetual twilight, and the current whispered through the ancient ruins. Here and there, the glow of bioluminescent flowers penetrated the deep blue, bathing the tombs of those who had someone alive who still loved them in an ethereal light.

"I've met a girl. You told me that love destroys us and that I should do my duty, but I wonder if you were wrong." My voice was thick as I looked at my mother's lifeless stone eyes.

It was said that on the night of the full moon, the spirits of our lost royalty stirred, their whispers carried by the currents. Few dared enter on such nights, but I always visited then, because my mother had died on a blood moon fifty-six years earlier.

I sensed a presence behind me and spun around.

My father. His dark hair was floating around his shoulders, and he wore his blood moon crown. The sight of it inflamed my anger.

"How can you still celebrate this night?" I clenched my webbed fingers into a fist.

"When you become a man and stop behaving like a boy, you'll learn that emotions cannot get in the way of running a kingdom." His face was impassive.

"You never deserved her," I spat, pushing past him.

"That, my son, I know."

I stopped, shoulders hunched, and turned to see my father's gaze on me. The stern expression he usually wore and the madness that always gleamed in his eyes was gone, and his face only showed sadness.

50.

MORGANA

I was given a room on the third floor, and my mouth fell open as I stepped inside. Walls of deep cerulean faded into the watery backdrop, contrasting with the golden furnishings, and wispy aureate drapes framed an arching window that looked out on the sea beyond. There was a long gilded mirror, a human-style ensuite bathroom with golden amenities, and glittering chandeliers winding down from the roof. The space made me think of sunlight on the ridges of deep blue swell as it dipped toward the horizon. The bed, woven from thousands of strands of seaweed, hung from the ceiling on bronze chains. It swayed gently with the current—perfect for beings with tails.

There was a knock on the door.

"Are you in there, my dear?" a kind female voice asked. A matronly mermaid with a crimson tail and silver hair piled on her head in a messy bun swept into the room. "I'm Laoise. Prince Aigéan asked me to dress you for the ball." She clicked her tongue as she surveyed me.

"Dress me?" I raised my brows. Surely, the Mer didn't wear gowns for these things.

The lady chuckled at the look on my face.

"Beautiful red hair like fire, and eyes like the ocean on its best day . . . I have the perfect thing for you." Clucking, she shuffled out of the room.

She returned holding a wooden box inlaid with shells. Inside, a sponge cushion cradled the most exquisite dark green jewels I had ever seen—a necklace, earrings, and a matching shell clip.

I ran my fingers over the stones. This was the moment in my blockbuster where I was supposed to reject the jewels and stick to my old, tatty suit—but there was no way I wasn't wearing these!

After Laoise had finished with my hair and fastened the jewelry, she covered my body with purple and silver glitter flourishes from a little terracotta pot.

"This is how the Mer dress." She led me to the gilded mirror so I could survey her handiwork.

The earrings and necklace, which clasped my throat like a choker, shone in the aquamarine light. My eyes glimmered turquoise underneath a winged line of kohl. Laoise had pinned my usually wild hair into an elegant bun with a sweeping fringe, adorning it with the shell clip and an array of more glittering green jewels.

"It's beautiful," I gasped.

Laoise's cheeks glowed.

⁓🐚⁓

After Laoise left, I paced back and forth until a note was slipped under my door.

His Majesty King Neptūnus cordially invites you to attend the Blood Moon Ball. The grand ballroom awaits you at the far end of the hall.

Seriously? I bit back a snort of laughter.

I followed the green-tinged banisters to a set of large wooden doors.

Two guards stood at attention outside, their breastplates gleaming and spears poised, but their helmets had been replaced with glittering white masks. With mouths drawn in their usual stern expressions, they held the doors open, and I drew in a sharp breath as the ballroom unfolded before me.

The space held a magical glow, illuminated by bioluminescent chandeliers hanging from the vaulted ceiling. The walls, crafted from what looked like mother-of-pearl, reflected the soft blue light, creating an atmosphere that reminded me of moonlight under the ocean's depths.

At the far end of the room, a long table held an array of what must have been Mer delicacies. Platters of sea fruits, kelp sushi rolls, and jewel-like caviar pearls were paired with crystalline goblets that the Mer filled with a luminescent substance.

Several Mer twirled gracefully on the ballroom floor in the room's center, their tails creating ripples that danced alongside the hauntingly beautiful melody played by a group of musicians near the stage. Four thrones carved from deep blue lapis lazuli overlooked the festivities.

How many thrones does one king need?

King Neptūnus sat upon the grandest one, his chin resting on his fist. He was surveying the room with a faintly bored expression in his dark eyes. A golden crown encircled his head, and part of his ebony hair flowed freely, while the rest was tied into a topknot.

Finn was seated beside him, and I could see their likeness; they both had the same thick, obsidian brows. Next to Finn sat Pisceon. He shared the dark Neptūnus features, though his skin was a coffee-colored tone where Finn's was fair. The sapphire tips of his tail curled elegantly around the back of his chair, and he offered me what seemed to be the faintest hint of a smile.

Princess Glacies sat on the king's other side. She was looking radiant and cold as always. Her white-blonde hair fell over the glittering scales that decorated her bare breasts, and her pale eyes caught my stare. Guilt curdled my stomach, and I swallowed loudly. Her eyes held no malice; she simply surveyed me from top to bottom with a cool distaste. Strings of pearls hung around her neck, and little sea flowers were pinned artfully into her wavelike curls.

If I was supposed to be an all-powerful Selkie, my outfit could have been a bit more flattering. My furry bodysuit didn't have much on her tail, which glistened like a black pearl as it slithered up the side of her throne.

I sighed in relief when I spotted Edward sitting at one of the gilded tables surrounding the dance floor. His eyes were wide as he surveyed the room.

I hurried over and slid into the chair across from him, and he grinned. "Can you believe this?"

I shook my head.

The music ceased as the herald who had delivered our sentence in the throne room stepped onto the stage. This time, I recognized him. It was Mr. Inegar. The familiar scowl had given him away. So Finn hadn't been lying when he'd said the man was an old family friend—perhaps a relative, given that he could walk on land.

"We are gathered here to celebrate the blood moon and thank the ocean that gives us our power. We invite you to feast, dance, and be merry whilst leaving your offerings." He gestured to a crystalline pool beside the entrance, where a stone statue of a woman cradling the moon in her arms leaned forward to scoop the water from it into her mouth. Offerings rested around the edge: strings of pearls, shells, and sea flowers.

"Prince Aigéan and Princess Glacies will now dance an ode to the blood moon."

Mr. Inegar retreated to the sidelines.

Jealousy spread through my veins like venom, bitter and uncontrollable, as Finn glided over to Glacies's throne and held out his hand. Her expression remained cold as he led her onto the now-empty dance floor.

I turned back to Edward, whose eyes were narrowed on me.

"What is this stuff anyway?" I plastered a grin onto my face, gesturing to the vat of luminous liquid on the table before us.

"If I was to guess, Mer moon wine." Edward's brow creased. "I wouldn't drink it if I were you."

The music was soft and haunting, like the full moon shining over the waves at night. Despite myself, I glanced over my shoulder. Finn was holding Glacies gently against him, a hand clasping her waist. His movements were fluid yet commanding, and his tail shimmered aqua as it flicked through the water. Glacies's hair cascaded around her like threads of spun gold, catching the light with every turn. Her slender arms reached out to him, their fingers brushing as they spun apart and came back together in perfect unison.

Heat crept up my neck, flushing my cheeks, and I poured myself a glass of the luminescent liquid.

"I'm going outside," I muttered, gesturing to the grand glass doors leading toward what looked like a balcony.

"Mer wine is much stronger than anything you'll be used to!" Edward called after me.

I sucked in another breath as I pushed open the doors. If the ballroom had been beautiful, this . . . *this* was something else. From the ornate granite-sand balcony, a garden of coral spread out below like a sky full of colorful stars.

The coral bloomed in crimson, gold, and lavender, each colony glowing as tiny spawn drifted upward like scattered orbs across the dark sea. Twisting spires reached toward the surface, their tips dusted with bioluminescent specks, while delicate sea fans swayed gently in the currents. I thought of Taranis and Abalone. This must be the garden where they used to meet.

I took a little sip of my wine. It was like nothing I'd ever tasted, the freshest blueberry popping in my mouth mixed with what I imagined it would be like to drink moonlight shining on a pool of ice. The substance traveled through my veins, almost immediately relieving my inhibitions.

A giggle cut through the silence, and I spun around. Princess Glacies's face was alight with laughter as she burst outside with a mermaid on her heels. The mermaid giggled as she reached for Glacies's hand, the glass doors swinging shut behind them. She was breathtakingly beautiful, with long black curls, dark skin, and a golden headdress complemented by an array of gleaming bracelets and bangles.

I slunk into the shadows on the other side of the terrace as Glacies, still laughing, pulled the woman to her. My jealousy evaporated, and my soul ached for her. Perhaps she was so withdrawn and cold because her heart was with this woman, yet, like Finn, she remained a prisoner to her duty.

The mermaids continued to laugh as they made their way to the balcony's edge. I slipped back into the ballroom before witnessing more of this intimate moment I should not have been privy to.

Finn had taken my vacated seat and was deep in conversation with Edward, much to the dismay of the other Mer, who cast sidelong glances of disapproval.

He rose as I approached. "Could I have this dance?"

"I don't know how." My cheeks burned as I put my empty goblet down on the table.

"I will lead." A devilish grin split Finn's face as he held out his hand.

Sensible Morgana wanted to say no, but the moon wine in me said "Yes!" and I let Finn lead me onto the dance floor.

"You look very beautiful in our jewels," he murmured, putting one arm around my waist and pulling me into him. "Put your hand on my neck."

King Neptūnus watched us from his throne, something like amusement dancing in his dark eyes. He was now the only one still sitting. Glacies remained outside, and Pisceon had taken a partner to the dance floor.

"Thank you." I toyed with the crystal choker as Finn pulled me closer, heat rising within me as his hand settled on the small of my back. "It seems to glitter even when there is no light."

"They were my mother's." Finn exhaled, his gills quivering with the movement. "Mer from the Kingdom of Thálassa can store fragments of magic in objects."

A hauntingly beautiful song drifted around us, and I let my webbed fingers graze the back of Finn's neck. He was wearing his seaweed coronet, and his dark eyes locked on mine as we began to move.

"I saw Glacies in the garden with a woman."

"Ah, yes. Princess Aarna Okeanós is staying with us for the event. I'm glad to see her happy," Finn said with a sad smile.

The water provided a sense of weightlessness, allowing me to spin fluidly. Finn's tail propelled our movements, compensating for my lack of natural aquatic grace.

"You don't like balls," I stated as the dancing Mer around us became a blur of color.

"I don't like *this* ball." A wrinkle deepened between his brows. "My mother was murdered on a blood moon. I see nothing that warrants celebrating."

I glanced over Finn's shoulder at the king again. He was staring toward the back of the room, a vacant expression now in his eyes, as if he was lost in the past.

We moved in silence, and I let the music swell within me. It was like the song I'd heard on the rocks, but a merman was singing in a language I didn't know. I could tell from his tone that it wasn't a happy song.

"It's the old language of the ocean," Finn said softly.

Maybe it was the wine, but something about the song and the dance allowed me to relax into his chest, resting my head against his.

"What's it about?" I asked.

"This is the ballad of Siana and Kyano."

"Kyano?" I pulled back, searching Finn's eyes. "What happened to him?"

"No one knows." He sighed.

We continued to spin, the world melding until only our bodies gliding to the haunting tune remained. The chandeliers above became golden smudges against a blurry sky. Dizziness consumed me, and I put a hand to my temple.

"Did you drink our wine?" Finn's brows drew together as he pulled back from me in concern.

I nodded, blinking. My vision had started to contract.

"I'm glad you haven't changed." He let out a low chuckle. "Our wine is practically a sedative for humans, and you are still part human."

"Do you know how much I like your V muscles?" I slurred, attempting to make a V shape with my fingers and stumbling against him.

"I will call Laoise to take you to bed." Finn tangled his hands in my hair as I nuzzled his neck. "I wish I could take you myself, but it wouldn't be appropriate."

51.

MORGANA

King Neptūnus sat at the head of the stone table in the center of the war room. His long, dark hair was braided at his back. Glass bulbs illuminated the space, casting a soft glow on the stained glass mosaic adorning the back wall: a merman, his spear held high as he battled the largest octopus, the Kraken, while a mermaid, her hair rendered in hundreds of red glass shards, prayed for his safety.

In the middle of the table was a 3D map of what must have been the world, but under the sea. Little stone figurines—Mer, Sirens, monsters, Drowned—were carved out. It was perfect for plotting a battle strategy.

"Welcome again, Morgana," croaked the Mer version of Mr. Inegar, but his eyes narrowed on me. "King Neptūnus would like to invite you to sit on his council. Please take a seat." He gestured to the table, where Finn, Pisceon, and Glacies were already positioned around the king.

Was everything down here this formal? It was no wonder they liked visiting the human world.

I eased into the seat beside Glacies, now facing Finn directly.

The colors from the stained glass window danced across all our faces, tinted by the azure water outside. Now and then, the panes would darken with the shadow of an oceanic creature passing by.

There was a short, awkward knock on the door. Mr. Inegar slid over to open it, and Edward walked in.

"You're late, Drowned boy. Take a seat quietly, and be quick about it," Mr. Inegar grunted.

Edward hurried over and sat down on the opposite side of Princess Glacies. I leaned behind her head to check on him, and he grinned. He was shooting furtive glances at Pisceon's oversized chest, which tensed as he conversed with Finn.

"It looked like you enjoyed our hospitality last night." King Neptūnus's lips twisted into a smirk, his gaze darting around the room before locking onto mine.

I flushed. When I awoke, I had expected a crushing hangover, but I'd felt fine—spritely, even, like some of the moon wine's magic lingered.

"So you finally broke the wheel but needed a girl's help." The king's eyes dripped with disdain as he turned to Finn.

Finn ignored his father and addressed the table. "Enough time has been lost. With the wheel broken, Taranis won't be able to create storms for a while, but his cronies bragged about having an army, and the girl confirmed it."

The girl?

Finn's expression was unreadable.

"Yes, Your Highness." I lifted my chin and met the king's black eyes. "I came here with Finn to—"

"Who are you to address him thus?" Princess Glacies turned her light blue eyes upon me. "Who is this Finn? He is a prince, and you are—well, I don't know what you are. A consort of the Drowned, perhaps." She moved her eyes across my uneven fur covering.

"I apologize, my prince." I rolled my hands in a mock bow toward Finn. "As you can all see, I am *not* Drowned but a descendent of the ancient Selkie seals." I gestured to my body. "But you already knew that, didn't you, Your Majesty? Isn't that why you asked Finn—*Prince* Aigéan—to follow me on land?"

All eyes were turned on me now as I glared at the king.

"You were on land to follow this, this . . . mutant? I thought you were investigating the storms," Glacies hissed at Finn.

"We are gathered here for a reason! Let's get to the point before more Mer end up dead." Pisceon slammed his fist on the table.

"Silence!" The king's voice rumbled over the table like a nautical wind blowing through rocks. "Let us hear what they have to say." He was eyeing me now, and I noticed again the small crescent tattoo on his forehead—the same pattern I had on my back.

"Taranis's cronies confirmed he has an army of thirty thousand Drowned and plans to attack." I let the breath whoosh from my chest in a sea of bubbles as I studied the king.

"Father, we need to protect our people. The Drowned are stronger under Taranis's blood magic." A vein throbbed in Finn's temple.

The king rubbed his chin with his silver-ringed fingers, muttering under his breath as if piecing together our words.

"So my brother has his army . . ." Cold amusement frosted his face. "Aigéan, how many Mer do we have?" He whipped his gaze to Finn.

"We have around four thousand." Finn leaned back in his stone chair and lifted his chin in thought. "The Okeanós, Krumós, and Pācificus could each offer another thousand." Finn turned to the map on the table and moved pieces representing each house into one corner. "The Mors army is small and needs to remain guarding Mortimer, so they're out." He left their pieces placed somewhere in what must have been the South Atlantic.

"That leaves Niveus with another two thousand." He smiled at Princess Glacies as he moved a stone Mer from the Arctic Ocean into the cluster in the North Atlantic. "And I'd guess a thousand from Thálassa—"

"Ten thousand!" Pisceon interrupted, raising his dark brows. "To their thirty?"

"So they have more men." Finn rubbed his chin. "But we have the magic—"

"The strength of our magic is good for nothing but party tricks these days, and you know it, cousin!" Pisceon's brows drew together in frustration. "Plus, *they're* immortal." He glared at Edward.

"Arrogant ass," Edward hissed under his breath.

Finn sighed. "Yes, and the Drowned men we fought at the wheel seemed to have some *other* power. Whether it was blood magic or necromancy, I couldn't tell."

Edward shot me a concerned look, and I nodded in confirmation.

"Do you think you can go to the Sirens and ask them to join the cause?" Princess Glacies suggested, toying with her long pale hair while she studied the stone pieces on the board.

"There's like fifty of them left!" Pisceon exhaled a long breath and then turned away from the table, as if trying to keep his frustration in check.

"No, she's right." Finn angled his head as he studied the map. "Their fifty is worth a thousand drowned. They still have their powers."

"Will their powers be useful, though?" Pisceon toyed with the Siren figurine thoughtfully. "It's mostly mind illusions and light weaving—and, of course, allure, but we have that in spades." He smirked.

King Neptūnus glared at him. It was clear jokes weren't appreciated at his table.

"We should push up your marriage date." He turned to his son, and his black eyes glittered. "We need the Niveus close."

"My people will come to your aid, I assure you." Princess Glacies stiffened.

Finn brushed off his father's comment. "We should marry after the battle. I see no time for festivities."

"You will marry when *I* say you will marry," the king snarled, looking between Princess Glacies and his son.

I swallowed and looked at Finn. His eyebrows were drawn and mouth tight as he surveyed the pieces on the board. Was he purposely ignoring his father? I glanced at the king, but his eyes were on me. They had taken in my stiff throat and lingering gaze on his son. His lips curled back from his teeth, amusement flickering in his dark eyes. I made my face neutral, cursing the heat I felt spreading from my ears to my cheeks.

"Do you think Taranis has reforged Manannán's alliance with the sea monsters?" Finn let his hand hover over the squid-shaped statue on the board and made eye contact with his father, perhaps trying to change the subject.

"The beasts were always quick to join Manannán, but their strength is not what it once was." The king nodded slowly as he surveyed the board.

"What about the Lugh Sirens?" Pisceon leaned forward and let his tattooed forearm flex somewhere over the Irish Sea. "Their magic is more practical than the houses of Kaimana, Sundara, and Agápē."

"Are you serious?" Finn turned to face him. "They're too busy lining their pockets with the coins of man. They wouldn't even remember the ways of the seas." His voice was icy, and his gaze flicked to me.

"At least they have survived the Shadow. That's more than we can say," Pisceon muttered, rubbing his neck.

"By sleeping with humans? They are but half-breeds." The king swung his head around to survey Pisceon in a beast-like manner. "*Humans* are the ones who got us into this mess in the first place . . . with their need to conquer . . . their endless greed. *They* created the Shadow. It was *their* God who brought this curse upon us."

The voices around the table began to blur as they continued arguing. Something wasn't right. I grasped the arms of the sandstone chair, the grains digging into my palms as bile licked at the back of my throat. Manannán had returned, and I was descended from Siana. Was Finn, Prince Kyano, Siana's other lover who had made Manannán jealous enough to start the great battle?

No, no, no! I had not come here to start a war, but to end one.

"Wait a minute!" I slammed my webbed fist upon the table, rattling the stone pieces. "Can't you see what you're doing?" All eyes snapped to me. "If you go to war against Taranis, you are repeating history—just like the curse wants!"

"How very Selkie of you." King Neptūnus threw back his head and laughed. His hands, which rested on the table, shook with him, his many rings tapping the table in unison.

Finn was leaning back with one arm draped over his chair. He ran the other through his dark curls as if contemplating what I had said.

"We are *all* creatures of the ocean." I pulled my cherry hair off my shoulder and gestured to the crescent moon on my back so the king could see it reflected the same inky pattern as the one on his brow. "Shouldn't we be working together to stop this . . . this shadow?"

"The Shadow is man's fault!" he roared, glowering at Edward. "We must defeat my brother, or Drowned will rule the Kingdom of the Deep. First, he took my wife, and now he comes for the throne." The whole room rattled like a tidal wave had crashed across its roof.

"But you cannot win," I cried. "All your people will die! Is that what you want?"

"Morgana." Finn brought his forearms back onto the table and shot me a look of warning.

The king laughed again, and his black eyes shone. "But we have some thing that my brother does not have . . ."

"Oh yeah? And what's that?" I breathed, narrowing my eyes on him.

He stopped laughing, and the gills in his neck flared as he snarled, "*You.*"

Time froze as fear flooded my being. I looked from the king's glistening eyes and over to Finn. He was staring at his father, mouth agape.

"What are you waiting for? Seize them!" the king bellowed, turning to Pisceon, and the war room reverberated.

"Please, no," Edward whispered to my right.

Pisceon pushed back his chair and moved around the table toward us.

"Father, what is the meaning of this?" Finn cried. His dark brows were knotted in confusion.

I felt Pisceon's presence at the back of my chair.

"Do not touch her!" Finn's snarl rumbled through the room like a clap of thunder across a stormy sea.

"You dare to challenge me, boy." The king swung his head to his son as he spat out the words.

Finn didn't flinch.

"I said seize them!" the king cried again.

A pearl-cloaked guard from the door rushed to grab Edward. He let out a frightened squeak but then turned and punched the Mer right in the face. His fist collided with the guard's jaw and the side of his helmet simultaneously.

"Argh, bollocks." Edward sucked in a breath and shook his wrist.

The guard blinked, then lunged at Edward again.

I drew my dagger. I was not going back down to those dungeons. *We* were not going back. With a kick of my webs, I was out of my stone chair and facing Pisceon.

A second guard had helped his colleague detain Edward. He thrashed as they held both of his arms. His face was pale, and his eyes were defeated.

A cold knot formed in my stomach.

Pisceon lunged for me, but he was thrown against the wall by something—a force I couldn't see but felt move past us. A crashing wave.

"I said don't touch her, cousin!" Finn was out of his chair, eyes flashing, and his fists were claws again.

The water in the room started to swirl. His dark hair was astray, and he continued to hold Pisceon against the sandstone wall with the force of an invisible wave.

The king swung his head from his son and back to me and laughed—a hollow, chilling sound.

One of the guards left Edward's side and approached Finn, drawing a shining silver sword. He lunged, but Finn was ready.

He met the blade with a blade made from particles of water and mist, barely visible against its watery surrounds. The guard's metal sword and Finn's watery sword clashed. They held them there while staring each other down.

A sharp, manic laugh tore from the king. "Foolish *boy*!" he cried.

With an effortless flick of his wrist, lightning skittered from the tips of his fingers, and Finn was encompassed by it. The lightning forked across his muscular torso, simmering in jagged lines like a network of glowing scars. Finn's face contorted in pain, and his watery sword disintegrated.

I tried to rush to him, but Pisceon, now freed from his place on the wall, grabbed me and held me against his chest. "Sorry for this," he whispered into the side of my head. "What Daddy Neptūnus says goes."

Finn's body convulsed as the lightning continued to crack across it, and his face buckled with agony, but he didn't cry out. He kept his eyes on his father, and they were cold.

I twisted in Pisceon's grip, loosening one shoulder and flailing as I tried to escape. Somehow, his fist found the side of my face—whether by accident or on purpose, I couldn't tell.

Pain blinded me, and my ears rang. That moment was all it took for Pisceon to use his strong biceps to put me in a headlock with one arm while holding my dagger wrist with the other.

"Where did you get that blade?" The king's eyes widened with what looked like fear.

"Enough!" I cried, shaking my shoulders against Pisceon's grasp.

Finn floated above the table as the lightning continued to wreath him, unconscious now. Or at least I hoped that was all he was. Surely, the king wouldn't kill his only son and heir.

"Can't you see that hate has created more hate for many years? This is exactly what the curse wants. Violence is *not* the answer."

"Take them away and destroy the girl's blade!" the king roared.

"No," I pleaded. This was wrong. I knew it in every inch of my being.

No, no, no—

I thrashed against Pisceon's grasp, clawing at his biceps with my webbed fists. We would *not* be returning to those dungeons. I closed my eyes and relaxed my shoulders within his firm grip.

I focused on my breathing: in and out. In and out.

I scrunched my eyes and searched for that power I knew was inside me.

The silver orb flickered.

Power comes from the heart.

I reached for it as I imagined myself free of Pisceon's grasp. I imagined it not as something I wanted but as something that already existed in the plane of the unlimited. That was when I felt the surge. Power traveled up my arms until it crackled from every inch of me, a light-calming power that filled the room with gentle strength and ancient presence.

52.

MORGANA

The Mer were all floating belly-up, just like my dead goldfish had as a child, a look of contentment spread across each of their faces.

The explosion—a bomb of what appeared to be calm—had seemingly come from my webbed fists. I looked down at them in awe.

A whimper from my side alerted me to Edward's presence under the table.

"What happened?" I swallowed as I looked around the room.

"Y-you—" he stammered, pointing at my hands. So it had been me.

The last thing I remembered was Pisceon's rough hands on my shoulders. That was when the bomb had gone off, rendering all the Mer in the room senseless. The glass panes from the window threw colored shadows on their faces as they drifted to and fro in the swell.

"A-are they dead?" Edward breathed, curling himself out from under the table.

Princess Glacies was hovering above my head, and I pressed my palm to her chest.

"Her heart is beating." I exhaled the words. Thank god it was beating. Thank god I hadn't turned them all to dust. There was no doubting that I had powers, but not being able to control them made me dangerous.

"We ought to leave at once," Edward hissed. The cape of the pearl-cloaked guard floating above his head stroked his cheek.

I rushed to Finn and pressed my fingers against his neck. He had a pulse. His father's lightning was no longer scorching him, but he floated motionless like the others. His dark locks wafted in the swell, his eyes were closed—the lids bruised indigo—and his lips had parted slightly. I brushed his hair from his forehead.

"Are you coming?" Edward pushed past me.

"I can't leave him." I nodded at Finn's lifeless body.

"We have to. He can't be trusted." Edward's voice was icy. "There's a reason the Mer are stunned, and I am not."

I didn't move. Some of Finn's actions had been questionable . . . but he was still *Finn*.

"I—I can't." I shook my head, and tears built inside me. I was putting Edward in danger by lingering.

"Do you believe they'll allow us to leave the castle with an unconscious Mer draped over your shoulders?" Edward gripped my arm and pulled me toward the doorway.

I swallowed.

"Morgana . . ." Finn's voice was weak.

I swung around to see that he had righted himself.

"What happened?" He dragged his gaze over the other floating Mer. Angry red streaks still decorated his body where the lightning had struck.

"I don't know. I did something." I looked at my hands again, as if expecting to see answers.

Something welled in Finn's eyes as he surveyed me.

"We need to leave before the king wakes up," Edward said anxiously, tapping his foot as he stood in the doorway.

"He's right." Finn's dark eyes surveyed his father's lifeless body. "You need to go *now*."

"What about you?" My throat constricted.

"I need to handle my father. He will never stop hunting you if he thinks you are the key to one of his plots."

"Are you going to kill him?" My eyes were wide. "But, the trident . . ." I reached for him, remembering how the lightning had encompassed his body.

"I'm not going to kill him." Finn's face darkened. "I'm not a monster. Even though he's tried his best to make me into one, he is still my father and all I have left." He exhaled a breath, squeezing my hand. "Although I must admit a part of me wants to kill him for what he's done to you . . . for what *we've* done." His thumb brushed gently across my fingers.

"When he wakes up, he might kill *you*," I choked out.

Finn chuckled, but there were dark rings under his eyes. "That was nothing." He waved his other hand. "I would let him burn me to splinters if I knew it would keep you safe."

"You promised you wouldn't talk to me like this anymore," I muttered, pulling away from him, but I didn't mean it.

"Don't you get it?" He cupped my face. "I've never been scared of death, but now I'd go happily just knowing that we've had this."

"H-herm." Edward's cough reminded me of his presence.

"Go," Finn said gently. "I need to stay here and ensure he doesn't send guards after you."

I didn't move.

"My father may be stronger than me, but I know his weaknesses and how to manipulate his mind." His eyes glimmered. "He must be convinced of my allegiance so we can figure out what he's up to."

I reached for Finn's tattooed arm once more, and he pulled me against his chest.

"There is a second half to the prophecy," I said hoarsely. "My grandmother confirmed it."

He ran his hands through my hair, his tail beating slowly as he hovered above the floor. "Then we will find it together," he whispered, thumbing my jaw and lifting my face to his. "We will find the whole thing before we decide what to do."

He gently released me and moved back, pulling my hand onto his chest so that his heart beat against my palm. "We will save my people together and bring peace to the clans."

Utter silence filled the room as we stared at each other, broken only by Edward tapping his foot impatiently behind me.

"You asked me about destiny once, and I realized when you cried for peace that we were meant to meet." Finn caressed my hand, which was still pressed against his chest.

"Why do you think that?" I asked, looking up at him. Tears were trying to fall from his dark eyes, but the ocean was quickly claiming them.

"My father is incapable of love, and my mother was scared of it. But you have shown me that the best way to protect my people is to love them, and that means trying to keep the peace before going to war." He looked away from me at his father's floating body, and when his eyes found mine again, they were filled with fire. "I never cared that I was in an arranged marriage because my mother taught me to focus on my duty. 'Love destroys us,' she told me. *Amor perdot nos.*" He sighed. "But I realize now it destroys us in the most devastatingly beautiful way, and I would destroy myself a thousand times for you."

My blood thrummed as he ran his thumb across the top of my hand. "What are you saying?" I breathed.

"We need to go!" Edward tugged on my elbow. Finn allowed me to be drawn away but didn't release my hand. I kept my eyes locked on him as I stepped toward the door.

"Wait—the guards." Finn shook his head as if pulling himself together. "I could use my magic, but when they awaken, they'd know it was me. We need to find the prophecy before my father, or Taranis does, and the best way to do that is to convince him that I am using you to help find it." His eyes were pleading as he looked at me.

Edward yanked on my arm.

Finn kept my hand against his chest. "Can you trust me?" he asked.

"Not on your life!" Edward cried, his eyes blazing. He tried to pull me away again.

I shrugged him off and slipped a hand into Finn's dark hair, my gaze searching his weary eyes. His arm wrapped around my waist, pulling me against him.

"Yes, I trust you." My eyes burned as I said the words.

Finn kissed the tears that formed on my lashes. "I can't take back the things I've done, but from the moment I saw you on that jetty, you began working your way into my heart. I don't deserve your love—not now. Maybe I never will, but I can promise you that I will spend every waking moment of every day trying to earn it." His voice was hoarse.

I was crying now. I could barely see Finn through the tears bursting from me. He pressed his lips to mine, and I shut my eyes, savoring his closeness.

"Oh, for pity's sake!" Edward's cry startled me.

I choked back my sobs and, despite it all, stifled a giggle.

"You need to leave." Finn let me go, flicking his tail and gliding backward. "If you need me, I'll be there in a second."

Edward grasped my arm again, and Finn let him pull me through the door this time, but his eyes remained locked on mine.

I pressed myself into the sandy wall, hardly breathing as I monitored the passage ahead. The hallway outside the war room was deserted, and we hurried along it. The glass bulbs flickered eerily as we passed.

"If we see anyone, act normal, purposeful," I told Edward confidently, but my voice was shaking.

"Can't you just knock them out?" he whispered as we reached the slimy banisters that ran along the open areas of each level.

"No! We can't count on that. I don't know how to control my power." My nostrils flared, and I stopped him at the top of the final set of stairs.

Inhaling, I steadied my breathing as I scanned the curved banisters and roughly hewn steps. Two guards were waiting at the bottom with their backs to us. Their cloaks billowed in the swell, and I noted the tall spears gripped at their sides. They turned their fierce eyes on us but did not apprehend us as we passed.

I breathed a sigh of relief. How long did we have until King Neptūnus woke up? Would he hurt Finn again? I shook the thoughts from my mind. I needed to get Edward out of here.

More guards stood at the front entrance, their presence blocking the way. Beyond them, the blue ocean awaited us. My heart pounded, and it took all my willpower not to dart through the exit, dragging Edward with me.

"And where are you two going?"

I winced at the cold voice behind us as we slipped through the archway. Edward stiffened at my side.

Drawing myself up to my full height, I turned. It was Alga. *Damn.*

"We are acting on Prince Aigéan's orders." I moved my shoulders around in a manner I imagined was regal.

Alga's eyes narrowed. He twisted his magnificent steel-clad torso and looked over his shoulder to his comrades at the foot of the stairs. Noticing no disturbance in our wake, he surveyed us slowly before nodding.

My breathing steadied only once we'd passed beneath the archway etched with the Runes of the Ocean and descended the jagged path winding through the Mer village below.

"Oh, bollocks. I quite forgot about this part." Edward pulled me to a halt.

Shit, the ravine.

The dark cavern stretched before us, the black rock bridge a mere crack across the center. Finn and I had swum right over it, but Edward didn't have that option.

"If I recall correctly, these waters had no guards." A grin split Edward's pale face, and he stepped onto the bridge.

I followed, trying not to look down. He was right; I couldn't see any guards ahead, only the backs of their chipped likenesses on the archway at the other side. I focused on visualizing the Mer suspended in calm, hoping to use my powers to hold them there until we were safe.

Edward spun around and winked at me as the slippery rock bridge dissolved into solid ground and sand. "Hah, that wasn't too dreadful."

"Edward!" I cried as his leather boot slipped.

Fear widened his eyes, and he teetered precariously. His foot hesitated on a narrow ledge. Then, the stone beneath him crumbled with a sickening crack. His arms flailed as he slipped, his scream swallowed by the cavern.

I dived for him, using my webs to thrust me forward. He had managed to grip the rock face, but his hand was slipping.

I dropped to my knees and reached for him. My fingers had barely brushed his wrist before he slid further. The dark cavern yawned before us, its jagged walls glistening.

"Hold on!" Tears burned my eyes as I gripped his arm with all my strength.

Edward's wide eyes locked on mine, his other hand scrabbling for a hold. The weight of his body strained my muscles, but I dug my knees into the rock, anchoring myself.

I pulled, inch by inch, until Edward's free hand found the ledge. When I heaved him back onto the bridge, our breathing was ragged. For a moment, we lay there, side by side, the ocean's silence broken only by our gasps.

"I'm quite ready to indulge in a gallon of fine rum and enjoy several hours of chess." Edward moaned.

I rasped a chuckle, and he snorted. Soon, we were laughing uncontrollably, until tears tried to fall from our eyes and grains of sand stuck to the sides of our faces. It was a hysterical, cathartic release. Then Edward stood, pulling me up to walk beside him again.

We didn't relax our pace until we got back to the kelp forest where I had once swum with the seal pod. That felt like so long ago.

"Edward," I choked. "I am so sorry that I dragged you into this."

He shrugged. "It may sound mad, but I feel revitalized. I believe I had been dwelling in a sort of gray for so long that I had quite forgotten what it felt like to live truly—to face heartbreak, danger, death . . ." He stopped to empty sand from his boots while I squinted nervously into the gloom.

"That's how I felt when catapulted into this world." I sighed. "I just wish I could control my stupid powers! I don't even know what I did to those Mer."

"I—I think I might." Edward shuffled from foot to foot, sending a group of small white crabs scuttling.

"You do? *How?*" I studied his face in the emerald waters.

"Yes, well, after our quarrel"—his cheeks flushed at the thought—"I retired to my room. I still had that silly children's book the merman at the Taberna had given you, so I decided to leaf through it." He trailed his fingers across the soft, treelike coral we were passing. "It was written in the Runes of the Ocean, but as I turned through the pages, I realized it contained tales of the old gods."

"The words were few, so I asked the Captain for a rune key to decipher it. Siochain and her daughter, Siana—whom you are descended from—were the Gods of Peace, as you well know." He glanced sideways at me to ensure I was following, and I nodded.

"The book claimed they were the most powerful of all the gods, yet they chose not to wield that power due to their nature. Instead, they safeguarded it and protected the ocean."

"So you think what happened in that room was . . ." I rubbed my chin.

"The power of peace, yes," Edward said, watching me intently.

"Seriously?" I huffed a laugh.

"You were crying out for peace just before the explosion, so it stands to reason." He puffed out his chest, pleased with himself for solving the riddle.

"But when the Drowned attacked me on land, I turned them into dust."

Edward's brow furrowed, and then he shrugged. "I think that was a form of peace also, but maybe you wished for a finite end for them. Perhaps your powers are operating on the will of your unconscious mind."

"Honestly, where would I be without your brains?" I slung my arm over his shoulder.

Edward looked at his feet, grinning. "What's between you and the prince, anyway?" His smile faded, brows drawing together in frustration.

My heart twisted as I thought of Finn. He had chosen to stay behind and face his father's wrath so we could escape, but he had also lied to me and pursued me on his father's orders . . . and still, I had given myself to him—all of myself. I didn't regret it.

Edward was watching me expectantly.

"I met him on land, that's all." I brushed off the question, a school of fish scattering in the wake of my palm.

"Don't tell me he's the one you saw when you Mourned?" Edward's mouth popped open as he surveyed me.

I nodded, staring intently at the green waters surrounding us

"Oh no, surely you can't be in love with a merman. They're wicked!" He wrung his hands.

"No, they're not wicked." I chewed on my cheek. "There is good and evil in every species—and I never said anything about love." I tossed my hair over my shoulder.

"You didn't need to. When we Mourn, we see only those we love—it is a gift from your ancestor, Siana." Edward looked at me sadly. "I wager he never mentioned he was a merman when he met you on land, did he?"

The terrain had grown increasingly rocky, and we could see the first plumes of Therme Skótos.

"No, but I didn't tell him my secret either." I swatted a school of krill from my face.

"Yes, but I bet you *wanted to.* You didn't tell him because you thought he wouldn't believe you—these darn things." The krill had now surrounded Edward.

"Your point is?" I reached for one of the prawn-like creatures and nibbled on it, glaring at him.

"My point is, he didn't tell you because he didn't want you to know, not for any other reason," Edward grumbled.

53.

Finn

I should kill my father. I let my webbed fingers unfurl, molding to the curve of his throat.

I should kill him for everything he's done to Morgana . . . to me. But I can't. He's all I have left. I clenched my fingers into a fist, pulling it tight against my chest.

I would tear out enemies' throats for Morgana with my teeth, feasting on their flesh. I would break the world apart if she asked and I'd kill any man who made her shed tears. But not him—he's the one man who holds me in chains.

My father's long dark hair floated in the swell, and weary lines ran beneath his closed eyes. He seemed so weak, so peaceful. It would have been too easy to run my sword through his throat, but that would be a cowardly move and no way to ascend to the throne. He had stripped me of my choices and shaped me into a weapon, but even now, with every reason to strike him down, I couldn't. Because who was I without him?

I could hate him. I should hate him. But hatred was too clean, too simple. What I felt was a tangled mess.

My father would be angry, but it was nothing I couldn't handle. Dealing with this situation would require a performance. Fortunately, I'd spent a lifetime mastering the art of concealment.

I tore my gaze from his lifeless form and drifted into the dark hallway that led from the war room, breathing a sigh of relief. At least Morgana had left our castle unharmed. *Morgana.* Her name was like wine to the mind. I could get drunk from whispering it to myself.

I would tear through the tides for this girl, defy the currents, and battle the deep itself if it meant keeping her safe, and if it came to it, I would end my father's life.

She was not a girl you loved gently. She was the kind you loved with your whole being—or not at all.

Yet everything between us felt so precarious. Would she still love me if she knew the real me? If she knew all of the things I'd done?

No, she could never find out. Even if I lost her now, she'd haunt me forever, just as the tide lapped persistently at the shore.

"Aigéan!" My father's roar crashed through the palace like a thunderclap.

A half-human shifter had bested the mad king. I gave a low chuckle.

54.

MORGANA

It had been three days since our escape from the castle, and my mind was plagued with thoughts of Finn. Had his father awoken? Was he okay? Had the Mer started preparing for war?

I had been up to the surface for air and rejoined Edward in the games room on one of the regal—yet slimy—velvet couches. I was sipping my rum and surveying the rowdy Drowned at the roulette wheel.

There was going to be a war—a war between the Mer and the Drowned, my father's people—unless I could stop it. But how? I had powers; I knew that now, but I didn't know how to control them. All I knew was I needed to find the rest of the prophecy, and Finn had said we would find it together.

"H-herm." The cough startled me, and I spun around, reaching for my dagger.

It was only Edward's friend Daniel. He was hovering nervously.

"Care to join us, old sport?" Edward nodded at the space on the couch beside him.

"No thanks, Ed. I have promised Mrs. Vanderbilt a game of poker."

Daniel grinned, toying with the buttons on his military uniform. "I was just returning from the Taberna after picking up preservation potion for my medals," he said, flicking one of the gleaming bronze stars on his chest, "when a gray dolphin approached me."

A gray dolphin—the prince's dolphin. *Finn.*

"It had a piece of paper in its mouth. It's for you." He handed me the scroll, my name scrawled on its front.

Finn was alive, and he wanted to talk to me.

I unraveled the paper with shaky hands.

Come outside. That was all the note said.

I threw my chair aside, ignoring Edward's grumbling, and raced from the games room, taking the rotten steps to the bar two at a time. Bursting through the swing doors, I scanned the darkness. I couldn't see Finn, only the shimmering plumes of Therme Skótos.

A glimmer of white caught my eye—Pháos. The beautiful creature clicked gently, angling its head as it surveyed me. Stepping from the ship's light, I made my way toward it.

The dolphin swam in a wide arc around me, its movements deliberate, almost playful, before pausing just a few feet away. Then, with a sudden motion, it flipped and circled back, nudging something with its snout.

I had been so mesmerized by Pháos that I hadn't noticed the orbs. Tiny light spheres like bubbles gently drifted with the current, yet remained anchored to their path. They created a glittering walkway leading into the pillars of Therme Skótos. Pháos swam through them, careful not to disturb their delicate arrangement. Then he turned back to me, bobbing as if to say, *Follow.*

I stepped tentatively onto the pathway as Pháos repeated the gesture, swimming ahead just far enough to guide me and then pausing to make sure I was coming. The glowing orbs illuminated the trail, their light rippling across the sand and surrounding water.

With a final flick of his magnificent tail, the dolphin disappeared, leaving me alone with the trail of tiny lights. I was used to swimming above the forest, but the illuminated sandy track led me between the pillars. The landscape was otherworldly, a maze of towering heat vents belching plumes of liquid warmth into the surrounding water. The vents were gnarled, streaked orange, red, and black. Bubbles spiraled upward from the cracks, and schools of luminescent fish darted between them.

I swam deeper into the forest until the path opened into a clearing framed by twisted pillars, its ground blanketed in soft, silvery sand. Finn was standing at its center. His emerald tail shimmered faintly in the dim light. I took in his bare, inked chest and his dark hair, floating gently in the water, framing his angular features.

"I believe I owe you a proper date." He grinned. "You know, one where I'm not trying to hypnotize you to extract information."

"You seem to be forgetting that you're engaged . . ." I muttered.

The tiny lights gathered around him were flickering like fireflies.

"Once we break the curse, there will no longer be any need to merge the kingdoms. Glacies and I will be free." His eyes glowed with quiet intensity as they met mine. A smile curved his lips, and he reached out, beckoning me forward.

It felt like the entire ocean was holding its breath, waiting for me to step toward him. I let him take my hand, noticing the burn marks lining his arm. These were not the same burns from the war room; they were thicker and deeper. Red and angry, they stretched across his shoulders, curled down his arms, and faintly traced his tail.

"Your father . . ." I choked, reaching out to brush the nearest blister. Finn flinched but didn't pull away; his gaze remained on mine, purple rings haunting his eyes.

"He punished me well." Finn's voice darkened. "But it was nothing I couldn't handle." He replaced the shadows with that arrogant smirk.

"Your scars . . . " I lifted my eyes to his.

He nodded but waved a hand as if he didn't want to dwell on the topic.

I traced his arm, following the skin between the fresh burns. In the center of his chest, there was a small heart-shaped tattoo. I had never noticed it before, and the skin around it looked tender, like it had just been cut.

"Is this new?" I asked, running my fingers over the lines of the heart. His body shuddered beneath my touch, igniting a flicker of something inside me.

"Yes." He brushed off my question, his voice becoming grave. "My father believes you're the key to the prophecy, but I have convinced him to find the whole thing before he does anything rash. We have a lead in the Kingdom of Thálassa. Will you come with me there?"

"What about Taranis?" I asked.

"Pisceon and Glacies will travel to each of the Mer and Siren houses, calling them to attend a summit where we will determine the best way to deal with Taranis's threat. If we can find the prophecy before he attacks, we may be able to prevent this war."

I swallowed.

"If the rest of the prophecy exists, it could be the answer to obtaining the peace you desire, which is best for my people." Finn ran a hand through his dark hair, again drawing my attention to the shadows beneath his eyes.

"If I come with you to Thálassa, will I end up in another dungeon?" I raised a brow.

Finn chuckled. "You will be safe under the Mer emissaries' order of protection. We can visit Thálassa and then go to the summit together."

I remained silent, processing everything he was saying.

When I didn't respond, he continued, "I understand it may be hard for you to trust me, which is why I need to tell you the truth. My father believes I'm here courting you under his orders, luring you into our grasp to use your powers in uncovering the prophecy."

"And are you?"

"No, I'm not." He ran a thumb over my chin.

"Show me." I narrowed my eyes.

He sighed, placing my hands on his chest. A ripple washed over us, and the clearing was engulfed in darkness. This time, I knew what to look for: the light. This time, it wasn't a single flame. Every little orb he'd placed around us continued to glow, and although I could no longer see Finn, his heart thrummed against my palm. I took a deep breath and let his emotions wash over me in the darkness. The pain and loneliness were still there, but in each of the little lights, something flickered: *hope . . . and . . . love.*

My throat bobbed as the clearing swam back into focus. Finn was before me again, his shields in place, my hands still pressed against his tattooed chest.

"I need to ward the castle and prepare my people should Taranis attack, but if you want to come, meet me under the archway of Archōn Agorá at the next full moon."

I thought about the rune-covered ruins stretching into the blue waters and remembered I'd passed under an archway.

Finn's gaze was steady as he surveyed me. His shimmering tail moved faintly, keeping him balanced, and his dark hair floated in delicate strands around his face. His expression was a mixture of vulnerability and something deeper.

"I'll come," I whispered, turning from him, but he lunged forward, pulling me back.

"I am done caring what my father thinks. I am done with duty . . ." He ran a hand through his dark hair again, the turbulence of his mind visible in all his features. "You are my moon among parting clouds, guiding me through the storm, a light that breaks through my darkest waters, the song of the sea always calling me back . . . You, *you* are my horizon, offering me a hope I never knew existed. I need to know there's hope for us. Even if it's just a single drop, barely enough to taste. Without that drop, I can't survive."

I kissed him—a quick, gentle kiss that said *goodbye for now.* I laughed softly as I pulled away, saying, "There is hope."

One of his hands slid into my hair while the other pulled me back into him. I could feel the scales of his tail against me as I opened my mouth to let his tongue sweep in. We were suspended in time, the glow of the lights casting a dreamlike shimmer over the silvery sand.

I moaned as the kiss deepened. Unable to help myself, I slung my legs around his tail. He grasped my ass and let me arch into him. I moved up and down with the kiss, allowing his scales to stroke the right spot.

Keeping one hand on my ass, his other found my hair again, angling my head to deepen the kiss. My hands roved his muscled chest, passing gently over the burn marks.

The ache between my legs began to build as I felt his muscular body tensing. There was a pressure, stroking me there—water was undulating between my thighs, its intensity building with the kiss. Was Finn using his magic to pleasure me with our surroundings?

I pulled back from his lips; a wicked grin played on his mouth.

"Did you like that?" His voice was low.

The water between my thighs applied a stroking pressure again. Up and down and then around and deeper, teasing me.

Finn's mouth twitched up at the corners as he did it again, and my eyes fluttered. I wanted to let them roll back and give myself to the feeling.

Once you've been with me as a Mer, you'll never scream a mortal man's name again.

I let out a little gasp as the water caressed me. At the same time, Finn pulled me into another heated kiss. I could feel his packed abs pressed against me, the scales of his tail, and the water stroking, stroking between my thighs...

Oh, holy gods.

Stop, we had to stop! I pulled myself from him. We couldn't do this—not yet, anyway. A war was coming, and we had to end it. Taranis had killed my grandmother, and I couldn't let him kill any more innocent Mer or drown more innocent humans in his quest to rule the ocean. I couldn't lose myself in whatever *this* was. Not right now. First, we would find the prophecy and save the clans, then Finn could break his engagement, and I would let him do whatever godforsaken Mer things he wanted to do to me.

Reluctantly, I released my legs, my feet padding against the soft sand. I turned from Finn, but he put his hand atop mine, which was still on his chest.

"Do you ever wonder if this thing between us is the curse prompting us to reenact Siana and Kyano's story?" My throat was dry as I asked the question that had been troubling me.

"No," he said simply.

As I pulled my hand from him, our eyes met. I let my gaze linger on him before turning away. I felt the absence of his body, his taste, and whatever he had been using the water pressure to do to me.

"I'll see you soon." His words caressed my body as if he'd sent them traveling after me on the current.

As I made my way back down the sandy track still hung with glittering lights, for the first time, the ocean depths didn't feel so vast or lonely.

55.

MORGANA

My cabin bed creaked in protest as I settled onto it, mind whirring. I was magical—possessed of an ancient magic. Finn and I would try to find the prophecy before King Neptūnus or Taranis and save the Kingdom of the Deep.

What the hell?

My life had officially become a blockbuster.

I'd come to Ruadán's Port to care for my grandfather. Instead, I'd found a town filled with dark family secrets and Finn, a man whose feelings remained a mystery to me. I was never sure if I should trust him, yet somehow, he was the only place I felt at home.

We were the eclipse of sun and moon, the collision of peace and pain, the whisper of fate and fire. Yet I feared that, when such elements collided, it could only end in darkness.

So many questions remained unanswered. Where was my father, and what had really happened to him? What lay in the second half of the prophecy? The thought gnawed at me, along with the lingering fear that Finn and I were merely puppets, doomed to reenact Siana and Kyano's fate.

Maybe if we found the prophecy—if we broke the curse—we'd finally know if what was between us was real.

I scanned my senses for signs of what to do next but only found sleepiness. My eyes were just beginning to droop when a knock at the door jolted them open. I sat up and instinctively reached for my dagger on the slimy dresser.

"It's I, Edward." His posh English accent filtered through the keyhole.

"Come in." I relaxed against the grimy headboard.

He emerged in the gloom, looking bashful. "Your room is quite different from mine." He cast his eyes over the green-tinged dresser and patchwork quilt. "But not what I expected."

I raised my brows at him in question.

"Given that you're descended from a line of gods and all, I expected a grand princess's bed with a stack of five pillows and plenty of ruffles." He huffed a laugh.

I rolled my eyes and patted the quilt beside me. Edward's face darkened as he sat down.

"Whatever did the Mer prince want?"

As I recounted Finn's words, his face morphed into a scowl. I left out the part where I'd climbed his Mer body like a jungle gym.

"Please, don't tell me you believe this or that bollocks he spun at the castle?" He scoffed.

"There is another side to him. It's hard to explain." Heat rose in my cheeks. Edward had never seen the Finn who wasn't prince-like, whose emotions were a void of pain and loneliness, who broke when he thought about the burden of his duty—the one who had a light inside him that burned only for me.

Edward was still scowling.

"What's your problem, Edward? Out with it."

He sighed, running a hand through his copper hair. "The morning after the Blood Moon Ball, a note was slipped beneath my door, requesting my attendance at the council. It was just down the hall, so no guard was sent to escort me. I must have arrived before you all, and as I was about to knock, I heard voices spilling from the room. One belonged to the king—there was no mistaking his deep, authoritative tone—and the other was the herald."

"Mr. Inegar," I whispered.

Edward raised his brows at me.

"That is the herald's name. Go on." I nodded at him, dread creeping into my belly.

"The door was ajar, so I quietly crept forward and caught sight of the two mermen through the opening. This is what I overheard—"

I was staring hard at Edward. He seemed to be racking his brain for the best way to put it, then he exhaled a slow breath and began:

"The herald—or this Mr. Inegar—approached King Neptūnus and asked what was happening. King Neptūnus replied: 'My son has returned with the girl I instructed him to shadow on land.'"

"Wait," I interrupted Edward, holding up a hand. "Finn told me he had sought information on me on his father's orders." Relief coursed through me.

"Would you let me finish?" Edward spluttered.

"Sorry," I muttered, the niggle in my gut returning.

"King Neptūnus nodded and said, 'The girl we had in the cells *is* Iona's granddaughter. She is a shifter, and my son kept that from me, but now that we are certain she is a Selkie, do you know what that means?'

"Mr. Inegar replied, 'Blood taken when it need not be taken, but we must do it right this time, sire. This may be our final chance. We can't afford another loss like with her grandmother.'"

Her grandmother? My stomach tightened, and Edward reached for my hand in understanding.

I nodded at him to continue with the tale, choking down the emotions clawing at my insides, desperate to get out.

"Then, the king glanced toward the doorway, flicking the tip of his golden tail. I pressed myself against the wall, not wishing to be discovered, and quietly retreated. That's why I arrived late to the council." Edward squeezed my hand, and a veil of sadness clouded his features. "I am sorry I had to tell you all this."

My ears were ringing, and I felt like the world was collapsing. A weight pressed down on my chest, making it difficult to breathe. My grandmother's vision had come true. A merman had killed her, but it wasn't Taranis; it was King Neptūnus, Finn's father.

My stomach twisted, and my throat ached as the room swam back into view.

Did Finn know? Bile rose in my oesophagus, and I clutched at my chest as I drew sharp, ragged breaths. Was he the one who killed her?

A flash of anger ignited within me, and I welcomed its arrival. It consumed the shock, the sadness, and the pain in one fiery gulp. I clenched my fists. I would make them pay.

"I'm still going." My voice was mercilessly calm despite my thundering heart.

"It's not safe." Edward's blue eyes had turned pleading in the gloomy light.

Only with blood that need not be taken is the curse shaken.

Taranis must have reported this one sentence to the king when he was fighting the spirit of Manannán, or perhaps the king had found it in his chambers.

All the blood in my body was rushing to my head, making the room spin. The police officer had said my grandmother suffered a cardiac arrest. Her heart stopped—a bolt of lightning would do that. A wave of nausea washed over me with the realization. He'd described a gash on her palm but no knife. They must have believed taking her Selkie blood by force was the key.

Pisceon had known where my grandfather lived. Had I truly regained consciousness and told Finn my address that night at the jetty, or had he already known all along?

Had Finn found my grandmother first and then, when her blood didn't work, set his sights on me?

Edward's face was pale as he watched me process the information.

"I need to find the rest of that prophecy—there must be more to it." I thought about everything that was known:

> *Evil begets evil. Sin begets sin. All love will be lost, and you'll know no peace. In shadowed depths where silence reigns, a curse was cast, eternal chains. The spirits of Manannán and Siana must return, for only then shall the clans truly learn. One of both Drowned and Selkie lines is the answer, the curse's sign.* And the line that had sealed my grandmother's fate: *Only with blood that need not be taken is the curse shaken.*

Resolve masked my pain as I turned back to Edward. "What's that saying? Keep your friends close and enemies closer. I won't tell Finn what we know, and I will pretend to believe his sentiments when he bestows them. If he does have a lead on the prophecy, then we need to know what it is." I chewed my cheek thoughtfully. Could he have been the one to do the deed? I didn't want to believe it. *I couldn't.* But the gnawing doubt remained. Finn had told me that he was always entangled in his father's schemes.

"I forbid you to go. It's too dangerous!" Edward slammed his fist down on the bed, which groaned in protest.

"Whatever Finn's done, I don't think he would hurt me now. H-he showed me his soul." My voice wavered with the underlying truth I was fighting. I wasn't sure anymore.

"He's *magic*, Morgana!"

I stood up and began pacing the room. I needed to shake off the nausea that was eddying in the pit of my stomach. Think. I needed to think. I thought of the time Finn and I had spent together, the understanding he'd shown at the loss of my grandmother. Could it have all been just an act?

He had seemed sincere. When he had reached for my hand and devoured my body with his eyes, it had seemed genuine. When his body had been atop mine . . . No. I shook away the thought.

Edward was watching me intently; concern etched into the lines of his face.

"The next full moon is one month from now." I brushed my hair behind my ears and met his gaze. "I will go to land, see Louisa, and learn how to harness my powers."

Heat crept up my neck as I clenched both my fists. The Neptūnus Mer might be able to control the Atlantic, but I was magical, too, and my powers would not be stunted.

Edward sighed and rose to his feet. "I hoped it wouldn't come to this, but I'm coming with you to the Kingdom of Thálassa and this . . . this summit." He folded his arms across his chest and gave me a pointed look. "After all, they should have a Drowned emissary there." His face broke into a cheeky grin. "Just be sure you learn to harness enough power to wipe the smug smile off that Mer bastard's face if it comes to it. "

Epilogue

MANANNÁN

I lounged across the stone couch in my fortress beneath the waves, idly flicking my opalescent tail. The ocean's hush surrounded me as I drifted through memories—of the past, the nothingness I once was, and how I had clawed my way into this new Mer form.

Taranis had tried to fight against my consumption of his being when Abalone was alive, but he was an easy target once King Neptūnus killed her. I laughed out loud at how it all worked out—it only took thousands of years.

I surveyed myself in the gilded mirror set into the stone wall. I liked what I saw: the high cheekbones, the sandy hair and dark features, and of course, the red irises. They were my touch.

I had to admit I missed Taranis. It had been fun being there with him when he made love to Abalone. It was desperate and passionate—the type of lovemaking that comes from knowing you can never be together.

He couldn't block me out at the height of his passion, so I'd go along for the ride. I smirked at the memory. I used to run my hands through

Abalone's fuchsia hair and cup her green-tinged breasts alongside him. All the while, I thought of another . . . Siana.

Siana, it had *always* been you, and I'd had thousands of years to miss you. Now you were here again. I'd seen you at Samhain when the veils between worlds parted, and I could walk upon the land. I could feel you in her—the one they called *Morgana*.

My shadow latched onto Taranis when he visited a cave in Orkney. It was cut out of the cliff face, just under the sea. There, I had laid for centuries, a shadow of despair, barely a whisper. I had chosen those waters to mourn you because that's where your people were from.

Taranis must have come there to learn about you, hoping to end the curse your death created by finding the rest of the prophecy. When he entered the cave, he was but a boy, dispatched on endless quests at the king's behest. Forever fated to be a half-prince, never to ascend as king.

I made Taranis a man when he returned to the Kingdom of Neptūnus with my shadow. I sensed how he pined for Abalone, and I showed him how to woo her. Without me, without my ancient strength coursing through him, they might never have fallen in love.

I ran a hand through my pale hair and watched the muscles in my bicep bulge in the mirror. I had grown rather fond of the tattoo inscribed upon this body's chest: *Amor perdot nos*. Love will destroy us. Fitting.

I moved away from the mirror, and the scales of my white tail glimmered in the glow of the blown-glass bulbs lighting the cavern.

There was a knock on the door, and a mumbled, "Dinner is ready, my lord."

My lord, they call me—Lord of the Drowned.

I made my way down the hallway to the dining room, gilded paintings hung here and there as if trying to hide the trickling sediment drips that found their way down every wall in this fortress. They shimmered like obsidian under the lamps hanging at intervals in the passage. I had the Drowned start on this place when my necromancy returned.

As I passed, I straightened the edge of an opulent frame. Water lilies. A Monet. The Drowned had decked the castle out in all of their finest loot.

The glow from the dining hall leaked into the path before me, and that feeling overcame me—the one I always got in this grand room, at this huge table. Loneliness.

The table stretched before me, its dark wood gleaming under the flickering of five elaborate candle holders. Each one was crafted from gold, twisted into the shapes of sea serpents, their mouths open to hold the candles. The flames—a gift from the Neptūnus lightning powers I'd retained from Taranis—danced subtly, battling the ever-present current that swept through the cavern.

Behind the table, an enormous oil painting hung—Mer and sea beasts in a swirling ocean storm, waves crashing and lightning striking, frozen in time. The figures' eyes seemed to follow my movement within the cave. Their presence afforded me some small comfort, making me feel less alone.

The Drowned cooks had outdone themselves as usual. Dishes had been carefully laid out—pots of urchin stew, plates of kelp salad, and a shell filled with carved fish slices. This body required sustenance, so I asked my staff to replicate the Mer's diet.

I slid into the velvet-backed chair at the head of the table. Plucking a goblet from among the golden utensils laid out for me, I brought it to my lips. Ah, the rum was so sweet . . . I'd missed this amber elixir. After all, I'd been the first to concoct this spiced fusion for my Drowned to savor.

I settled back into my chair, thinking of Taranis again, of the moment he had lost all his humanity and surrendered himself to me. He'd left the Kingdom of Neptūnus on the day of Abalone's wedding to the king, taking my shadow with him. When we returned some fifty years later, Abalone met us in the gardens. She fell into our arms among the curated corals. They were spawning, and their colorful flakes danced around our bodies as we held one another.

But that insidious herald had followed us, hastening back to King Neptūnus, who stormed into the garden and found us in each other's arms. Lightning fire filled his eyes, and he held Taranis behind a shield of pure heat, forcing him to watch as he slit Abalone's throat. Her blood shimmered in the water around us, mingling with the colors of the coral spawn. Sex and death intertwined, as they often do. It was rather a pity . . . for I did enjoy fucking her.

To my great delight, King Neptūnus spared his brother's life. He wished for him to endure the weight of his loss for all eternity. It was then that Taranis relinquished his humanity to me.

I toyed with my goblet. Yes . . . what luck. Now he was gone, but I had his body, his humanity.

After this, King Neptūnus weakened. He began descending into the madness I hear plagues him now. I laughed out loud. No one could handle death, the toll it took—no one but me.

Ah, the irony of it all: the gods created their worst enemy when they made me. They never foresaw my rise to such power, nor expected their beloved Siana to fall for me.

I stiffened, knocking my knife onto the stone floor with a clatter. Siana, had I just heard the soft echo of your voice?

I looked over my shoulder, but no one was there. I scanned the room, and it was empty. I was alone with my dinner. What was it about this place that consumed me with thoughts of you?

One of my Drowned-serving men bowed his head as he entered. "My Lord, can I get you anything?"

My hands were shaking, my heart—Taranis's heart—hammering at my chest.

"Get out!" I roared the words, and the serving man hurried away.

I was alone again, with my trembling hands, that fucking monstrosity of a painting, and my memories—memories that I had pushed away for thousands of years.

Siana . . . They say it was you who shattered my storm wheel, who reduced my men to dust. A low chuckle escaped me. Perhaps now, you and I are not so different after all.

You made me a better man, but destruction was how I showed my passion. Only you knew that, didn't you? You fell in love with *death*.

Darkness curled around me as I thought the words, and I threw back my head and laughed.

Acknowledgments

I feel incredibly lucky to have worked with such creative and inspiring people while bringing *Sea of Evil and Desire* to life.

First and foremost, my deepest gratitude goes to my sister, Eve. We started writing this story together when we were barely teenagers, and holding onto those original ideas hasn't been easy—but I managed it. And to Eve, again, for using her *whole* ass to do the final developmental edit on this book.

Thank you to Vivien Reis, my talented cover designer, who patiently worked with me through every revision (allowing me to change the synopsis ten times). Also, thank you to Gustavo, my map designer, who endured my endless tweaks and morning grumpiness due to our time difference.

Thank you to all my developmental editors (Michelle, Ann Leslie, and Lesley), my line editor Jenny DePierre, and my grandfather, who read the first rough draft of *Sea of Evil and Desire* ten years ago and told me bluntly that it was terrible. To my mother, who read me *The Hobbit* and *The Dark is Rising* before I was old enough to read them myself and took us to her poetry slams, those moments shaped me into the writer I needed to become.

Thank you to the dark-haired man with near-black eyes who walked into the quiet store beneath the shadow of a broken Ferris wheel where I once worked and asked me about myself. The only logical explanation was that he was a merman sent to follow me on his father's orders.

And finally, to you, my reader. Whether you simply read this book, shared it with your friends, or left a review, thank you. I have given everything to this book, and I cannot thank you enough for your support. The characters in this world exist because of *you*.

www.ingramcontent.com/pod-product-compliance
Ingram Content Group UK Ltd.
Pitfield, Milton Keynes, MK11 3LW, UK
UKHW041353150425
5472UKWH00017B/113